UNPLEASANT CREATURES

UNPLEASANT CREATURES

MAHALIA SMITH

"According to legend,

the Devil sent his Imps out to play,

and some of them blew all the way to Lincoln..."

Prologue

Sam remembered waking with a start and sitting upright. Outside her room something had crashed to the floor. She rubbed her eyes and considered lying down again and pulling the duvet over her head, as she had been instructed on previous occasions to do. But the sounds continued...

Thwack...Thump... The sound of something being dragged along the thinly carpeted floor. The sound of something not very nice.

Sam reached over to the packing crate that doubled up as a bedside table and switched on the little star night light that had been a present from Pops – because, he said, she was his little star. This had pleased her immensely at the time and she had drawn great comfort from the light in the months since it had been given to her. However, the little star wasn't capable of giving her comfort now, not with the terrible noises outside her room – was that a gurgling sound she could hear?

She pushed the duvet to one side, swinging her legs off the bed, her feet almost immediately finding the fluffy cat slippers – another present from Pops, another beloved possession and a much favoured alternative to the cold, bare floor that the thin rug didn't quite reach.

Another loud thwack resonated down the narrow hallway as Sam opened the door to her bedroom, almost causing her to slam it back shut. But instead, she opened the door wider. She glanced back at her bed; should she take Benny? Instantly deciding against this, she walked out the door and towards the source of the not very nice sounds, her fluffy cat slippers padding soundlessly along the floor.

She walked the length of the hallway towards the front of the flat, and the sitting room. The door was slightly ajar, and she could just make out the edge of the settee. Stepping closer to the door, she could also make out the outline of a hulking dark figure crouched in the gloomy light, its legs writhing up and down like a monster. She scrunched her eyes shut for a few seconds and forced down the scream that so wanted to be let out.

Sam nudged the door so it opened a little more, and could now see the legs belonged to her mother, along with the gurgling sound. He was sitting on top of her, his hands around her neck. She opened the door a little wider. Her mother's eyes swivelled in her direction and locked onto hers. She knew what her mother's eyes were saying – for her little girl to get back to the safety of her bed. To not, under any circumstances, try and intervene. And her eyes also conveyed that she was frightened. Very frightened indeed.

She started to take some deep breaths, gathering what little strength and courage she had. She balled her hands into fists and, without giving it too much thought, charged through the door and towards the crouching figure.

'Urrrrgggghhhh!!'

It took a few seconds to realise that *she* was making the growling sound. Sam hadn't meant to make a noise, but it sounded good. Hopefully it would scare him enough to stop the horrible thing he was doing to her mother.

She hurled herself at the hulking creature with all her might, expecting to topple him over with the force. However, it was like slamming into a brick wall and she almost winded herself. He turned and looked down at the minor interruption, removing a hand momentarily from her mother's throat to wipe the spittle from around his mouth. His eyes were red and bulging and, as he bent lower, she could see the veins pulsating in his forehead. He looked like a monster, although she didn't believe in monsters.

'You want some too, do you? Little bitch!'

With one swift motion, she was lifted off the ground and flung against the wall near the door she had so bravely entered, the force causing the lamp in the corner of the room to topple over. Instinctively, she curled up into a ball, unsure whether he was coming after her. But no, there didn't seem to be any movement, only the sound of heavy breathing and her mother's sobs. Tentatively, she peered out from under her arm. He was now slumped on the settee, his hand around the remote control. Her mother was still on the floor, her head turned towards her.

'Are you OK, baby?' She whispered, in a rasping voice that didn't sound like her mother. She nodded, but didn't move her position.

'Go back to bed now, it's all right.'

She looked from her mother to the figure on the settee. He had switched the TV on and was flicking through the channels as though nothing had happened. Slowly, she uncurled herself and rubbed her elbow. It felt sore. So did her head, but not too badly this time. She started to crawl towards her mother.

'Sammy! Please! Please go back to bed!'

The urgency in her mother's voice stopped Sam in her tracks. She noticed that one of her fluffy cat slippers had come off and was lying beside the settee.

Near him.

Sam didn't dare move any nearer to reclaim it, resolving to get her slipper back in the morning, or whenever it felt safe again to do so.

She walked back down the hallway, wearing the remaining fluffy cat slipper. She entered her room and closed the door behind her, as she'd been told to always do. She went to her bed and looked down at Benny in contempt. What would he have been able to do anyway? He was only a stupid bear.

And she was only six.

With a shuddering breath, she crawled into bed, scooped up Benny and pulled her duvet over both their heads.

Chapter One
Twenty years later

Sam often found herself thinking back to the night her mother was almost strangled to death by Eddie – she could say his name now without shuddering – and how helpless she had felt to stop him. There had been numerous other occasions where things had been positively frightening, but none that were quite that bad. Thankfully Pops was called the next day (he never said who made the call so Sam hadn't anyone to thank) and he'd come straight round, taking one look at the state of his daughter and granddaughter, and charging at Eddie with his stick – whacking him over and over again whilst the coward (they always are), hastily pulled on his clothes and scarpered. But not before turning to her mother and saying:

'I'll be back, Denise.'

Of course, that meant yet another move. Not that Sam minded leaving; the flat was damp and dingy and the people upstairs played their music till all hours, causing her to lie awake at night and be grumpy and miserable in the mornings.

Unfortunately, Eddie was right. He did come back into their lives within a matter of months, as her mother's addictions found her begging at his doorstep for supplies that he was only too happy to provide. And, in return, she was his punch bag, on and off, for several miserable years.

After that particularly bad night, they had been placed in a hostel temporarily until another flat became available. This pattern repeated itself over the course of Sam's childhood, as her mother lurched from Eddie to other violent relationships and, horribly, back again.

How Sam hadn't been taken into care was beyond her, but she knew from a very young age to mask her feelings: to not ask for help; to keep her predicament secret. She couldn't risk being taken away from her mother. Her mother wouldn't be able to cope without her.

'Oh dear, Sammy, what's wrong with you today? Did you get out on the wrong side of the bed?' Miss Hattie, the class teacher would say, bending down to Sam's eye level and smiling inanely.

Not knowing what that meant, Sam would reply, 'Only my mum calls me Sammy,' giving Miss Hattie a hard stare, already perfected from the age of six, before going to hang up her coat.

Sam felt that Amy, one of the class assistants, was better at understanding her. Amy had noticed Sam's dishevelled attire (on the occasions she'd had to pull her crumpled school uniform from a suitcase following the latest move) and give her a shirt or cardigan – whatever was most obviously needed – from the spares in the school cupboard. Amy wouldn't make an issue of it, just handed over the needed item to Sam. The most memorable time was when Sam was meant to bring in a packed lunch for a trip to Southend but her mother had had to go to hospital to get her wrist seen to (due to another of Eddie's outbursts). She'd been dropped off at Katya's, one of the few neighbours her mother spoke to on account of her kids going to the same school, at 6.30am. Katya wasn't best pleased but had taken her in, seeing the state of her mother.

'Pops will collect you today,' her mother had said, patting her on the head with her good hand, the other hung limply at her side. 'Not a word to him about this, OK?' Sam nodded solemnly; even at her tender age, she knew her mother didn't want Pops to know that she'd taken back Eddie, not after all he'd done to help her get away from him. But as she drew near to school, trailing behind Katya and her three kids, it suddenly dawned on her that this was the day of the school outing. A day she'd been really looking forward to, that is until the events of the night before. Not only was she meant to bring a packed lunch but also to wear shorts and bring pocket money for ice cream. She briefly considered saying something to Katya, but Adrian, her youngest, had just fallen over and was screaming.

Tears welled up in her eyes then, threatening to spill over, so she scrunched them shut and quickly counted to ten, which usually worked. And by the time she entered the classroom, her mouth was already set in a firm line, determined not to let her true feelings show. She didn't care if she was the only one wearing her uniform, or that she didn't have the money for an ice cream. None of it mattered.

However, Amy had foreseen any problems. 'I brought some extra things, just in case you forgot,' she said, passing Sam a pink canvas sports bag. 'Go and get changed before Miss reads out the register,' she continued, patting Sam's arm.

Sam waited until she was in the privacy of the toilet cubicle to peer into the bag. There was a bright yellow T-shirt and a pair of white shorts and underneath this was a Tupperware box which contained perfectly cut ham and cucumber sandwiches, an apple, a carton of Ribena and a packet of crisps. But that wasn't all, Amy had even added a plastic wallet with two pound coins – she'd be able to get an ice cream after all.

She didn't say anything to Amy when she re-entered the classroom, fearful that she might cry and that, this time, she wouldn't be able to stop. Instead, she bought herself the cheapest ice lolly, leaving her with enough change to buy Amy a pretty shell, which she pressed into her hand before she got back on the coach. She also bought one for her mother, who turned it over in her hands, staring at it vacantly as if she didn't know what it was.

'Thanks, Sammy,' she eventually said, placing it on the windowsill by the sink, where Sam found it the next day, upturned and filled with cigarette ash.

Of course, Pops had had a large part to play in her upbringing but he was an old man weighed down with a melancholy that Sam always noticed, even when he was being upbeat.

She had begged Pops for her and her mother to live with him. Only once, during a particularly tough time, when her usual defences were down.

'Come now, child, you know that can't happen. I'm an old man now and your mommy needs to learn to take care of you herself. Not the other way round. It's not right.' He leant forward in his armchair, near enough to Sam that she could smell the rum on his breath.

'You're not her protector,' he whispered, an urgency in his voice. 'Lord forgive me for saying this, but she'll drag you down.'

'But why can't we both come and live with you?' she had asked imploringly, her eyes brimming with tears. 'Then we can all look after each other.'

Pops just sucked his teeth and shook his head. 'I can't do it all any more. I can't watch her do this to herself and Lord knows, I can't help.'

Sam had looked at Pops in bewilderment as he leant back in his chair and closed his eyes. How could he be so harsh? But as she grew older, she understood that her mother and Pop's relationship had always been fractious, mainly due to her mother's heavy drinking from a young age and the succession of brutal men she invited into her life. He was right, he was too old to keep stepping in and saving them from one disastrous situation to the next. Her mother would have to change, be the strong one.

Chapter Two

As Sam buttoned her jacket, surveying their new surroundings, she felt a little wave of something ripple through her, something akin to optimism. They had finally left London and made the move to Lincoln, a small city in the East Midlands. Their house (she felt strange saying 'my house' out loud, having always lived in flats) was a small two-up two-down at the top of the hill. It wasn't actually that much bigger than some of the flats they had lived in, but the novelty of going upstairs to bed was something she thought she'd never get used to. That, and not being at the mercy of whoever lived above or below, making loud noises in the middle of the night. They even had a garden! But the best thing was getting her mother away from the abusive relationships that put them both in constant danger; a time she was determined never to revisit. With Pops gone, it was up to her to keep them both safe.

'I'm going now.' She walked to the foot of the stairs. 'Shall I pick up something for dinner? Or d'you want to?'

'Uhhhmmmmmmmm,' came the response, then, 'It's OK, Sammy, you can get something.'

'OK,' she replied, feeling ever so slightly narked that her mother always managed to make it sound like *she* was the one doing Sam a favour, instead of the other way round. Her mother rarely went out on her own since they had made the move, and even when out with Sam, she was anxious and jumpy. Sam wanted to shake her and say, 'You don't have to keep looking over your shoulder now!' but she knew it would take time. Her mother wasn't as strong as her.

She slung her bag over her shoulder and had a quick glance back at the living room and the tiny kitchen beyond. Everything neat.

Everything in its place – just how she liked it. No more scrabbling through suitcases for clothes. No more coming home to strange men that her mum invited in. She wouldn't allow it. No way. *She* was the one in control now and she was going to make sure it stayed that way.

And here she was, going off to work and about to embark on a counselling course at the local university. Not bad considering they'd only arrived in Lincoln three months before, blinking in disbelief as they stood on the cobbled stones, taking in the uneven medieval buildings that were so different to anything they had seen before. She took one last look at herself in the mirror by the door. Her poker straight weave was immaculate, foundation applied evenly and eye lash extensions in place. But no amount of concealer could hide the dark shadows under her eyes; all those nights where she would find herself being shaken awake by her mother; to hastily pack up her things, or to go and hide in the wardrobe, had taken their toll. Even now, all these years later, she still woke in the early hours, the adrenaline coursing through her veins, her body drenched in sweat. She frowned then grimaced at her reflection.

Sam turned right on to Occupation Road and breathed deeply. The air seemed so much cleaner up here and with the gentle breeze and the signs of the summer to come, she slowed her usual brisk pace and took in her surroundings. It was a world away from the overly populated and polluted streets of south London, where it felt a constant battle to get from a to b, dodging the hoards of idiots who didn't look where they were going or were walking at a snail's pace in the middle of the pavement, oblivious to others. She found herself growling under her breath at them, willing them to move out of her way. One time she noticed a woman giving her an odd look and realised she must have been snarling louder than she thought.

But there was no need to growl in Lincoln. There simply weren't enough people to get in the way. As she approached the top of Steep Hill, Sam slowed her pace and looked up. This was her favourite part of the journey into work. With its foundations laid in 1072, Lincoln Cathedral was the oldest structure Sam could imagine to still be standing. In her eyes, it was the most magnificent and imposing place she had ever seen, and she never tired of gazing at it. On the days she had more time to study the cathedral, she would always come across a new detail – terrifying figures carved into the stone, panels portraying lust, sodomy and avarice. The latest one she'd discovered depicted the torments of Hell, which she particularly liked.

She was also fascinated by the legend of the Lincoln Imp, turned to stone by an angel for causing havoc. It had taken her a while to locate him, grinning down at her from the top of a pillar to the back of the cathedral, a reminder that even in a holy place, evil may not be far away. She was irresistibly drawn to the place and would often sit in one of the cathedral pews, or lately, walk into the morning chapel to light a candle for Pops – not that she was remotely religious. She had stopped believing there was a god long ago.

Chapter Three

The health centre was a bright, modern affair which looked slightly at odds with the higgledy piggledy, old-fashioned shop fronts along the cobbled street.

'Spare any change?' said a man huddled in a duvet near the entrance.

'No,' replied Sam, aggravated by continually being asked by him. Hadn't he got the message yet? 'You'll need to go before security moves you on.' The homeless man stared blankly from dark eyes that contrasted starkly with his pallid skin. Sam scowled as she stepped around him and entered the centre. She didn't have time for hopeless, weak people, other than her mother.

Sam's mood didn't improve when she saw Nigel sitting in *her* chair! What the fuck did he think he was playing at? He gave a little wave that died in the air as she stalked straight past him and down the corridor to the staff kitchen. She was determined not to have to ask him to move from her desk. Entering the kitchen, she took her mug from one of the cupboards above the sink, glad that she no longer had to go through the rigmarole of retrieving it from the locked cupboard behind the reception desk. Still, it would be difficult for someone else to use it without feeling awkward, what with the words 'THIS MUG BELONGS TO SAM' printed in bold, red letters across it – a present from Denise after her first week there. She slammed it down on the counter, instantly regretting doing so as she didn't want to risk breaking it.

'I've got you a little something,' Denise had said when Sam arrived home after her first week's induction into her receptionist role.

'You've been out then?' Sam had asked sceptically. Her mother had nodded, finding it difficult to hide the delight on her face as she brought her arm from behind her back to reveal the small gift bag she was clutching.

'What's this in aid of, then?' Sam had asked, clearly confused. She wasn't used to receiving unexpected presents from her mother.

'Oh, it's just a small pressie for getting your job and for... well...' she had shrugged and raised her arm in a gesture to encompass their new home, 'for sorting all this out.'

Sam had smiled and taken the bag from her mother. She'd pulled out the mug and turned it slowly, taking in the words that could not be more apt. Her mother must have mistook her bemused expression for something else, her face dropping as she said anxiously, 'What, you don't like it? I just thought it would come in useful.'

Sam set her new present carefully on the counter and smiled. Pulling her mother in for a hug, she said 'Mum, it's exactly what I needed! Thank you!'

Sam tapped her nails on the counter whilst waiting for the kettle to boil.

'It'll take even longer if you watch it,' came a nasal voice behind her. It was Nigel. He'd obviously become bored waiting for her to reclaim her desk.

'Enough water for me?'

She glanced in his direction and twitched her mouth slightly into something approximating a brief smile. She knew that as the new girl she really must try to get on with everyone and create a good impression. But it was proving difficult with the podgy creature who stood a little too close to her, his fat fingers splayed out on the counter as he propped himself up, trying to look all jaunty. How she'd love to chop those fat little fingers off with one fell swoop of an axe, or some other sharp instrument capable of causing maximum pain and injury. Instead she said, 'Of course Nigel, I always make sure I fill the kettle up,' edging a few steps back as she spoke. A part of Sam's brain told her she was thinking irrationally, she knew Nigel wasn't a threat, not really. But his mere presence infuriated her. She clenched her fists to stop them shaking.

'Good to hear! I could murder a coffee,' said Frances, bustling in with her hair awry and the belt from her coat trailing along the floor. She threw her bag onto the table and went over to the cupboard, where Nigel was still propped.

'C'mon, out of my way. Woman in need of coffee here,' she said, towering above Nigel and nearly smacking him in the face with the cupboard door. Sam smiled, properly this time. Frances was one of the senior doctors at the centre, not that you'd ever guess by her unruly appearance and haphazard manner. And with her forthright way of speaking, she sometimes came across as rude, but Sam liked the fact that with Frances, you knew exactly where you stood. Added to that, when Frances smiled, her whole face lit up, positively beamed, and there was something so kind and warm in her expression that was instantly appealing.

Clearly disgruntled, Nigel flounced out of the kitchen muttering something along the lines of '… getting out of the way of the stampede'.

'Morning, Frances,' said Sam, gesturing to the older woman to pour her drink first.

'No, no, you were here first and the water has to be just off the boil for coffee. Ah, there you are,' she said, after rummaging through the cupboard again and producing a cafetière. Sam paused a moment, intrigued by the coffee brewing device. She and her mum only drank instant. She remembered seeing a cafetière in the kitchen of Zoe's house, one of her few friends from school, but hadn't known what it was. Noticing her hesitation, Frances said, 'Would you like some coffee?'

'Er … OK, thanks. Are you sure?'

'Of course, I wouldn't have offered otherwise,' replied Frances.

As Sam made her way back to the reception desk, she could see that several people had already made their way in. A woman with two young children was already seated and a man wearing a duffle coat, who she instantly recognised, was standing purposefully by the reception desk.

Sam placed her mug of coffee down and smiled, 'Hello, Colin.'

'D'you know what?'

'What, Colin?'

'I went to my sister's yesterday. And d'you know what?'

'What, Colin?'

'We had chicken and chips. And d'you know what?'

'What, Colin?'

'The cab cost me a fiver.'

'Did it?'

'Yeah.'

This was a rather stilted conversation that Sam now knew off by heart as it was the exact conversation that took place every Monday morning with Colin when he came in for his latest prescription. At first, Sam hadn't been aware of the rules and would try to interject with a new line such as, 'Did you have a nice weekend, Colin?' or 'Does your sister ever come over to you for dinner?' but Colin would just stare blankly back at her. In truth, the first time Sam had encountered him, she had (even by her own admission), been a little rude. When Colin had greeted her with 'D'you know what?' she had stared at him and said briskly, 'Do you have an appointment?'

When Colin hadn't answered, Sam had continued to stare at him, willing him to speak but he just carried on standing there with a stupid expression on his face. It was only when Frances walked past and said, 'Good morning, Colin', prompting him to address Frances with, 'D'you know what?' and, as she responded, 'What, Colin?' and he explained, 'I went to my sister's yesterday. And d'you know what?' Sam could see the pattern of the conversation. She soon ascertained that he had a learning disability and found it difficult to veer off his usual few sentences.

'Why don't you go and take a seat, Colin, and Josie will be ready for you soon?'

Colin nodded and, with his arms folded, took his usual seat in the front row.

Sam took a sip of her surprisingly tasty coffee and looked enquiringly over at the woman who was unbuttoning the coat of her younger child, a chubby little boy with a shock of red hair who looked to be around two. The woman looked up and smiled wanly at

Sam, 'It's OK, I've already checked in at that machine over there. My appointment is with the Health Visitor.'

'That's fine,' Sam replied, remembering to smile back. She then turned her attention to the computer, lowering it to the correct level from where it had been left by Maria, one of the other receptionists, who was around six foot tall. There didn't appear to be that many appointments so far, but it was only early and they could soon fill up, as Sam had experienced. What annoyed her the most were opportunists who just walked in and expected to be seen right there and then and would demand to speak to the centre manager, Alan, rather than taking Sam's word that there wasn't a hope in hell's chance that they could be seen.

Sam's eyes flickered back over to the woman, who had taken a toy truck out her bag for the boy. The girl, who could have been about five and had the same red hair as her brother, was sitting at the little table and chairs set out especially for little children. She was studiously colouring in one of the mermaid printouts with a set of crayons, both of which were also provided for entertaining bored children who don't yet understand the concept of having to wait your turn. The boy, clearly delighted with his truck and eager to show it off, toddled over to his sister and crashed it into the middle of her drawing, jolting the arm she was colouring with and thus causing her to colour out of the lines. The girl looked furiously at her brother but didn't say anything. She looked at her mother, who had her head in a copy of *Heat* magazine, then she grabbed the truck from her brother's little hands and deftly dropped it behind a nearby radiator. *Clever girl*, Sam thought, as the boy screeched his outrage to his disinterested mother. Sam looked scornfully on at the woman, who looked haggard and worn out as she half-heartedly tried to appease her son. Sam knew she would never let herself end up looking like that. She caught the girl's eye and smiled; *you go girl*, she thought to herself.

'Ahem.'

Sam almost jumped and looked up to see a tall, young man with the bluest eyes she'd ever seen. How could she not have noticed him coming in?! Not liking being caught unawares, she said sharply, 'Have you arranged an appointment?'

'Yes, I'm Jack Sutton. I'm here to see the Physio, I—'

'That's upstairs,' Sam interrupted, jabbing her finger in the direction of the stairs to the right of the entrance.

'Er... OK, thanks,' he smiled, causing Sam to feel a little guilty. Even worse, he was walking with a limp.

'You can take the lift if you want, it's just round that corner,' she called after him, by way of apology.

He turned back and smiled, 'Thanks.'

In that instant, Sam also noted his straight white teeth. He was, she had to admit, bloody gorgeous. She smiled back briefly before turning her attention to the phone that had just started ringing.

'Good morning, This is the Hill Health Centre. How can I help you?' she said automatically, looking at his retreating figure.

Chapter Four

Sam walked back along Eastgate Road to pick up sausages for dinner. She could just go to the local Co-op nearer to home, but she really liked walking into the old-fashioned butchers, with its scattering of sawdust on the floor. She even liked the smell of the raw meat, and although conversation with others didn't come naturally to her, she found exchanging pleasantries with Kenny, the shop owner, enjoyable. The bell over the shop door tinkled as she entered.

'Well, hello there, lass. How're you finding the weather?'

'Not too bad, but I'm playing it safe for now,' Sam replied, clutching at the collar of her jacket.

'And how's your mother?'

'Not bad,' Sam smiled; her mother had come with her on a few occasions to the butcher's and Kenny had definitely taken a shine to her. It was quite amusing really, how his eyes hadn't left her mother's face since she entered the shop, to the expense of the other customers waiting to be served.

And it wasn't surprising; Denise was a good looking woman, especially when she made herself up, tonging her long, thick hair into loose waves and adding a touch of makeup to her flawless skin. At the age of forty-eight, she could easily pass for thirty and Sam found it somewhat irksome when they were all too often mistaken for sisters. Although Sam knew she was pretty, with the same large eyes and slim figure as her mother, she didn't have the natural beauty her mother possessed, which was remarkable really, considering the years of drug and alcohol abuse Denise had put her body through. With thin hair (made thick, at times, with the addition of a weave), and brittle nails (made long and strong with acrylic veneers), Sam had to work harder at looking beautiful.

With a palette of makeup and careful blending, she could paint over the dark circles under her eyes and even out her blotchy skin – which she attributed to the stressful years of her childhood. However, softening the hard expression on her face proved difficult and at school she was always being reprimanded for being insolent, or sullen – her 'resting bitch' face, as her mother so thoughtfully called it. Sam had to remind herself often to relax her features and smile.

'That'll be £3.86, lass,' Kenny said, winking at Sam as he added a couple more venison sausages to the bag, free of charge.

'Thanks,' said Sam.

'Oh, and say hello to your mother for me.'

'I'll think about it,' she replied, smiling as she walked out the shop.

Cutting through the grounds to the back of the cathedral, Sam pondered the possibility of her mother and Kenny getting together. He seemed like a decent kind of a bloke (though you never could tell, not for sure), and although he looked older than her mother, he wasn't too out of shape.

She paused for a moment as she walked past the parade of grand old houses facing the back of the cathedral. Her favourite house was the one painted duck egg blue, with large windows and an intricate wrought iron balcony running the length of the middle section. It had an imposing air to it that shouted affluence, travelling first class and garden tea parties. It was a house that symbolised the upper classes, a life that was so alien to her and yet she couldn't help wondering what it would have been like to grow up in a house like that, with a normal mother – and a father, maybe someone like Kenny. Her thoughts turned, inexplicably, to the image of the man at the health centre earlier; his blue eyes and perfect face. It had been a long time since she'd actually fancied someone and she wondered if she might be ready for a proper relationship. She noticed a woman with a severe bob standing at one of the ground floor windows of the grand house, holding a cigarette and looking deep in thought. Sam took her in; the silk, high-collared blouse and cashmere cardigan draped over her bony shoulders. Suddenly the woman focused on Sam, her piercing blue eyes fixing hers with the coldest of stares before abruptly pulling the curtains shut.

'Is it 'cos I'm black?' Sam said under her breath. She laughed and shook her head, but deep down, couldn't help feeling stung; she was quite sure that the woman wouldn't have reacted like that if she were white.

'Hi, I'm back,' she said, on opening the door to her more modest home. The front door led straight into the small living room which led to an even smaller kitchen beyond. It didn't have a window but the frosted glass back door, which they often left open when cooking, even in the winter, saved it from feeling like a rabbit hutch

'Hi love,' Sam's mother said, popping her head through the arch that separated the living room and kitchen space. She had a pair of Marigolds on, and was scrubbing the kitchen counters. 'Just thought I'd do a bit of spring cleaning.'

'Oh, right.' Sam wiped her feet on the mat before stepping into the sitting room, noting the smell of Fresh Pine dust polish. It had been tidy when she'd left for work but now everything positively sparkled. Her mother had been busy.

'What're we having?'

'Guess,' Sam entered the kitchen and plonked the bag of sausages on the cooker hob.

Her mother laughed, 'Let me think.' She pulled off one of the Marigolds and placed her forefinger on her chin, an exaggerated thoughtful expression on her face, 'Sausage casserole?'

'You guessed correctly,' Sam laughed.

Sausage casserole was one of three meals that Sam had learnt to cook from the age of eight. The other two were spaghetti bolognese and fish pie. She could also whip up a baked potato with a variety of toppings, or a plate of scrambled eggs (though not her favourite, she would make them as her mother liked them).

Prior to learning how to cook these meals, Sam existed on a diet of things that could be warmed up in the microwave or brought to life with the addition of boiling water. From a young age she had mastered the art of microwave cooking and especially liked Pasta 'n'

Sauce packets. But all that changed when she was invited back to Zoe's house for dinner one day after school.

Zoe had been one of her few friends during her brief period attending Campsbourne School and they had become firm friends following an incident in the playground in which Sam had stood up to a boy who was bullying Zoe, getting punched in the stomach in the process. Zoe's mother had made spaghetti carbonara and to Sam's deprived taste buds, it tasted exquisite, much better than the Pasta 'n' Sauce packets. Seated at the dining table with Zoe, her dad and Ben, Zoe's older brother, Sam had quietly observed Zoe's mother serving dollops of the carbonara onto Ben's plate, urging him to help himself from the bowl of green things (runner beans, she found out later).

'Oh, muuuum! You know I don't like vegetables!' Ben had protested. Ben's dad cracked a joke she didn't understand and they'd all started laughing, including her. She wasn't sure why she joined in, but it felt good to be sat with Zoe and her nice family, talking about nice things and eating nice food. When Sam asked if she could have a second helping, Zoe's mother, clearly delighted, had said, 'Of course you can, sweetie,' and, looking around the table, she'd added, 'Such a polite little girl, you ungrateful lot could learn a thing or two.' It was such a happy experience, so different to eating in solitude, with only the TV for company.

Going to Zoe's house for dinner on Fridays soon fell into a pattern. It was something that Sam looked forward to more than anything – especially when things got hairy at home, like coming back from school one day to find her mother passed out on the sofa, vomit trailing down her chin, or to find Darren, one of the succession of brutal men, laying into her mother and screaming, 'You fucking bitch, that was my best vodka. I'll slit your throat next time!'

Then one Thursday afternoon, Sam had come home from school to find her mother packing their meagre belongings into the two battered suitcases that hadn't time to get dusty before their next use.

'Mum? What's happening, where are we going?'

'It's OK, Pops is going to pick us up soon. Go and see if I've missed anything from your room.'

'But Mum?' Sam's bottom lip trembled; this was the third time they'd moved in the space of a year, and for the first time in what felt like ages in her short life, Sam had felt happy despite the constant fall-outs between her mother and Darren. Sitting at the dining room table in Zoe's house had become a beacon in the storms, giving Sam a glimpse of what it was like to live in a normal family.

But any further protests froze on Sam's lips as her mother looked up from packing to reveal a black eye and blood trickling from the corner of her mouth. Silently, Sam had turned heel and walked the short distance to her bedroom. After a quick glance, her vision blurred with tears, she walked back out, closing the door behind her, the star night light from Pops left unnoticed on the shelf. Years later, Sam still wasn't sure what she missed most, those happy, cosy family dinners at Zoe's house, or the comfort from the night light.

'How's your day been then?'

'Good,' Sam replied, putting the oven on and placing the sausages onto a tray.

'Blimey, there's loads! Are we expecting guests?!'

Sam gave a snort of laughter, 'As if!' They never had guests, except Pops, but that didn't count as he was family and besides, he'd been dead for the past fifteen years.

'Kenny, your admirer, gave me extra,' Sam winked. It was so easy to tease her mother.

'Oh really, Sam, would you give it a break?! The man doesn't fancy me and I definitely don't fancy him!'

'Well, he always asks after you. You should go in sometimes – it would do you good to get out, and it would make Kenny's day.'

'I'll get the veg chopped,' her mother said, abruptly changing the subject and turning her attention to rummaging in the fridge to produce carrots, parsnips and a wilted bunch of parsley.

'What about the onions?'

'I thought you might do those, you know they play havoc with my eyes.'

'Uh uh,' Sam shook her head. 'You know the drill.'

Her mother's role as sous chef had come about after a brief

stint of cooking sessions, provided by the Mental Health Team Denise was under following a spectacularly bad time. If there were any period in her childhood during which Sam was at risk of being placed into care, it was then. But thankfully, Pops had intervened, against his daughter's wishes, to get the help that was so desperately needed.

Sam and her mother were moved from the women's refuge they had stayed in since her mother's major fall-out with Darren, and placed in a small, newly decorated flat off Tooting High Road.

Sam had been completing her homework when she heard the doorbell, followed shortly by the sound of an overly enthusiastic female voice she hadn't recognised.

'Hello, Ms Campbell, I'm Alice Haines, Occupational Therapist from Wandsworth Mental Health Team? Er ... do you remember we spoke on the phone?' Judging by the silence that followed, Sam ascertained that her mother hadn't remembered a thing about it.

Laying on her front on the bed, her head propped up with her hands, Sam frowned. She knew she would have to rescue her mother; something she had tried to do since she was little: always feeling the need to defend her in some way. But why should she? She bet Zoe never worried about her mother like she did about hers. Looking down at the maths exercises that she couldn't understand, she suddenly pushed the book onto the floor and sat up. She knew there was no point in asking for her mother's help after her visitor had left. She could barely get out of bed some mornings, let alone sit with Sam and work out maths equations, or just sit with her full stop. Sighing, Sam picked up the book and placed it on the bed. Maybe she could ask Pops for some help, he was good with maths, having helped her before, sitting with her patiently whilst she scrawled her workings out in her notebook. Reluctantly, she left the tranquillity of her bedroom and walked down the hallway towards the kitchen.

'So, just to recap, following your care review, you were referred to our team for a course of cooking sessions, with your consent, of course.'

Sam hovered by the kitchen door to see her mother staring

blankly at the colourfully dressed young woman looking enquiringly back at her. She looked nice, Sam thought to herself, not someone to be afraid of. Feeling herself being scrutinised, the woman suddenly looked in Sam's direction, 'Oh, hello there! My name's Alice. I've come to do some cooking with your mum.' Her eyes flickered back in the direction of Sam's mother, 'If that's still OK with you, Ms Campbell?'

'Denise,' Sam's mother muttered, 'you can call me Denise.'

After some preliminary questions and a short discussion on the aim of the cooking sessions, namely for Denise to be able to prepare healthy, nutritious meals for herself and her daughter, Alice proceeded.

'I thought we'd start with something fairly simple,' Alice beamed, apparently oblivious to the sceptical expressions on the mother and daughter's faces. 'Scrambled eggs on toast.'

Sam looked from Alice in time to see her mother's brow furrow.

'I'm not stupid, you know, I can cook bloody eggs!' She folded her arms in a show of defiance.

'Great! I've got everything we need right here.' Unfazed, Alice produced a box of eggs, bread and butter from her rucksack. Obviously deflated, Denise shrugged and said, 'Oh all right then, let's get started.' Curious to stay, but aware that her mother might not want her there, Sam edged slowly away from the door.

'Why don't you stay and help too? Sam, isn't it?' Alice asked. Sam nodded slowly.

As they commenced, Sam looked on in dismay as her mother fumbled her way through the preparation of the meal. Her hands trembled, causing her to spill some of the gooey contents of the eggs all over the counter top.

'Bollocks to this!' she exclaimed, slamming her hand down on the counter, causing Sam to jump. If the woman was shocked, she didn't show it, instead she smiled kindly and said, 'Happens all the time to me. Don't worry, there's plenty of eggs.'

It made Sam upset to see how badly her mother was doing, especially in front of the woman and she knew she would have to try and make things better.

'Mum,' she said, going over to her mother and tugging at her arm.

'What!' Denise said impatiently, trying in vain to turn on the stubborn hob ignition.

'Why don't you make pancakes instead?'

'There!' Denise said with a look of triumph as the cooker ring finally burst into a small circle of flames.

'Mum?' Sam tried again.

'I'm not making bloody pancakes, Sammy, I'm not in the mood!'

'But you make really good pancakes,' Sam said quietly, before retreating to her bedroom.

Pancakes were the one thing her mother could make well, Sam thought, perching on the edge of the bed and reopening her dreaded maths book. She loved the smell of pancake batter, and her mother seemed better when they sat together, enjoying a pancake on Saturday mornings, which, sadly, didn't happen often.

'Sammy,' Denise called, 'the eggs are ready. Come and have some for your dinner.'

Again, Sam reluctantly walked down the hallway and into the kitchen. Her mother had set three places round the small fold-up table. The woman was already seated – *what the hell did she think she was doing?* They never had visitors round for dinner.

As if reading her thoughts, Alice said, 'Your mother's kindly invited me to stay for tea. I hope that's OK with you?' Sam shrugged noncommittally, and sat in the chair the woman pulled out for her.

'What do you think?' her mother asked, almost as soon as Sam brought the first forkful of scrambled eggs to her mouth.

'Hmm, it's OK,' Sam nodded, but she much preferred having fried eggs, especially when Pops sometimes took her to the greasy spoon across the road on Sunday mornings – usually when her mother was nursing a hangover, or a black eye, or worse.

'Well, that was lovely. I really enjoyed it,' Alice said, wiping her mouth on the piece of kitchen roll provided by Denise. 'Same time next week?'

Denise shrugged, 'I suppose so.'

It soon became apparent to both Sam and Alice that Denise had little motivation to learn how to cook. She wasn't able to maintain her attention to the task at hand and would lose track of the order in which to plan a meal, agonising over the quantities of ingredients, even with the recipe in front of her. If it hadn't been for the skinny little girl, avidly watching during the food preparation with her beautiful, sad eyes, Alice might have been tempted to bring their tuition to a premature close. But instead, she turned her attention to Sam, giving her a little more responsibility each week when deciding on recipes.

Thus it was Sam who learnt to cook; her mother designated the more menial tasks of tidying away the mess or scrubbing the potatoes. When Alice announced their cookery lessons were coming to an end, Sam had felt a wave of sadness. Alice's cheery calmness had been the perfect antidote to her mother's low mood and, she had to admit, to her own sullenness. And when Alice produced a purple folder containing all the recipes they had cooked together and a small box with some cupboard staples, Sam had hugged her in an uncharacteristic display of affection. Alice hugged her back and then, pulling away, she placed her hand under Sam's chin, gently tilting her face upwards, and said, 'You take care of yourself, darling, and your mother too,' before turning briskly, so Sam wouldn't see her tears. Finally, she walked out of the flat, closing the front door gently behind her.

Sam really enjoyed learning to cook, and she soon fell into a pattern of stopping off at the local grocery shop after school, basket over her arm, to get the needed ingredients for dinner, affording curious stares from her peers as they picked out their sweets and comics, the usual items that eight-year-olds craved. She'd even learnt the art of lighting the ignition on the crappy cooker.

Pops had been invited round on one occasion, after much persuading from Sam, and the three of them had sat around the fold-up table, eating spaghetti bolognese and drinking orange squash from plastic beakers. And Sam had felt as if she was part of a normal family, almost. But then her mother had to spoil things yet again by introducing another brutal thug into their lives, putting a temporary end to Sam's cooking.

'So, tomorrow I'm going to get my nails done after work,' Sam said, spearing a piece of parsnip from her plate. Her mother looked slightly disappointed.

'Oh, OK.'

'Why don't you come too? Then we could maybe go out for something to eat?'

'Maybe... I'll think about it.'

'Well it's not as if you've any other major plans, is it?' Sam said, more sharply than intended, noting the reproachful look on her mother's face. Instantly feeling both guilty and angry, her stomach churned and she stood up abruptly. 'I'm going upstairs, I need to read through the stuff the uni sent me about my course. It starts next week – remember?'

'Yes, of course I remember – on the Tuesday isn't it?'

Sam nodded.

'Why don't you stay down here? I won't disturb you.'

'It's OK, I know you like watching that horrid botched bodies thing.' By way of appeasement, she added, 'I'll come down later and make us a hot chocolate. OK?'

Her mother nodded and smiled. Sam hesitated a moment, watching her clear up their dishes, and tried to reconcile the feelings of anger and guilt roiling inside her. Even though she was now twenty six, Sam couldn't imagine being able to live her life independently; to move into a place of her own, maybe meet someone special. The thought of being stuck with her mother nearly brought her to tears.

Chapter Five

As Sam approached The Hill Health Centre, she was relieved to see that the homeless man wasn't sitting outside in his usual place.

'Good morning, Sam,' said Alan. Sam smiled, not having to remind herself to do so. Like Frances, she knew where she was with Alan. No prying questions. No hidden agenda. No threat.

'Morning.' They entered the centre together.

'Right, I'd better get the agenda printed for the team meeting,' said Alan, looking briefly at his watch.

Sam noticed that Frances' cafetière was on the staff room counter, left to brew its delicious contents. Opening the cupboard above the sink, Sam immediately saw that her mug was missing. She opened the other two cupboards, but no luck. Shaking her head, she returned to the first cupboard; she must have overlooked it somehow. But no, her mug wasn't there. Taking a deep breath, she selected a couple of small cups for herself and Alan – the preferred choices from the over-used looking items available. Maybe she had left her mug on the reception desk, but she knew she would never do that.

Picking up the cups that held a disappointingly small amount of tea, Sam made her way towards the seminar room.

'Well, I think young mothers make unsuitable parents. A woman should be in her thirties at least before even thinking about reproducing.' Nigel was holding forth, as usual, a haughty expression on his saggy, unpleasant face. A couple of the team members shuffled uncomfortably in their seats, including Anna, one of the nurses, but didn't say anything.

'Ah, Sam! Good morning! Just in time for our little debate. What are your thoughts on young mothers?'

Her mother had been twenty-two years old when she had become a mum and definitely hadn't done a good job bringing her up, but she wasn't about to divulge that titbit of information to the smug arsehole. Besides, she didn't believe age was a factor when it came to motherhood (unless the poor cow was twelve or something), more that some women were suited to motherhood and others just were not.

'I don't think age is relevant, it's more to do with—' The rest of the sentence froze on Sam's lips as she watched Nigel bend down and pick up his mug of coffee. Except it wasn't his mug. It was *her* mug!

'What are you doing with *my* mug?' Sam said, a dangerous tone to her voice. Nigel looked at the mug as if seeing it for the first time, then gave a low chuckle. 'Oh, yes. Sorry, Sam, I just grabbed the first mug I saw – you don't mind, do you?' He made a ridiculous giggling sound and took a large slurp with his rubbery, moist lips. Sam stared murderously at him: her first impulse to hurl the cups of tea she was holding at him – hopefully the contents would still be hot enough to cause serious damage. But no, that wouldn't do. It wasn't civilised behaviour and she couldn't risk getting sacked. She gritted her teeth and clenched the cups so tightly, she felt she might break them. She couldn't afford to lose it. Not here in front of everyone. She didn't like feeling like this, it scared her: all those times during her school years, where she had to be physically pulled off other kids who had angered her, or later on, as a temperamental teen, taking offence to anyone and everything. She thought she was managing to curb her temper since the move to Lincoln but her destructive thoughts kept returning, threatening to overwhelm her and alienate her from those around her.

Sam didn't take in a word of the meeting, all her attention directed towards the fat, balding creature across the table, his podgy hands clasped around her mug, the grinning face from his staff badge taken when he had more hair and stating that he was Dr Nigel Simmons.

After the meeting had finished, Sam went to the kitchen and washed up the small cup that wasn't hers. She slammed it down on the drainer, her thoughts fixed on the image of the creep suctioning onto her mug. She visualised cutting off his rubbery lips with a sharp blade before cutting out his tongue. She didn't have many possessions in her life and although it was only a mug, it was a rare present from her mother. Standing at the sink, she felt, rather than heard the presence of someone behind her. Turning round, she was greeted with the sight of the fat slug. He was standing too close for her liking and she shivered with revulsion as he leaned over her to turn the tap on and she felt his arm brush against her.

'I'll just give your mug a good wash then it's all yours. Nice skirt, by the way,' he said, giving Sam a cursory up and down glance. 'There we go, nice and clean.' He held out Sam's mug and she took it, her hand involuntarily touching one of Nigel's podgy fingers. He did an annoying little bow and left the room, side stepping Frances and her stern stare on his way out.

'Take no notice of him,' Frances said, placing her cafetière on the counter. 'The silly man has a crush on you, as he does with all the attractive young women who start working here. But I do believe that he is harmless. Just try not to rise to his bait and he'll soon get bored.' Sam nodded and gave the older woman a faint smile.

'Right-oh, better get back to the front line,' said Frances briskly, leaving Sam alone in the kitchen. Glancing down, she saw that her hands were trembling from her encounter with Nigel, not from fear or anxiety, but rage. Pure, white-hot rage.

Sitting at her desk in reception, Sam placed her mug in the drawer where she kept her bag and tried not to think about those moist rubbery lips. She shuddered and locked the drawer.

Chapter Six

A blend of Toluene, Formaldehyde and other noxious chemicals hit Sam's nostrils as she entered the nail salon. Su, one of the technicians, looked up from her workstation, nodded and pointed to the waiting area. Sam nodded back and went to sit in the only seat available. Considering it was 4:30pm on a weekday, the salon was busy, with all three technicians attending to clients and four people waiting.

Sam didn't mind waiting and inhaled deeply as she lowered herself into the seat, enjoying the harsh chemical smell. There was an immediate scraping of the chair next to her and turning her head, she saw a mousy woman, probably in her fifties, shunting herself away, a look of disdain etched on her shrew-like features. And it didn't take much to work out why; a quick glance round the salon and there was one factor that set Sam apart from the rest of the clientele: she was the only one there who wasn't white.

Even in these times, the inhabitants of Lincoln were largely white and although Sam had found the people she encountered to be friendly on the whole, she had been acutely aware of the instances when she was being regarded in a less favourable light. That was the one thing that Sam missed about London; being able to go about her business without giving too much thought to being judged on her colour – that and memories of her time with Pops. All these years later, and she still missed him so much.

Sam settled herself in her seat with the magazine she had bought on her way to the salon. She took another deep breath and shrugged, then released her shoulders. This was her time. She wasn't going to let the shrew bitch spoil it.

Flicking through the pages, she stopped at the hair section, admiring the model sporting her corkscrew curls. She herself was sporting a poker-straight weave, but she'd been considering a different style recently, maybe something softer.

Deciding she might as well contact her hairdresser in the hope of getting an appointment any time soon, Sam pulled her mobile from her bag. Just as she located her number, Sam's mobile started to ring, affording another look of disdain from the shrew sat next to her.

'Sammy, oh God!' This was followed by a gasping sound. Sam paused a moment before answering, well used to her mother's outbursts. The last time was about three weeks ago when she'd received no less than twelve missed calls from her mother due to someone knocking on the door.

'He keeps knocking, Sammy, he won't go away!' Her mother had wailed down the phone, causing Sam to hold her mobile away from her ear.

'Why don't you just ask who's there? And how do you know it's a man?'

'Oh, I know the sound of a man knocking at the door, Sammy. Like they have a bloody God-given right to be let in!' More hyperventilating. 'Oh God! Sammy! He's at it again! What shall I do?!'

It turned out to be the woman from a few doors down, enquiring about a parcel that had supposedly been left at number seven (their house) but turned out to be for number one.

Now, Sam took a deep breath, scrunched her eyes shut and waited to hear what her mother was agonising about this time. The technique worked to stop her tears as a child, but wasn't quite as effective in dampening her anger.

'What's wrong, Mum?' She gripped her phone tightly to her ear and started counting soundlessly, in a bid to remain patient and not scream, *what the fuck's wrong now?!* Her mother made a few more gulping noises before whimpering, 'He's got my pendant.'

'What?'

'Mummy's pendant. I was looking for it and ... Oh God!' Sam bent her head away from her mother's wailing and thought for a moment. She had never got the chance to know Grandma Eden as she had died long before she was born and when she had tried once to get Pops to talk about his late wife, it made him cry, so she never asked him again. Her mother was always vague when she tried to bring up the subject, leading Sam to conclude that they must not have been close, so it surprised her now to hear her mother's distress.

'Mum,' she said, as calmly as she could, which only produced a fresh round of wailing in her ear. Sam pinched the bridge of her nose. 'Mum! Listen to me. Now!' She didn't want to have to raise her voice in public but this was getting out of hand, and the only way to get her mother's attention was to speak with authority. When she was sure her mother was listening, she continued, 'Have you looked in the box under the stairs?'

'Yes.' Her mother was still breathing rapidly but at least she was listening and responding.

'What about the—'

'SHE CAME INTO THE ROOM AND SAW ME PASSED OUT ON THE FLOOR,' announced the shrew suddenly.

Sam glanced over to see if she was addressing her, but no, she was looking down at the book in her lap.

'Sammy?' Her mother's voice brought her back to the conversation.

'Yes Mum, I was just thinking, did you check in the basket on top of the—'

'I WASN'T EXPECTING ANYTHING TO HAPPEN, BUT THEN IT DID AND WHAT A NIGHT THAT WAS,' came the voice of the shrew, her monotone a little louder this time. Again, Sam looked at her but she had held her book right up to her face, blocking Sam's view. There was a picture of some ageing rock star on the cover and it looked like it might be an autobiography from what Sam could make out from the words between the woman's pale fingers.

'Sammy? Sammy? Can you hear me?'

'Er ... yes, Mum, I was just—'

'ANOTHER TIME I'LL NEVER FORGET WAS WHEN WE TOURED AUSTRALIA AND THE BUS BROKE DOWN.'

She was reading out loud, Sam had sussed that much out. But it only seemed to be when she was speaking to her mother. And each time she stopped, the shrew stopped. She looked around in bewilderment at the other customers in waiting, but they didn't seem to notice.

'Sammy?'

'Look, I'll be back soon and help you look, OK? Bye.' This last response prompted another snippet from the autobiography, affording a curious glance from one of the other women. She caught Sam's eye and gave a 'loopy' gesture with her forefinger. Somehow through the red mist of fury, Sam managed a tight smile. Thank God someone else had noticed, it wasn't all in her head.

Abruptly, Sam stood up and walked towards the toilet at the back of the salon. She needed to get away from the shrew, who was now fastidiously placing a bookmark on the page she had got up to, not once looking up to gauge Sam's reaction.

Sitting on the toilet in the cramped cubicle, Sam placed her fist in her mouth and bit down hard to stop herself from screaming. It hurt like hell. When the urge had passed, she withdrew her fist, noting the teeth marks that had nearly drawn blood on the worst affected fingers. She didn't like being this angry, it churned her insides and made her feel uncomfortable and jittery. Normally, she'd be able to laugh it off, look back at the other woman who'd noticed the shrew's reading aloud and roll her eyeballs in response – *look at the poor crazy woman. Thank God we're normal*, communicated silently between them.

It was that fucker using her mug which had started things off on a bad foot. All day there'd been the feeling of a dark cloud hanging just above her head and even Frances' words hadn't managed to placate her. It was also probably due, in part, to it being that time of the month, she reflected, as she eased out the bloody tampon from herself. She was about to discard it into the toilet bowl but stopped as an idea formulated in her head.

Pulling a bunch of tissues from the dispenser, Sam wrapped up the soiled tampon. Walking back out to the waiting area, she saw her chance. The shrew was standing at the counter to get a better look at the vast array of nail varnishes. *Nothing's going to brighten up those insipid fingers,* Sam thought, as she sat down and bent forward to place the wrapped up tampon in the shrew's unattended bag (*more fool her for leaving it there*). As luck would have it, the stupid cow had made it easy, leaving the bag open with her book perched on the top. In one deft move, Sam wedged the tampon in between the pages of the book and sat back up, suddenly feeling like a weight had been lifted from her.

Justice had been served.

Chapter Seven

The lightweight feeling didn't last long as Sam opened the front door and took in the disarray of the sitting room. Her chest tightened. The cabinet drawers had been pulled out, their contents strewn across the table and the floor. All the items on the shelving unit had been moved about or taken off. Nothing was in its usual place. And amidst all the mess was her mother, crouched on the floor sobbing, her shoulders heaving theatrically.

'Eddie's got it,' she said, by way of a greeting, 'I must've left it there. Oh God, Sammy, what shall I do? I promised Daddy I'd look after it and I have, all this time haven't I?' She looked up imploringly, her palms held out in supplication.

Sam stood for a moment, regarding the excuse for a mother in front of her; the weak, snivelling cow that she'd had the misfortune to be born to. Her hands twitched with an urge to do something bad, so she folded her arms. Why couldn't *Denise* be the strong one? Just for once in her pathetic life! She closed her eyes to shut out the image of her mother cowering on the floor amongst all the mess. The mess that Sam would now have to clear up.

She started to feel a strange sensation then, like the floor was moving beneath her feet; the room started to blur as her vision went in and out of focus and for a moment all she could hear was her own breathing: In, out. In, out.

Her mother was standing in front of her now, and Sam wondered how she'd got up so quickly. She noticed her mother's expression change. Something wasn't right; her eyes were open wide and bulging, arms flailing and she was making a strained, rasping sound as if she were struggling to breathe.

Sam then became aware of her own arms, no longer folded, but extended in front of her, her hands gripped tightly around her mother's slender neck, and she now recognised the strange expression on her mother's face. It was the same as when faced with the wrath of Darren, Eddie, or one of the others that her mother had allowed into their lives. It was a look of pure terror.

She gasped, immediately releasing her grip. 'I'm sorry,' she said, watching her mother slump down to the floor; she was trembling and whimpering, her head bent downwards revealing the stray hairs at the nape of her neck that had escaped her ponytail. And, for a brief moment, Sam considered picking up the heavy glass vase from the nearby shelf and smashing it over that neat little head, watching as the blood slowly seeped into the carpet, contrasting sharply with the pale blue pile. But only for a brief moment.

'I'm sorry,' she said again, kneeling down. Her mother looked up and then suddenly grasped Sam tightly, 'It's OK, Sammy, it's OK.'

But it was far from OK and they both knew it.

****

Sam didn't take kindly to the sound of her alarm; she'd had a restless night. However much she tried, she couldn't get that image out her head: the terrified expression on her mother's face, of her being the cause of it. It made her feel queasy. She had never lost it to that extent before, not with her mother. Sam wondered, not for the first time, if she should get some help. Maybe some kind of anger management sessions might go some way to helping her contain the molten lava that resided in the pit of her stomach. She had ambivalent feelings after her first counselling session – a requirement of her course – but hoped they might help.

After showering, she sat at her dressing table and applied the various pots of foundation and powders that gave her the confidence to face the world: a presentable self. But no amount of careful blending and applying seemed to cover the dark circles under her eyes, or soften her 'resting bitch face' features. And was that the beginnings of a spot? She leaned in for a closer inspection of her hardened features. Keeping up the pretence that everything was all fine with her mother was taking its toll on her sanity. She had hoped the move to Lincoln would be the fresh start they both so desperately needed; a new life away from the dangerous men and drugs that Denise was so helplessly drawn to. But Sam knew that even without these constant threats to their safety, her relationship with her mother was difficult. Lifting the corners of her mouth, she attempted to smile, but the reflection looking back at her was more of a grimace.

Tentatively, she opened the door to her mother's bedroom. 'Bye Mum,' she whispered, to the recumbent form in the bed, before closing the door gently behind her.

Sam noticed the homeless man as she approached the health centre. He was sitting a little further down than usual, in the recess of a newly vacated shop front. He was munching happily on a sausage and egg McMuffin and waved to Sam, seemingly oblivious to the scowl he got back in return.

And there he was, his flabby arms perched jauntily on her desk, a twinkle in his piggy eyes as she entered. 'Ah, Sam, just the person!'

She paused for a moment, before walking purposefully towards the door to the side of the reception. Wrenching it open, she gave Nigel one of her death stares.

'What are you doing in here?' she asked, her voice low and dangerous.

'Getting myself acquainted with my appointments for the day,' he said, beaming.

'But you can look at your appointments on your *own* computer in your *own* office.'

Nigel swivelled round to face Sam, leaning back in the chair, his legs splayed out in a proprietary manner. 'But I like this computer, it's got a bigger screen. Look, don't worry, I'll be out of your hair in a minute, I just can't get the calendar up for some reason. Could you help me? Pretty please?' He fluttered his stubby eyelashes in what Sam took to be an attempt at looking coy.

Cursing silently under her breath, she strode towards the desk and with a few clicks of the mouse, had the calendar up in a matter of seconds.

'Nice nails,' Nigel said. 'The pink really suits your colouring,' he added, his usual nasal tone a shade lower as he reached towards her hand.

Quick as a flash, Sam slapped his hand away, 'Don't you *dare* touch me!'

'What's going on?' said Alan, poking his head around the door.

'I— I was only paying her a compliment, just saying her nails looked nice and then she hit me!' replied Nigel, nursing his hand. The usually mild-mannered branch manager gave Nigel a hard stare. 'I suggest you leave and let Sam get on with her work,' he said, a look of distaste evident on his face.

Sam exhaled in relief as both men left. Pulling out a cleaning wipe from the packet on the desk, she wiped down the computer, keyboard and chair and when content that she had erased Nigel's residue, she sat down, adjusted her seat and began her work. But not before sending a quick text to her mum:

I won't be home late, then we can plan how we're going to
get your pendant back xx

It wasn't until the end of the day that Sam encountered Nigel again, this time in the kitchen, as she was washing up her mug and plate from lunch.

'Sorry about earlier, it wasn't my intention to scare you,' he said, propping against the counter, too near to her.

'You didn't,' Sam replied curtly, squirting some washing up liquid onto a scourer.

Nigel turned so his body was facing the counter, elbows taking some of his weight, he whispered conspiratorially, 'Sambuca.'

'Wh— what?' Sam said, almost dropping the plate in her hand. 'Why did you call me that? How do you know?'

'Aha,' said Nigel, tapping his finger on his fleshy nose, 'I have my ways.'

Sam had been named after one of her mother's favourite tipples, and detested it. But there were some small mercies; at least she hadn't been called something floral, like Rosie, or Daisy, God forbid. And at least she could shorten it to Sam.

She had toyed with the notion of changing her name by deed

poll at some point in the future, when her mother was dead and couldn't be upset by her daughter shedding the name she had given her.

'Sambuuuuuuuucaaaaaaa,' repeated Nigel, jolting Sam from her thoughts, 'I think it suits you .... I ...'

Without giving too much thought to what she was doing, Sam lunged towards Nigel, gripped his podgy arm and bit down hard.

'Aaaaaaaaaaaarrrrrrrgggggggghhhhhh!'

Releasing her grip, Sam took a step back and saw the blood oozing out from the perfect indentation her teeth had made on Nigel's flesh. Holding his arm, Nigel started to make his exit but Sam grabbed him. 'Leave me the fuck alone from now on,' she hissed. Nigel whimpered as she dug her acrylics into his flesh and she enjoyed the terrified look in his eyes as she bared her teeth, his small eyes opened wide in terror at the blood – his blood – glistening in her mouth.

'And don't even think about saying anything or I'll tell Alan you tried it on with me, which you did. Frances thinks you're a pervert, I know everyone will believe me. Do you understand?' Nigel nodded, desperate to make his escape. A small movement caught Sam's eye; the cleaner hovering by the kitchen door, mop bucket in one hand, rubbing her forehead with the other. 'I'll come back later,' she said.

'It's OK, we're all finished here,' Sam said, not taking her eyes off Nigel.

Chapter Eight

It took several swills of TCP to wash the taste of Nigel's blood from Sam's mouth and for a moment, she looked in disbelief at her reflection in the staff toilets – disbelief at what she had just done and what she would say to her supervisor at her next counselling session.

Stepping outside the centre, she took a deep breath and looking up, noticed the cumulus clouds in the early evening sky. There was a definite sense of spring in the air, and she felt as lightweight as she had when getting her own back on the shrew in the nail salon. Only this was better, a rush of blood to the head that made her dizzy. But she knew it wouldn't last and would soon be replaced by the low-lying anger that was ever present.

At the top of Steep hill, Sam turned right instead of straight on towards home; she couldn't face her mother just yet, not with this jittery feeling. She felt a sudden urge to be inside the cathedral. Nodding brusquely at the robed man near the entrance, she rushed into the morning chapel and, tossing some coins into the collection box, lit a candle and placed it in the sand. Closing her eyes, she conjured up Pops, his beige cardigan frayed around the edges, the flat cap perched on his head but with horror, she realised that his features were blurred from years of not seeing him. But then he smiled; the twinkle of a gold-capped tooth just visible, the crinkles around his eyes. And she felt calm then, just standing there staring down at the candle and the image of Pops alive inside her head.

****

Opening the front door, Sam was relieved to find no evidence of the disarray from the previous evening. A smell of something garlicky hit her nostrils as she walked through to the kitchen.

'Hi Sammy, dinner's nearly ready. The table's all set,' her mother said in an overly cheerful voice.

'Great, did you go out?'

'No, I found some chicken kievs in the freezer and I've used up the last of the potatoes and parsnips.' Sam studied her mother for a moment, taking in the nervous way she was twirling her hands, flitting from one kitchen utensil to another without actually doing anything.

'Are you OK, Mum?' she eventually asked, reaching for her mother's arm to steady her and feeling an imperceptible flinch.

'Yes, I'm fine, Sammy.'

'I mean about yesterday. I'm really sorry, I don't know what came over me.'

'I'm fine,' her mother replied, before abruptly turning away to open the oven. Miraculously, the kievs weren't burnt, unlike most of the items she attempted to prepare.

They ate in silence, an unusual experience since they had moved to Lincoln. Gone was the twitter from her mother, recounting the minutiae of her day, or the questions she asked Sam about her job. Every now and then, Sam felt Denise looking at her, but when she looked up, her mother immediately averted her gaze.

Carefully placing her cutlery on her unfinished plate, Sam looked across the small table, willing Denise to look at her. To speak, to shout, to cry. Anything to replace this weird silence. Just when she could stand it no longer, her mother spoke.

'You reminded me of someone yesterday. When you were angry.'

'Mum, I said I'm sorry, I don't know what else to say.'

'I know you're sorry, Sam. I am too, for making you feel like that.' Sam watched as her mother stood up and came towards her, her arms outstretched. She sighed with relief as her mother's arms encircled her.

'Who did I remind you of?' Sam mumbled, through her mother's embrace. 'And please don't say one of your exes, I'm nothing like them.'

'My dad.'

Sam pulled away to look at her mother. 'Pops?' she said incredulously. Her mother nodded, clasping and unclasping her hands.

Sam stood up, almost knocking her chair over in the process. 'I ... I don't believe you!'

'Oh he never hit me Sammy. I don't want you thinking he was some kind of monster. He would just get really angry sometimes and the look in his eyes – it was like he was trying to stop himself. I know I was the cause of a lot of that anger, but still ...' Her mother shook her head and inhaled sharply. 'It was almost like he was possessed with something. I sometimes wished he'd just hit me and get it out of his system. But he never did Sammy, I want you to know that. He never did.'

Sam slumped back onto the chair, deflated. It was devastating to hear her dear Pops being described in a menacing light and it horrified her to think she was the same.

'I can't imagine him being like that,' she whispered.

'He was calmer as he got older.' Her mother smiled, 'I think that having you was the turning point. He doted on you, especially with Mummy dying so young.'

'What was grandma like?' asked Sam, intrigued; Grandma Eden had died of cancer at the age of fifty-seven and had never got to meet her granddaughter.

'She was lovely. Everything a mother should be. Nothing like me,' she said bitterly, before snatching up their plates and taking them into the kitchen, indicating the end of the conversation.

'We'll get your pendant back,' Sam called after her mother.

****

Walking into work the next day, Sam couldn't help but notice the homeless man, now a permanent fixture on the narrow, cobbled street. He was fast asleep, cosy as you like in one of those silver, shiny expensive looking sleeping bags.

Bracing herself for the sight of Nigel nestled in her chair, she was relieved to find it empty. She wondered if the pig had squealed to Alan about what she'd done to him but somehow didn't think he'd dare, so pushed the thought from her head. Whatever happened, she would deal with it. Retrieving her mug from the locked cupboard, she made her way into the kitchen.

'I know, it's really scary. She's only in her twenties. I can't believe it's happened on my street!' Anna exclaimed, staring fixedly at the pages of the *Lincolnshire Herald* splayed out on the table.

Standing with her, one of the physio's from upstairs shook his head. 'I didn't think things like this happened in Lincoln.'

'What's happened?' asked Sam, switching on the kettle. Anna glanced up from the newspaper, a troubled expression on her face. 'Oh, hi Sam. It's one of our patients, she's gone missing. The family live on my street. The police have been doing their door to door enquiries but I never really knew them that well.'

Sam nodded, not really knowing what to say, and rearranged her features into what she hoped approximated a look of concern. Having lived in London, she was used to hearing unsettling news, posters with the beaming faces of missing people, not yet aware of what was to come. She turned to make her tea.

'Morning all' said Alan, popping his head round the door. 'Ah, Sam, can I have a quick word?'

Sam froze. What if the fat slug *had* actually grassed on her? Shown Alan the teeth marks, *her* teeth marks so perfectly indented in his fleshy arm. She turned and gave Alan what she hoped was a smile. 'Yes, of course Alan.'

Stepping into the corridor, Alan said, 'Nigel's called in sick and I don't think he'll be in for the rest of this week.'

'Oh?' Sam replied, waiting to see if she was to be cited as the reason for his 'sickness'.

'So, you'll need to do a block cancellation for all his patients and I wasn't sure if you've been shown how to do that on the system?'

'Oh, right,' said Sam again, struggling to hide the relief that swept over her. The slug had heeded her threat. He wasn't going to say anything. 'Er, no I haven't been shown how to do that.'

'That's fine.' Alan gave a reassuring smile. 'Go and get your tea and I'll show you.'

She had just sorted out the appointments, slotting some onto the other GP lists and rescheduling some for the following week, when she became aware of someone standing before her. It was Jack Sutton, the gorgeous looking bloke she had seen earlier in the week. He'd managed to startle her again, approaching the reception with such stealth she hadn't noticed.

'Hello again,' he said, smiling to reveal those perfect, white teeth. Sam returned his smile. She couldn't help it. He really was as perfect as the image she held in her mind. An unexpected jolt of pleasure rippled through her, it had been a long time since she had felt so strongly attracted to someone and she wondered if he had a girlfriend.

'How can I help you?' she said.

'I'm seeing the Physio and, before you say anything, I know his room is upstairs. I just wanted to say hello.' And, with that, he limped towards the lift, turning back to give Sam a wink.

'Ahem.' Sam dragged her eyes away from him and smiled to herself before turning to another patient.

'Edith, how lovely to see you.'

'Wish I could say the same, and it's Miss Mowbray to you.'

Sam's smile widened; she looked forward to her encounters with the blunt-speaking elderly woman before her. On a good day, she was even allowed to greet her by her first name.

'My apologies.'

'What are you apologising for?'

'For calling you Edith.' Edith nodded her head sharply. 'And how can I help you, Miss Mowbray?'

'I have an appointment with Dr Simmons.'

Sam's eyes flickered towards the screen in front of her. 'I can't see your name here, Miss Mowbray,' she replied, shaking her head. 'Dr Simmons isn't in today so we've had to reschedule some of his appointments, but you weren't on the list.'

'Nonsense, girl, I have an appointment for today. Check again, you must have made a mistake.' Edith folded her arms in a resolute manner.

Sam made a pretence of checking the screen again. 'No, sorry,

Miss Mowbray, you're definitely not on today's list.'

Just then, Frances came striding down the corridor towards the waiting area and, holding her hand up to shield her eyes from the bright morning sun, peered around the door to the reception. 'You can have your appointment with me since I have a cancellation.' Edith's shrewd eyes blinked uncomprehendingly for a moment before focusing on Frances.

'Hrrrrmmmmmppphh,' came Edith's reply as she was ushered along the corridor to Frances' room.

The rest of the morning passed by in a blur, and it wasn't until later that Sam realised with dismay that she had missed Jack leaving the centre. Not that she would have known what to say. '*Would you like to go out for a drink later?*' seemed inappropriate, and besides, she wasn't that forward, especially when she was uncertain whether he actually fancied her. She wasn't used to getting attention from a white guy. But the way he had purposefully come to say hello, instead of just going straight upstairs, his eyes shining as he winked at her, made her think otherwise.

She shook her head as she collected her bag and walked out of the centre; she was reading too much into what was most likely politeness on Jack's part. She needed to get a life and, besides, she didn't need a man in her life; in her experience they brought nothing but trouble. Apart from Pops, of course, despite what her mother had said.

The brilliant sunshine caused Sam to squint, and she made a mental note to start taking her sunglasses out with her. She was about to cross the road to the café when she noticed him. He was crouched in a rather awkward position (possibly due to whatever was wrong with his leg) and was talking to the homeless man who had grasped his hand and appeared to be thanking him. She hesitated a moment, unsure whether to approach him, and, as if feeling her gaze, he suddenly looked up in her direction. The sun caught his hair, making it look like a golden halo, and Sam was once again reminded of how good looking he was. He raised his hand in greeting and she hesitantly returned the gesture. After saying something to the homeless man, he stood carefully, clutching what Sam guessed was his bad leg.

'Hello again,' he said, limping towards her. She returned his smile without having to think about it.

'Hello.'

'I'm Jack, by the way, I told you my name when I came for my first appointment, but I doubt you'd remember. What's your name?'

'Sam.'

'Short for anything?'

'Just Sam.'

It was a few moments before Sam realised she was just standing there, staring up at him. 'Right, well nice to see you Jack. I'm off to get my lunch,' she said, averting her gaze from those blue eyes that dazzled in the sunlight, and had momentarily mesmerised her.

'Well, as it happens, I was just going to get myself something. Are you going over there?' Jack said, pointing towards the café.

'Yes I am. But I'm getting something to take away.'

Unfazed, Jack shrugged his shoulders and smiled. 'Well, I'll just have to make the most of your company whilst I can.'

Together, they crossed the road and entered the café. Sam felt a rush of pleasure as he opened the door for her, then silently reprimanded herself for being so easily pleased. As they stood in the queue, Jack turned to her. 'Look,' he said, nodding towards an empty table by the window. 'That's my favourite spot to sit and it's usually occupied. Why don't you join me?'

Sam was about to say no, but the hopeful expression on his face stopped her. 'OK,' she said with a shrug of her shoulders. She couldn't help smiling at the enthusiastic look on his handsome face.

'Great!' he said, looking like a boy who'd won a prize at the fair. Despite her protests, he had insisted on buying her lunch and not used to being bought anything from a man, except Pops, Sam felt a little uncomfortable as she pulled out a chair and sat down. Noticing the homeless man looking at her from across the road, she shifted her position so that she was facing in towards the café. Jack had moved to the front of the queue and, by the amount of smiling and laughter coming from the woman serving him, he was obviously a regular. How was it that Sam hadn't seen him before? Maybe their paths had crossed and she simply hadn't noticed.

She noted, with a hint of disdain, how the woman's face positively lit up as she conversed with Jack. All Sam got from her was the bare minimum needed for the transaction of requesting food and purchasing it. But Sam knew that was mainly down to her – she wasn't in the habit of exchanging pleasantries.

Over lunch, Sam found out that Jack was in his final year of studying Journalism.

'So, how old are you?' she asked, thinking he must be a few years younger than her.

'Twenty-seven. And you?'

'Twenty-six.'

'Hmmm ... both late starters.'

'Yep,' replied Sam curtly, not wanting to explain her turbulent journey into adulthood as the reason for only now embarking on a course that would hopefully lead to a fulfilling, secure career. As if noting her reticence, Jack filled in the silence that followed, talking in that relaxed manner that comes easily to people secure in who they are.

He had taken not one but *three* gap years following his A Levels, making a joke of it in between large mouthfuls of his Panini – *it took me that long to get over the stress of revision!*

He had his own house in the trendy new development on the Brayford Waterfront, almost exactly across the water from the university, the only drawback being there was no excuse for being late for lectures, he'd said with a laugh. His parents lived near the Cathedral, his mother was a County Court Judge, his father an antiques dealer. The sore leg was the result of a recent skiing trip, where he had fractured his right femur.

The relaxed, fluid movements of his body as he spoke made Sam, in turn, relax. She found herself enjoying the experience of just chatting with someone who wasn't her mother, or a colleague or patient. Any friendships growing up had been impossible to sustain, what with all the frequent moving and having to cover up her miserable home life.

Sam looked down at her watch and was surprised to find her

lunch hour was nearly up. The saying 'How quickly time flies when you're having fun' couldn't be more apt.

'Hold on a second, I just need to get something,' Jack said when she told him she'd need to be getting back.

'Something for later?' she said, raising an eyebrow as Jack returned clutching two paper bags and a takeaway tea.

'One's for you,' he said, proffering one of the paper bags. 'Go on, take it.'

Bemused, Sam took the offering and looked inside. It was one of the beautiful little cupcakes that were placed tantalisingly on the counter, defying the local custom not to purchase one. Sam had given in quite a few times since she had started working at the health centre.

'Errr, you didn't have to do that. I don't know what to say,' she said, looking up at Jack who was staring intently back at her.

'No big deal, just a little something to keep you going for the afternoon. I hope you like those ones.'

'Yes, the chocolate ones are my favourite,' she said, smiling without the usual effort. 'Thank you,' she added, shyly.

The other bag of food wasn't for Jack, Sam found out, as he escorted her back across the road and, before she could protest, towards the homeless man.

'Hey, Billy, this is Sam. Sam, Billy.'

Sam's mouth twitched into an apprehensive smile, half expecting Billy to ignore her. After all, that's what she had done to him on the many occasions she had noticed him slouched in the doorway. But she was greeted with, 'Hi, Sam. How's it going?' He was proffering his hand towards her and she shook it for as brief a time as she could without seeming rude. She'd have to give her hands a good scrub when she got back to the centre and she resisted the urge to wipe the contaminated hand on the side of her skirt.

'Here we go, something for later,' Jack said, placing the paper bag he was holding in Billy's lap.

'I told you, I'm fine!' Turning to Sam, he continued, 'Thanks to this good man here, I now have a brand spanking new sleeping bag.'

'I'm just sorry the shelter didn't work out for you,' said Jack, overlooking the compliment.

'It's not your fault, you did your best,' said Billy with a shrug of his shoulders. Turning to Sam, he said, 'Not only did he get me this sleeping bag, he rang round some homeless places to see if I could stay. He's a real living saint, I tell you.'

'But what happened, Billy? They said there was definitely a vacancy.'

Billy looked down, a sheepish look on his prematurely haggard face. 'They caught me with this,' he said, lifting part of the sleeping bag to reveal a bottle of whisky.

Jack sighed with exasperation. 'Billy, I told you they have strict rules about alcohol. What did you think you were doing?'

'Old habits die hard, my friend. Old habits die hard,' Billy said with a sad smile.

'The proper good Samaritan, aren't you?' Sam said, approaching the entrance to the health centre.

Jack shook his head. 'Not really, no. I just can't walk past someone on the street and not try and help in some way. Do you know Billy's only a couple of years older than me? It's scary to think that with a bad twist of fate, I, or you, could've ended up like that.'

Looking at Sam with a serious expression on his perfect face, he added, 'We should count ourselves lucky.'

Talk for your bloody self! Sam thought, the beginnings of a sneer forming on her face, but Jack's sincere expression stopped her and she simply nodded.

Walking home later that day, Sam felt a strange, nervous flutter in her chest as she thought of Jack. Standing outside the health centre, he'd asked her out that weekend and although her first instinct had been to decline, she found herself accepting. She was fed up with the tense, almost claustrophobic atmosphere at home; it would be good to spend time with someone other than her mother. With an exchange of phone numbers, Sam had gone back into work feeling slightly light headed, her cheek tingling pleasantly where he had, rather chastely, kissed her.

She returned home to find her mother sitting at the table; clasping and unclasping her hands in that way of hers that meant she was more anxious than usual. Sam's shoulders slumped, the light feeling leaving her body almost immediately.

'Hi, Mum,' she said tentatively.

'Oh Sammy, have you seen this?' her mother answered, gesturing towards several newspapers laid out in front of her. Sam walked towards the table and instantly recognised the story of the missing woman.

'Yes. They were talking about it at work; her family are registered at the health centre and she lived on the same road as one of the nurses.'

'Oh God, that's awful!' her mother said, bringing her hand up to her mouth.

'Come on mum, it's sad, but how many people go missing in London every day? It's not that big a deal in the scheme of things,' Sam said, already feeling put out by her mother's overreaction to the story.

'Yes, but this is a small town, Sammy, and it says here another woman went missing just a few months back,' her mother said, jabbing a finger at one of the newspaper columns. Sam's jaw tensed as she considered the fact her mother wouldn't leave the house to do anything for her own flesh and blood, but she'd apparently been perfectly capable of going far enough to get all these papers for some stranger, who'd been fool enough to get herself taken.

'Sarah Hollins.'

'What?'

'Her name was Sarah Hollins. Only twenty-six, same age as you.'

'Well you shouldn't talk about her in the past tense, she might still be alive.'

'Oh Sammy, don't say that!' her mother said, bringing both hands to her mouth this time and making Sam feel like she wanted to shake her, to bring her back to her senses and make her get a fucking grip. She swallowed down the surge of anger that threatened to emerge and loosened her hands, which she'd realised were clenched into tight balls. 'I just can't stand the thought of anything happening to you. I worry all the time when you're out. Did you know that?'

If only you'd had the same fucking level of concern when I was growing up, Sam thought, grudgingly.

'I'd better make a start on dinner. Unless you had something planned?' Sam said, with an edge to her voice that went unnoticed by her mother.

'Sorry, I got a bit carried away. Let's cook something together.'

The resentment Sam was feeling quickly dissipated as her mother approached her, holding out her arms for a hug. 'I don't think I could carry on if anything happened to you, Sammy,' her mother mumbled into her neck as she clutched Sam fiercely to her. Sam managed not to mention all the things that had already happened to her, thanks to her mother's poor parenting. Instead, she let her mind wander to Sarah Hollins, and whether she'd deserved to be hurt, like Nigel.

Chapter Nine

A shaft of light entered the dingy room through a gap in the curtains, warming her left arm and, although she couldn't see it, instinctively she turned her head towards it. She felt the light bathe her face and took a deep, shuddering breath, amazed at how, even in these horrific circumstances, she still had the ability to draw comfort from such a small thing.

This place was infinitely better than the dungeon, with its cold, stone floor and complete and utter darkness – apart from when he was there, shining a torch in her face. The best thing was being able to distinguish between night and day and, although she had no idea how long she'd been in the dungeon, she now knew that she had spent three nights and two days in this new place.

He put her in a bath on the first night and washed off the dried blood and excrement with a sponge. The pain was excruciating and she cried out when the sponge came into contact with the open wounds, especially the one on her abdomen; the one she'd been made to do herself and, because the results hadn't pleased him, he'd gone over it again. She must have blacked out after that because when she came round, she was here, lying on a mattress in this new place. The rest of what happened that night in the bath haunted her every moment.

'Hollins … Sarah Hollins … hmm. Has a better ring to it than plain old Smith, don't you think?' She quickly nodded her agreement, not wanting to anger or provoke him as he gently washed her face, carefully dabbing round the blindfold with a soft flannel, and, despite the horror of her situation, a small thread of hope inveigled its way prematurely into her mind.

'Why did you change it? If you don't mind me asking.'

'M— my mother went back to her maiden name after my parents' divorce.'

'Ah, I see. Well, it's a good thing; gives us a bit more time together before connections are made.'

She was about to respond, but all of a sudden his hands were gripping her head and pushing her under the water, the force sending water whooshing up into her nostrils and her mouth. If she'd had more forewarning of what he was about to do, she'd have taken a deep breath, like she did just before diving into a pool, only coming up for air when she'd completed the length – one of the things she'd been proud of, in that other world.

And as her lungs felt ready to explode and her body to convulse, she was pulled, spluttering, from the water.

When her coughing fit finally dissipated, she heard him clicking his tongue. 'What a fuss over getting your hair washed and look at the mess you've made!' It was then that she smelt something foul and realised that she'd shat herself. 'I'm not putting my hands in that filth. Pull the plug and stand up.'

She remained still, not sure whether it was some kind of trick.

'Now!' he roared in her ear. She scrambled blindly through the stinking water till she found the chain to the plug and pulled. 'Good girl. Now stand up so I can shower you.'

She gasped, as the first jets of icy water hit her body.

'Too cold for you?' he asked, and she tried to shake her head, because she knew what he was going to do, but her body didn't seem capable of following her instructions anymore.

His laughter mingled with her cries as the unbearably hot water seared her skin.

****

Saturday morning dawned brightly, waking Sam prematurely. She'd been dreaming about Pops. They'd been sitting in the greasy spoon and he had bought her a large chocolate milkshake, the frothy top threatening to spill over the rim of the tall glass. Pops was laughing as she took several big gulps of the drink, a chocolaty outline framing her mouth. The scene still imprinted on her mind, she wanted to climb back into it.

She lay back in bed, planning how to tell her mother she was going out on a date later that evening. She'd tried several times to broach the subject the previous day, but the words seemed to die on her lips at each attempt. Her mother was still obsessing over the missing woman, which wasn't making Sam spending the night with a virtual stranger any easier to broach as a subject. Having tried very hard to engage with her and to distract her with almost any other news story, Sam had finally got her talking about their garden. It was only a small space but had obviously been neglected for some time, judging by how over-grown it had become. After a few fretful protestations, she had eventually persuaded her mother to come out with her to the local market where there were several stalls selling a variety of plants.

The brilliant sunshine belied the chill in the air as they walked towards the market and Sam linked arms with her mother, drawing closer for warmth. She felt her mother's pace slow as they approached the playground in the park.

'Isn't it lovely seeing the children playing? They all look so happy,' her mother said, turning to look at her, a smile lighting up her face. Sam smiled back but kept her thoughts to herself. To her, the children all seemed to be screaming and the mothers looked miserable, the desperation visible on their faces as they clawed at the chain link fence – *I'm a human being, get me out of here!* their imploring eyes seemed to convey. Sam shook her head; she knew she was being silly.

'I would've loved to have had another child, you know.'

Sam was jolted from her thoughts by her mother's surprising comment. It was the last thing she'd ever expected to hear her mother say.

'I can guess what you're thinking, Sammy. I know I've made a mess of motherhood. But wouldn't it have been nice to have a little brother or sister for you? Another little you?' Her mother stopped walking and Sam realised a response was required.

She didn't hold back this time. 'I think it would've been the worst thing you could have done. I had to practically bring myself up for most of the time and if it wasn't for Pops, I honestly don't know if I'd be with you now today.' Sam's voice rose to match her increasing anger. 'I had to take care of *you* a lot of the time. Do you remember? No, I didn't think so!' she shouted, causing a few stares from passers-by. With a sense of satisfaction, she saw her mother's face crumple. 'I couldn't have coped with the responsibility of bringing up a little brother or sister as well.'

There was a shift in mood after that and, although they both made an attempt at light-hearted chat, whether to invest in some of the perennial plants over some of the shorter-lived annuals, was it too late to plant bulbs? Or just get some already established plants? In the end, they returned home, a bag in each hand containing a mixture of geraniums, marigolds and impatiens.

'Shall we make a start on the garden now?' Sam's mother asked, an expectant look on her face.

'No Mum, I've got some work to do for my course.'

'Oh, OK,' her mother replied. 'Well maybe later on then?'

'I can't, I'm going out.'

'Oh?'

Sam watched her mother's face drop as she blurted out that she had a date with Jack that evening. And although she did her best to appear happy about it, the clasping and unclasping of her hands stated otherwise. *Tough*, Sam thought to herself as she marched upstairs to her room, slamming the door behind her. Looking at her reflection in the mirror, she took a few deep breaths and willed herself to calm down, to suppress the increasingly regular surges of anger that rose up from the pit of her belly, threatening to overwhelm her.

****

They met outside a swanky bar on the waterfront. He was already there, looking effortlessly cool in a brown leather jacket and dark blue jeans. Sam felt the unfamiliar flutter in her chest as he turned, his perfect face breaking into a grin on noticing her.

'Hi Sam,' he said, bending down to give her a kiss, on the lips this time. The feel of his mouth brushing gently against hers made her insides somersault and he smelt so good. 'You look amazing,' Sam smiled, glad that she'd opted for the yellow jumpsuit instead of her usual choice of short black dress. The shop assistant had said the colour complimented her skin.

'You scrub up well yourself,' she said, feeling a sudden, unfamiliar wave of shyness.

Instead of a dark, noisy bar, Sam was surprised to find them entering a brightly lit lobby. She looked up at Jack enquiringly but he just smiled and she felt the warmth of his hand in the small of her back as he gently guided her into a nearby lift.

'Wow!' Sam exclaimed, as they exited the lift into an impressive room mutely lit by gothic-style chandeliers suspended from the high ceiling. A mixture of tables and booths filled the floor space, all dressed in pristine ivory tablecloths, huge paintings depicting pale women in languid poses and flowing robes adorned the marbled walls. But the most striking feature was the floor to ceiling window that offered a panoramic view of the brayford waterfront. Sam was glad to see a few black and brown faces dotted amongst the mainly white clientele.

'This is where I take a girl I want to impress,' Jack said. Sam turned to look at him, her features softening when she realised he was only teasing.

'I've booked us a booth,' he added, catching the eye of a waiter.

'Very organised,' said Sam, trying to inject a little sarcasm into her tone but secretly impressed.

'You really do look amazing,' Jack said, as they settled into their seats.

'So you've already told me.'

'Well it's worth repeating. I love your weave by the way.'

Sam smiled, relieved that he actually knew what a weave was and wouldn't later be gobsmacked when she had it taken out to reveal her much shorter hair - *Wow, where's all your hair gone!* – assuming their *relationship? Affair?* lasted that long.

'I don't know about you, but I'm starving,' he said, peering at the menu in front of him. Sam thought back to the ham sandwich she'd eaten hours earlier, taking it up to her room so she wouldn't have to face her mother's anxious looks from across the little dining table.

'Me too. But are they serving food? I can't see anyone having anything.'

'They have a good tapas selection.'

And they certainly did, Sam found out later, as she tucked into the delicious little dishes of calamares, gambas pil pil and tortilla, washed down with cold, crisp cava.

'You've definitely been here a few times then,' Sam said, patting the corners of her mouth with her napkin, *silk, if you please, how very posh.*

'Oh, only a couple of times,' Jack waved his hand noncommittally. 'So,' he said, setting his glass on the table and leaning forward, 'tell me a bit about yourself.'

'Like what?' Sam said, alarmed, she wasn't used to small talk.

He shrugged. 'I don't know, anything – your favourite colour? Where you live? Who your friends are?'

'I don't really do friends,' she said abruptly and instantly regretted it, on realising how absurd she must sound. As if on cue, a trio of women walked past them, chatting animatedly with their arms linked as they made their way to the bar. 'I ... er ... it's just always been me and my mum. She gets quite anxious so I need to make sure I'm around for her,' Sam added, hoping she hadn't already put him off, but when she dared to meet his eyes, all she saw was kindness and concern.

As the night wore on, and onto their second bottle of wine, Sam found herself opening up and revealing a little about her past; telling him about the all too frequent moves and the violent men her mother brought into their lives. The alcohol definitely had something to do with loosening her usual reserve but she also found him so easy to talk to, with no pressure or expectation; unlike the previous men she'd met on her lonely nights out in London, who had made it clear they were only after one thing. If he was shocked or disgusted as she spoke about her childhood, he didn't show it. She even very nearly told him about that awful night when she had tried to stop her mother being strangled to death and been hurled across the room for her efforts, but managed to suppress that – she didn't want to overload him with too much baggage.

He had reached out and held her hand. His eyes filled with so much concern, she wanted to tell him about the anger she harboured like molten lava in the pit of her stomach, flowing through her body, ever upwards, and the constant effort to contain it, but, although the cava had uncharacteristically loosened her tongue, she thankfully held back. She didn't want him to be put off by the real her.

'So, do I get to see you again?' Jack asked later, standing outside the unremarkable two-up, two-down. He had insisted on walking her home.

'Yes,' said Sam simply, cupping the side of Jack's face. He gripped her hands and pulled her towards him. He kissed her then. Properly this time, leaving no doubt in Sam's mind about whether or not he fancied her. As he drew away, a movement caught the corner of Sam's eye. It was the curtain being pushed to one side. Only slightly, but just enough to make out the outline of her mother's face staring anxiously back at her. Defiantly, she turned her back to the window and pulled Jack to her for another, lingering kiss.

Her mother could go to hell.

Chapter Ten

'Hello Colin.'

'D'you know what?'

'What Colin?'

'I went to my sister's yesterday. And d'you know what?'

'What, Colin?'

'We had sausages and chips. And d'you know what?'

'What, Colin?'

'The cab cost me a fiver.'

'Did it?'

'Yeah.'

Sam smiled. She found she had been doing that a lot since her date with Jack. She had entered the health centre in a jubilant mood not usually suited to Monday mornings.

'Hi Frances,' she said in a sing song voice she didn't recognise.

Frances gave her a studied look before replying, 'Who's the lucky man then?' and at that moment, Sam was thankful for her dark skin which hopefully dulled the blush she could feel creeping up from her neck and on to her cheeks. Even the knowledge that Nigel was back at work hadn't dampened her mood.

'OK, Colin, take a seat and Josie will call you in soon,' Sam said, noting that Colin was giving her an odd look and realising that she was still grinning like a Cheshire cat.

Colin gave a brisk nod and turned to sit in his favourite seat. However, it was already occupied and he turned back to Sam with a look of bewilderment.

'It's OK, Colin, why don't you sit there?' Sam said, pointing to the seat at the end of the front row. 'Josie won't have any problem seeing you now, because it's closer to her room.' Reassured, Colin turned and ambled off towards what would be his second favourite seat in the centre's waiting area and Sam settled into checking the appointments for the day.

A moment later she looked up from her screen as two women entered the centre. The older one was propping up the other, who looked like she might crumple to the floor at any moment. They took slow, measured steps, the older woman fixing her eyes on the reception desk with a look of such concentration as if her own and her companion's lives depended on reaching it. Sam found herself shifting forwards in her seat, in an unconscious attempt to lessen the gap between them.

On reaching their destination, the older woman smiled faintly at Sam, 'Hello love, we haven't got an appointment but my daughter here really needs to see a doctor.'

Sam looked from mother to daughter, whose eyes had still to leave the floor. 'I'm sorry, we're fully booked this morning but I can book you in for this afternoon?'

The woman shook her head.

'I don't think we can wait till then. You see, she's not eaten a thing or slept since it happened and I think she'll pass out soon if the doctor can't give her something ... I don't know what to do ... I ...'

The woman's voice cracked as she tried, and failed, to suppress a series of rasping sobs that came from somewhere deep within her. Her daughter carried on staring at the floor, seemingly oblivious to the distressed sounds coming from her mother.

'Errrr, can I take your name please? I'll see if I can slot you in,' Sam said, her eyes flitting from daughter to mother.

'I'm Mrs Burton and my daughter is Amanda Hollins.'

At the sound of her name, the younger woman looked up and Sam instantly recognised who she was, her eyes mirroring the hazel eyes of the missing woman's in the papers.

'Oh,' was all Sam could say. With her sallow, crepe-like skin and hollow, haunted eyes, Amanda Hollins looked older than her mother.

Luckily, Frances was able to see her straightaway – at least she was in safe, stable hands. Although Sam doubted whether there was anything Frances could prescribe to help the poor woman.

The morning passed uneventfully after that; Sam eventually found her thoughts returning to Jack and his dazzling blue eyes, his soft lips as they kissed. When she had woken the following morning, her mother asked how her date had gone, but didn't mention spying on them. Sam didn't bring it up either, and they had both spent the rest of the day avoiding one another.

'Welcome back, Nigel,' Sam said, entering the staff kitchen and seeing him standing over the kettle. He jumped, causing her to smile. She walked towards him with a confident stride. 'I hope you're feeling better?' she enquired, noting him visibly blanch. 'Any water left in the kettle?'

'Y ... yes. There's plenty,' he mumbled, backing away as she grabbed the kettle from him and switched it on.

'Good,' she said, her voice low as she gave him a hard stare. With a deep sense of satisfaction, she watched as he scuttled humbly out of the kitchen.

Taking her cup of tea back to her desk, Sam found she couldn't stop glancing down at her watch; her date with Jack had ended with a plan to meet for lunch and, when 12.30pm finally arrived, she grabbed her bag and stepped outside.

'Hi there, Sam, how're you doing?' It was the homeless man, Billy. Sam hesitated before giving him a brief smile. She didn't want the burden of having to talk to him every time he clapped eyes on her.

She half expected to see Jack sitting at the table in the window, but there was another couple there, she noticed as she entered the café, ignoring the enquiring look from the waitress. Surveying the small space, it took several seconds to register he wasn't there so she picked a table at the back.

Fifteen minutes later and he still hadn't turned up. Feeling humiliated, she picked up her bag and left. Back at the health centre, she couldn't stop checking her phone, just in case. There was nothing – a missed call or a message to explain why he hadn't turned up. During the course of the afternoon, she felt increasingly restless, causing her to snap at an unsuspecting old man who'd come in to see if there were any emergency appointments. There weren't any, she told him, in no uncertain terms.

By the time she left, the acid in her gut was simmering away and, as she reached the top of Steep Hill, she felt she might explode. *How dare you, Jack?!!* She wanted to scream down over the good Lincoln folk. *How dare you make me feel like this!*

She should've known it was too good to be true. Why on Earth would someone like Jack, with his perfect looks and perfect life, be interested in a fucked-up freak like her? Regaling the horrors of her childhood had probably scared him off. She was damaged goods after all.

But that kiss, only two evenings ago, his lips on hers, sending a warm thrill through her body and making her feel lightheaded. What was that all about? Had it really meant nothing to him?

'Sam! Sam! Wait up!'

She whipped round and there he was, just a few yards down the hill. His limp appeared more pronounced as he tried to run, clutching his bad leg. *Good*, she thought, *I hope it hurts.*

She turned back and continued on her way. She wasn't going to make it easy for him.

'Sam. Sam! Please, just stop a minute, would you?'

She carried on walking but slowed her pace.

'Christ, Sam. Please stop walking and hear me out!'

She turned and waited for him to catch up. He was limping quite badly now, wincing every time he put weight on his right leg.

'Thank you,' he said, between rapid breaths. She could see a sheen of sweat on his forehead, which he wiped away with the back of his sleeve.

'Well? I'm waiting,' she said, scowling at a nosy passerby.

'Can we at least sit down? How about there?' he suggested, pointing to the Wig and Mitre pub behind Sam. She gave him a hard stare and shrugged.

'OK.'

A few moments later, they were seated in a small booth. Like the majority of buildings in the Cathedral Quarter, the pub was an old building with low ceilings and snug little booths. Sam was glad for the poorly lit dark wooded interior that lessened the blueness of Jack's eyes. She didn't want to fall for him all over again.

'I'm so sorry Sam. A friend of mine was in a bit of a state. He's got family problems and needed to travel to Leeds to sort it out. He missed the train so I gave him a lift.'

'And it didn't occur to you to call?'

'I left without my phone and Nick's ran out of charge so I couldn't even call you on that. I'm so sorry Sam. I'd never intentionally stand you up.'

'Did your friend sort his problem out at least?' she asked, more harshly than intended. She couldn't help it, she still felt angry.

'I don't know,' Jack shrugged. 'I just dropped him off at his sister's house and drove like a maniac so I could get back to you.'

She looked up then to see a small smile playing on his lips and thought how much she wanted to feel those lips on hers again.

As their plates of food arrived (Jack had persuaded her to let him treat her to dinner), Sam felt a definite shift in mood as she picked at her beef wellington, her appetite leaving her as she fought to quench the fluttering sensation that had started in the pit of her stomach and was steadily making its way to her chest. She suddenly didn't feel herself. He seemed different too.

An uncomfortable silence had prevailed after he told her about his friend when what he had told her should have cleared the air. His relaxed manner was gone as he shot her furtive glances when he thought she wasn't looking. What had happened to the easygoing conversations they had had previously? Maybe he was just worried about his friend. Or maybe he realised that he didn't actually like her; the thought struck her, causing her to lose her appetite altogether. Maybe he was just going to let her down politely because he was a nice guy and that's what nice guys did.

The sensation in her stomach started to burn and she shifted uncomfortably in her seat. Staring intently at her plate, she resisted the urge to pick it up and hurl it at him. How *dare* he make her feel like this? All open and vulnerable. But then he reached over, placing his hand over her clenched fist, and the burning sensation began to dissipate.

'What's wrong Sam?' he asked, a look of concern etched on his perfect face.

'I don't know,' she eventually whispered, realising that she was trembling. 'I think I ... I ...'

'Go on?' Jack urged, gently stroking her hand until it began to unfurl from its tight ball.

'I've never felt like this and it's ... weird.'

'Weird in a good way?'

She looked up at him and smiled shyly. 'I don't know about you, but I've never done this before,' she said finally, averting her gaze from his.

'You mean you've never had a boyfriend?' Jack asked, eyebrows raised.

'Not properly, no,' said Sam, trying to blot out the flashbacks of those seedy one night stands in London. Of going out on the hunt, dressed to kill, all fired up. Throwing herself at almost any man that looked her way.

Beginning during her teenage years, Sam attempted to alleviate the feelings of hurt and anger that threatened to consume her. Looking back, she knew it had a lot to do with Pops, the realisation that he was truly gone taking several years to hit her, so that when it did, it came with such a force she didn't think she could bear it. At his funeral, she had remained dry-eyed, watching her mother cry copiously and had wished she could do the same. But she just felt an emptiness, a detachment. Then came the anger, hot and terrible, making her insides churn. Anger at being left alone in the world with only her pathetic excuse for a mother. *How could Pops do that to her?*

'Don't worry, I'm not an innocent little virgin,' she said, nervously twiddling the stem of her wine glass. 'I've just well ... never really had a proper relationship with someone. Not that I'm calling this a relationship,' she said quickly, worried that he would think she was reading too much into what had only been a couple of dates after all. He probably thought she was mad.

'I was really hoping we could call this a relationship,' he said, his voice low as he stared at her intently. 'You've already blown me away Sam, I've never felt like this about anyone.' He leant forward then, his lips brushing hers as he kissed her gently and caused her insides to melt.

'Thank you for being straight with me,' she said, meeting his gaze.

'I'm not into playing games,' Jack replied, pulling her in for another kiss, harder this time, more insistent and, had she been standing, it would've no doubt made her legs go weak. 'Anyway, what about you?' he said, eventually pulling away.

'What about me?'

'I've just laid myself on the line here, so how about telling me how you feel?'

'I like you,' she said, leaning in for another kiss, 'a lot.'

Chapter Eleven

Sam woke up to the sound of birds singing and, although the blinds were closed, she could tell that it was sunny outside. Stretching herself out fully, she sunk back down into the bed, revelling in the softness of the Egyptian cotton sheets and fluffy pillows – Jack's bed was without a doubt, the most comfortable she had ever slept in.

She smiled, mulling over the past couple of days. Jack had brought her back to his house on Friday evening and it was now Sunday. She really hadn't planned to stay beyond Saturday but he had been too hard to resist. She smiled again at the thought of him. His smell. His touch. *That body.* The way he made her feel like she was the most desired object on earth. She felt a contentment she had never felt before. However, her thoughts soon turned to her mother, no doubt anxiously waiting for her to return home. She pushed the feeling of guilt aside; at least she'd texted to let her know where she was and besides, she was a woman now. She couldn't be expected to babysit her mother forever.

'Morning, sexy,' said Jack, appearing at the doorway with a tray of coffee and crumpets.

Sam raised her eyebrows. 'Breakfast in bed again? How long's this going to last?' Jack faked a hurt look, setting the tray down on the bed in between them.

'I don't know what you mean. This is how I treat all my women.'

'Oh, I see. I thought it was too good to be true. So there are others then?'

'Only you, baby. Only you', Jack whispered, gripping the back of her head and pulling her towards him. He kissed her, hard, nearly spilling the coffee. 'Only you' he said again, continuing to hold her head so tightly in a way that made her feel slightly uncomfortable. She was about to say something but the sound of another voice, unexpected and unfamiliar, cut her short.

'Hello there.'

Sam gasped at the sight of another man in the room, a smirk on his face as he looked directly at her.

'For fuck's sake, what have I told you about sneaking up on me like that?!' Jack shouted savagely, making Sam jump. She looked incredulously from Jack to the stranger standing in the doorway. At least Jack knew him. He wasn't an intruder.

'Yeah yeah,' the man replied, seemingly unfazed by Jack's violent outburst. 'Aren't you going to introduce us?' He then walked right up to the bed and held out his hand to Sam. 'I'm Nick.'

She couldn't believe the audacity of him and hiked up the duvet to cover her nakedness.

'Sam,' she said, offering him a hard stare in place of her hand to shake.

'Nice to meet you, Sam,' he replied, lowering his hand and perching on the edge of the bed. 'Hasn't Jack told you about me? No?' he asked, crossing his legs and clasping his hands around one of his knees as he looked quizzically from Jack back to Sam, like a spectator at an event.

Jack let out an exasperated sigh. 'Sam, this is my friend, Nick. Sorry, I meant to mention he's staying here for a while. He went away for the weekend and I wasn't expecting him back till this evening.' Jack fixed his friend with an accusatory glare.

'I know mate, I'm sorry. Things didn't go too well.'

'What happened?' Jack asked, his expression changing quickly to a look of concern.

'I found her in her usual drinking hole, smashed off her face.'

'Fuck no! I can't believe it! Don't the bar staff know not to serve her by now?'

Nick nodded, 'Yeah, I know, you'd think not after last time, right?'

Sam looked on in confusion and an increasing sense of irritation. What the hell were they talking about? And why wasn't Jack bothered about his *friend* sitting on the bed ogling at her? Maybe he hadn't noticed, but she did; the way his eyes kept swivelling in her direction, seemingly penetrating the duvet to her naked body underneath. She felt exposed, vulnerable.

As if reading her thoughts, Nick held his palms up in a conciliatory gesture and stood up. 'I'm sorry Sam, please forgive me for bounding in on you both. Jack's used to it, but I can see it's freaking you out.' He hesitated, waiting for a response, but when it didn't come, continued, 'I've been visiting my sister up in Leeds and, to put it bluntly, she's an alcoholic. I sometimes feel like just washing my hands of her but she has a daughter, my niece, and I don't want to see her ending up in care.'

Sam nodded slowly, regarding him. So this was the friend for whom Jack had missed their lunch date. She found her initial feelings of irritation towards him dissipating slightly. She knew only too well what it was like to be in his niece's position.

'How is Kayleigh?' Jack asked.

'Angry, but she's holding up. She's staying with a neighbour for the time being.' Then, addressing Sam, 'Kayleigh's the only good thing my sister's ever done.'

'How old is she?' Sam asked, genuinely interested.

'Eleven, going on twenty. She's had to grow up fast.'

Sam nodded. 'I know how that feels', she said quietly. Nick looked at her inquisitively and might have gone on to say something before Jack intervened.

'Look mate, let me get myself sorted and I'll catch up with you downstairs.'

'Yeah sure', Nick answered and turned to leave, but then hesitated before turning back and, to Sam's alarm, walked right up to the bed, a small smile on his face as he leant over her and plucked a crumpet off the tray. 'My favourite,' he said, winking.

****

The wind tugged at Sam's jacket as she trudged back up Steep Hill towards home. She silently cursed herself for falling for that saying about March coming in like a lion and going out like a lamb. As the month drew to an end, it definitely felt like the opposite was happening as the cold blast whipped around her ears making her wish she'd brought a hat.

Jack had offered to give her a lift, but she'd declined, insisting that she wanted to walk when really what she wanted was time by herself to reflect on the odd encounter she'd experienced when Nick had entered Jack's bedroom uninvited, bursting their romantic bubble. The way he had walked right up to the bed, leaning over her to help himself to a crumpet – like he had a right to do so – unsettled her. But then, she reasoned, there was the fact that he and Jack went back a long way. That was obvious as they conversed with a familiarity that could only be gained through years of knowing one another. There was also the fact that he cared about his young niece.

How she wished she'd had someone, other than Pops, looking out for her. She remembered blowing out the candles on her birthday cakes after Pops had gone, making the same wishes year on year; *please can a long lost aunt or uncle appear and take care of me; please keep my mother safe.* But her wishes remained unanswered, leaving Sam to face life's challenges alone.

Shrugging off the inauspicious feelings that crept into her head, she ducked into the Co-op for a pint of milk and bread, certain that her mother wouldn't have gone out and bought any provisions in her absence.

'Hi Mum, I'm back,' Sam called, closing the door on the rain that had just started.

'Mum?' she said, standing at the bottom of the stairs. She walked through into the kitchen and placed the milk in the fridge and the bread in the bread bin, slamming it down in the process. If her mother wanted to ignore her then fine, she could play that game too. But then she caught sight of the note on the table. The familiar untidy scrawl of her mother's writing:

Sam, I'm not sure if you'll be coming home this weekend but just to let you know I'm going to London to get my pendant back today (Sunday). I can't sit around here any longer knowing he's still got it. It's doing my head in! Going to try and make the 12.45 train. Wish me luck.

Mum x

Sam stared at the note then back towards the clock above the T.V. – 11:58am. If she ran, she could make it. Her mother couldn't have left that long ago. Grabbing her bag, she slammed the front door and ran down Steep Hill towards Lincoln Central railway station.

Chapter Twelve

It was by now pouring down, the wind pushing the rain horizontally into Sam's face, forcing her to squint her eyes as she stumbled down the street. Her heels caught in the cobbles, making her wish she'd had the presence of mind to change into her Converse. She briefly considered getting a cab, but quickly dismissed the idea; it wasn't like catching a cab in London, where there was an abundance. The two cab offices she knew would mean a detour from Steep Hill and then she would probably have to wait for one anyway. No, she couldn't risk it. The only way was to walk, or run, as she was trying to do, in a straight line towards the town centre.

At nearly 12:40pm Sam rounded the corner of St Mary's Street and waited impatiently to cross over the road to the station. There probably wasn't enough time now to buy a ticket and she felt anxious at the thought of having to persuade the guard to let her onto the platform. But, as she approached the station, she could see that the gates were all open and there didn't seem to be any guards in sight. Small mercies for it being a Sunday, she supposed.

The little train that would take her mother to Newark for a connecting train to London was just approaching platform 1 on the other side of the tracks. Sam knew she would have to hurry if she had a chance of making it. Taking the stairs three at a time, she sprinted across the bridge and down the stairs on the other side, just as the train was about to set off.

'Wait! You have to let me on!' she yelled, running alongside the train, tugging wildly at one of the doors. There came the sound of a whistle and the train immediately ground to a halt, almost sending Sam flying. A guard further up glared at her, but she didn't care as she yanked the train door open. She was about to step up inside the train, but something stopped her. Through the train window, she caught sight of a familiar figure sitting huddled on the platform opposite.

Sam slammed the door shut, ignoring the shouts from the guard and the disgruntled faces of the passengers, as the train trundled back into motion. It didn't matter. None of it mattered. She had found her mother and she would keep her safe, as she always had done.

The huddled figure didn't look up as she opened the door to the small waiting room. Thankfully, they were the only occupants.

'Mum?' Sam said tentatively. As she drew closer, she could see that her mother was shivering.

'Mum?' she said again, sitting in the seat next to her mother, 'It's me, Sam.'

Her mother looked up then as if just realising there was another person in the room. She turned to Sam, the vacant expression on her face turning to one of recognition as her eyes focused on her daughter.

'Sammy?' she said, hesitantly reaching out to touch Sam's arm. 'Why are you here?'

'Oh Mum, why do you think? You left a note saying you were going to London to get your pendant. Remember?' Sam sat next to her.

'The note,' her mother replied vaguely. 'Oh yes, the note.'

'What did you think you were doing, Mum? Going off by yourself like that! You gave me such a scare!'

'Really?' said her mother. 'I didn't mean to do that Sammy. I just wanted to get my pendant back and I couldn't even manage that.' She started to cry then, leaning her head on Sammy's shoulder.

'It's OK, I'm here now. It's OK,' Sam said, encircling her mother in her arms. 'Mum, you're shaking, are you cold?'

'Just hungry, I think.'

'When did you last eat?' Sam drew back from her mother so she could study her. She could see that her skin had a greyish tinge and her eyes were a puffy mess.

'I had something earlier,' her mother said dismissively.

'What did you have?'

'A sandwich.'

'Really?' said Sam, thinking back to the empty fridge she had placed the milk into that morning. 'Mum, I know you haven't had anything today.'

'OK, OK, it was yesterday. I had a sandwich yesterday.'

Sam smiled, 'Well, you know what this calls for, then?'

Sam waited whilst her mother cleaned herself up, splashing her face with cold water in the waiting room toilet.

'Thank you Sammy,' her mother said, meeting Sam's gaze in the mirror. Then they walked out of the station arm in arm, huddled together under one umbrella.

A welcome blast of warm air hit Sam as she entered Brown's Pie Shop, her mother following closely behind. They had only frequented the cosy little restaurant a handful of times, but they didn't need the menu to know what they both wanted. Tucked away in an alcove, they dug into giant Yorkshire puddings surrounded in rich meaty gravy, washed down with a bottle of house red. Sam didn't mind her mother drinking when she was around to monitor quantities and, besides, it was well and truly called for when she thought of what might have happened if she hadn't arrived at the station on time and her mother had caught the train.

'Mum, promise me you won't try and do anything stupid again,' Sam said, setting her glass down.

'What, like wussing out of getting on a train to get my pendant back?' her mother asked. 'I can't even do that, can I? I'm pathetic!'

'Mum, just think about what would've happened if you had travelled to London. Just rocked up at Eddie's place out of the blue? That would've gone down well, wouldn't it?'

'I know, I know. I just had to try and do something,' her mother said resignedly.

'Well, we'll plan something together, OK?' Sam said, reaching over to clasp her mother's hand in hers, 'I promise.'

As they tucked into their crème brulee's– another shared favourite – Sam shyly told her about Jack.

'I can see you're serious about him,' her mother said, reaching over to pat Sam's hand.

'Don't be ridiculous! We've only been out a few times!'

'And a whole weekend,' her mother said, one eyebrow raised.

'I'm sorry,' said Sam.

'What for?'

'Leaving you.'

'Oh Sammy, I'm the one who's sorry. You shouldn't have to feel guilty. I know I get a bit anxious about being alone, but I'm just going to have to get used to it. You deserve to have a good time. OK?'

Sam raised her wine glass. 'Here's to good times for both of us.'

'I'll definitely drink to that!' her mother said, smiling as they clinked glasses.

Chapter Thirteen
Summer 2007

Sarah let out a muffled sob, which brought on another round of coughing and made her nose run. She knew she must make herself stop, she couldn't afford to block her only airway and besides, it only served to worsen the throbbing at the back of her head. She forced herself to concentrate on her breathing – in 1 ... 2 ... 3, out 1 ... 2 ... 3. Just like her mother did when she was meditating. In 1 ... 2 ... 3, out 1 ... 2 ... 3.

But then she thought of how today should have been; her last day in Landsdowne Primary school. After a final assembly, they had been mostly left to their own devices. Mrs Turkington had put Shrek on the DVD player but she'd already seen it in the cinema and couldn't be bothered sitting through it again. Besides, she'd had a falling out with her best friend, Nina, who had decided to sit next to that cow, Lorna, arms linked. Both of them had been making smug, sideways glances at her. So when Mrs Turkington had left the class unattended, making it clear she wasn't coming back any time soon, a group of them had decided to leave the classroom and explore the school.

It was an old school; 'Boys' room' and 'Girls' room' engraved in stone above some of the classrooms, an era long gone, and there were several, older buildings at the back of the main part of the school. There was one building in particular to which the group were headed: the old drama department. There was a rumour that a teacher had killed herself there in the 1960s and it had remained locked ever since. Of course, Mrs Turkington and all the other teachers had denied this, stating that it had been closed due to asbestos, but, Sarah thought, they would say that, wouldn't they?

The door to the building was padlocked but one of the boys had found a way in round the back, levering up one of the small windows with a palette knife he had nicked from his home economics class. Being the smallest, he'd wedged himself through the tiny space – quite brave of him, Sarah had thought at the time – then had opened the back door to let them in, a triumphant grin on his face. The other two girls in the group had chickened out of going in but she had remained, finding it quite exhilarating to be the only girl.

Entering the large, bare studio, she'd been a little disappointed at how normal it all looked and nothing like she had imagined. But then one of the boys had shouted, 'Come up and have a look at this!' and they had all run towards his voice and discovered a thin, winding staircase at the back of the room. The staircase led up to a narrow corridor with a door at the end, which was closed but with a key visible in the lock. As they hovered at the entrance, what they saw definitely did not disappoint.

The room had a dank air, despite the shaft of sunlight coming from the window at the far end, making Sarah feel suddenly cold. She had seen immediately that it was where the costumes and other paraphernalia from past theatre productions were kept. As she walked around for a closer look, she had noted that some looked ancient, as if they had been there for hundreds of years, although Sarah didn't think the school could be that old. A couple of mannequins stood side by side at the far end of the room, both dressed in those old, creepy dresses with bustles. She picked up a gaudy necklace and put it on, turning to show it to the others, but they had all gone. Except for him, the boy with the cute smile, just standing in the middle of the room, staring at her. He dared her to try on one of the creepy dresses and because she wanted to impress him, she did.

Stepping behind a screen, she had taken off her school tunic, relishing in the thought of how jealous Nina would be when she told her what she had missed out on, this definitely trumped sitting in class watching a rerun of Shrek. He handed her one of the dresses and she gingerly stepped into it. But when she popped her head back round the screen, he had gone. She laughed, making it clear she wasn't scared of his little prank – rummaging through the piles of costumes, opening up a huge chest – in an effort to find his hiding place. But there had been no sign of him. It was then that she noticed the door was now closed – how had she not noticed? She had already known it would be locked;

something in the way he smiled. But she'd tried anyway, twisting and pulling at the doorknob in an increasingly desperate bid to get out, away from this place. A horrific thought had struck her then; what if this was where that teacher had killed herself? Sarah shouted out then, kicking and clawing at the door as she did so, but then she felt something heavy to the back of her head, first making her see stars then nothing at all.

She wasn't sure how long she had been unconscious for but guessed it couldn't have been too long, otherwise surely she would be feeling thirsty, and there was still a thin beam of sunlight from the window, although it was duller now. She knew that if she could just calm herself down, she could work out what to do. That was what had got her the certificate in Maths at that morning's assembly; her methodical approach to working out solutions. But she was finding it difficult to concentrate with the smelly rag tied around her mouth. The blindfold and fastenings binding her wrists together definitely weren't helping.

If she could just work her hands free, then everything would be ok, even if she couldn't get the door open, she could smash the window and shout for help. Surely the caretaker would walk by at some point; the shed where he kept his cleaning tools was only a few yards away. Just the thought of a fellow human being somewhere nearby gave her some comfort – the thought of not being alone. But then, as she wriggled and squirmed her way into an upright position, her arm brushed against something warm and soft and then came the sound of a low chuckle. And as she felt the sudden, sharp pain of being pinched on the cheek, she realised there was a lot more to fear than being alone ...

Chapter Fourteen

Sam smiled as she took the cassoulet from the oven. She was glad she had followed Jack's recipe; it looked and smelled perfect. And that was what she wanted this evening to be. Perfect.

Several weeks had passed since her mother had tried, and failed, to go to London and get her pendant back. And although she hadn't come any closer to working out what to do (Eddie was a mean, mean man – he wasn't going to simply hand it over, assuming that it was even in his possession still), the predicament had brought her closer to her mother. Ever since that wet and windy day, in the waiting room at the railway station, the tense atmosphere surrounding them had all but disappeared and her mother was really making an effort to start afresh. She had even started yoga and Spanish classes at the local community centre, something Sam would never have imagined her mother capable of.

Sam briefly wondered what her mother was having for dinner, but pushed the thought aside. She made a promise to herself *not* to ruminate on the day to day aspects of her mother's life; this was *her* time. She had built up to this moment slowly, leaving a fridge full of food, had spent time listening to her mother's continued fears for Sarah Hollins, which seemed even more pointless now the woman had been gone for three long, silent months. Sam had expected resistance when she told her mother about moving in with Jack, but Denise had never waited to move in with a boyfriend in her life and so had stayed tight-lipped.

After some rummaging in various drawers, she found a couple of night lights, which she placed on the table, along with some bright purple napkins. She stood for a moment, admiring her handiwork.

Their first evening of officially living together was going to be perfect. She smiled again, shaking her head at how quickly things had progressed between her and Jack over the past few weeks. She hadn't experienced anything like this before – the feeling of overwhelming love for a man. Jack made her feel like a different person. A better person. She found herself viewing the world in a different light when she was with him.

The only blot on the landscape was Nick, with his ever-watchful gaze and that unpleasant way he had of catching her unawares. She couldn't believe it when one morning she and Jack had been brushing their teeth and Nick had sauntered into the bathroom, taken his toothbrush from the cabinet and, standing beside Jack, had proceeded to brush his teeth. It would've made a weird scene to an onlooker; Jack, seemingly unbothered by the intrusion, whilst Sam fleetingly met Nick's smirking expression in the mirror. She had got her own back later though – taking his toothbrush and scraping it round the rim of the toilet. That had made her feel better.

Then there was the way he always seemed to be around when they went to the supermarket, walking alongside them down the aisles, happily throwing stuff into *their* trolley and never offering to pay. When she brought it up with Jack, he always seemed taken aback, as if Nick's behaviour was normal, causing her to reflect on whether she was just being petty. It wasn't as if she had any longstanding friendships of her own to compare.

But thankfully, Nick hadn't been around much these past few days, being preoccupied with his new girlfriend. *Poor cow*, Sam thought as she lit the candles. She prayed he'd move in permanently with her.

Perfect timing, she thought, on hearing the front door open. Pulling her dress down to reveal more cleavage, she turned to give him a special smile, the sexy one she reserved just for Jack.

'Wow! This looks fantastic, Sam! I didn't realise you had missed me so much!' Nick said, pulling his jacket off and throwing it carelessly over one of the chairs. Sam's smile froze momentarily before transforming into a scowl.

'What are you doing here?' she growled, making no attempt to hide the animosity she was feeling.

Nick's eyes widened in mock incredulity. 'What do you mean? I live here. Remember?'

Sam fought the urge to pick up one of the dinner plates and hurl it at him, her hand actually twitching at the thought. But no, she wouldn't give him the satisfaction. Changing her snarl into a smile, she said, 'Hasn't Jack told you?' She let the question hover a moment, enjoying the glimmer of uncertainty on Nick's face.

'I'm moving in.'

Sam scrutinised Nick, searching for any signs that she had unsettled him. But no, he remained unpleasantly impassive. Then he laughed, an abrupt bark, causing Sam to jump.

'Is that all? I thought you were going to say you were pregnant or something. You've been practically living here for the last few weeks anyway! He does like to move quickly in a relationship, our Jack.'

They stood facing each other for what Sam felt was an eternity, her eyes locked onto his. The sound of the front door opening eventually caused her to look away.

'Oh, hi Nick. I wasn't expecting you back tonight,' Jack said, looking uncertainly from Sam to his friend and seemingly sensing the tension in the room.

'Didn't realise I had to receive an invite first,' Nick said, and then frowned, noting the sparkling wine and flowers Jack was holding.

'Ah, mate, I've disturbed a special evening for you both. I'm sorry.'

'It's fine,' said Sam, eager to interrupt and control the conversation. 'I was just saying to Nick how this is our first official evening of living together,' she continued, walking towards Jack and kissing him seductively and slowly, pulling him in towards her when she felt him draw away.

'Err, yes. I hadn't got round to telling you,' said Jack, extricating himself from Sam's grasp and looking uncomfortably towards his friend.

There was a moment's pause before Nick went over to Jack and clapped him on the back. 'That's OK, mate. Congratulations,' he said, turning to Sam with a small smile. 'Don't mind me, I'll go upstairs and leave you two lovebirds in peace.'

Sam watched as he walked towards the living room door before turning back to get his jacket draped on the chair next to her.

'By the way, I hope you haven't forgotten about Josh's stag do,' he said, so close to Sam, she could feel his breath on her arm as he stooped to pick up his jacket.

'Christ!' said Jack, slamming the palm of his hand into his forehead. 'Tonight?!'

Nick nodded. 'I can go and give your apologies, if you like. I'm sure he'll understand. He's only been planning it for the past year and all that. Sounds like you're tied up, and I know how you like things tied up,' Nick said mildly as he stood in the doorway, that infuriating smile playing on his mean lips. Sam noticed a strange look pass between them. Something knowing and menacing.

'No, no. It's fine, I'm coming,' said Jack finally, looking slightly ruffled as he placed the flowers and wine on the table.

'Sam, I'm so sorry, I forgot all about this.' Jack looked briefly at Nick as he spoke, to Sam's annoyance. Do you mind?'

Mind? Do I miiiiiiinnnnnnddddddd? What the fuck do you think? she screamed inwardly, fighting to keep her face neutral. She didn't need to look in Nick's direction to feel his scrutiny.

'Of course I don't mind,' she said, recovering herself, careful to keep her voice soft and even. 'I was hoping to catch up on my *Sex and the City* box set anyway.' Standing on tip toe, she pecked his cheek before whispering into his ear, 'I'll keep the bed nice and warm for you.'

'You're one in a million, d'you know that?' Jack said, returning her kiss – on the lips this time. Glancing over in Nick's direction, she thought she caught a glimpse of something in his eyes. Something hard and cruel.

'Bye, have a good time,' Sam said half an hour later, standing at the front door to wave them off. She waited to hear the sound of the taxi driving off before walking back to the kitchen. She counted to ten and, when that didn't work, picked up the cassoulet and hurled it into the bin with such force, the dish broke in two.

Chapter Fifteen

'D'you know what?'

Sam jumped, startled by the sight of Colin standing at the desk. She had been hiding behind her computer screen, brooding on the issue of Nick, her thoughts cloudy and distorted as she mulled over what she had planned to be a special weekend, the first of many with the beautiful new man in her life.

They had returned from the stag do in the early hours of the morning, merry with drink. She had long given up on greeting Jack with welcome arms and, instead, with the duvet wrapped tightly around her, was feigning sleep. From what she could hear, she ascertained that Jack was the worse for wear, shouting unintelligible utterings whilst Nick encouraged him up the stairs. She flinched as the bedroom door flung open.

'There we go, mate, have a good sleep,' she heard Nick say as she felt Jack stumble into the bed beside her, almost instantly passing out. Then, in a quieter voice directed at her, Nick muttered, 'I brought him back, safe and sound.'

Sam lay rigid, waiting to hear the door close. But no, it remained open and she could feel his insidious presence. When she thought she could stand it no longer, would have to physically push him out of their bedroom, he whispered,

'Sweet dreams.' Then the sound of the door being closed, quietly and gently, allowing Sam to finally stop holding her breath.

'D'you know what?' Colin repeated, jolting Sam yet again from her thoughts.

'What, Colin?' she said in a sharper voice than intended, not feeling like investing in the usual verbal transaction.

'I went to my sister's yesterday. And d'you know what?'

'What, Colin?' she replied exasperatedly, keen for the stilted conversation to be over.

'She wasn't there.'

'Wha— Oh ... er, how come?' said Sam, stumbling to catch up with the unexpected change in direction.

'She's dead.'

'What?!' she said, suddenly alert.

'She went to the hospital and then she died,' Colin replied, speaking in his usual matter of fact tone.

'Oh my God, Colin. I'm so sorry! What happened?'

'She went to the hospital cos she wasn't feeling well then she died.'

'I'm so sorry, Colin,' Sam repeated, at a loss for words.

'Yeah,' he said simply, as if talking about the weather. If it weren't for the fact that his duffel coat was done up unevenly, causing one half to be lower than the other, there were no other signs that anything was wrong. Thankfully Josie, the nurse, came out then and ushered him straight to her clinic room, patting him reassuringly on the arm as they walked. She must have been informed of the sad news by the hospital.

The rest of the morning passed quietly by, apart from Edith coming in again to insist that she had an appointment with Nigel. There was something not right with the old woman, Sam reflected, as she crossed the road to the cafe for lunch. With stains visible on her coat and greasy looking hair that was in stark contrast to her usually smart and prim appearance, there was definitely something wrong. And what of Colin? It was obvious he didn't have any other family or friends to support him – who would he have now to eat his Sunday dinner with?

With a shake of her head, Sam forced the thoughts out of her head; she wasn't used to caring for others apart from her mother, and now Jack.

Although Jack was skating on pretty thin ice these days, seemingly oblivious to Nick's encroachment on their relationship. The weasel could do no wrong in Jack's eyes and it was starting to infuriate her.

Since their 'official' first evening together, she had left early the following morning and had had no intention of returning until Jack begged her. She played it cool, of course, stating she had a shed load of work to do for her counselling course and needed a quiet space to study. When he asked why she couldn't do this at his home, she just smiled, citing 'too much distraction' before giving him a lingering kiss on her way out. She wanted to remind him of what he was missing.

He was slumped on the sofa and, as she left, she popped her head round the door to address him. 'Bye Nick. Thanks for bringing Jack back safe and sound. Have a good weekend.' She'd made sure to keep her tone as light as possible. No need for him to think he had anything to worry about. Not yet ...

Chapter Sixteen

Summer 2009

The sun shone brightly, casting its rays across the bedroom, making everything more appealing somehow, despite its small size. He had asked Mother if he could move into his sister's considerably larger room, now that she had left home, but was given a blunt no.

He bent down so he could look at his reflection in the baroque mirror as he knotted his tie. Tracing a finger gently over the gold leaf frame, his thoughts turned briefly to its former owner, his nan. She was the one person who had truly loved him in the short time he had known her. Now all he had were a few happy memories and the mirror that he had begged Mother to let him keep. He had grown quite a bit since his time away and the mirror was now placed too low.

He took the mirror off the wall, attempting to pull out the hook it had been hanging on, but it wouldn't budge. No matter, he thought to himself, he would sort it out when he got back later.

Making his way quietly down the stairs, so as not to wake Mother, he stopped short at the sight of her already up and dressed, pushing her fat feet into shoes that were too small. She had a hospital appointment, she said, her eyes not quite meeting his. Opening the front door, she hesitated, causing a premature feeling of warmth to flow through his veins. She was going to wish him well on his first day, reassure him that it was going to be OK, that it didn't matter that he had missed out on the first year. He was a bright boy; he was capable of catching up. But no. She didn't say any of that. She just wanted him to know that the milk was off and that he would have to make do with toast.

But then, what did he expect? He had tried so hard to make her love him but no matter how hard he tried, his attempts were always rebuffed. He vividly remembered instances throughout his childhood when there was no doubting the lack of feelings his mother had for him. There was the time when he was six, his small legs running to match Mother's strides as they walked to school. There was a fallen flower on the pavement, a rose. Its deep pink petals stood out in stark contrast to the grey pavement. Slowing his pace, he stooped to pick it up, inspecting it in the palm of his hand. It was beautiful. Running to catch up with Mother, he tugged at her arm, handing her the flower like he'd seen on that American sitcom where they all smiled a lot, revealing their bright, white teeth. Looking up into Mother's eyes, he smiled, hoping she would be pleased with his offering. But instead, she batted the flower out of his hand and shouted, 'Put that bloody thing down! A dog's probably pissed on it!'

Then there was the time he'd made her a mother's day card at school, placing it within the pages of his reading book so it wouldn't get crushed in his rucksack. She'd taken it, reluctantly, her lips pursed in disapproval. Later that day he'd found it, torn in two in the bin. She couldn't even put it up for one day. He had gone up to his room then and stared at his reflection, as he often did, wondering what was so wrong with him that he couldn't be loved by his own mother.

But as the sun shone brightly down on him, he pushed these thoughts aside; today was going to be a good day.

A fresh start.

Entering the grounds of Greenchester Secondary school, he walked purposefully towards the group of boys he knew from primary school. They all stopped talking as he approached, muttering their hellos. Eyes down, none of them met his gaze. Then, thankfully, there was Jack, welcoming him back like a long lost hero and breaking the awkward atmosphere. Taking their cue from Jack, the others resumed the usual banter and they all had a kick about with Jack's ball until the bell went.

The day had gone well, he'd even been invited to David's birthday – paintballing that Saturday. He wasn't stupid though, he could tell that David had invited him under duress, he didn't really want him there. He had Jack to thank for that; being friends with the popular boy had its perks. But that wasn't why he was Jack's friend; he knew that he'd always stay loyal to Jack. They were partners in crime. Soul mates. He knew that sounded gay but that was how he saw their friendship. They'd even talked about sharing a place together when they were grown up.

Returning home, he'd been bursting to tell Mother about the birthday invitation – 'See, I have got friends. I am normal, see?' Of course, he hadn't said any of this, choosing his words carefully so as to make it sound as though being invited to a party was a normal event. Well it was, to boys like Jack. With his easy smile and hero good looks, he was like a magnet to all those around him, the other kids and teachers alike. He'd tried to emulate him but stopped when he saw the piteous expressions on the other boys' faces, as he tried to drape his arm casually over the next boy's chair in an attempt to copy Jack's relaxed style. He had been accused of being gay, whereas if it had been Jack, the boy wouldn't have blinked an eye. He just couldn't carry it off.

But if Mother heard him come in, she didn't make a show of it, just kept her eyes trained on that inane quiz show she always watched.

By the end of the week, with no mention of the 'incident' – no mention of Sarah – he felt he could finally put that whole dreadful experience behind him. And thankfully, Sarah wasn't around anymore, her family had packed up and moved away. So it truly was a fresh start, for all concerned.

But Saturday morning started with a call from Jack. He had come down with chicken pox and wouldn't be able to make paintballing. His jubilance sunk instantly to the pit of his stomach, making him nauseous. He was so looking forward to it, the first good thing since being in the detention centre. He couldn't go now, not without his friend, his only ally. But Jack talked him round, he always did in the end. And that was that, he was going.

It hadn't started well. After much agonising over whether to go or not, making his insides churn, he turned up late to the designated meeting point to find no one there. He was only a few minutes late though and he felt sure that if he had been Jack, they would have waited.

He waited for the next bus anyway. Might as well see it through now, he thought resignedly. As he entered the centre, he spotted them immediately, sitting in a gaggle surrounding the birthday boy, drinking cokes. He hesitated for a moment, reasoning it wasn't too late to back out, *but David spotted him, shouting him over to join them. To his surprise, and joy, he was greeted warmly by the group, David even gave him the money for a coke, 'My mum gave me it, wants me to treat everyone,' he said.*

They all chatted and joked whilst David opened his presents, placing them in the large carrier bag his mother had left for him. Very thoughtful of her, Nick reflected, if only his own mother were capable of such consideration. A carrier bag, only a small thing, but a gesture to show she cared enough to think about how David would manage with bringing his presents back.

For those few moments, sitting with the boys, watching David open his presents, Nick felt an inexplicable joy, a rare feeling of belonging. He wished Mother could see this. And when he handed David his birthday card, with a fiver stuffed inside (he'd had to use some of his savings, there was no point asking Mother), David had looked up and said, 'Cheers mate. Ace,' and they had high fived across the table. Nick was so glad he'd come.

It was when they were donning their overalls that he noticed the atmosphere change, charged with something he couldn't quite put his finger on. But, as David caught his eye and winked, he shrugged it off, putting it down to excitement. Going through the rules, the instructor had to caution them at one point, as they were all fidgety, glancing back and forth to each other as if communicating in some secret code. Something that he wasn't part of.

But still, he shrugged it off. He had to stop over-thinking things.

Luckily they were a large enough group to make up two teams, negating the need for randoms to join. He couldn't believe it when he had been chosen to join David's team. 'Too good to be true' was one of Mother's favourite sayings and looking back, he could've kicked himself for not realising that.

They stood, huddled around David to examine the map, the 'battlefield' was set in an area of forest and they had to plan their strategy. Standing so close to David, he could see the fine hairs running down from the nape of his slender neck and, fighting the urge to stroke them, he forced himself to look at the map.

After agreeing to separate into three groups of pairs, they quickly dispersed into the surrounding woodland and, as Nick crouched side by side with David, he felt like pinching himself; David had picked him. The birthday boy had actually picked him. And as they made their way to the final destination, a wooden hut, Nick felt such an overwhelming feeling of happiness; this was what it was like to be normal, to be like David and Jack.

It hadn't taken long to get to the little clearing where the hut stood and, as they crouched behind a clump of bushes, Nick had wanted to make a run for it. He didn't mind if he got shot, he told David, distracting the others long enough for David to make it to the hut, and be the rightful winner. But no, David insisted on going first, telling Nick to lie low for a couple of minutes before following.

As he sat there, Nick began to wonder where the others had got to. It seemed strange that they hadn't encountered any of them yet; hadn't had to dodge any shots. But then he heard something, a low whistle. Was it David signalling him to follow? Standing slowly, he peered cautiously over the bushes. It was all clear, all he had to do was make it to the hut.

Leaving the cover of the bushes and with his gun at the ready, he started to run. With each stride bringing him closer to the hut, he kept expecting to feel the impact of a pellet. But, as he got closer and with still no sign of the enemy, no sign of his own group for that matter, he could almost taste victory. And then there he was, at the door to the hut, he'd made it! Giving it a push, he found it didn't budge, so he pushed harder. It gave way slightly but then slammed shut again – almost as if someone was pushing it from the other side. 'David?' he whispered, 'It's me, are you in there?' He walked around to the side of the hut, jumping to get a look into one of the windows, but it was too dark and he couldn't see a thing.

Puzzled, he walked back round to the front of the hut. Maybe the door was stiff and he just needed to give it more of a shove. But all thoughts to this next action froze as he saw Kevin, one of the enemy group, standing in the clearing, only ten yards away from him. Without a second's hesitation, he jumped into action, aiming his gun and firing at the enemy. To his amazement, he managed to hit his target, right in the centre of his chest. Kevin flinched but remained standing, raising his gun to shoot back. Nick frowned. He wasn't playing by the rules, he was supposed to play dead now.

He was about to tell Kevin this, but then came a flurry of movement from the surrounding trees and bushes, as the others emerged and came to stand beside Kevin. Nick looked at them in bewilderment, there were nine of them in all, three from his group. What was going on? But, as they raised their guns in unison, the dreadful realisation dawned. Of course, this had all been planned right from the start. As they took aim and fired, he turned back to the door of the hut, pushing at it in a desperate attempt to gain entry. As he pushed, he could just make out the faces of the other two boys, one of them David, laughing at him through the crack in the door. 'Let me in! Let me in! Please!' he sobbed, the impact of the pellets becoming increasingly painful as the other boys advanced.

Falling to his knees, he held his arms up in surrender, but still the shots kept coming, until he was completely covered in paint. Curling himself into a tight ball, all he could think was that he was glad Jack wasn't here to see this. But then Jack wouldn't have let this happen in the first place.

When the shots finally stopped coming, he slowly raised his head from his arms to see with relief that they were walking away. Except David, who paced back and forth several times. 'Did you think we'd all forgotten about what you did to Sarah?' he said, coming to a stop in front of him. 'Jack might be able to, but we can't' he hissed before booting him painfully in the leg, 'Fucking weirdo,' he added, before walking off to join the others.

Curling back into a foetal position, he scrunched his eyes tightly shut. It took every bit of strength left in him to suppress the sobs that were threatening to surface. It took a few moments, but he started to feel calmer, his breathing pattern slowed and he began to find it peaceful lying there in the woods, breathing in the earthy aroma and listening to the sounds of various birds chirping in the trees. He contemplated just staying there and never returning home, to Mother, to school, to the cruel, cruel world. Maybe he could survive right here, in the woods, he thought to himself. But as he felt the first few drops of rain and heard the distant voices of other groups, he realised that unfortunately wasn't an option.

Forcing himself up, he walked back in the direction he remembered coming, anxious to not be seen and ridiculed; he knew he must look a complete state. But he needn't have worried; no-one noticed the skinny, bedraggled teenage boy hobbling back to the paintballing central building.

By the time he returned home, the weather had well and truly turned. From being bright and sunny, it was now pouring down with an uncomfortably cool wind. Opening the front door, he had meant to rush past the front room, where Mother would invariably be, but he found himself pausing, forever hopeful that this might be the day Mother sat up, a look of concern etched on her chubby face, and said, 'Darling, what happened?' But as usual, she was sitting in front of the TV. Her eyes flickered to where he was standing, long enough to register his soggy, paint-covered attire, before returning to the glass screen that took up the majority of her time.

He removed his ruined trainers and trudged up the stairs to the bathroom, closing the door firmly behind him. As the bath ran, he peeled off his clothes, which was a painful and slow process. Taking in the bruising across his back and some of his chest, he gasped; the pellets had been more lethal than he'd realised. Lowering himself slowly into the steaming bath, he placed his flannel in his mouth to stifle the sobs that could no longer be suppressed.

So much for the fresh start.

Chapter Seventeen

Sam let out a sigh as she left the health centre. It was now Thursday, a whole six days since she had last seen Jack and, she hated to admit it, even to herself, but she was missing him like crazy. Annoyingly, he seemed to have heeded her excuse of having to concentrate on her coursework and had left her alone, not contacting her once since the weekend. She was now beginning to doubt what they had together, had she just imagined it? Her insides churned with the uncertainty, she hated feeling like this.

And they were beginning to notice at work: her snappy retorts; the 'resting bitch face' she could no longer be bothered to hide. Even Frances had caught the sharp end of her tongue when she had asked Sam what the matter was. With her fists balled, she had secretly hoped Frances would reprimand her in some way, not let her get away with being so rude. But to her dismay, Frances had simply given her a curt nod and walked away.

It was all down to that little creep with his ever-watchful gaze. How she wanted to wipe that cruel smile permanently from his nasty face – erase it forever. The anger she felt burned so searingly hot, the Pepto-Bismol she had started taking was no longer having an effect. The way she was feeling was also taking its toll on her skin, causing her to spend longer and longer applying increasing layers of makeup in a desperate bid to cover the dark circles and spots. She was even setting her alarm an hour earlier so that she could apply make up before going outside. She couldn't let people see the real her. The monster.

A little voice inside told her she was overreacting, that she was making too big a deal of Nick. She knew she was on the brink of losing control, like those nights out in London. All fired up. On the hunt for someone, or something, to console her.

Her mother had only increased her rage. Sam had not become physical with her again – there had been no repeat of the strangling - but she'd sneered at every kind gesture. Denise's careful, overly attentive handling of the fact Sam had suddenly moved back in had proved hugely irritating. She tip toed around her on egg shells, consciously avoiding the subject of Jack, instead twittering about what might or might not have happened to Sarah fucking Hollins – was she still alive? And why had she been chosen in the first place? Until Sam felt like she might explode.

Thankfully there had been some outlets for the pent-up rage seething inside her. Only yesterday, she had stopped at the entrance to the staff kitchen, about to walk away on seeing Nigel standing with his back to her, waiting for the kettle to boil. But then, having checked that nobody else was there, she had crept right up to the fat slug and said 'Boo!' in his ear, causing him to spill boiling water on his hand as he attempted to make his coffee. Letting out a startled yelp, he ran from the kitchen, abandoning his unmade drink. *Good*, she thought, opening the fridge to retrieve her lunch. She had been about to close the fridge door, but hesitated on noticing the familiar green container. Nigel's container.

Without giving too much thought to what she was about to do, she pulled it out and unclipped the lid. It contained the sort of lunch that reminded her of the packed lunches her friend Zoe used to bring to school; sandwiches cut into perfect little triangles, a pot of yoghurt and another mini container with grapes. How she'd longed to have packed lunches like that. Bending over the container, she hawked up a lump of phlegm all over those perfect little sandwiches, made by 'Mummy', no doubt (it was no secret that Nigel still lived with his mother).

Replacing the container in the fridge, she took a deep breath, the swirling rage in her stomach momentarily quelled.

And only earlier that day, Billy had greeted her with his usual, 'Hello there Sam, how's it going?' and she had walked over to his resident spot in next door's entrance and said, 'What makes you think you have the right to speak to me? Like you're some long lost friend of mine?' and then kneeling down so her eyes were level with his, 'I think it's time for you to jog on before I report you for harassment.'

Billy opened his mouth, as if to say something, but then simply nodded. Without another word, he picked up his rucksack and ambled off down the street. It was only when he had disappeared around the corner that Sam turned back and entered the health centre. Sadly, that did nothing to ease the burning in her gut, the reproachful expression on his face as he gathered up his meagre belongings stayed with her for the rest of the day. She wasn't used to feeling guilty.

Chapter Eighteen

'Mum, I'm back,' called Sam, as she opened the door to her old home. Her voice resounded around the empty front room telling her no one else was around, no other fellow human being to absorb the sound of her voice.

Suddenly feeling very alone, she slumped onto the settee but immediately got back up on noticing the piece of paper on the dining table, propped up by the vase her mother had recently purchased on one of her now regular expeditions into the town centre.

> Gone to Spanish class. I've made a casserole (impressive eh?)
> and left on counter as too hot to put in fridge.
> Enjoy!

Typical, Sam thought to herself, letting the note flutter back down to the table. She had expended so much energy worrying about her mother isolating herself away from society, and now that she was actually going out, Sam found herself resenting her mother's newfound freedom. She should be here, waiting at home to console her, to reassure her that everything would be OK and to advise her on what to do.

It wasn't fair; all throughout her childhood, she had managed to muddle through somehow without the parental guidance that was taken for granted by most people. People like Zoe, like Jack. Maybe even Nick, though instinctively she knew he'd had a shit childhood. He was damaged goods.

Just like her.

Sam stifled a yawn in the staff meeting the following morning, she hadn't taken in a thing and sat up in an attempt to appear attentive. After a troubled night of tossing and turning, she'd finally got up and showered at 5am, slipping out of the door not long after and pounding the ancient cobbled streets under a newly risen sun until her feet ached. Walking down to the canal, she watched the swans for a while, but soon felt restless, needing to be in the one place that made her feel at peace.

Turning to walk back through the town centre, she had been tempted to knock on Jack's door, even making a slight detour so she could walk past his home. But no, she couldn't just turn up like that, especially at such an ungodly hour. She didn't want to risk looking feeble and desperate.

Her pace slowed as she viewed the familiar red brick building, willing for some sort of sign that Jack was awake and feeling desperate like her. But the house gave nothing away to what was happening within.

Except for a slight gap in the stylish grey slatted blinds in one of the top windows. At first she thought she was mistaken, but then the gap grew larger, as if someone were forcing them open. Then it dawned on her with a sickening realisation; it was Nick's bedroom. He was the one behind that blind, pulling the slats apart to peer out.

At her.

Abruptly, she carried on walking, hoping against hope that he hadn't seen her, or better still, that the blind just hadn't been pulled down properly to begin with. But after walking a few yards, she dared to look back to see that the slats were now evenly aligned, with no apparent gap.

Panting from the exertion of jogging up Steep Hill, she reached her destination. Wrenching at the great doors of the cathedral, she howled in desperation to find them locked. But then what had she expected?

'Are you OK? Sam?'

Sam was brought back to the present. The team were gathering up their diaries and coffee mugs and leaving the meeting, except for Alan, who was peering at her closely, his brow furrowed.

'I'm fine,' she replied, forcing a smile. 'Just fine.'

At 12 noon the following day, Sam was standing in the staff kitchen, about to place a rather sad-looking ready meal in the microwave. Her mood hadn't improved and everyone who'd come into contact with her had been subjected to curt remarks and cold glares. Even Edith had been rudely disposed of when she had come into the health centre yet again, insisting that she'd made an appointment for that morning. Sam shook her head, regretting the way she'd treated the obviously troubled, old woman.

'You might want to pass on that,' a voice behind her said, causing her to whirl round abruptly.

'What?' Sam retorted.

'I said you might want to pass on that,' Frances repeated in her matter-of-fact way, stepping nearer to Sam and taking off her glasses as she inspected Sam's lunch. 'There's a much better offer waiting for you at reception. Well, a damn sight better than consuming that dreadful concoction of artificial substances that seems to pass for food these days,' she continued, wrinkling her nose in disgust. If it had been anyone else, Sam would have been infuriated.

'Er ... who is it?'

'Male, around six foot tall. Good looking specimen. Goes by the name of Jack, if I'm not mistaken. It might do you good to spend some time with him. Your unhappiness hasn't gone unnoticed,' she said in her characteristically blunt manner.

Suddenly feeling ashamed, Sam found herself struggling to meet Frances' level gaze.

'Has it been that obvious?'

Frances nodded.

'I'm sorry,' Sam said eventually, her shoulders slumping.

'Apology accepted,' said Frances, stepping closer to Sam and placing a hand gently under her chin. 'Forgive me if I'm wrong, you can tell me again to mind my own business, but I sense that life has been harder for you than most.'

Sam wanted to shrink away from Frances' appraising gaze, it was as if she could see right into her. But with her chin clasped firmly, there was nowhere else to look but into the older woman's eyes and what she saw was kindness and acceptance.

'You're a lovely, strong young woman and you deserve to be happy,' Frances said, finally releasing Sam from her grasp. Sam nodded and attempted a smile. She couldn't believe that those intelligent brown eyes could be so fooled, couldn't penetrate to her red, seething core and see her for what she really was.

A monster.

'Hello there,' Jack said, as Sam approached the reception area. His sheer presence seemed to light up the whole area and when he smiled, she was once again taken aback by his beauty. Tara, one of the new young nurses did a double take when she walked past, and gave a flirtatious smile in Jack's direction.

He's mine, Sam wanted to scream. But she needn't have worried as Jack's eyes locked onto hers, making her feel like she was the only person there.

'Hi,' said Sam, as lightly as she could muster. 'What are you doing here?'

'I've come to see you, of course. I was hoping we could have lunch? But if not, I brought you this,' he said, proffering a paper bag. Sam peeked inside and saw that it was one of the nice cupcakes from the cafe. If he thought he could win her round that easily, he was mistaken, but without saying anything, she took the paper bag and placed it on the shelf below the desk. Picking up her jacket and bag, she returned to Jack's side.

'You're in luck, I haven't eaten yet,' she finally said, looking up into Jack's eyes. She didn't return his smile.

****

'I'm sorry.'

Sam paused, a spoon of curried parsnip soup midway to her mouth. They were sitting in the cafe, not in the usual spot in the window, but at a table near the back. Sam was glad on this occasion; she didn't want to be on show.

'For what?' she said innocently, wanting Jack to spell it out.

'For being insensitive. It was supposed to be a special weekend for us, with you moving in, and I blew it. I'm so sorry.'

Sam took another sip of her soup before answering. 'It's OK, we're not shackled to each other.'

'I wish you were shackled to me right now,' he said, his blue eyes appearing a couple of shades darker as he stared at her intently. 'I've missed you,' he said quietly, reaching for her arm and grasping it tightly, causing an unwanted pleasurable feeling of expectation to ripple through her. She didn't want to feel so desperate and needing of him, feelings that she had long learnt to suppress as part of building her defences to survive her childhood. She didn't want him to see her like this, so open and vulnerable, and tried to pull her hand away but Jack tightened his grip.

'I'm not going anywhere,' he said fiercely. 'I meant what I said before. I've never felt this way about anyone else. I'm not going anywhere, Sam, so can we start again?'

She tried to look away from his beautiful face, but found it impossible to not be drawn back to him.

'Please, Sam,' he whispered, taking hold of her other hand.

She hesitated a moment, not given to taking a chance on another human being, but eventually found herself nodding. Maybe now was the time for change. Maybe she deserved a stab at happiness.

'From tonight?' Jack asked, a hopeful expression on his face.

Sam nodded again, 'I'll have to go home first and pick up a few things.'

'Fine by me. I can pick you up after work in the car then you could pack up a load of stuff.'

With a tentative smile, Sam squeezed Jack's hand. 'I'm not sure Jack, maybe I'll just go back on my own. I need to talk to my mum.'

'Well, I think it would be good to meet her. Put her mind at rest about who you're about to share your life with.'

Sam laughed.

'That's better,' Jack said, almost to himself.

'What's better?'

'Seeing you happy.'

With some persuading from Jack, Sam eventually gave in; agreeing that he would collect her later and she would introduce him to her mother (no furtive glances from behind the curtains, but properly this time).

Settling herself back behind the reception desk, Sam caught sight of the paper bag containing the cup cake and decided she would take it home for her mother. Something to soften the blow when she told her she was moving out; for definite this time.

Chapter Nineteen

Sam glanced up at Jack as she turned the key in the lock. She had a slightly sick feeling in the pit of her stomach, but if Jack was feeling the same, he didn't show it. He returned her gaze with a reassuring smile. However, as they both caught sight of the woman whimpering at the dining table, Jack's smile dropped as he looked uncertainly back to Sam.

'Mum! What's happened?' she said, quickly closing the distance between herself and her mother, leaving Jack to close the door quietly behind him.

'I spoke to Eddie,' her mother mumbled through her cradled arms.

'What?!' Sam struggled to comprehend what she just heard. She had deleted Eddie's number from her mother's phone ages ago but she must have written it down, or memorised it.

'Mum?' Sam said, touching Denise's arm, 'you didn't tell him where we are, did you?' she continued in as gentle a voice as she could muster.

Raising her head from her arms to reveal her mascara-smudged face, her mother was about to speak when she noticed Jack, still standing awkwardly by the door.

'Oh!' Denise said, jumping at the sight of the unfamiliar man in her home.

'Hi, I'm Jack. So sorry, I didn't mean to scare you.' He raised his arms in a conciliatory gesture. 'Should I leave?' he continued, looking at Sam.

'No, no. It's fine' said Denise, hurriedly wiping her face with the scrunched-up tissue from her sleeve. 'Any friend of Sam's is welcome here.' She stood up and attempted a wobbly smile.

'Mum!' Sam said, struggling to contain the urgency in her voice, 'did you tell him where we live?'

Denise's attention returned to her daughter. 'Of course I didn't. I'm not that stupid!' she said indignantly.

Sam took a deep breath.

'Good.'

'I would invite you to stay for dinner but ... well ... I haven't got round to getting anything in. It hasn't been a good day.' Denise said, addressing Jack.

'No problem,' Jack replied. 'I'm more than happy to get us a takeaway.'

'That's if you want me to, of course,' he added hastily, turning to gauge Sam's reaction.

But before she could say anything, her mother jumped in. 'That sounds lovely, Jack. What a nice thing to suggest.'

Sam groaned inwardly as she observed her mother positively beaming up at Jack through her tears. Was she actually trying to flirt with her daughter's man? *In the state she was in?* But as soon as he left, with instructions to bring back a Chinese takeaway from around the corner, Sam found herself being tightly embraced in her mother's arms.

'You hold on to him. He's definitely a keeper,' her mother said, releasing Sam so she could look at her. Sam regarded her mother sceptically. Since when did her mother have the right to start dispensing advice?!

As they sat around the table, tucking into the veritable feast that Jack had brought back; including two bottles of expensive-looking wine, Denise relayed her conversation with Eddie. He had told her that the pendant was still in his possession and that if she came back and asked nicely, she could have it back.

'Uh, uh,' said Sam, interrupting her mother. 'There's no way that's happening. I can't believe you'd even consider going to see him!'

'No, Sammy, I didn't say I was going to do that. But ...'

Sam watched in alarm as her mother looked down and started fidgeting with her hands – a sure sign she was contemplating exactly that.

'Oh, I just wish your Pops was still here. He'd know what to do,' Denise said, standing up abruptly and stacking the mostly empty takeaway containers onto a tray.

'Leave that, Mum. I'll do it later,' Sam said, placing a steadying hand on Denise's arm. She hadn't needed much persuading as she almost immediately slumped back onto her chair.

'I'll go.'

'What?' Sam said, looking across the table and meeting Jack's eyes. He had remained largely silent throughout the meal, glancing occasionally in Sam and Denise's direction to indicate he was listening.

'I said I'll go,' Jack repeated firmly.

'Thank you Jack, but no. This is my mess and I've got to sort it out,' said Denise, attempting a smile. 'Now, how about I make us a nice cup of coffee?' she added, getting up and walking into the kitchen. 'I think I've got some chocolates somewhere too.'

'Are you serious?' Sam whispered as her mother made coffee. Jack nodded solemnly, reaching across the table and gripping Sam's hand. 'Then we'll go together. But don't say a word to my mum,' Sam said, squeezing Jack's hands tightly.

He had no idea who Eddie was; what level of risk he was taking in going to his house to demand something, and yet Jack was going to do this, for her. Any final doubts about him fell away.

Chapter Twenty

Collecting the plates and the rest of the takeaway debris, Sam rose from the table. Standing at the entrance to the kitchen, she paused for a moment, watching her mother as she made the coffee. She could see that her hands were shaking, causing the boiling water to spill onto the counter. She could also see that there was no way she could go back with Jack tonight. With a sigh, she placed the dishes by the cooker and went up to her mother.

'It's OK, Mum, go and sit down and I'll bring the coffee through.'

As the evening went on, Sam observed her mother with a mixture of fascination and trepidation, as she laid bare the details of their former life. It was strange to watch her speaking so candidly about it all, she even spoke of that terrifying night, when Eddie had nearly killed her. They hadn't spoken about that night. Until now.

Maybe it was the second bottle of wine that had loosened her mother's tongue, but Sam could see that it was also due to Jack's listening skills, intuitively knowing when to, and when not to speak. A sudden rush of warmth travelled through her body as she looked at the man she loved. Yes, loved. She smiled at the thought.

It was well past midnight when Jack staggered to his feet, saying he would walk home as he was well over the limit to drive.

'Don't be silly,' Denise said instantly. 'You're more than welcome to stay,' and turning to Sam with a wink, 'I'm sure Sammy won't mind.'

'I'm sorry,' Sam whispered later into Jack's chest as they laid on her bed.

'For what?'

'My mother.'

'Sam, there's no need to apologise. We couldn't have left her like that, she was in a right state!'

Sam lifted herself from her comfortable position and sat upright.

'As I said, she's like that a lot. It's nothing out of the ordinary.' She let out a sigh and reached for the glass of water on the chest of drawers by her bed.

'Can you shut your curtain properly?' Jack said, reaching out to stroke Sam's back, raising the hairs on her neck.

'Why?' she replied, turning to face Jack, a look of amusement on her face. 'Nobody can see us from here.'

'I know, but I don't want to be woken up by the morning light.'

'OK,' she replied, turning back to pull the curtains together, but not before taking one last look at the view of the floodlit cathedral in the distance; the very reason she left the gap in her curtains, positioned perfectly so that she could see the cathedral from where she lay in bed, taking comfort from the glorious sight on those all too frequent nights when she couldn't sleep. She couldn't help but feel a little resentful at being deprived of the view but didn't protest.

Later, as the cathedral bells chimed to let the good people of Lincoln know it was 3am, Sam let out a sigh of satisfaction. She still didn't feel anywhere near sleepy but felt instead a sense of total wellbeing, having Jack lying beside her. She turned to face him, starting slightly when she saw his eyes were open. She brought her hand to his face and smiled, but he didn't reciprocate.

'What's wrong?' she said, alarmed to find that his cheeks were damp.

'I can't stop thinking about what your mother said,' he finally replied, taking her hands in his. 'Your life's been really tough, hasn't it?'

Sam nodded slowly, there was no point in denying it. She felt Jack's grip on her hands tighten.

'It makes me so angry to think of you trying to defend your mother like that. I don't know how anyone could hurt a child.'

Sam didn't reply. Although that night was definitely the worst, there were numerous other times when she had been hit and shouted at, when her mother's attempts to stop the violence had failed. She soon found that she didn't cry after all of the beatings, but that sometimes made it worse, as if the men thought that they had failed somehow and would hit her harder. She then learnt to feign her cries, all the while clenching her fists so tightly, her knuckles turned white.

'I could kill that bastard for what he did to you and your mother,' Jack hissed.

'Let's just get the pendant back,' Sam said, pulling him closer for a kiss. 'It won't be easy. Eddie is older and tougher since those days. I'm not sure what he would be capable of doing to us now.'

Chapter Twenty One

'There it is, on the end,' Sam said, pointing to a row of tall houses.

'OK, I'll see if I can park round the corner,' said Jack, flicking the indicator switch.

'Watch out!' Sam shouted as a car suddenly swerved out from behind them with a prolonged beep of its horn. As the car drew level to Jack's Fiesta, the driver, an ancient looking woman wearing massive sunglasses, stuck up her middle finger and with a sneer, accelerated away with a screech of tyres.

'Bloody Hell! Can you believe that?!' Jack said, turning to look at Sam, a look of incredulity on his face. 'I only slowed down to turn the corner!'

Sam shook her head and smiled, 'Welcome to London.'

After Jack had pulled into a parking space and turned off the engine, he didn't make any attempt to open the car door, instead staring straight ahead. Finally he spoke, after several enquiring glances from Sam.

'I think you should stay here.'

'What? No! No way! We've been through this already, Jack, we go together!' She fixed him with one of her hard stares, satisfied to see his resolve crumbling before her eyes.

'OK,' Jack sighed, running his hands through his hair. 'But I want you to promise me you won't do anything stupid, I need to keep you safe.'

'OK, He-Man,' Sam said, with a roll of her eyes but deep down, she was touched.

As they rounded the corner onto Trinity Road, they were immediately confronted with Eddie's house, a ramshackle, crooked building that stuck out like a rotting tooth at the end of the gleaming Edwardian terrace. Quite fitting really, Sam thought, as she walked up to the front door and boldly knocked. There was silence for a moment, and Sam glanced up at Jack standing beside her. She could see a flicker of uncertainty in his eyes and wondered whether he was thinking the same thought as her, *what if Eddie wasn't there? What if he'd gone away, or had given Denise a false address?*

But then came the sound of scampering footsteps and Sam braced herself. The footsteps stopped abruptly behind the door and then nothing. Sam balled her hand into a fist, ready to give another round of short, assertive knocks, when something in her lower field of vision caught her attention. Looking down, she saw that the rusty letterbox was open.

'Careful,' said Jack, as she knelt down level with the letterbox, mindful of keeping her distance prior to Jack's warning. However, all caution melted away at the sight of the two large brown eyes, framed by long, thick lashes, staring back at her.

'Hi there, sweetheart,' Sam heard herself say in a voice she didn't recognise. 'Is your mummy or daddy in?'

The large brown eyes blinked back at her a couple of times. Sam tried again. 'Sweetie, it's really important that I speak to your ... er ... daddy. He has something that belongs to me. Could you open the door?'

The eyes carried on staring back at her, but then a small voice said, 'My mum said I mustn't open the door to strangers.'

'That's right, but if you could just go and—'

'But if you know my dad then you're not a stranger, so that's OK,' the small voice interjected. Before Sam could reply, the letterbox closed abruptly and the scampering footsteps retreated from the door.

Sam straightened up and braced herself for coming face to face with Eddie. She was relieved to feel Jack's warm hand finding hers and gripped it tightly.

They waited for what felt like ages before the sound of something scraping along the floor could be heard from the other side of the door.

'What the hell's that?' Jack said, an alarmed expression on his face. Instinctively, they both took a step back as the fumbling and scraping sounds stopped and the door was eventually opened. The smell of cannabis hit Sam's nostrils instantly and she was surprised to find herself looking down at the same large brown eyes framed by a mass of unruly corkscrew curls. Sam was mesmerised by the little girl's beauty, which shone through her dirty face and grubby attire.

'I thought you were going to get your daddy,' she said, smiling down at the girl as they stepped into the dark hallway. The little girl shrugged her skinny shoulders.

'Dad's not back yet and Mum's sleeping and, anyway, I can open the door when I stand on this,' she said, pointing at the source of all the scraping sounds, a wooden stool.

'I'm seven now so I can do things by myself,' she flashed an unexpected, brief grin, which revealed a gap in her front teeth.

'My big teeth are coming soon. See?' she said, tapping her gums to show Sam the white stumps that were starting to poke through her pink gums.

'Could you get your mum for me?' Sam said, suddenly wanting to get this over and done with.

Peering past the girl, she could make out a dim light at the end of the hallway.

'Uh, uh, uhhhhh. Uuuuuuurrrrrrrrhhhh!' came the sound of a baby's cries.

'I'm coming Lee, don't worry,' said the girl. 'That's my little brother. Come on,' she said, tugging at Sam's sleeve. With no further option, Sam followed her down the narrow hallway and towards the source of the increasingly demanding cries.

As she walked down the hallway, Sam noted the cracks in the walls and the peeling wallpaper, reminding her of the depressing dumps she had spent her childhood in, and she looked down at the spindly little figure with the huge mop of curls with a deep sense of sadness at the prospect of history seemingly repeating itself.

She glanced back, relieved to see Jack following close behind, the expression on his face inscrutable. The girl let go of Sam's sleeve and ran towards her baby brother, sitting in a bouncy chair in the middle of the sparse room. Glancing around, Sam noted they were in a dining area with a kitchen at the far end. She took in the grimy counters and broken blind before resting her sights on the girl crouching over her brother, rocking his chair back and forth vigorously as she tried to placate him.

'Do you want some milk, Lee? Are you hungry?' she said, continuing to rock the chair, causing the baby's head to jerk back and forth. There was a momentary silence whilst the baby gave his sister an appraising stare before emitting a loud, indignant squeal.

'OK, OK, Lee, I'll get your milk.' The girl sprang upright and, with startling agility, dragged a nearby chair towards the fridge, standing on it to reach a bottle of milk on the middle shelf. Sam noticed there was very little else in there. She looked on with a growing sadness, as the girl dragged the chair over to the microwave, loosening the bottle top before placing it inside with the practised ease of having done so many times before. Whilst the bottle spun round behind the glass door she turned back to Sam and grinned, clearly enjoying having an audience. Sam smiled back encouragingly, trying to hide the pity she felt for the girl, who, at seven years old, shouldn't even know how to use a microwave, let alone have the responsibility of caring for another human being.

But then she thought back to what it was like for her at around the same age, of knowing when it was safe to leave her room, or when she needed to keep a very low profile to avoid being in the firing line of Eddie, or another one of the brutish men in her mother's life. She thought of her mother saying she'd wanted another child and she suddenly felt weak from the realisation of just how bad her upbringing had been.

'You OK?' said Jack, a look of concern etched on his face as Sam found herself gripping the kitchen counter.

'Fine,' she said, managing a faint smile which faded immediately at the sight of the emaciated figure that had just entered the kitchen.

'Who the fuck are you?' croaked the figure, a scrawny woman who couldn't have been much older than Sam. Without waiting for an answer, she pushed past Jack and grabbed the baby out of his chair, causing him to emit another indignant squeal. She then grabbed hold of the little girl's arm and pulled her off the chair.

'It's OK, Mummy,' the girl whimpered. 'They said they know Dad.'

'Layla, what did I tell you about not opening the door to strangers?' said the woman in a vicious tone, as she looked down at her daughter. Snapping her head back up, she said, 'So you're not from the bloody council then?'

'No, no we're not,' said Sam, quickly wanting to reassure the young woman who resembled a trapped animal as she pulled her children tightly to her. The last thing Sam wanted to do was scare her. She knew only too well what it was like living with a monster like Eddie.

'Well, well, well, what have we got here?' came another voice, startling everyone in the room. Standing in the doorway was Eddie. He didn't look as big as Sam remembered, although his malign presence caused an unwanted ripple of fear to course through her veins.

'Hello Eddie,' Sam said, breaking the silence and making every effort to keep her voice level.

Maintaining his stance in the doorway, Eddie jutted his head forward and squinted his eyes as he concentrated on Sam's face. Then all of a sudden he clapped his hands and threw his head back, 'Ha haaaah!' he bellowed, causing Sam to jump despite herself. 'Sammy!' he said, 'How nice of you to visit your old Pops!'

'Only my mum calls me that and you're not my Pops,' Sam said, through gritted teeth, fighting the urge to scratch his eyes out.

'Awwww, c'mon, Sammy, I was your daddy for a while. I tried my best. You just never made it easy for me, did you? You never knew what was good for you. But it seems that's changed.

'Who's the pretty boy?' he said, abruptly, gesturing to Jack, his eyes not leaving Sam's.

'I'm Jack,' said Jack, moving into Eddie's line of sight, but Eddie's eyes didn't so much as flicker in his direction, preferring to keep his gaze trained on Sam.

Sam stepped forward, determined to get this over and done with as quickly as possible. 'I've come to collect something that belonged to my mum.'

'Hold on, hold on,' said Eddie, raising his hands up in what could have been taken to be a conciliatory gesture – to someone who didn't know him. 'Let's back track a bit, shall we?' He stepped forwards, taking a cigarette from a packet on the counter. Patting his pockets and not finding what he was looking for, he simply held the unlit cigarette in his fingers.

'Here, Eddie,' the woman said, proffering a lighter with a hand that trembled. Eddie ignored her, moving closer to Sam until he loomed over her, making her feel like she was six years old again. It took all her strength not to take a step back.

'My my, who would've thought, eh? My little Sammy's all grown up,' Eddie said, his eyes taking a slow journey up and down her body.

Sam forced herself to hold her stance but felt nauseous with fear. How could she have been so naive as to think he would just hand over her mother's pendant?

'Eddie, I'm not here to make small talk, I just want my mum's pendant back then we'll leave.'

'But just look at you. You're the image of your mother. How is she, by the way?'

'Fine,' Sam said, through clenched teeth. She cursed inwardly, wishing she wasn't wearing such a tight top, as Eddie's eyes lingered on her breasts.

The baby let out another cry which cut through the momentary silence like a knife. Eddie whipped round and grabbed the woman's arm, almost causing her to drop the baby.

'Go upstairs. Now.'

Taking the bottle from the microwave, the woman turned and fled from the room. Sam saw the fearful look on the little girl's face as she followed her mother.

'Look, you heard Sam, just give back the pendant then we'll be on our way.' Jack said, moving to stand by Sam's side. Eddie cocked his head to one side as if in contemplation, then, in one swift movement, drew his arm back and punched Jack in the face. Eddie's time spent in the boxing gym hadn't gone to waste; it was a powerful punch, causing Jack to lose his balance and fall to the floor where Eddie immediately gave him a vicious kick in the stomach. Sam screamed and dropped to the floor beside Jack.

'Jack? Jack? Are you OK?' She could see blood spewing from a split in his right eyebrow and, pulling a tissue from her bag, tried to stem the flow by dabbing at it. Jack emitted a groan.

'He'll be just fine. No major arteries damaged, he just won't look so pretty for a while. Now, where was I?' Eddie said, examining the cigarette he still held between his thick fingers.

'Oh, yes,' he walked over to the cooker and lit the cigarette from one of the rings. Holding the cigarette to his lips, he took a long drag, before exhaling slowly. Looking up at him from her position on the floor, Sam's skin pricked with fear as a distant memory of Eddie stubbing his cigarette into her mother's flesh suddenly re-emerged.

He knelt down to Sam's level and took another long drag. She resisted the urge to cough as he blew out the smoke in her direction.

'Now, despite what you might think, Sammy, I'm a reasonable man. I looked after you and your mother to the best of my ability. Seven years. Seven long, long years. Managing her mood swings and addictions. She was a bloody nightmare.'

'You didn't help her,' Sam snarled.

'I know things weren't always easy, Sammy,' Eddie continued, as if he hadn't heard her. 'But I would have given her the world if she'd only done what I asked, made a bit of an effort. And I'm gonna give you some valuable advice so listen up.' He paused and holding his arm out, flicked cigarette ash over Jack's recumbent body. Sam immediately went to brush the ash from Jack's jeans, but Eddie took hold of her wrist, his large hand gripping her like a vice.

'Get the fuck away from your mother,' he hissed, pulling her towards him so she could smell his stale breath. 'She's a snivelling little bitch, one of life's needy little losers and she'll suck the life out of you. Like she did me.'

He tightened his grip, causing Sam to yelp in pain and, as he leant in closer, for one unbearable moment, she thought he was going to try and kiss her.

'That's the advice bit over. Now listen very carefully. If I hear another word from you or your mother, I'll come looking for you and I won't be so accommodating next time. But there won't be a next time, will there, Sammy?' He twisted her wrist suddenly, causing a searing pain up the length of her arm. She gasped, shaking her head violently.

'Clever girl, you know what's good for you. Now get the fuck out of my house and take pretty boy with you.' He stood up and leant against the kitchen counter.

'Come on, Jack, you need to get up,' Sam said, kneeling over him and shaking his shoulder. He let out another groan.

'Come on, put your arm around me. Please, Jack!' She let out an involuntary whimper as she looked up at Eddie. He had discarded his cigarette and was just standing there, his fists balled, ready for another go at Jack, or perhaps her, she couldn't be sure. With all the strength she could muster, she hauled Jack up to his feet and dragged him in the direction of the hallway. She half expected Eddie to block their way, to keep them from leaving for his own amusement, but he stepped aside.

As they reached the front door, Eddie let out a low whistle.

'Aren't you forgetting something?' he said, greeting Sam with a leering smile as she manoeuvred Jack round awkwardly to look back in his direction. He pulled open one of the kitchen drawers and took something out.

'Here, take your rubbish with you,' Eddie said, tossing the object onto the floor. Sam glanced down at something that gleamed in the dark hallway. It must be the pendant, she thought, disbelievingly.

'Come and get it then. Before I change my mind,' Eddie said, the smile dropping from his face in an instant. Carefully, Sam lowered Jack onto the stool that had been left by the girl in what seemed like ages ago. For one awful moment, she thought Jack would fall to the floor as he slumped over to one side, but he managed to hold his position.

Tentatively, she took a few steps back down the hallway, keeping her eyes fixed on the pendant. As she drew near to it, she hesitated and glanced up at Eddie. He gave a curt nod to convey his consent for her to take the object from the floor. She knelt down, but, as her fingers reached for the pendant, she felt an excruciating pain as Eddie's shoe came into contact with her hand, pinning it to the floor.

She cried out, causing Jack to stir from his slumped position and attempt to stand up.

'Leave her alone!' he shouted, spitting out the blood that was trickling into his mouth.

'Take one step closer and I'll fucking finish you off for good, pretty boy!' Eddie said, jabbing his finger in Jack's direction.

'Please, Jack, he means it,' gasped Sam as Eddie pushed his weight down on her hand.

'Good girl,' said Eddie, peering down at her. 'Now you won't go forgetting what I said, will you?'

Sam shook her head vigorously, willing herself not to burst into tears as Eddie finally took his foot off her hand.

'Come on, then, get a move on,' he said, punctuating each word with a loud clap of his hands.

Sam looked towards the pendant as Eddie kicked it into the kitchen before she retreated back down the hallway towards Jack as quickly as she could. Placing his arm around her shoulder, they both stumbled out of the door and into the daylight, almost crashing into a suited man who immediately averted his eyes on seeing the blood trickling down Jack's face. He walked up the path of the house directly next door, closing the gate firmly behind him. So much for neighbourly concern, thought Sam but then she couldn't really blame him, God knows what he had to put up with living next to a brute like Eddie.

Before rounding the corner towards Jack's car, Sam glanced back at the house, fearful that Eddie might change his mind and come storming after them. Thankfully the front door remained closed. A movement in one of the top windows caught her eye and she saw the little girl, Layla, staring back at her with those beautiful brown eyes. Layla raised her hand to wave but a large hand – Eddie's – yanked her away from the window and out of Sam's sight.

Sam scrunched her eyes closed tight for a second before leading Jack to the car. She tried to usher him into the passenger seat.

'What are you doing?' Jack mumbled.

'I need to get you to a hospital,' she said

'No hospital and I'm driving.'

'It's OK, I took a few lessons before me and mum moved.' She tried again to move him towards the open door. 'You can't be serious about driving, you might be concussed. You've got to go to A and E!' she called after Jack desperately, as he stumbled round to the driver's side.

Peering in through the car door, Sam was about to protest further but stopped when she saw the steely expression on Jack's face, his knuckles white from the force with which he gripped the wheel.

'Get in the fucking car, Sam,' he said, in a low voice she didn't recognise. Too stunned to say anything, she slipped into the seat beside him as he turned on the engine and revved the car into life.

'Wait!' Sam said, placing her hand over his as he manoeuvred the car into first gear.

'Please just let me wipe your face.'

Jack didn't reply, but shifted the gear back into neutral, turning his head slightly so that Sam could reach his affected eye. She dampened some tissue from a bottle of water and dabbed gently at his face. The blood was coming from a split in his eyebrow, he was lucky Eddie had missed his eye. She attempted a smile but he didn't reciprocate; it was as if he was staring straight through her.

'That's enough,' Jack said, grabbing Sam's hand and placing it firmly in her lap. He pulled the car out of the parking space, causing another car to brake abruptly behind him.

Sam didn't dare say anything as Jack swerved in and out of traffic, his foot pressed down hard on the accelerator. How they weren't pulled over, she didn't know, but thankfully Jack's driving hadn't caught the attention of the police.

Shortly after entering the county of Lincolnshire, Jack pulled into a small service station.

'The tank's nearly empty,' he said, by way of explanation. Until then, the journey had been in complete silence. Although Sam had wanted to say so much, taking furtive glances in his direction, the set expression on his face put her off.

Jack turned the engine off but made no attempt to get out of the car. Instead, he placed his hands in his lap and Sam noticed they were trembling.

'I'll put the petrol in,' she said and got out of the car. She closed her eyes as she filled the tank, grateful to feel the cool breeze on her face. Placing the nozzle back in the slot, she started to head towards the service station.

'Sam, wait.' She turned back to see Jack had got out of the car and was leaning against the bonnet.

'I'm sorry,' he said, his voice breaking slightly.

'Sorry?' Sam said incredulously, 'You're the one that was beaten up trying to help me and *you're* sorry?' She shook her head and started to walk back towards the car. Towards Jack.

'I'm the one who's sorry, Jack, you didn't deserve any of this.' She ran into his waiting arms and hugged him fiercely. 'I thought you were angry with me,' she mumbled into his chest. 'You should be.'

'I— I could never be angry with you after that. After him. I'm angry with myself, I ... I wasn't able to protect you. What must you think of me?'

Sam pulled away and looked up into Jack's face. The area around his eye had begun to swell and, despite her efforts to clean his face, there were still patches of dried blood evident. He lifted her hand and inspected it, shaking his head when he saw the imprints of Eddie's shoe still visible. He gently kissed each finger, letting his lips brush slowly over each one, causing an unexpected shiver of pleasure to run up Sam's spine. How he could manage to make her feel like this after what they had just been through, she didn't know.

'Right,' she said firmly. 'We're going to stop here for a bit and get you cleaned up and have something to eat. OK?'

Jack nodded and, hand in hand, they headed towards the service station.

Chapter Twenty Two

Nick was on the settee when they eventually got back to the house. With his feet curled up under him, he looked quite effeminate, Sam thought.

'What the fuck!' said Nick, straightening up.

'Not now, Nick,' Jack said dismissively and went upstairs. Nick raised an eyebrow in Sam's direction, but she gave him a blank stare before following Jack out of the room.

In the privacy of Jack's bedroom, they unpeeled each other's clothes and made love with an intensity that made Sam feel like she was going to explode. She heard Nick's door slam shut at one point but couldn't care less. Let the creep know how much she was loved and wanted by Jack. He belonged to her now.

Lying back on the pillows, Jack gently took her hand and examined it, the skin hadn't broken, thankfully. She flinched as Jack carefully manipulated each finger.

'I'm sorry, baby, I'm just checking to see if there's anything broken.'

'I'm fine,' Sam smiled. 'But I wish you'd get checked out at the hospital, or how about I book you in at the health centre tomorrow? I'm sure I can squeeze you in.'

'Sam, for the last time, I'm not going to the hospital, OK? Now let's just try and draw a line under it.'

'OK,' Sam eventually conceded, detecting the irritable edge to his voice. Several hours later she found herself still wide awake. Glancing over at Jack's face, illuminated by the moon from a slight gap in the blinds, she could make out that he was awake too.

****

Sam woke with a start and groaned inwardly when she saw the time. She was supposed to be at a lecture for 9.30 am and it was already 8.45 am. She could make it if she got a move on but first, there was something she had to do. Pulling on her dressing gown, she left the bedroom, closing the door quietly behind her so as not to wake Jack.

Perching on a stool at the little kitchen island, she looked up a number on her phone and pressed call. After negotiating the automated voice stating too many options, she pressed 5 and after several minutes of tapping her nails on the counter, was eventually connected to a human voice.

'Access team, Children's services, how can I help?'

'Oh, hi, yes, I want to report something about a child ... er, actually, two children.'

'Please go on,' came the voice.

'There are two children who are being neglected and abused. They live at number eighty, Trinity Road, Tooting,' Sam said firmly.

The call took longer than expected as Sam answered a number of questions by the Duty Social Worker. She gave her name and address, but the one question she wouldn't answer was her connection to the two children. She just hoped she had given enough information for Social Services to do their job properly. The thought of those large brown eyes nearly broke her heart.

'My my, it's a bit early in the day to be the good Samaritan, isn't it?'

Sam jumped; she hadn't heard Nick come down the stairs.

'I'm guessing this has something to do with what happened yesterday?'

Sam nodded but didn't say anything.

'Sounds pretty serious,' he continued, walking over to the kettle. 'Tea?'

'No thanks, I'm meant to be in a lecture in twenty minutes.'

Nick nodded and Sam was thankful that for once he didn't feel the need to reply with a clever retort or snide comment, something to niggle away at her and make her insides churn. But she had been too quick to assume, and as she neared the door she heard the sound of his voice, low and soft.

'I'm sure I'll get the lowdown from Jack. There's no secrets between us.'

Her stomach gurgled uncomfortably as she crept into the lecture hall, affording a disapproving glance from the tutor at her lateness. She settled down at the end of a row near the back, cursing inwardly at her decision to attend. The thought of Nick having a cosy little one to one with Jack made her head spin and there was the problem of what to say to her mother, how to explain their failure in getting the pendant back. But, despite these worries, she soon found herself absorbed in the content of the lecture, as the low rumble of the lecturer's voice gradually entered her consciousness, crowding out the uncomfortable thoughts that frayed her nerves and turned her stomach into a bunch of knots.

The topic was Personality Disorders and there was a slide on the PowerPoint with a list of types and characteristics.

'Now I want you all to have a think about the people you know. It may be a relative, a friend, or work colleague,' the tutor said, pointing with a ruler at the screen. 'There's always someone – or some people – we come across in life who have the ability to really get under our skin. They will say, or do something that will make you feel mad, or upset, and they will do this on a consistent basis.'

The tutor paused as a large number of students nodded in recognition, some of them murmuring in little clusters. Sam remained silent, having no cluster to discuss her thoughts with. She wasn't there to make friends.

Stuffing his hands in his pockets, the tutor stepped round the lectern and sauntered towards the front of the PowerPoint.

'I don't want you all to leave here today and start diagnosing the surrounding population, but have you ever thought that these people – these particular individuals – who have a particular knack for getting under your skin, could actually have a personality disorder?' Freeing a hand from his right pocket, he waved it nonchalantly. 'Of course, I don't want you to start self-diagnosing, not just yet. They could just be awkward buggers.'

This last comment afforded a rumble of laughter in the room but, try as Sam might to muster a smile, she just couldn't stop thinking about *him*. That small smile. Those little remarks that went seemingly unnoticed by Jack yet caused her to see red.

Chapter Twenty Three

In the end, it had been easier than Sam thought to explain about the pendant. Jack had come home with her and, taking one look at his face, Denise had burst into tears. She didn't ask questions and Sam had already decided there was no need to tell her about the mother and the children suffering the same fate they had endured. Her mother was very apologetic that they had gone to retrieve her pendant and been hurt in the process, although Sam knew that before the bruises healed, she would be muttering about her pendant again. But for now at least, there was peace.

As they said their goodbyes at the front door, Sam couldn't help the rising tide of anger. Anger at what she and Jack had had to go through. Anger at having, yet again, to step in and try to save the day for her mother and at a huge cost to herself. And anger that she had ever thought Eddie had a decent bone in him.

****

Standing in Jack's plush kitchen, Sam smiled as she poured the freshly boiled water from the kettle into the cafetière. To think, just a couple of months back she hadn't even known what one was. Now she had become quite obsessed with trying out all the different blends of ground coffee the local Co-op had to offer. But the best, by far, had to be the Blue Mountain blend served in the Highbridge, the beautiful timber-framed café, unique in its location atop an ancient bridge over-looking the canal.

Jack had taken her there a couple of weeks ago, thoughtfully asking her mother if she would like to join them. She cringed at the memory of her mother emitting a girlish titter as she accepted the invite, a sound that had oddly infuriated her.

'Ahhhhh, there's nothing better than the smell of freshly brewed coffee in the morning.'

Sam jumped, nearly spilling the contents of the cafetière. She turned to see *him* sitting at one of the place settings at the table, the places she had set so carefully for her and Jack. She hesitated a moment before moving towards the table and placing the cafetière down as far away from Nick as possible, which was difficult, given the table's small dimensions.

'Hmm, enough for me, I hope?' he said, toying with the lilac napkins she had picked out in Binns the day before.

'Probably not,' she said, not bothering to disguise the sharpness of her tone. She cursed inwardly at dismissing Jack's earlier suggestion of going to the Highbridge for breakfast, at wanting instead to surprise him with poached eggs and smoked salmon. A small gesture to show him how much he meant to her.

Not meeting Nick's eyes, she stalked back over to the counter, furious at herself for hoping that Nick's unwelcome appearances would stop now he had met someone.

Jack had told her, when she had noted Nick's frequent absences for a few days at a time, *noticing that he wasn't lurking in corners, always watchful*, but she didn't say that, of course. She had been ecstatic at the time, secretly hoping that he just might not return from his next stay away.

But he always did return. And as she sat across from him now, watching in growing disgust as Jack generously gave up half of his breakfast to him, fetching another mug and measuring out the coffee that was only meant for two, she wanted to reach across the table and scratch his eyes out, rake at his skin until she had erased all facial features and only a bloody pulp was left. But in her mind's eye there would always be that taunting little smile.

Sam eventually excused herself from the table, taking her half-eaten breakfast with her as Jack and Nick chatted happily away. She scraped the gooey contents of her plate into the bin, swallowing the bile that was rising in her gut.

'Can you believe it, Sam?'

'Sam?'

She turned to see them both staring back at her, the questioning expressions on their faces indicating a response was expected. She hadn't heard a thing they had been talking about. The blood pumping in her ears had drowned out all other sound.

'Are you OK?' Jack asked, his expression changing to that of concern. Nick's face stayed the same, his cold, little eyes fixed on hers.

'Yes ... sorry, I'm fine. Just zoned out for a moment there. What was it you were saying?' she said, turning back to place her now empty plate in the sink.

'June twelfth!' Nick said triumphantly, picking up his plate and moving towards the counter. 'We share the same birthday,' he continued, his arm brushing gently against hers as he placed his plate in the sink. 'We'll have to have a joint celebration,' his voice quieter this time. In her ear. Causing her to recoil in repulsion. There was something else too – in his menacing low tone that reminded her of how Jack sounded in the car after that awful experience at Eddie's - something that bothered her far more than his proximity.

Not knowing how to respond, Sam turned on her heel out of the room, desperate to get away from him. Reaching Jack's bedroom (too early to be calling it 'their' room), she slammed the door shut behind her and sat at the small desk by the window. Adjusting the vanity mirror she had brought from home, she took a long, hard look at the reflection staring back at her.

The light did nothing for her features, she thought, leaning forward to inspect her face more closely. The dark shadows under her eyes seemed to be spreading, fanning out to her cheeks and above her eyes, making her skin blotchy. She reached for her make-up bag and took out the MAC foundation, a recent pay day treat, and was in the process of applying the powder thickly over her face when she saw the door opening, causing her to freeze momentarily, horrified at the thought of Nick coming in to impart some more of his nasty little comments. But thankfully it was Jack peering round the door, a sceptical expression on his face.

Sam met his gaze in the mirror, continuing to dab around her eyes with the powder.

'Are you OK?' he asked, walking into the room.

Sam shrugged. 'Why wouldn't I be?'

She continued dabbing furiously around her eyes, why weren't the shadows disappearing? She jumped at the feel of Jack's hands on her shoulders. Her nerves still jangled from Nick's voice in her ear.

'Hey, what's got into you?' he said, bending down to caress her neck with his lips. Sam closed her eyes for a moment and willed herself to relax and enjoy the tingling sensation on her neck; the reassuring pressure of Jack's warm hands as he massaged the knots in her shoulders.

'You don't need all that stuff on your face,' he whispered. 'You're beautiful just the way you are.'

'Awwww, I didn't know you felt that way about me!' Sam's eyes flew open to see Nick standing in the doorway and before she could do anything, he ran up behind Jack and hugged him, moving his face to one side so she could see him in the mirror's reflection. He looked like an evil little gargoyle, sprouting out from Jack's side, grinning back at her.

She stood up, almost knocking over the stool in her haste to get away. Grabbing her jacket and bag, she fled from the room and down the stairs.

'Hey, I was only joking!' Nick called after her. She whipped around to see him at the top of the stairs, his hands held up in a placatory gesture. Jack was standing just behind him looking bewildered. He couldn't see what she could. The usual smile had widened into a huge grin on Nick's face.

She opened the front door to see it was raining. She had left her umbrella upstairs but didn't care. She so desperately needed to get out. To get away from Nick's malevolent presence.

She walked hurriedly to the end of the street and was about to turn the corner when she heard Jack's voice calling after her.

'Sam, Sam! Hold up!'

Sam briefly considered running, but realised she was being childish so stopped and turned to face him.

'What's wrong?' he said, jogging up to her. The fury she had felt just a few moments before started to dissipate at the sight of him standing there getting wet in the rain for her, the raindrops trickling down his cheeks, his breath fast at the exertion of running. The man she now knew she loved with every cell of her being.

'Look, I'm sorry about Nick,' he said, wiping the rain from his face with the back of his hand. 'He can go too far sometimes but he doesn't mean it, he's just a bit of a piss taker. Please come back.'

He went to take her arm, but she shrugged him off. She couldn't go back there, not yet anyway. She was scared of what she might do if she saw that face leering at her, knowing that he had succeeded in getting to her.

'Please, Sam. Don't let this spoil our day together, I was planning to take you to see my parents later.'

'What?!' She couldn't quite believe what she was hearing. 'You can't just spring that on me!'

Jack held up his hands, much like Nick had a moment ago, however, unlike the evil creep's gesture, it wasn't in malice.

'Look, it doesn't matter, it would only have been for a quick introduction.'

'I ... I'm not ready for that.'

'Like I said, it really doesn't matter,' said Jack, stuffing his hands into his jean pockets. 'You can meet them another time.' He stepped closer to her, lowering his head so their foreheads touched.

'I'm sorry,' he whispered, brushing his lips gently over the top of her nose. 'I'm not used to feeling this way about someone. About you.'

He lowered his head further until his lips found hers, kissing her so exquisitely, her heart sang. If only Nick could see them now. But she immediately pushed away this thought and forced herself to concentrate on how turned on Jack was making her feel.

Eventually she pulled away and, looking up into his clear, blue eyes. She smiled.

'Please come back,' he whispered.

Sam raised her arm and touched his face. 'I will, but not now. I need to see my mum, it's been ages since I last went over. But I'll come back later,' she said hurriedly, hating to see the hurt expression on Jack's face.

'OK,' he said eventually. 'I'll be waiting for you.'

She took a few paces before turning back to see him still standing there. He raised an arm to wave and she waved back before turning left into the park and out of sight. Opening her bag, she dug around until her fingers found the packet of tissues. She pulled several out and wiped her face dry, sighing at the thought of what the rain had done to her weave, not to mention the expensive Mac make-up, but at least it had stopped now, replaced by a wind that had seemingly come from nowhere. The park was deserted.

With a sudden urge to get to her destination, she ran the last few yards out of the park and onto Michaelgate, the street that ran parallel to Steep Hill. The wind had begun to really pick up and she clutched at her thin jacket, wishing she had worn her parka instead. It was now beginning to rain again, a light sprinkling at first before the drops became heavier and more frequent. She started to run again, cursing at the crap weather that belied the time of year. A discarded umbrella caught her eye and she slowed her pace but after a quick assessment, taking in the broken spokes and torn material, ruled it out as a possibility for shielding her from the rain.

Reaching the cathedral entrance, she sighed with relief to see the great doors stood open.

****

Entering the cathedral, Sam closed her eyes briefly, letting the familiar sense of calm wash over her. Sunday service was about to start and the priest stood near the entrance greeting the parishioners. She didn't meet his expectant gaze, instead ducking into the morning chapel and out of sight. Thankfully she was alone. She didn't think she could bear it if anyone else was occupying this sacred space. Not today.

She peered inside her purse and counted out the last of her change, which amounted to the grand sum of forty-seven pence. Letting the coins drop into the donation box, she refused to feel guilty, thinking of the numerous times she had given generously and how she would most likely continue to do so. There were no other candles lit in the square of sand. Hers would be the only one.

Sam soon found what she was looking for on a ledge above the donation box. Striking the match, she hesitated, momentarily mesmerised by the quivering flame before letting it touch the wick of the candle.

She placed it in the middle of the square and sat down on the hard bench. Scrunching her eyes firmly shut, she forced herself to clear her mind and make space to conjure up the image of Pops. Initially, the sounds from the Sunday service grated on her; she didn't exactly like choir songs at the best of times and a woman was definitely singing off key, her shrill voice soaring unpleasantly above the rest. But thankfully the singing eventually gave way to the low, rumbling recital of prayers, allowing Sam to focus her mind.

She gradually opened her eyes and shrugged off the brief sense of disorientation and something else; a feeling that she wasn't alone. But a quick glance around the chapel revealed no other signs of human life.

The low hum of voices from outside could no longer be heard and for a moment she wondered if she was completely alone in the cathedral. Her legs felt numb from being seated on the uncomfortable bench for so long – over an hour, judging by her phone. She stood up and walked stiffly towards the arched entrance to the main chapel.

Most of the congregation had left, apart from an old couple, deep in conversation with the priest who was nodding in earnest at whatever they were saying. Sam walked out of the morning chapel and was about to leave the cathedral when her attention was drawn to the great rose window. There had obviously been an improvement in the weather and the stained glass looked aflame with the sunlight streaming through it. Turning slowly, she walked towards it, mesmerised by the refracted light cast across the stone floor.

A small group of Chinese tourists were studying an information leaflet about the cathedral, and on seeing Sam one of them thrust it towards her, pointing at an image on the paper and then gesturing around the cathedral. Sam would have been tempted to ignore him in usual circumstances, but considered it mean not to reveal the whereabouts of the little figure perched on the column directly behind him. She jerked her head in the direction of the column and watched as the man looked up, searching for the grotesque stone creature. It didn't take long for his eyes to settle on what he was looking for and he immediately pointed it out to the rest of the group, before smiling and nodding his appreciation to Sam. But she was no longer looking. Her attention focused now on the object of interest: the Lincoln Imp.

It was grinning down at her from its perch and Sam was suddenly struck by how much it resembled Nick, with its sharp little features, and cruel smile. She returned its smile and nodded. She knew what she had to do.

Chapter Twenty Four

'Here,' he said, throwing something at her feet, 'Eat.'

She wasn't remotely hungry anymore but picked up the package of sandwiches, salmon and cucumber, she read before the light from the torch was directed away from her towards the wall.

'I can't hear you!' he said, in a sing song voice. She made a listless attempt to open it, but it was so difficult with her right hand out of action. Securing the package between her knees, she clawed at the packaging and managed to rip it open to the sound of his foot tapping impatiently on the stone floor.

Seven nights and six days. That was the amount of time she had spent in the new place before being brought back here. So much for that tiny bud of hope.

The torch swept back over her and she brought the sandwich to her mouth and took a bite which made her gag but she managed to keep it down.

The dark figure behind the torch lowered down to crouch in front of her. 'Good girl,' he said, reaching out to stroke her hair.

She didn't even flinch and lowered her gaze from the torchlight. There was nothing left in her. She wasn't Sarah anymore, just a bag of pain.

'It's nearly time, isn't it?'

She looked up at the dark outline of her tormentor, the all-powerful demon that presided over this new world, and tried to grasp what he was saying, but her mind, like every part of her being was running on empty.

'You've done your best and I want you to know I'm impressed, Sarah, I really am. But I can see you're waning and ... well ... it just isn't fun anymore, is it?'

She kept her head lowered and remained silent until he grabbed her fringe and yanked her head back, causing her to yelp.

'You're really struggling to please me now and although it's not in my nature to hurt people's feelings, I have to say, you're really beginning to stink quite badly.'

'G ... give me a bath then, in the other place.'

'What?'

'Take me to the other place so I can get clean. Please ... please,' she said, moving painfully to kneel before him because, despite the degrading, unspeakable things she'd had to do and the pain she'd endured from his torturous games, despite the all-consuming cold and darkness, where she imagined all types of horrors lurking in the corners until she thought she'd lose her mind, despite all this, that tiny bud of hope still remained. She so badly wanted to stay alive.

'My dear Sarah,' he chuckled. 'You've gone way past the point of no return.'

'Please, please, please,' she heard herself say in a voice she didn't recognise. 'Please!'

She clutched at his leg but was kicked with a force that knocked her back. Instinctively, she began to curl into a foetal position, but she was so weak now and her languid movements were not fast enough to fend off another vicious kick to her stomach.

'Don't you fucking dare touch me!' he screamed from somewhere above her. She braced herself for another kick but it didn't come and, for a while, all she could hear was the roaring sound in her ears.

'I'm sorry,' he eventually said, 'I didn't want to lose my temper with you, not now.'

She felt her hair, once again, being stroked.

'I want you to know you've been great, Sarah, really fucking fantastic. You've more than made up for our little get-together in school, such a precious time that was snatched away too quickly. Don't you remember? In the theatre department?'

Sarah gasped for air as her brain grappled to comprehend what he was saying, the buried memories of that last day of term slowly coming back to her. Could it really be him? She opened her mouth to speak but only a low whining sound came out. She winced at the feel of his hand *brushing against her cheek.*

'It's OK, my sweet, no need for words. I can see you remember.' She *held her breath as he stroked her hair before giving her a vicious pinch on the cheek, causing her to yelp out in pain as she did when locked in that old school room all those years ago.*

'But all good things come to an end,' he said, standing up abruptly. 'It's inevitable and there isn't anything you can do now to change it. Just be rest assured that you have done your utmost.

'Now, I've left a bag just behind you on the ledge with more food and water and I've emptied your bucket. See, I'm not that bad, am I?'

She nodded, despite herself, reeling from the misfortune of having her life not once, but twice in the hands of the demon. She felt her head being patted, much like a dog that had pleased its owner.

'I have a few things to do so won't be around for a while, but don't worry, I promise I will be back as soon as I can.'

She felt him push her hair aside and then his breath, hot against her ear as he spoke. 'And when I do come back, I'll be introducing you to our new guest.'

Chapter Twenty Five

The torrential downpour did nothing to dampen Sam's spirits as she entered the health centre at exactly 8.40 am, her shoes making a squelching sound as she walked towards her desk. Even the fact that it was a Monday couldn't stop her from smiling, opening up the text message Jack had sent earlier.

I so wish you'd come back yesterday. I couldn't sleep without you, please come back tonight. I miss you baby xxx

She smiled again before switching her phone off. He wasn't going to get away with letting Nick come between them. She would make sure of that. Thank God she had kept her resolve and not gone back yesterday, instead, going shopping after she left the cathedral to buy the items for a roast dinner, much to her mother's delight.

They had such a lovely evening, chatting away together; her mother's usual anxieties dampened by the bottle of wine Sam had also bought. And as her mother linked her arm through hers on the settee, laughing at some stupid sitcom on the TV, she couldn't help but feel a little guilty at the real reason she had gone round: to teach Jack a lesson.

Sam had just switched on her work computer and was in the process of logging on when she was aware of someone entering the reception area. She started at the sight of Edith Mowbray standing before her, clutching a plastic bag between her gnarled fingers. Sam was momentarily rendered speechless. Edith's once neatly tied-back hair was hanging in lank strips across her face and she was dressed in a strange, mismatching ensemble that made her appear even more out of character than the last time she had visited the health centre.

'Edith ... are you OK?' Sam asked, breaking the silence when it was clear that the old woman wasn't going to. Sam cursed inwardly at forgetting to address her by her surname but judging by the blank expression on Edith's face, she hadn't noticed. Coming out of the small reception area, Sam approached the elderly woman.

'Miss Mowbray?' she said, catching the distinct smell of stale urine as she drew closer and, on seeing the look of pure fear in the old woman's eyes, she held her palms up. 'It's OK, it's OK,' she said, gently taking the old woman's arm and leading her into the nearest empty room.

'Where are you taking me?' Edith asked, suddenly shaking off Sam and whirling round towards the health centre's exit.

'I thought you might like to sit here for a bit and I'll bring you a nice cup of tea,' she said, surprised by the unfamiliar soft tone to her voice. She gently led Edith back into the room and seated her in the comfortable chair behind the desk, hoping that the escape route would now be less easy. Luckily Alan was just walking past as Sam approached the door, and he stopped in his tracks when he caught sight of Edith.

'My God,' he whispered. 'What's happened to Miss Mowbray?'

'I don't know, she just turned up out of the blue. She didn't look her usual self when she was last here but now ... well ... she's even worse,' said Sam, glancing back at Edith who was still clutching a plastic bag in her hands, twisting and untwisting it as if her life depended on this repetitive action.

'Well, something's clearly very wrong. I'll see if Frances can see her now, I think she's still in the kitchen. Just stay here and keep an eye on her.'

Sam nodded and perched on the edge of the desk. Edith was now staring vacantly at the plastic bag in her lap. Sam was shocked at her frailty; she had always been a trim and tiny woman but what she lacked in stature, she more than made up for with her usual sharp wit and bristly character.

'Morning' said Frances, nodding at Sam as she entered the room.

'Now, how can I help you today Miss Mowbray?' she asked,

approaching Edith and kneeling down beside her.

Edith looked up for a moment before returning her gaze to the plastic bag which she'd now tied in a knot. For a moment it didn't look like she was going to say anything but then she muttered, 'Well, I ordered some tea but it hasn't come yet.'

'Oh yes,' said Sam, relieved that Edith had at least remembered her offer of tea. 'How do you like it, Edith?'

'Three sugars and a dash of milk. And it's Miss Mowbray to you,' Edith retorted, a brief return to her normal self, making it all the more sad to see the usually forthright old woman so frail and lost. A brief glance in Frances' direction told Sam she wasn't alone with this thought.

'Yes of course, Miss Mowbray,' Sam said. Edith nodded curtly before returning her gaze to the plastic bag in her lap.

Sam returned to find Frances gently trying to prize the bag from Edith.

'Edith, you're going to have to let go so I can examine you.'

But Sam could see that Edith was having none of it, holding on stubbornly to the bag as if it contained her life's savings. Sam moved forward into the room and set the tea and two slices of thickly buttered toast (both of which belonged to Nigel) on the desk. She was relieved to see Edith's eyes flickering in the direction of the desk before fixating on the toast.

'Here. Look after this, will you?' she said, thrusting the plastic bag towards Sam.

Sam took the tightly knotted bag and held it up for closer inspection whilst Edith grabbed a piece of toast and took a large bite.

'Why did you bring this, Edith?' she finally said, waiting until the old woman had swallowed her last mouthful, followed by the tea which she finished in three large gulps. Again, Sam was saddened by what she saw. It was clear that Edith had not been looking after herself for some time.

'What?' said Edith bluntly, not bothering to wipe the trail of melted butter from her chin.

'This,' replied Frances, pointing to the plastic bag.

'That's my handbag!' Edith exclaimed. 'Give it back!' she said, leaning forward and making a snatching motion to grab the bag back.

'Edith,' said Frances, gently but firmly, 'I suspect you may have a urinary tract infection that's causing you to feel a little confused. I'm going to arrange for you to have some tests at the hospital and then we can get you started on a course of treatment to get you better.'

Not waiting for a response, Frances left the room to make the necessary arrangements.

In the team meeting later that morning, Frances confirmed that Edith did indeed have a urinary tract infection and that Lincoln General were going to keep her in for the next few days to monitor her condition. Sam was relieved to hear this, she hadn't realised until now how fond she had grown of the old woman. But the news that followed pleased her even more. Alan announced that Nigel was leaving for a new post in Derbyshire and would be gone by the end of the week and a locum would take over his patients for the time being. Sam closed her eyes briefly, letting Alan's voice wash over her. Her tactics had paid off and the slime ball was leaving. Because of her.

And as she stepped out into the late sunshine, she smiled. She now knew that she had the power to evoke real change, to make her life with Jack perfect. To get Nick out of their lives. And with this thought, she headed off towards the shops to buy the ingredients for dinner.

It was time to take action.

Chapter Twenty Six

Sam let herself into the house to find Nick sitting on the settee, one arm slung proprietarily over the back. With great effort, Sam threw him a dazzling smile.

'Oh, hi Nick, I'm so glad you're here. I'm cooking dinner tonight.' She held up two shopping bags. 'I've even bought wine.'

Nick didn't say anything at first, just stared at her, not changing his position on the settee and making her feel uncomfortable, causing her smile to waver.

'I was just about to put a pizza in the oven,' he eventually said, keeping his gaze fixed on her through narrowed eyes.

'Oh well,' she said with a shrug of her shoulders. 'Now you don't have to.' She walked through to the kitchen and emptied the contents of the carrier bags onto the counter. 'I'm making a chilli con carne,' she continued, keeping her voice light, 'just to say sorry for the way I behaved the other day. I ... I hope you'll join us?'

'Well then, how can I resist?'

Sam jumped at the proximity of Nick's voice, and whirled round to find him standing right behind her. How had she not noticed?

'That's great,' she said, forcing herself not to flinch. 'Here, put this in the fridge, will you?' She held out the bottle of Pinot Grigio, grateful for having something to give him to do, to get him away from her. But instead of taking it, he just stood there, the beginnings of a sneer forming on his unpleasant face.

'Sam! I'm so glad you're here!'

She felt a surge of relief at the sound of Jack's voice.

'And look, she's brought wine!' Nick said, grabbing the bottle from Sam's outstretched arm as he turned to face Jack. A strange look passed between them before Jack eventually spoke.

'Well, I don't know if it's meant for you too,' Jack said slowly, his eyes boring into Nick.

'Of course it is,' said Sam, not waiting for Nick to jump in.

'How can I help?' Jack said, breaking eye contact with Nick and pulling her in for a hug. She closed her eyes briefly and took a deep breath. She couldn't even begin to put into words how good it felt to be encircled by Jack's strong arms and feel the beating of his heart on her cheek. And he smelled so, so good. She drew in closer to him but then remembered they were not alone. Opening her eyes, she saw Nick scrutinising them; his head cocked to one side and his mouth curled up in a grimace.

'Why don't you two relax and have a beer whilst I get dinner ready?' she said, pulling away from Jack and ignoring Nick's dark looks.

'Are you sure?' said Jack, massaging the small of Sam's back, causing her spine to tingle. She nodded and gently ran her hand down Jack's arm, enjoying the fact that Nick was witness to this tender moment between her and her man. A moment that he was not part of. Could never be part of.

'Well I could definitely get used to this,' Nick said, walking towards the happy couple and for one awful moment, Sam thought he was going to try and join their embrace but instead, he brushed past them and put the wine in the fridge. Retrieving two bottles of beer, he passed one to Jack.

Sam watched as they settled onto the settee to a game of Call of Duty. The tense moment between them seemingly forgotten. They were so comfortable together, she thought, observing them both putting their feet up on the coffee table, bending forwards to take a swig of beer, their movements mirroring the other's. *Not for too much longer,* she thought. No, this would soon be coming to an end. Suddenly Nick turned round and met her gaze. She struggled to smile but was too late to change whatever he saw etched on her face. He raised his eyebrows and gave her an overly exaggerated smile before turning back to the game.

Unsettled by being caught off-guard, Sam busied herself

with preparing her ingredients. As the chilli simmered away in the pan, she reached into her bag and retrieved the most important ingredient: a pack of laxatives. Looking up to see the back of Nick's head, she smiled. She almost felt sorry for him.

Almost.

She set the table with care, putting out napkins and trying not to think of the last time she had done this – all that effort with the cassoulet to mark her moving in with Jack. To mark the beginning of something special. All ruined by that small smile and vicious tongue. But as she mixed the crushed laxatives onto Nick's plate, she smiled. This was going to be more satisfying than taking down that slug, Nigel.

'This is delicious baby. Thank you,' said Jack, momentarily putting his fork down to stroke Sam's arm. Sam smiled and glanced across the table to Nick. She hadn't dared look in his direction until he had eaten a few mouthfuls of his meal, scared that somehow he would be able to read from her eyes what she had done.

'How is it for you, Nick?' His name stuck in her throat and she took a large gulp of wine to help ease it down. For a moment, Nick didn't say anything and just gazed upwards as if deep in thought, making Sam want to reach across the table and pierce those eyes with her fork. She took another large gulp of wine.

'Come on mate, don't take the piss,' Jack said, finally breaking the uncomfortable silence.

'Only kidding – it's dee-li-cous.' Nick chortled. 'Is there any left?'

'Of course,' said Sam, standing up abruptly to take Nick's plate.

Jack placed a restraining hand on her arm. 'You're not his maid, you know. He can help himself.'

Sam shook Jack's hand off and laughed. 'Don't be silly, you can both be on washing up duty. D'you want some more too?'

She smiled as Jack nodded and passed his plate, pulling her in for a kiss as he did so. She didn't need to look in Nick's direction to feel the scathing expression on his face.

She hummed quietly under her breath as she mixed another liberal helping of the crushed laxatives into Nick's plate, making sure that her back was blocking her actions from Nick's sight.

'Allow me.' Sam nearly jumped out of her skin to find Nick directly behind her, catching her unawares for the second time in one evening. She pushed the saucer with the remnants of the laxatives to the back of the counter behind her and prayed that he hadn't seen.

'C'mon then, hand them over,' Nick said, with an edge to his tone that made Sam wonder if he knew what she was up to. With no plausible excuse to hand, she passed the plates into Nick's waiting palms.

'The one on the left is yours,' she said, aware that her voice sounded strained.

'What, my left or yours?' Nick said, a mock quizzical expression playing on his unpleasant features.

'*Your* left,' Sam replied and attempted a smile.

Nick nodded and started to walk towards the table but stopped and turned to say, 'It doesn't really matter anyway, Jack and I are used to sharing things, so if I give him my plate by mistake, I'm sure he won't mind.'

Sam clenched her teeth as she watched Nick take the two plates to the table. She couldn't be sure now which contained the laxatives and felt so helpless. Slowly, she returned to the table and sat in her chair, wondering if or how she could stop Jack from eating the food. But he had already started and she knew that whatever excuse she came up with would sound suspicious. At least she hadn't put quite as much of the laxative powder into the second helping, she thought, trying to console herself. And hopefully he was eating from the plate that was meant to be his.

'Are you OK, baby?' said Jack in between mouthfuls, pulling Sam from her thoughts. She saw Nick was staring at her with a curious expression. It was only then that she noticed the shreds of purple napkin in front of her, the last bits of it secured tightly in her hand.

'Oh!' was all she could utter.

Later, tucked up in bed in Jack's arms, Sam's eyes were beginning to droop as the adrenaline left her veins and exhaustion finally took over. She had waited pensively for any signs that Jack was in discomfort but it was now several hours after they had eaten and he seemed fine. She watched the even rise and fall of his chest and raised her head slightly to see if he was asleep. To her surprise, she saw that he was wide awake.

'What's wrong, Sam?' he said, moving to lay on his side so he could look at her. 'You seemed so on edge earlier.'

Sam lowered her gaze. *Well, I've just put laxatives in Nick's food and it was all going really well until he insisted on carrying your second helpings to the table and now I don't know if I've given you an overdose of laxatives too!*

Instead she told Jack about her day at work and how Edith had shown up in a confused state. She told him how worried she had been, and still was. At least this was all true, if not the real reason why she had been on edge all evening. But thankfully, Jack just nodded and encircled her in a tight embrace, kissing her forehead with the softest of kisses until she drifted into a deep sleep.

She woke up with a start and looked over to the digital clock to see that it was only 4.30 am. A sound came from outside the room, a long, low groaning and Sam realised that was what had woken her. Then came the sound of the toilet flushing and a door opening and then closing. Nick's door across the small landing. She smiled and, turning over, went back to sleep.

All too soon, Sam was woken by the alarm on her mobile and, turning it off, she swung her legs out of the warm bed. Pulling on her dressing gown, she looked down at Jack. With his mouth slightly open, he had clearly been undisturbed by the noise. She slipped out of their bedroom and went downstairs to put the kettle on. She had a couple of lectures in the morning and then a shift at the health centre and wanted to prepare a quick lunch to take for the long day ahead.

She jumped at the sight of Nick sitting at the kitchen table. His face was pale and drawn and he was gripping a mug.

'You're up early,' Sam said, recovering herself quickly. She walked over to the kettle and filled it up.

'I know what you did.'

Sam whirled round, expecting to see Nick standing right behind her but no, he was still seated at the table.

'What?'

'What? What did I do?' she repeated when Nick didn't respond. She glared defiantly at him, her fists clenched. The familiar turmoil in her belly beginning its painful journey up to her chest. She would have to take a dose of Pepto Bismol. But not now, not in front of him.

The beginnings of a smile played on Nick's mouth, the small, cruel smile he reserved especially for her.

'Mustard seeds in the chilli last night,' he said, standing abruptly. 'It's OK, you weren't to know I'm allergic to them.' He turned and left the room before Sam could say anything.

The kettle came to a boil and switched itself off but Sam didn't notice. She continued to stare at the spot where Nick had been seated.

She hadn't used any mustard seeds, but she knew now she had to be careful. If something like this happened again, Nick would blame her and Jack might well believe him.

Chapter Twenty Seven

Sam selected the shiny new key from her bag and let herself in to Jack's home - hers too now, so he kept reminding her. It had been almost a month since she had placed laxatives in Nick's dinner and since then she had kept up a continuous stream of nasty little things; a drop of washing up liquid in his coffee, piercing the ready meals he bought for himself and replacing them in his reserved space on the second shelf of the fridge, ensuring she kept a full diary of things for her and Jack to do that didn't include him, whilst all the time, keeping up a sickly sweet façade. Quite frankly, it was exhausting. But she was determined to see her mission through. To get him out of their lives for good.

'Hello?' she called into the empty space. She pulled off her sandals and rubbed the big toe on her left foot vowing never again to buy cheap Primark footwear.

'Hello?' she called out again, but still no response. She walked past the sitting room to the kitchen and switched the kettle on. Whilst she waited for it to boil, she walked back into the sitting room, trailing her hand across the various fixtures and objects along the way, enjoying the contrasting feel of the different textures, from the coolness of the marble-top counters to the soft velvet sofa and the smooth, leather armchair, all of which must have cost a fortune and made Sam wonder – not for the first time – how much money had been spent on kitting the place out so expensively.

Jack had brushed away her questions about his finances with a vague, 'My parents are helping me out for now'. And when she had tried to push him further, just once, when she was curled up next to him on the settee, his fingers gently swirling her shoulder, he stopped and got up abruptly. 'Stop now' was all he said in that cold tone she had heard so rarely, standing over her, the vein in his neck visibly pulsing, his fists bunched. That had put an end to the subject.

But she later found out that Jack's parents had bought the house outright for him and also paid for the refurbishments and the household items (a generous titbit of information from Nick when he was in a rare, genial mood). Jack had been adamant that he didn't want any money towards the bills which made her feel uncomfortable, but with the new found knowledge of how much his parents had actually been 'helping' him out, she felt a little less uneasy. And at least this meant she could still help her mother out when needed.

She didn't press Jack further about his financial situation, seeing how it made him so uncharacteristically angry, but she was fairly certain that he had never worked and that his lifestyle was completely bankrolled by mummy and daddy. She usually despised people like Jack, with their easy, privileged lives – so different to her own. But then she hadn't banked on how he made her feel; of how she would fall so deeply for him. She approached the foot of the stairs.

'Hello?' she shouted this time, just to make sure she would be heard. But again, she was greeted with silence. She climbed the stairs and opened the door to their bedroom (she was getting used to the idea of it belonging to her as well now). The duvet was pulled back, just as Jack must have left it when he got up. Shaking her head, she walked up to the bed and straightened the duvet; she could see Jack still needed some training. She went back out to the landing and glanced over to the bathroom, which was clearly empty, so Sam turned to go back downstairs. But not before pausing by the door to Nick's room. She pressed her ear to it, listening out for any signs of life but was met with silence.

Back downstairs, she made herself a cup of tea and settled onto the sofa to watch the TV. But after a few minutes of flicking through the channels and finding nothing to hold her interest, she started to feel fidgety. Swiping the screen of her mobile, she could see that apart from a message from her mother sent earlier in the day, there was nothing else. Her thumb hovered over Jack's number but she willed herself to not press it. To not look like she was some desperate, insecure loser. Instead, she picked up her mug of tea and took a sip then thought why on earth was she drinking tea on a beautiful warm Friday evening? Like some old, sad woman. She went back to the kitchen and made herself a vodka and coke. Opening the door to the back garden, she considered sitting outside to enjoy the last of the sunshine, but immediately changed her mind on hearing the racket from the kids playing next door, their ball crashing against the fence every few seconds. Instead she went back to the sofa, picking up the fan from the bookshelf on her way. Placing it on the coffee table, she switched it on and sat back, taking a large gulp of the vodka and coke and hoping it would settle her growing unease.

She had just made a second drink when her phone pinged, making her jump and spill some of the liquid down her top. 'Shit,' she cursed, wiping her mouth before swiping the screen.

Hey baby I'm out with Nick. Sorry meant to txt u earlier.
I won't be back too late xxx

Sam stared at the screen for a moment, watching the words blur in front of her. Slamming her phone down on the coffee table, she suppressed a scream. The familiar pain weaved its way from the depths of her gut and up into her chest. She hurled the glass of vodka at the wall, immediately regretting it on seeing the dark liquid contrasting with the white wall. Taking several deep breaths, she forced herself to calm down. She knew she was being irrational; Jack was only out for a few drinks and he would be home soon. But clenching her hands into fists to stop them from trembling, she knew exactly why she was feeling such an uncontrollable rage. It was the fact that Jack was with Nick. All her hard work over the past few weeks that she thought was beginning to pay off, all those false smiles to cover her little ploys, all the effort taken to drive a wedge between them. All for nothing. She felt the pressure starting to build up again so closed her eyes tightly and started to count.

Twenty minutes later, she stood back to assess her work. She had scrubbed the wall until the drink stain had disappeared and, with the broken glass hidden away in a plastic bag in the outside bin, there were no traces left of her outburst. She then placed the bottles of vodka and coke on the coffee table with a fresh glass. No need to keep getting up now, she thought, preparing herself another drink. But the downfall of having a liquid dinner invariably leads to a full bladder and she soon had to get up.

After going to the toilet, she paused again outside Nick's door. At least she now knew he was definitely out. 'Nick?' she said, giving three sharp knocks to his door, just to be sure. But of course, there was no response. He was out, busy plying Jack with drinks. Keeping him away from her. Again, she felt the pressure building up in her temples, fuelled by rage and, no doubt the several large vodkas she had gone on to drink after wasting one on the wall.

Taking a couple of deep breaths to ground herself, she turned the door handle and stepped inside the room. She stood motionless, surveying the unfamiliar surroundings. She'd only had a brief glimpse when Jack had shown her round for the first time, introducing it as 'the spare room' as she hovered at the threshold. But not for much longer, she thought, imagining it with a desk and office chair for her to study, she could use the wardrobe too, thinking of her clothes fighting for space in Jack's room.

The room was smaller than Jack's; a double bed was pushed into one corner with a small chest of drawers to one side. She walked over to the window and peered through the grey slats of the blind. She could see directly out onto the street, unlike the view from Jack's room which looked out to the river. She stepped away abruptly on the sickening realisation that this was where Nick would have stood, watching her through the gap in the blinds when she had walked past the house, desperate to see Jack on that early morning.

She imagined him standing there, smirking at her distress from his vantage point. Suddenly she felt an unpleasant surge of bile rise through her and for a moment, she thought she was going to throw up. Closing her eyes, she clenched her hands tightly into fists until the feeling of acrylic nails digging into soft flesh became unbearable, taking over the need to be sick. But the excess saliva in her mouth remained. Moving over to the bed, she bent over and spat into the dark blue pillow. That made her feel a little better.

Perched on the edge of the bed, she surveyed the room. It was incredibly neat. Much like she strove to keep things, but then Sam shrugged this thought away, hating to think of having anything in common with the creep.

The room was devoid of anything that might give her a sense of Nick, his tastes, what made him tick. But then this wasn't his room, or his house to stamp his mark on. One of the only items that looked out of place was a strangely old-fashioned mirror; its ornate, fussy gold frame at odds with the sparse, modern room. Leaning forward, she took the other item that clearly belonged to Nick, a silver framed photo of him with his arm round a little girl, around seven or eight, Sam guessed. She had long brown hair and a sweet face. She must be the niece, Kayleigh, or was that the name of the alcoholic sister? Sam mused. What really struck Sam was the large, open grin on Nick's face, no signs of malice, his eyes cast downwards in the girl's direction. She was also smiling, her head leaning into Nick's arm. They both looked incredibly happy.

Sam carefully placed the photo back on the chest of drawers and stood up, feeling unsettled at what the picture projected; a side of Nick that she didn't know. She walked over to the wardrobe and opened it. Several pairs of jeans, a few jumpers, a suit and a jacket hung in an orderly line from the horizontal pole. She pushed the suit to one side to get a better look. '*Bloody cheek!*' she muttered, running a hand inside the soft felt lining. It was Jack's blue jacket, the one that matched the colour of his eyes, her favourite. She was tempted to take it out of Nick's wardrobe and return it to its rightful place on the coat stand by the front door, but she couldn't risk Nick knowing she'd been rifling through his things. Regretfully, she straightened the coat so it hung back in the uniform line and closed the wardrobe door, wondering whether Jack knew that his friend just helped himself to his belongings. He probably did.

There were several drawers at the bottom of the wardrobe containing T-shirts, underwear, socks and a couple of belts – all ordered neatly into their own compartments. She pushed the last drawer shut and straightened up, not really knowing what she was looking for. She knew she should leave, they could come back at any moment and she didn't think Nick would take kindly to her snooping through his belongings.

But as she went to leave, something caught the periphery of her vision; a flash of something colourful and familiar poking out from under the lid of the laundry basket near the door. Sam lifted the lid and stared down at the striped shirt she had bought for Jack a few weeks into their relationship. She hadn't bought it for any particular occasion or reason, other than it had caught her eye when she was out shopping and she knew the alternating shades of orange, blue and grey would make Jack's eyes dazzle. He'd been really touched by it and had worn it a few times now. *What the hell was it doing in here!* she thought, pulling it from the laundry pile. Had Nick even asked if he could borrow it?

Sam took a deep breath and again, willed herself to keep calm, which was a losing battle considering the questions swirling around her head: Did Nick know she had bought the shirt for Jack? Had he asked if he could borrow it? Or had he just sauntered into Jack's room and taken it, like he'd taken the jacket? And if so, had he gone snooping through *her* stuff? She shivered with revulsion. But there wasn't any way she could get the much-needed answer without giving away the fact that she'd been trespassing. She felt like screaming with frustration. Clutching the shirt, she left the room, slamming the door behind her.

Returning to their bedroom, Sam dropped the shirt into the laundry basket and was about to close the lid, but the sight of her red, lacy knickers stopped her. Smiling, she bent down to retrieve them and took both garments back to Nick's room.

Back downstairs, Sam poured herself another vodka and coke and sat back. It was after midnight now and she had long given up hope that Jack would be back any time soon, his text stating he wouldn't be back late just an empty promise. She lay down, enjoying the cooling sensation of the fan as it oscillated back and forth, lulling her to sleep.

****

He watched Jack stumble up the stairs in a desperate bid to empty his bladder.

"You all right, mate?" he called after him.

"Yeah, I think I can handle it from here."

He was about to follow him up the stairs but a slight movement in the living room caught his eye. He went to switch on the light but stopped when he saw her curled up asleep on the sofa. He stood, poised in the doorway, looking for any signs that she might not be as fully asleep as she outwardly appeared. If she suddenly opened her eyes, he would turn on the light and pretend to be surprised to find her there. But no, she was completely still, apart from the slow, even rise and fall of her chest.

Emboldened, he entered the room and carefully knelt in front of the sofa, lowering his head level to hers. Finally, a chance to scrutinise her to his heart's content without the worry of being caught, of her returning his stare with her contemptuous glare, which cut right through him and made him feel like he was thirteen again; a time he wanted to erase from his memory.

The fan, which was set to 'swivel' mode, moved a strand of hair across her face each time it directed its cool air in her direction. Her lips were slightly parted and he could just hear her breathing.

She looked so vulnerable asleep, so sexy, he didn't know whether he wanted to throttle her or kiss her and his hands twitched with temptation.

He watched, mesmerised, for what seemed like hours but could only have been a few minutes, as he heard the flushing of the toilet upstairs and the subsequent slamming of the bathroom door.

He sighed as he quickly got up and left the room. He knew that when Jack found the bed he shared with Sam empty, he would come downstairs looking for her.

****

When she was sure Nick had left the room, Sam opened her eyes and exhaled deeply, a relief from the shallow breaths she had taken whilst the creep stood over her. She knew it was him by the cloying smell of his aftershave and it had taken every last ounce of reserve to feign sleep; to not open her eyes and scream at him to fuck off. The thought of him being in such close proximity repulsed her. She had never been sure about Nick's feelings towards her: hatred, definitely, at her taking away his beloved Jack, but now she knew that his feelings were also fuelled by lust.

Chapter Twenty Eight

'Well? What d'you think? Shall we go?'

Sam took the flyer from Jack's hand. It was advertising a student comedy night at the university the following evening. She could think of nothing she would rather do less, but it had come with perfect timing. She needed a good excuse.

She gave it a moment to appear as if she were considering it then smiled, 'Why not? I could do with a laugh.' She moved closer to him, putting her arms around his waist. 'Then why don't we go for something to eat? And you can wear the shirt I got you. You know how sexy you look in that.' She looked up at him suggestively, tightening her grip.

'Hmm, sounds good to me,' Jack murmured, his lips finding hers. 'There's something else that would also be good. Something we can do right now.' Suddenly pulling away from Sam, he took her by the hand and led her upstairs.

Later, Sam pulled on Jack's dressing gown and went downstairs to make them both a cup of tea. She stopped dead at the sight of Nick sitting at the kitchen table, turning the student comedy night flyer over in his hands. He looked up at Sam and raised an eyebrow.

'No need to guess what you've been up to.'

'Mind your own business,' Sam said, walking past him to the counter.

'I wish I could, but you could hear the racket you two were making out on the pavement!'

Sam chose to ignore him and made the tea, not bothering to ask him if he wanted some. She was getting sick of keeping up the pretence.

'This looks like it could be a laugh. Are you and Jack going?' he said, just as Sam was on her way back upstairs. She turned and saw him holding up the flyer.

'Oh that. Yes, we're going. It's just for students though,' *Not for you.* She smiled to herself as she carried on up the stairs, not bothering to wait for a response.

Thankfully there was no sign of Nick as she left the house to start an afternoon shift at the health centre. It had been last minute, to cover for Maria who was off sick, but she didn't mind. The extra money was good and it would be a welcome diversion from the agonising wait to see if Jack would discover his shirt and her underwear that she'd placed in Nick's laundry. Maybe Jack didn't even know it was missing from his room and he wouldn't necessarily just go into Nick's room to find it. And what if Nick discovered her knickers instead of Jack? She suddenly realised what a stupid thing she had done. Fuelled by rage and vodka, she hadn't been thinking clearly. She arrived at the health centre early and immediately went to the kitchen to make a peppermint tea, hoping that would settle the all too familiar churning in her stomach.

Anna was sitting at the table, her head in her hands. She looked like she was crying and Sam, not liking to be put in a situation where she might have to console someone else, considered backing quietly out the room, unseen. But this was only a fleeting thought; she actually quite liked the woman, their mutual dislike of Nigel giving them something in common.

'Anna, what's wrong?' Sam asked, coming to sit beside the young nurse. Anna lowered her hands to reveal two bleary eyes.

'Oh, hi Sam, I'm sorry, I didn't hear you come in or I'd have tried to sort myself out.' She gave a small, hiccoughing laugh. Sam smiled and, pulling a tissue from her bag, held it out. 'Here, take this.'

'Thanks,' said Anna and proceeded to dab at her eyes. 'It's just something I found out today, about the missing girl, you know? Sarah.'

'Yes. Oh no, has her body ... errrrr ... has she been found?' asked Sam, remembering that the family lived on Anna's road.

'No, no, it's not that. Sarah's still missing. It's her mum, she was found dead in her house yesterday and it looks like it was suicide.' She rushed this last sentence out, gulping back tears before blowing her nose.

'That's so sad. I'm sorry,' said Sam, hesitating for a moment before placing her hand in between Anna's shoulder blades and gently rubbing in a clockwise motion like she had seen people doing in slushy movies. In truth, she felt nothing at the news. So what if the stupid cow had topped herself? And what if her daughter miraculously came back? Possibly escaping her kidnapper, if she had indeed been kidnapped at all. What then? To survive whatever atrocities she'd been through only to find her pathetic excuse of a mother didn't have the strength just to stay alive? To be there for her when she needed her most?

Sam's train of thought was interrupted by Anna taking her arm and gently removing it from her, making her realise she'd been rubbing her back a little too rigorously.

'I'm sorry,' she said again.

'No, I'm sorry for upsetting you, Sam. I don't know why this has affected me so much, it's not like I even knew the family that well.'

Well just get over yourself then, Sam thought, smiling back at her sympathetically.

When she came back to the house, she immediately sensed something was up; there was a charged atmosphere that was almost palpable. Jack was putting some washing onto the airer, his back was to her and he hadn't seemed to notice her presence. She stood watching him for a moment. The quick and abrupt way he was hanging out the clothes, so different to his usual, fluid movements suggested he was angry. Very angry. And then she saw it, the shirt hanging on the airer, and her red lacy knickers placed just beneath. She smiled, her plan had worked.

'You found it then,' she said, causing Jack to whip round, his eyes wild, face contorted in fury. 'Your shirt?' she added, taking a step back, shocked at the sight of him so out of character.

'Christ, Sam! You scared the shit out of me! How long have you been standing there?'

'N...not long. She stammered. 'Just admiring the view.' She added, attempting to sound light-hearted. It was deeply unsettling to see Jack like this and she wondered if she had gone too far with her little games to oust Nick. Tentatively, she moved towards him for a hug but stopped when she noticed him take a small step back.

'Are you OK?'

'Yeah, fine. You just made me jump, that's all.' He ran a hand through his hair and, seemingly recovered, pulled her to him. 'I'll make us some dinner,' he mumbled as he nuzzled into her neck.

'That would be nice,' she said, relieved at the quick turnaround in Jack's mood, emboldened, she risked adding 'And thanks for washing my stuff, you didn't have to.'

She watched Jack's eyes follow her gaze and settle on the red knickers, noting how his features hardened, his jaw clenching. She waited, hoping that he might say something. But no, his expression cleared and he smiled. 'It's my pleasure' he said, walking into the kitchen area. 'What d'you fancy to eat?'

'Oh, I don't mind. Will Nick be joining us?' she couldn't resist probing further. She noticed his body stiffen, but only for a moment before opening the fridge.

'Err, no. He won't. How about pasta with pancetta?' he turned back to look at her. She nodded and smiled but inwardly felt miffed. She wanted the satisfaction of hearing him tell her what had happened; about what he had come across in Nick's laundry bin and whether or not he had confronted him.

It wasn't until they were eating dinner that he said, 'Nick won't be coming back.'

Sam stopped mid-mouthful, unsure whether she had heard him correctly, he'd said it so quietly. 'What?'

'We had a bit of a ... falling out, I don't really want to go into it, but he's gone to stay somewhere else.'

'Oh ... I'm sorry,' Sam said, hoping she'd managed to keep the feeling of euphoria from her voice, but Jack smiled and shook his head.

'It's OK, you don't need to pretend. I know you don't like him.'

'Well, no, I don't but ...' Sam struggled to say something

convincing but couldn't.

'Look, it's OK. Really!' Jack reached over and took her hand. 'It's about time he found somewhere else anyway. He was cramping my style.'

Sam laughed as Jack winked at her. Then he reached over and, cupping her face in his hands, said, 'It's just going to be you and me from now on. I promise.'

She smiled, bringing her hand up to squeeze his, glad that Nick was finally out of their lives. She was going to make damn sure it stayed that way.

Chapter Twenty Nine

She hadn't planned to fall in love, it was just meant to be a bit of fun. But then he'd taken her hand, kissing each finger before placing it on his chest and saying fervently, 'I've got you, you know? You don't need to worry about a thing anymore.'

She'd looked up into his eyes and felt her heart melt; she'd known she didn't stand a chance. Nice men like him didn't go for women like her but there she was, encased in his arms, being made breakfast in bed, bought perfume and flowers when it wasn't even her birthday. 'Just enjoy it,' she'd thought to herself, as he nuzzled into her neck. 'You deserve this bit of happiness.'

A slight change to the interminable darkness transports her back to reality. Her eyes, sticky from a mixture of dried tears and mascara, flicker open. A weak light filters through the air bricks above, indicating that daylight has returned, bringing with it the realisation she has survived another night and the hope that this might be the day she escapes this hell hole.

She has never been so afraid. Crouched in the corner of this demonic place, dreading his return. Most of the men she'd had the misfortune to let into her life could be terrifying, but they had never done anything like this before.

Her mind is full of what is happening at home. Would she even have noticed her absence?? Would anyone else care? She was busy getting on with her life and she'd made it clear that she didn't care anything like as much as she should.

Her lower back spasms so she adjusts her position on the cold, stone floor, grimacing at the bolt of pain that courses through her body. Unwillingly, she pulls the filthy scratchy blanket up around her shoulders

162

and takes shallow breaths, not wanting to breathe in the stench. The stench of death. But she's cold; he took her jacket, along with any dignity she used to have. In that other life.

They were meant to be going on a mini break. 'It's a surprise!' was all he'd say when she asked for the second time as they drove through seemingly endless winding country lanes. But when she'd asked if they were nearly there as she needed a wee, he'd swerved onto the grass verge, slamming the breaks so both their heads jolted forwards and screamed, 'Go on then!' She'd been so shocked, she didn't move at first, just sat there, staring at him. His hands gripped the wheel and his shoulders moved up and down violently with his breathing. Then he'd turned to face her and said in a low, menacing voice, 'Get the fuck out of the car and take a piss.' And she'd done as he said, stumbling out of the car into the bushes, struggling to crouch and hold up her maxi dress as her tears mingled with the jet of hot wee running down her legs. She'd realised then she didn't have any tissue to wipe herself and cried even harder. She'd so wanted this to be perfect.

She hadn't asked where they were going after that, hadn't uttered a word as he'd turned abruptly onto an unnamed narrow lane dimpled with potholes, navigating the car around some, driving straight into others, causing the car to judder violently from side to side and making her feel sick to the core. She'd remained silent as they drove past a large creepy-looking building, only glancing at him when the car eventually came to a stop in between two outbuildings and he'd turned to look at her.

'Here we are, my love,' he'd said, smiling sweetly, reminding her of the man she'd fallen for. Maybe what had just happened had been a blip; maybe he was a nervous driver and just couldn't cope with her constant chatter. But where on earth were they? She'd thought, as he'd ushered her out of the car; there was definitely no cosy country hotel in sight. Maybe he was taking her camping? That could be romantic, she'd supposed. But then why pick this place?

'Wh ... where are we going?' she'd asked, as he'd taken her hand.

'You'll see,' he'd said, letting go of her hand briefly to pinch her backside. Hard. He'd laughed as she'd flinched before taking her hand again. He'd led her into one of the outbuildings, in the wasteland behind the main building, which used to be a school, he'd told her in an amiable, conversational tone. *It wasn't much more than a shed really. She'd pulled her hand from his as he'd walked into the gloomy space, preferring to stand by the door as an uneasy feeling weaved its way through her veins.*

'What is this?' she'd asked.

'You'll see,' he'd simply repeated, taking off his jacket and hanging it on a hook. To her astonishment, he'd then proceeded to unbuckle his belt and unzip his jeans.

'What are you doing?' she'd said, emitting a nervous laugh.

'What does it look like? I'm in need of a bit of light relief after that drive.' He'd pulled the belt from his jeans, letting it drop to the floor. 'Come here,' he'd said, his arm outstretched, beckoning her to him, all traces of amiability gone. She'd shaken her head and backed out the door, there was no way she was going to perform any sexual acts, not in this place. She'd walked towards the car, which was still open. She had decided to go home, with or without him. But then she'd found herself being pushed forwards so violently, the ground felt like it was coming up to meet her. And then had come a sharp stinging sensation, and then another, and then another, making her cry out in agony. Adjusting her head, she had only been able to make out his legs, and the belt gripped in his hand. And then he was on top of her, pushing her head into the dusty ground, pulling up her dress, ripping at her knickers. The expensive new lacy ones she'd bought for what was meant to be a romantic break.

She must have passed out momentarily because when she came to, she was lying in a foetal position in the shed. He was lifting big sacks of something from one spot to another, sweat pouring off him with the exertion. He'd stopped when he noticed her and smiled, 'Being such a gentleman, I won't ask you to help.'

She'd opened her mouth to speak but was incapable; a low whining noise took the place of words. Her body was on fire; she'd never felt pain like it.

'Ta da!' he'd said after moving the last sack. 'All finished. Your surprise awaits!'

She'd rolled over and started to crawl towards the door as he advanced but was dragged back.

'Now, we can do this the easy way, or the hard way,' he'd said, hauling her roughly onto her back. She'd felt like one of the sacks he'd been

moving. He'd pulled her up and towards the newly cleared space, where she watched on in horrified silence as he opened up a trap door revealing a metal staircase descending into darkness.

'No, no no no,' she'd sobbed when he held out his hand to her. But it was no use, as he'd grabbed her roughly by the arm and dragged her down the narrow stairs, her screams ringing out as her skin scraped against the stone wall.

'Here we are, my love,' he'd said when they reached the bottom. 'Welcome to your new world.' And then all she remembered was the fleeting image of his fist before it made contact with her face.

****

She can't remember how long it took her to realise she wasn't alone. Maybe it was the intermittent snuffling sound, or the stench, or a mixture of both. There was definitely something else with her in this dungeon; she could just make out a shape in the dying light from the airbricks, a shape that was solid but not static. At first she hadn't dared go near it but then as the light faded further, she realised she needed to find out what it was before being plunged into complete darkness. She knew she might lose her mind completely if she didn't know what else was in there with her.

Hobbling towards the shape, she hesitated before poking it gently with her foot. She was met with a grunting sound.

'H ... Hello?' she whispered, but there was no reply. Tentatively, she bent down and tugged the blanket covering the shape to reveal a mass of tangled hair and pale, bony shoulders. Slowly, the shape moved to reveal the profile of a face, or what was left of it. One eye was swollen and closed, the cheek a criss-cross of red, angry lines and as the head turned towards her fully, she stumbled backwards at the sight.

'Hel' 'eeeee,' came the sound from cracked, bleeding lips. The sound was repeated again and again before she realised what it meant.

'Help me.'

Now, as she pulls the blanket to her, she reaches over to tuck it around the shape that is solid but not static; the shape with the swollen eye and the criss-cross lines carved into her cheek; her roommate.

The missing woman. Sarah Hollins.

Chapter Thirty

Sam took a sip of her coffee and sat back, enjoying the breathtaking view from the cafe balcony overlooking the Champs Elysees. It really was true what they said about French women, she thought, admiring the tall, elegant woman walking below, in a powder pink pleated skirt and sky high blue heels, her hair scraped back in a low bun. She instinctively looked down at her own attire, a black and white polka dot halter neck dress, not her first choice, but Jack had insisted it looked good on her and was very 'French' looking, whilst out holiday shopping. Not having been to France before, she'd had to take his word for it and now she was here, she had to admit he'd been right. Pairing her dress with bright red wedge sandals, she almost felt she could pass for one of the elegant, Parisian women.

A waiter came over and placed a small silver tray with the bill on the table. She glanced towards the inside of the cafe to see Jack still standing in a queue for the toilet. He looked back, as if feeling her stare and rolled his eyes. She smiled back and crossed her eyes in a goofy gesture, so out of character for her.

She was happy, probably the happiest since Pops had died. And it was all down to that beautiful man, patiently waiting his turn in the queue.

She bent down and retrieved the compact mirror from her bag and, on examining herself critically, she found herself liking the reflection looking back. She'd finally got round to having the loose, curly weave just a week before travelling and it worked wonders with softening her features, which made her wish she'd done it sooner. Tracing a French-manicured nail under her eye, she was relieved to see the dark shadows were all but invisible under the carefully applied makeup. She had to admit, she was looking good and as she applied some more lip gloss, she had to stop herself smiling on catching sight of several men glancing over in her direction, when they thought their respective partners weren't looking.

All men were the same, she thought; basic, stupid, sometimes brutal, cowards. Except for Jack, of course, he was just perfect.

She picked up the bill and blinked several times, not sure if she was seeing correctly, but no, it clearly stated thirty-three Euros – way too much for two coffees and a strawberry tart! But then, she had been warned that this was one of the most expensive areas in Paris. Still, she thought, placing some notes on the tray beside the bill, it was worth it.

Just then, she heard a 'ping' sound. It had come from Jack's mobile, which he'd left on the table and what she saw briefly illuminated on the screen caused her jubilant mood to plummet. Two innocent words: 'Alright mate' and the name of the sender: Nick.

She glanced up to see Jack finally at the front of the toilet queue. Quickly, she reached over and grabbed the phone, briefly considering flinging it over the balcony, anything to stop Jack from seeing whatever that creep had to say. But she knew that was an irrational thing to do so instead, she swiped up to open the screen, noting with disgust how her hand trembled slightly as she did so. Disgust with how the imp-faced creep could make her feel this way without even being in the same country!

It had been over a month since Nick had left Jack's house and, as the weeks went by, with no mention or sight of him (she checked Jack's phone on a regular basis, just to be sure), she had slowly started to relax and had actually dared to believe that he might be out of Jack's life for good. But the long message on Jack's phone stated otherwise.

> *Alright mate,*
> *Afraid I'm in a bit of a mess at the moment and could really do with a chat. I knocked for you yesterday, and just now, but no luck. Chrissie's gone and done it – she's fallen off the wagon big time and Kayleigh's gone into care.*

It's only temporary and I told them I could look after her but they must still have records on me and said no. I can't believe it mate. My beautiful niece who's done nothing wrong. I know she won't be staying in a place like I did, but still, just the thought of her in care makes me sick.

Look I'm sorry about what happened. As I said, maybe Sam's stuff got mixed up with mine by accident, I really don't know how it happened. But I want you to know I'd never do anything to upset you. You're my best mate. My only mate.

Nick.

She stared at the message feeling a slight pang of sympathy for the girl and wondered what 'records' were held on him. What had he done? She stared at the small screen for a moment longer before remembering to look up, just in time to see Jack coming out of the toilet. He was smiling as he held the door open for a young woman with long, red hair. She was smiling back at him, obviously flirting. It didn't take Sam long to come to a decision. Pressing down on the message, she chose the first message option in the list.

Delete.

Grabbing her bag and Jack's phone, she stood up and together they walked back out onto the Champs Elysees, hand in hand.

Chapter Thirty One

Sniffing the pale pink roses, Sam smiled as she inhaled their delicate fragrance.

'Good choice. Beautiful, aren't they?' said the woman behind the counter.

'Yes, they are,' Sam smiled at the woman and handed over a ten pound note.

'Are they a gift? I've got some ribbon,' the woman disappeared under the counter for a moment before standing up, triumphantly holding a roll of cream ribbon.

'Yes, they are,' she said again to the woman, who proceeded to make a meal out of tying an intricate bow around the flowers. Eventually the woman stood back, clearly delighted with her work, and Sam didn't have the heart to tell her that the flowers weren't actually a gift. Well, strictly speaking, they actually were, a gift to herself.

Christ, what's happening to me? she mused, again burying her nose into the exquisitely scented flowers. But she knew exactly what had happened. She had met her soul mate; her mother was on an even keel; life was looking good. And after all the upheaval throughout her childhood, she damn well deserved to be happy and was going to bloody well enjoy it.

She looked guiltily up at the cathedral as she walked back down Steep Hill. She hadn't been in since before the trip to Paris, well over a month ago now. She thought of all the times she had needed to find sanctuary in there – in the small morning chapel – the one place she felt she could be near to Pops. But the need to do this had dissipated over time, causing a momentary feeling of sadness to wash over her.

But she refused to feel down, and with the decision made to light a candle for Pops soon, she carried on down the hill towards home.

With both hands full, she pressed the doorbell.

'Haven't you got your key?' Jack said, opening the door to let Sam in.

'Yes, but I've got my hands full, see?' Sam replied, feeling slightly put out at Jack's less than welcoming attitude.

'Oh. Yeah. Sorry, let me take that,' he said, relieving Sam of the heavy shopping bag she was carrying.

'Well, am I allowed in?' she asked, when Jack continued to stand in the doorway. She was beginning to get pissed off with his strange, off-hand manner. It was so unlike him.

'Look,' he said, running his free hand through his hair, 'I've got something to tell you.'

Sam gave him a hard stare, alarm bells starting to explode in her ears.

'What?' she said, sharply.

'It's Nick.'

Sam felt a sinking feeling with those two words. Just hearing the creep's name made her want to throw up.

'He just turned up this morning. I couldn't turn him away; he was in such a state. I think he's been sleeping rough.'

'Is he still here?' Sam heard herself say through the building fug enveloping her head. Jack nodded.

With a mounting dread, Sam followed Jack into the living room. *He* was sitting on the chair by the window, huddled up in the soft grey blanket she had bought for her and Jack to snuggle up with on lazy Sundays, watching re-runs of *Columbo*. She had never felt more happy and secure in those times, shrouded with Jack in the blanket, secure in the predictable plot unfolding on the TV; secure in the knowledge of Jack's love. The blanket was now touching Nick's skin. She felt another wave of nausea ripple through her.

'Come, let's go into the kitchen,' Jack whispered, ushering her out of the room that Nick hadn't noticed her enter.

She watched as Jack went over to the fridge, opened it and took out a couple of bottles of beer. She shook her head when he offered her one and waited whilst he opened a bottle, watching the up and down motion of his Adams apple as he took a large gulp. *Dutch courage*, she thought.

'D'you want me to put those in some water?'

She looked down at the bunch of roses she still clutched in her hand, the bow now crushed in her grip. The woman in the florist would have been so upset to see the devastation of her handiwork. She first noticed the blood on the ribbon; the red in stark contrast to the cream. She unclenched her grip and saw the source of the blood, oozing from the pierced skin of her palm.

'Oh my God! Sam! Are you OK?' Jack said, rushing to her side. She watched with indifference as he gently pulled out one of the thorns still sticking into her flesh. She let him lead her over to the sink, where he proceeded to run cold water over her opened palm, causing her to wince slightly with the stinging sensation.

'Didn't you feel it?' Jack asked, gently patting her palm dry with some kitchen towel. She shook her head.

'Here, keep that on it for now, until the bleeding stops.' He pressed several more sheets of kitchen towel into her hand.

'What's he doing here?'

'His niece has gone into care. Just temporarily whilst his sister's in rehab.'

'Oh,' said Sam flatly. 'Wasn't there anyone else who could look after her?'

Jack shook his head. 'No. His mother died a few years back and I don't think she would have been much help anyway.'

'But couldn't *he* have looked after her?' Sam asked, remembering the words *'they must still have records on me'* in the text she'd deleted.

'No, that wasn't an option,' Jack said, running both hands through his hair. 'Look, I know you don't like him and he can be well out of order sometimes, but he's my oldest friend. He had a tough childhood, you know that, and from your own experience, I think you should be able to have a bit of empathy right now.'

The last few words came from Jack in a raised torrent, making Sam feel like she'd been stung. She waited for him to come towards her, to say he was sorry and encircle her in his arms. But he didn't.

The thought suddenly occurred to her that he'd found out about the deleted message, but she instantly dismissed this. Mobiles always played up, not always showing missed calls and texts. And this was even more likely to happen when abroad. No, she had nothing to worry about, she was sure of it.

'*My experience?* Do you mean to say that I had a similar upbringing to Nick?' she said, struggling to keep her voice even.

'Similar in that you both had difficult childhoods, with mothers who didn't care for you in the way they're supposed to.'

'Why couldn't he look after his niece?' Sam asked again, determined to get to the bottom of what he'd done to have 'records' held about him. She tapped her nails on the counter, waiting for Jack to reply.

'He spent some time in a juvenile detention centre,' he said eventually, his voice lowered to a whisper.

'Why?'

'He locked a girl in a room.'

'*What?!*'

'It isn't as bad as it sounds, Sam, please just hear me out, OK?'

She found herself nodding, jaws clenched, forcing herself to take slow, even breaths.

'It was just kids mucking around on the last day of school. Nick accidentally locked a girl in the old drama department. He didn't mean to, the latch on the door got stuck and he hadn't realised. She was in a right state when the caretaker found her. She accused Nick of ... doing things to her.'

'What things?' Sam asked through gritted teeth.

'Well, we heard she had some bruising on her and bite marks. But Nick's always said he never did anything to her. Anyway, he had a bit of a meltdown with all the accusations, he went home and started trashing the place, really freaked his mother out. Social Services and the police made the decision for him to be packed away to a detention centre and Sarah moved away with her family. So that's that. I don't know exactly what happened except that Nick's always insisted she was making it up to get back at him for locking her in.'

'Sarah,' Sam said, looking intently at Jack.

'What? Oh yes, the girl's name was Sarah.'

'Did you know her?'

'God, Sam, what is this? Yes, of course I knew her. You know Nick and I went to the same school, we were in the same year group!'

She watched him take another gulp of beer, noting how his hand trembled slightly as he brought the bottle to his lips. Why hadn't he told her any of this before?

'I was going to tell you, Sam,' Jack said, as if reading her mind. 'But you seemed to take a dislike to Nick almost right from the start and I knew you would write him off completely if I told you.'

Too bloody right, she thought, but didn't say anything, instead waiting to hear what else Jack had to say that could go anywhere near explaining why he was friends with such a freak.

'It was a really hard time that Nick just wants to put behind him. It was difficult for me and the other kids too. We were all questioned by the police and it divided us all – into those of us that believed Nick and, well ... those that didn't.'

'How many believed him? Aside from you?'

'Not many,' said Jack, a defiant expression on his face as he looked at Sam. But then he looked down and his shoulders drooped. 'Just me,' he eventually whispered.

Sam leant against the counter and listened to Jack explain how he had stood by Nick, losing a lot of his friends as a consequence, all the while trying to imagine what horrors Nick had done to the girl, or not. Maybe he was telling the truth. But somehow she didn't think so. Maybe he wasn't just a warped little creep.

Maybe he was actually dangerous.

'I've told him he can stay. Just for a few days whilst he sorts himself out. Sam ... Sam? Is that OK?'

No, no ,no, nooooooooooo! It's not fucking OK! She wanted to scream whilst shaking Jack until she could make him see sense, make him see what she could see. Nick, the monster. But instead she found herself nodding as if she had no control over her movements.

She closed her eyes as Jack pulled her into his arms, amazed at the immediate sense of security that washed over her as he held her tightly.

'Just for a few days,' she said, her voice muffled against Jack's chest.

Chapter Thirty Two

Sam gasped as the jets of water came into contact with her skin. She had flipped the shower switch to cold for the last few seconds in an attempt to rid herself of the dull, pounding headache she had had since the day *Nick* returned. Pulling on her dressing gown, she opened the bathroom door and heard the sound of their banter drift up the stairs to greet her. Hurriedly, she entered the bedroom, slamming the door behind her in an attempt to drown out their voices.

Sitting at the dressing table, she stared at her reflection; the shadows were back with a vengeance, creeping down to her cheeks and making her look ill. She brought her hands up to her face and pulled down on the skin below her eyes. With her mouth drawn back in a grimace, she made a low growling sound. The reflection staring back at her looked demonic.

Getting to the bottom of the stairs, she could see them now, sitting side by side on the sofa, each holding a controller for the PlayStation. Her lips curled into a sneer at the thought of how *'just a few days'* had now turned into three weeks. *He* noticed her first, as he always did, and returned her sneer with a superficial grin that disappeared quickly and was replaced by something dark.

'Hi babe,' said Jack, looking up at her as he placed the controller on the coffee table. He stood up and came toward her. 'Would you like some tea?' She glanced over at Nick, noting with some satisfaction, the frown on his unpleasant face. She reached up on tip toe and kissed Jack on the lips, her eyes fixed on Nick's.

'Maybe later,' she said suggestively, taking Jack by the hand and leading him back upstairs.

'Hey, what about the game?' Nick called after them. There was a whining quality to his voice which made Sam smile.

****

'We're running low on provisions,' Sam said, peering into the fridge. She turned to see whether Jack had heard, but no, he was on the PlayStation, where he had returned shortly after they'd had sex. She concentrated her glare into the back of Jack's head, hoping that he might feel her disdain and get up off his backside and tell her how sorry he was for making her feel like this: second best. But no, there he sat, with *him*, both giggling like stupid school boys. She turned her focus to the back of Nick's head, this time imagining her eyes were two laser beams that could bore through his skull, frying the neurons and rendering him helpless. She almost jumped when he suddenly turned round and caught her stare, before turning back, rubbing the back of his head, she noticed with a degree of satisfaction.

She returned her attention to the fridge and retrieved a half-eaten packet of salami and some cheese and tomatoes. The tomatoes were mainly past their best, with wrinkly skins and the beginnings of mould visible on some. But a few were passable and she picked these out. Thankfully the last few slices of bread were still fresh.

Sitting at the table, Sam took a bite out of her sandwich. As if on cue, Jack and Nick both turned their heads in unison.

'Hope you've saved enough for us,' Nick said as he jumped up and walked towards the kitchen. Towards her. 'Fancy a sandwich, mate?'

'Sounds good,' Jack replied. 'I'll make us some tea.'

They sounded like a married couple, Sam thought, watching the two of them.

'Hey, there's nothing left!' said Nick, shutting the door to the fridge.

'I did say we were running low,' Sam said icily, 'but no one seemed to be listening.'

'No worries, there's tea and biscuits. That'll keep me going for now then we'll go out and get some shopping in,' said Jack, squeezing Sam's shoulder. 'We could stop off at the Magna Carta for a drink, if you like?' Sam couldn't help smiling as he nuzzled into her neck, his soft lips brushing against her skin.

'Sounds like a plan, mate!' Nick said, clapping Jack's back. Sam shuddered.

An hour later, she had her arm firmly linked through Jack's as they walked towards the High Street. The dark clouds that had oppressively covered the sky for most of the day had miraculously cleared to reveal a bright blue expanse, and despite being early evening, it had turned out to be the best part of the day, at least weather-wise. Sam was determined to focus on the beauty of her surroundings; the cobbled streets, the old-fashioned shop fronts, the firmness of Jack's arm and the way his eyes matched the sky. But, as hard as she tried, she couldn't block out the other figure beside him. The brief flash of an arm, a leg, sometimes the face in profile, with its snubbed nose that came into view when it occasionally fell out of sync with Jack's walking pattern.

But then this was how it had been since he'd returned, inviting himself along on outings, even mundane trips to the supermarket; a third wheel in their relationship. It had got even worse since his return, as if he were making up for lost time.

Sam hadn't dared say a thing. Not since last week anyway when, unable to sleep, she'd come downstairs to make a peppermint tea. He must have heard her because when she had made her tea, there he was, sitting at the table; his head cocked to one side, arms folded. Assessing her.

'Are you trying to scare me or something?'

Nick had slowly shaken his head, his cruel eyes glinting in the semi-darkness. 'No, Sam, I couldn't sleep that's all. I have a lot weighing on my mind. As I'm sure you do.'

'I don't know what you're talking about,' Sam had said defiantly. 'Don't try and pretend you know anything about me, you're—'

'It can't be easy,' Nick had cut in.

'What?'

'Being you.' He'd got up then and moved towards her. Not

wanting him to think she was scared, she'd felt angry with herself for backing away. 'It'll be a lot easier for you when you realise you can't win.'

Sam had laughed; a forced noise that she didn't recognise.

Nick had smiled. 'Jack and I go way, way back. We're like blood brothers and you're not going to change that. There have been plenty of other little sluts who've tried. Believe me.'

Stung by his words, Sam had raised her hand to slap him, but he was too quick, catching her wrist and making her wince as he tightened his grip.

'Now now, there's no need for that,' he'd chuckled.

'Is this what you did to Sarah?' Sam had asked, spitting the words out in his face. A look of surprise flickered briefly in his eyes, but then he'd suddenly grinned, moving his head closer to hers until their foreheads were almost touching. For one horrible moment she'd thought he was going to try and kiss her and she readied herself, almost looked forward to letting his tongue enter her mouth, to explore her teeth before she bit down hard, cutting through the pink, sinewy tissue until her jaw clenched shut.

But instead he'd whispered, 'You have no idea what you're starting here, Sam. Just back off now, OK?'

For a few seconds, he'd closed his eyes, his forehead still resting on hers. She'd briefly considered calling out to Jack, but then what was the point? Nick would have just denied what had happened and Jack would have believed him. She hadn't felt so helpless since she was a little girl. Even her last encounter with Eddie, which was damn scary, hadn't made her feel like this. She had to admit: at that moment, Nick had terrified her.

It wasn't until he'd released her and left the room that she'd taken a deep, trembling breath, wiping away the tears that had started to flow. She'd stayed where she was for a few minutes – as still as a statue, before making her way back to bed, the peppermint tea long forgotten.

Something profound had happened that night, but she still couldn't put her finger on exactly why Nick made her feel so deeply unsettled. After all, she'd had to stand up to many brutal thugs throughout her short life, or make herself as small as possible so they wouldn't notice her, whichever was the best option in a scary situation. But somehow the fight had left her and she now found herself just putting up with the constant intrusion. Of the ever-present evil imp in her and Jack's lives, lurking in the shadows. Watching and smiling.

But it wouldn't be like this forever. It couldn't be or else she risked losing her sanity. It was inevitable that there would come a point where Jack had to choose between her and *him*.

'Sammy ... Sammy!' The sound of her name being called lifted Sam from her dark thoughts; there was only one person who called her Sammy.

'Wow, I thought you were going to walk right past me!' her mother said. 'Hi Jack,' she said, giving a little wave that for some reason made Sam cringe.

'Denise, good to see you,' said Jack, taking a step towards her mother and kissing her on the cheek. Sam winced as she watched her mother look coyly up at Jack through her lashes; so openly flirtatious.

'I've just been to my Spanish class,' she said.

'Y como fue?' said Jack.

'Muy bien!' Denise replied, clearly delighted.

'I didn't know you spoke Spanish,' Sam said, giving Jack a sceptical look.

'Oh, I've just picked up a bit over the years.'

'From his yearly trips to mummy and daddy's holiday home in Malaga,' Nick chipped in, earning an annoyed glance from Jack.

'I'm Nick, by the way,' said Nick, giving a little bow whilst he proffered his hand to Denise.

'Pleased to meet you. I'm Denise, Sammy's mother,' she replied, taking his hand. Sam noted with disgust that her mother was using her posh voice, the one she reserved for people she was trying to impress. It made her want to be sick.

'We're going to have a drink in there,' said Nick, pointing towards the Magna Carta pub.

'Oh, nice. We've been a few times for lunch, haven't we, Sammy?'

'Why don't you join us?' Nick jumped in, before Sam had a

chance to respond. Her mother looked at her enquiringly, as if waiting for her permission.

'Yes, come and have a drink,' she found herself saying, feeling faintly uncomfortable with the intent way in which Nick was looking at her mother.

'Well, isn't this nice?' Denise said as they settled into a small alcove overlooking the cathedral. 'What's everyone having?' She raised her hand when Jack started to protest, 'No, no this is my treat. I still owe you for the Chinese takeaway and wine.'

The uncomfortable feeling increased as Sam noted how Nick's eyes followed her mother to the bar and for a moment she saw what he saw: a slim, attractive woman, her hair piled up on top of her head with a few tendrils hanging down sexily. And how she wished her mother wasn't wearing that dress, the way it just skimmed over her curvaceous backside. She could see Nick's mouth was open and practically salivating.

'I'll go and help her with the drinks,' said Jack.

For a few moments, Sam found herself left alone with Nick, something she had come to master the art of avoiding. Finally tearing his eyes away from her mother, she braced herself as he turned to rest his gaze on her.

'You kept that a secret, didn't you?' he said, settling back and folding his arms. 'Your mother's a stunner.' He let that hang in the air for a moment before sitting forwards suddenly. 'I've always had a thing for older women. They're always so grateful,' he added, smiling his terrible smile.

Convinced this time that she really was going to throw up, Sam ran from the table towards the back of the pub. Wrenching the toilet door open, she bent over the nearest sink and gagged, expecting the inevitable to follow. But she couldn't vomit and was left instead with an acidic, burning sensation in her chest. Finally, she splashed her face with cold water and leant back against the tiled wall, thankful for the coolness they brought and for being the only one in there.

When she felt able, she opened the toilet door and re-entered the pub; her eyes trained on the alcove where they sat. She barely noticed her surroundings, the woman who nearly dropped the tray of drinks she was carefully balancing as she knocked into her, the dog's tail she stepped on, causing it to yelp out in pain. No, she didn't notice any of these things. Only the way in which her mother was laughing at whatever Nick was saying; the way in which she held herself, like a teenager on a first date.

****

'Are you going to tell me what's wrong?' Jack said later, climbing into bed beside Sam. She was lying on her back, her eyes fixed on the ceiling, watching a moth fluttering into the light shade; its movements becoming more frantic as it hit the light bulb over and over again. Reluctantly, she turned to face Jack.

'I can't live like this anymore,' she whispered.

'What do you mean?'

'With him.'

'Oh,' Jack said, sitting up abruptly. 'This is about today in the pub, right? How Nick was with your mum?' Sam opened her mouth to speak but Jack continued, 'Look, I know he was flirting a bit, but he doesn't mean anything by it. And I didn't see your mum complaining.'

Sam bit her lip, willing herself to stay calm. She didn't want to fight with Jack. Not with that creep in the house, probably listening outside their door. She turned her head back towards the ceiling and noticed the moth had now gone.

Jack let out a deep sigh. 'Look, I wasn't going to tell you yet, but I'm going to ask him to leave. I was just waiting till after his birthday.'

'What?' She snapped her head back towards Jack, not sure if she'd misheard him.

'Don't think I haven't noticed,' he said, running a finger down her cheek. 'How miserable you've been since he came back.' I thought with time you might get to like him and I'm hoping that may still happen. But for now, I need to concentrate on me and you.' He tipped her chin and leant in to kiss her gently on the lips. 'I love you so much Sam, and I'm sorry for not asking Nick to leave sooner, but he was in such a state over his neice, it just seemed cruel.'

Sam nodded slowly, unsure of how she felt about this unexpected information – relief, elation – yes. No longer would she see him lurking in the shadows. But then she thought back to the photo frame in Nick's stark bedroom, his arm draped around his niece, the open smiles on both their faces, and wondered what Nick would do – would he go back to Leeds to support his sister and niece? She didn't know why she even cared.

Chapter Thirty Three

She tears another piece off her maxi dress and moistens it with water.

'Go easy on that,' Sarah croaks. 'We don't know when he'll be back with more.'

She closes the lid and sets the bottle down before using the ripped material to gently dab at the cuts and sores covering Sarah's body. Although the one on her leg is particularly nasty and looks infected, she's pleased to see that some of them are beginning to heal and likes to think this is down to her care. Sarah looks at her and attempts a smile; two of her front teeth are missing.

It has been three long days since he last came to visit. It was just after the last grids of sunlight faded, turning the slimy grey walls to an ominous black mass and all she could make out was a shape looming towards her.

'Sit down,' he'd said, shining a torch in her face then pointing it in the direction of the wooden stool in the middle of the dungeon. She remained in the corner, huddled with Sarah. The corner felt safe, hidden from sight, but if she left her position, she would be completely exposed.

'Do not let me come and get you,' he said quietly. With every cell of her being screaming out 'Nooooooooooo!' she stood up. 'Get back down and crawl.' She immediately obeyed, dropping to her knees, forcing her stiff, aching body to crawl towards the stool. Towards the monster.

'Look at me,' he barked, once she was seated, her head down, hands clasped, as if in prayer. Reluctantly, she raised her head, her eyes hovering in the direction of the devil; trying but failing to recall the man she once loved. She was still reeling from the revelation that Sarah knew him from school; that even as a boy, he was a monster.

He didn't do or say anything at first, just stood there, two devil eyes boring into her, the hint of a smile playing on his lips. The lips that used to cover her in butterfly kisses from head to toe; the lips that used to utter beautiful things to her; the lips she used to kiss fervently as if she couldn't get enough of him.

There was complete silence, as he stood there, not saying or doing anything, and she had started to wonder if he might, just might, be having second thoughts; that just maybe she meant something to him. But then he crouched down and tapped a brown leather case she hadn't noticed till then. He undid the metal clasps to reveal a set of tools: some she recognised – pliers, a chisel, scissors – and others she didn't. Slowly, he traced the outline of each instrument, watching her as he did so. And then he pulled a blow torch from the case and stood up. The click as he depressed the button made her jump and the swoosh of the flame made her pee herself as he approached her.

'If you move, I'll burn you,' he whispered, crouching down so his face was level with hers. She closed her eyes, her only defence against the sight before her and for a few, torturous moments, held her breath, bracing herself for what was to come; what piece of her flesh would he choose first. But then the hissing sound of the blow torch stopped and when she dared open her eyes, she saw it was turned off, on the ground next to his feet. She also saw that he was naked from the waist down, clearly aroused, and as he pushed her roughly onto the floor, all she could feel, despite the pain of what he was now doing to her, was relief.

She finishes cleaning up Sarah as much as she can and helps her into a sitting position. She is in awe of this woman who has endured so much in her short life. Sarah is a survivor. Like her.

She breaks off a piece of the stale bread and passes some to Sarah. They mainly pass the time in silence, trapped in their own nightmares, and not for the first time, she finds herself wondering if she will experience the same tortuous acts as Sarah. It's as if her companion has read her mind when she says, 'He was like that with me at first, showing me his instruments of torture before raping me. He obviously gets off on it and I thought, hoped, it would end there. But ... well ... it didn't. It was as if he needed to go further each time for his sick gratification.'

And as she takes in Sarah's battered, filthy, broken body, she wants to scream, so she shoves a huge piece of the bread in her mouth to suppress it, making her choke in the process. When her coughing fit is over (needing to drink more of the precious little water to overcome it), she asks Sarah about her own family. She discovers that like her, there were only the two of them, her parents separating shortly after the incident at school. She doesn't have the heart to tell Sarah the latest news, that her mother committed suicide. That would break her completely and she needs her to be strong for what they have planned. Sarah had broached the idea first, putting into words what she had already been thinking: they had to take action. Before it was too late.

The light has long gone and just as she is drifting into a fitful sleep, she hears it. The unmistakable scraping sound from above; the sound of heavy sacks being dragged across a cold, stone floor.

'Sarah. Sarah!' she hisses, nudging the recumbent figure beside her. 'He's here.' She jumps up, adrenaline coursing through her body, making her feel invincible. 'Are you ready?'

'Yes,' Sarah says, shifting herself into an upright position. 'Here.' She feels for the long, hard object that Sarah is holding out and grabs it. 'Be careful!' Sarah whispers after her, but it's OK, she's practised the walk in the pitch black, carefully navigating the uneven stone floor so she doesn't trip. She reaches the spiral staircase and squeezes herself into the tight space behind them. The weapon, gripped tightly in both hands, is one of the stool legs she smashed off as they put their plan into action. Sarah has the rest of the stool tucked into the blanket.

The trap door creaks open and she hears the steady, firm tread of his feet descending the stairs; his torch casting beams of amber light around the hellhole until it settles in Sarah's direction. She prays the bulky shape of the stool, placed under the blanket, will fool him into assuming it's her, if only for a few seconds. That's all she needs.

'Please! Please! She needs help!' she hears Sarah cry out, as practised – the needed distraction. She sees him walk towards Sarah and springs into action, she doesn't have long. Edging out of the tight spot, she runs silently towards him, weapon raised. But the dungeon is suddenly plunged into black, making her falter. She can't see a thing. She swings the stool leg blindly at the spot where she last saw him. And then an arm is around her neck, dragging her backwards, her feet scrape along the floor, desperately trying to gain purchase, but he's too strong and all the fight *in her starts to wane as his arm restricts her airway. She is flung to the floor like a rag doll. She looks up to see the beam of the torch, bouncing erratically as he paces the floor. Until he stops. She can see him trembling, not with fright, but with anger. A hot, terrible anger.*

Chapter Thirty Four

Sam brushed another layer of concealer under her eyes and sat back to assess her handiwork. Not bad, she thought, fluttering her newly applied eye lash extensions. She practised smiling and was pleased to find that the reflection in the mirror looked happy. Well, almost. She ran a finger along the silver necklace, presented to her earlier that morning by Jack, alongside a tray of croissants and coffee. It was the most exquisite present she'd ever received, making her feel like the luckiest woman alive. But then she'd gone downstairs and found Nick sprawled out on the sofa, causing her initial feelings of happiness to plummet.

'Happy birthday, Sam-my.'

He always referred to her as Sammy now since he had heard her mother calling her that, but only when they were alone; deliberating over the syllables with a faint smile playing at the corners of his mouth. 'Happy birthday,' he repeated, his voice just above a whisper, making her feel somehow violated. 'Aren't you going to say happy birthday back?'

'Happy birthday,' she said mechanically, wondering why she couldn't work up the courage to tell him to fuck off.

'I've got you a present,' he said abruptly, nodding his head toward the coffee table. 'Go on, open it.'

'I'll wait till later,' she said, having no intention of opening whatever it was he'd got her – something nasty no doubt, although she couldn't think what. She watched his expression change and braced herself for the next words to come from his mean mouth; chosen with care so they would swirl around in her head hours later, like undigested food. But then she heard Jack coming downstairs and felt his arms encircling her briefly before he moved towards Nick.

'Happy birthday, mate!' he said, clapping Nick on the back. 'I would've got you something but … well …' He paused, waiting for Nick to join in.

'It's the thought that counts!' they both said in unison. Sam looked on in disgust as they laughed at their in-joke, the words Nick had said so obviously true: *Jack and I go way, way back.*

'I'm going to make a move,' she said stiffly.

'Are you sure you don't want me to join you?'

'No, it's just me and my mum,' Sam said, shaking her head firmly. 'I'll be back in plenty of time to help set up for the party.'

'Don't you worry about that, Nick and I have got everything covered. Just go and enjoy yourself, OK?' He walked over to Sam and placed his hands on her shoulders.

'OK?' he repeated, gently.

'OK,' she said, trying to blot out the image of Nick in the background. Watching.

'It's a shame your mother can't make it to the party. Tell her I said hi,' Nick said after her. She felt, rather than saw his sneer and didn't bother to reply.

Sam watched the swans as she walked along the canal towards the Highbridge; it was strange seeing them up close, they looked quite evil. She wondered if she was the only one who thought that. There was a black one, trailing behind the others. It looked a bit dishevelled, one of its wings didn't look right, with some of the feathers sticking out at odd angles. It drew alongside one of the others, who immediately launched into a vicious attack, pecking at the black swan's already damaged wing. Apparently satisfied with its handiwork, it went to rejoin the others to carry on the journey up the canal. Sam couldn't help feeling sorry for the lone swan left behind and leaned against the railing next to it.

'That's life, I'm afraid,' she said. 'You're just going to have to suck it up and move on.'

The swan started moving towards her but she straightened up, 'I can't help you, you've got to sort yourself out,' she said, walking away.

As she walked, Sam tried to shift the perturbing image of

the swan from her mind. This was her birthday after all. But the unsettling sight was immediately replaced by another. An image that kept coming back to her. Again and again. It had happened last week, she'd skipped a lecture and come home early due to the beginnings of a migraine, the familiar, dull thud in her temples starting to take hold not long after she'd left the house.

Jack was at uni, then going to see his parents for dinner. She'd managed, yet again, to evade his invite to join them, stating the need to start on an essay, which was partly true. The real reason being they sounded so posh, she was afraid of not being up to their high standards; of letting herself down and being an embarrassment. Despite Jack's attempts to play it down, he couldn't hide his upper class background: the skiing holidays; knowing what wine to order when they were eating out (she was used to ordering the house red or house white when out with her mother – occasionally they'd have a bottle of something fizzy if there was cause for celebration); all these things told Sam that Jack was from a very posh background and the thought of meeting his parents terrified her.

Nick had been AWOL for the past couple of days so she was looking forward to having the house to herself. But as she stood in the hallway, she knew immediately she wasn't alone as a strange sound drifted down the stairs, like something being slapped repeatedly.

As she ventured past the sitting room she noticed a mug on the coffee table that wasn't there when she and Jack had left that morning. She picked it up and sniffed the remnants of coffee, the mug was still warm. She instinctively knew not to call out and give herself away; whatever was happening upstairs sounded unsettling and somehow private. Thankfully, with the house being a new build, there were no creaking stairs and she made her way up in silence onto the landing where she could see that Nick's door was partially open. She made her way cautiously towards it.

He was sitting on the floor, cross-legged on top of several plastic bags. Thankfully he was facing the back wall, allowing her to observe him unnoticed. The slapping sound was much louder now, caused by some kind of whip he was flogging his back with. The whip was made out of several pieces of rope with knots at the ends and before each rhythmical 'slap', she could see Nick's body tremble then tense, in preparation for the pain, the plastic bags catching the blood that trickled down his back. But even more disturbing than this was the sound that came from him, the sound of sobbing from somewhere very deep within him – ancient and almost inhuman. Sam backed away and down the stairs, picked up her bag and quietly left the house.

As she sat in the lecture she'd planned to skip, she considered telling Jack about what she'd seen but knew she couldn't; the whole scenario was so intimate somehow, like having sex. And that sound he made, it was something that drained her insides and hollowed her out. Yet it was a sound she could also identify with, when she was in the depths of her own despair; when the memories of her turbulent childhood, losing Pops and the increasing resentment at Denise's failings as a mother, were all too much to bear and an outlet was so greatly needed.

She forced the disturbing scene from her mind as she entered the High Bridge, where her mother was already seated.

'Hello, my birthday girl!' Denise said, standing up to greet her. Sam smiled, letting her mother hug her tightly for a moment before pulling away.

'Do you want coffee?' Sam asked, looking around for one of the waiters.

'Already ordered,' said Denise, beaming. 'Come and sit next to me for a minute, I want to take a picture with my birthday girl.'

Sam obliged, sliding onto the bench next to Denise and resisted the urge to pull away when her mother's cheek touched hers.

'Say cheese,' Denise said, grinning inanely into the camera on her phone. 'Awww, look at that, she said, showing the screen to Sam. 'We look like sisters.'

Sam was about to disagree, but was interrupted by the waiter setting two steaming mugs on the table. She poured some cream into her coffee and took a sip as she looked out of the window to the canal below, only half listening to her mother regaling her with how well her Spanish classes were going.

'Have you finished?' Sam tore her eyes away from the canal and back to her mother, who had set her mug down and was smiling at her expectantly. 'We don't have time to be sitting around drinking coffee all day when there's shopping to do!'

Sam couldn't help matching her mother's bright, enthusiastic smile. It was her suggestion, after all, to spend the day together, starting the day off with coffee in their favourite cafe, followed by shopping, where she would pick out a dress for the party later, and finish off with a boozy lunch in the nice Italian place just off Steep Hill.

She had considered not telling her mother about the party; there was no way she wanted her in the same proximity as Nick again, but Jack had stupidly let slip about it a few days ago, when they'd met her mother for dinner at the Thai Palace, a firm favourite that had soon become a regular place for the three of them to meet.

Sam had held her breath, waiting for her mother's response; she'd closed her eyes briefly and tried to disperse the vivid image of Nick dancing up close to her mother, with a huge grin on his nasty face. But she needn't have worried. Denise had instantly turned down the invitation, stating parties were for the young. Jack had been about to protest but had thankfully noticed the slight shake of Sam's head. At least that was one less thing to worry about; she so desperately wanted to enjoy the party, despite Nick.

As they were leaving the Highbridge, Sam noticed the range of mugs on display by the till, her gaze settling on one in particular.

'I'll take that one, please,' she said, smiling at the man behind the counter. She looked on patiently as he proceeded to wrap the mug in several layers of different coloured tissue paper before eventually placing it with extreme care into a gift bag.

'There we go,' he said with a flourish.

'Perfect,' Sam said. And she meant it. It was the perfect present for Nick.

Sam found them in the garden later, sitting on deckchairs and sharing a spliff. Jack was talking, whilst Nick nodded his head enthusiastically; it must have been something amusing as they both laughed, then Jack took a deep pull on the spliff before passing it to

Nick. They looked so comfortable together, Sam felt like an intruder as she stepped into the garden. With a slight shake of the head, she declined the spliff from Nick's outstretched arm.

'Come on, let you hair down. It is your birthday after all!'

'Leave it out Nick,' Jack said, throwing him a warning look. Sam bent down and kissed the top of his head, grateful for him sticking up for her. He knew she didn't touch weed, or any other drugs, not after having to live with a junkie mother in her former years.

'Good time with your mum?' he asked, looking up at her.

'Yes, good, thanks. She got me a dress for my birthday. I'm going to wear it tonight.'

'Ooooh, lovely!' Nick said, clasping his hands together in mock excitement, not bothering to hide the sarcastic tone in his voice. Sam ignored him, forcing herself to keep her eyes trained on Jack's as he looked up at her.

As she made her way upstairs to get ready, Sam tried to clear her memories of birthdays past, and all her fears - the nagging worry that she and her mum were on Eddie's radar again and her increasing feelings of unease around Nick.

Chapter Thirty Five

The party was already in full swing by the time Sam came downstairs. She glanced down at her watch and smiled; she would've only just started getting ready to go out at this time in London, but it seemed that Lincoln ran on an earlier timescale. The sitting room was empty but she could see a small group in the kitchen, grazing on the bowls of snacks Jack and Nick had put out whilst she was getting ready. She had to admit, they'd done a good job with the party preparations. There were silver and gold balloons placed strategically on the walls and a large variety of spirits lined up on a separate table along with party plates and plastic cups. She especially liked the fairy lights twinkling around the fence outside but then noticed Jack standing in the corner of the garden speaking to a couple of attractive blondes. They were transfixed by whatever he was saying and eager to show it, their heads bobbing attentively in unison.

She closed her eyes briefly; she so wanted to enjoy this.

A tap on her shoulder made her jump. Spinning around she saw Kate – or was it Jenny? – one of the students on her course. She felt Kate/Jenny's arms embrace her, drawing her closer until she was met with a light kiss on both cheeks. She then soon found herself surrounded by a host of various smiling faces, their arms outstretched as they grabbed her, pulling her in for air kisses and happy birthday wishes. With her fists tightly clenched, she managed to keep smiling somehow until it was over, at least she assumed it was over, as she saw them all stood round her with expectant looks on their stupid faces. She grimaced back (she knew she definitely wasn't managing to smile anymore), wondering what the hell she was supposed to do. She was fucked if she knew, never having had a party for her birthday. It had always just been her and her mum – and Pops, before he went and died on her. At least when he'd been alive, he'd made sure she got a birthday cake – a lemon drizzle, Tesco special – both their favourite. But now, here she was, trapped by these hyenas, hungry for a response she couldn't give, causing the blood in her veins to rush uncomfortably round her head and for sweat patches to appear on her new, lilac dress.

Then Jack materialised, effortlessly forging a path through the group and coming to stand in front of her. He was smiling and saying something but she couldn't hear above the thudding in her ears. He held her tightly and started moving, making her think at first that he was going to get her out of there. But as she felt her body moving back and forth with Jack's, she soon realised they were dancing, the group around them clapping in time to the beat. She no longer cared about them though, as she let her body be led by Jack, his body acting as a barrier between them and her.

'Are you OK, baby?' he whispered into her ear. She nodded.

'I am now.'

'You looked like you needed rescuing.'

'And that's exactly what you did,' she said, looking up into Jack's eyes. 'You rescued me.'

Suddenly aware that they weren't alone, Sam's eyes flitted beyond Jack and she was relieved to see the circle of bodies had dispersed – the expectant faces turned away from her, finally satiated as they talked and laughed amongst themselves.

'Come on, let's get the birthday girl a drink.' Jack led her towards the table of spirits. 'You look totally amazing by the way,' he said, winking at her.

With a vodka and coke in one hand and the other hand clasped tightly around Jack, Sam finally felt equipped to face the guests. She smiled and exchanged pleasantries, never letting any conversation get further than the light and superficial before moving on to the next face. At times she got lucky and was able to address a group of three or four at the same time, getting away with the fewest words possible. And then, as the night drew on and as everyone became more and more inebriated, conversation didn't matter at all.

Helping herself to a fourth vodka and coke, Sam finally started to relax. She felt her shoulders loosen and she leant back against the cool wall for a moment to survey the party. There were a few people dancing now, forming a small circle in the middle of the kitchen. She considered joining them, almost took a step forward, but stopped. It seemed so weird. So unlike the darkened clubs she'd frequented in south London – turning up on her own. To drink alone. To dance alone. Until she would attract a man's attention, which didn't take long, and then they would dance and invariably leave soon after – to his place, to an alleyway, whichever was most convenient. She wasn't proud of her actions during that time. A time when she felt so angry with her lot in life; with her useless mother, and Pops dying. Dear Pops.

With a deeper level of insight, thanks to the counselling sessions at uni, Sam now realised how desperately she had needed help during that time, to try and make sense of what she was feeling. But at least she was in a better place now and so was her mother, thanks to her actions.

She saw Jack in the garden, literally swamped by a group of women, and noticed the two blondes amongst them, vying for his attention. He looked across the tops of their heads and met her gaze with an intensity that made her go weak. She smiled. He was hers and she had nothing to worry about.

'You make such a gorgeous couple.' She tore her eyes away from Jack's to see Kate/Jenny standing next to her.

'Yes, we do,' Sam smiled.

'Black and Gold.'

'What?'

Kate/Jenny looked uncomfortable. 'Oh, it's just a song, 'Black and Gold'. It came to mind when I saw the two of you together, the way your colours contrast but compliment each other at the same time. Sorry, I've had too much to drink and I'm talking shite.' She hiccupped and let out an embarrassed laugh. Sam looked at her for a moment, considering what she'd just said.

'Black and Gold … hmm … I like it,' she said, smiling at Kate/Jenny.

'Thank fuck for that! I didn't want to offend you or anything. There aren't many black people in Lincoln.'

'No, really? I hadn't noticed!' Sam said, attempting a look of shock. There was a moment's hesitation before they both broke into laughter, laughing so hard Sam had to wipe tears from her eyes. It felt unfamiliar. It felt good.

'No, seriously,' said Jenny, her words slightly slurred. Sam had by now gathered that she was talking to Jenny, not Kate. Jenny gestured with her plastic cup, causing some of its contents to spill, Sam noticed. But never mind, it would be cleared up later and Sam didn't want to interrupt the moment to fetch a cloth; she was quite enjoying Jenny's company. With an assertive effort, she looked up from the spilt liquid on the floor and focused on what Jenny was saying.

'When you two started dancing earlier, it was like no one else existed.'

'Stop pissing with me!' Sam said with a laugh, thinking how only a couple of hours before she had been desperate to escape the group of hyenas surrounding her. It was strange to think they might have just liked what they saw.

'I'm not kidding! Everyone was mesmerised. Well, except for your flatmate. Nick, isn't it? He didn't look too happy at all. If looks could kill ... Phew!'

At the sound of his name, the merry feeling evaporated, changing to something heavy in the pit of her stomach. She hadn't even noticed him, but then he was good at that, lurking in the shadows.

'Are you OK? Sam?' She was distracted from her thoughts by Jenny gently patting her arm. 'I'm sorry, I didn't mean to upset you. I think Nick's a bit infatuated, that's all.'

'Well he's wasting his time. I'm not interested,' said Sam with a firm shake of her head.

'Oh no, I didn't mean you, I meant Jack. He's infatuated with Jack.'

Chapter Thirty Six

It was 3 am and the party was still in full swing. Jack had put some pizzas in the oven and was now dishing them out onto the plates that Nick was holding out. Sam had successfully managed to avoid him throughout the evening but she watched him now; watched for signs of his 'infatuation' with Jack. She knew, of course, that Nick was jealous of their relationship, jealous of her for coming between them. She was also certain that he was physically attracted to her. But the thought that he might actually be *in love* with Jack, in the same way that she was in love with him, made her skin crawl.

She had met his girlfriend earlier and couldn't help noticing how irritable he seemed, introducing 'Andrea' to them reluctantly, almost as if he was embarrassed. Andrea had said hello in a peculiarly childish voice and laughed shyly when Jack pulled her in for a hug, saying how nice it was to finally meet her. She was a poor looking thing, pudgy with a flat arse; Sam couldn't help feeling satisfied.

Alcohol had cured Andrea's shyness now, Sam observed; she was dancing up close with another bloke called Steve. He had tried it on with Sam earlier, but Jack had appeared, placing his arm around her shoulder. She could have dealt easily with Steve of course, but had wanted to test Jack. She saw Steve now, trying his luck with Andrea – his hands travelling down to her non- existent arse and, to her delight, Nick had noticed too. She watched his reaction with fascination. Watched his small eyes glint with unpleasant intent, watched as he went up and grabbed Andrea's wrist, pulling her away to a corner. Instinctively, Sam found herself moving closer, desperate to hear what he was saying to her, but she was apprehended by Jack offering her pizza.

'Look, I saved you the last slice.' Noting her hesitation, he added, 'Please have it baby, it's good to line your stomach to soak up the alcohol. You'll thank me in the morning, believe me.'

'Well then I can't really say no, can I?' she said, pulling him in close for a kiss.'You're so sweet, looking out for me.'

She was going to tell him about the altercation she had just witnessed between Nick and Andrea but stopped herself; Jack, being the good friend that he was, would probably try to intervene and make it all OK and she didn't want that. She most certainly didn't want things to be OK for Nick.

She started dancing with Jack and a few others, all the while looking around for Nick and Andrea. They must have gone upstairs to his room. She knew he would want somewhere private to let his cruel words flow. But then the couple dancing in front of Sam went to get more drinks, opening up the space and giving her a clear view into the living room where she could see the back of Nick's head above the sofa. She could also see the top half of Andrea's head, sitting in the chair opposite. Sam couldn't be sure, but she looked like she was crying. She was relieved to see no one else had noticed and edged slowly towards the living room. Drawing closer, she discovered that Andrea was definitely crying; huge, silent sobs racking her body. Moving closer still, she saw Nick in profile. Expecting to see his face contorted in anger, or disappointment, she was surprised to see he was in fact smiling; his leg slung casually over the other and his arms folded, his eyes trained on Andrea's shaking body. He looked like he was watching something funny on the TV and she was reminded of the first time she met him, perched on Jack's bed, scrutinising her. Sam watched the strange scene, engrossed. She didn't really know what to make of it. It was so bizarre and cruel, even by his standards. Watching Nick taking such obvious enjoyment in his girlfriend's misery made her feel cold inside. Somehow it was even worse than the way she'd seen her mother being treated at the hands of all those brutal men.

Nick tipped his head back and laughed, then stood up suddenly. Sam quickly backed away. Standing over Andrea for a few excruciating seconds, he slowly bent down and patted her on the knee. Sam watched Andrea look up at him, a hopeful, dog-like expression on her mascara-streaked face, but it didn't remain for long as whatever she saw in Nick's expression (Sam couldn't see from her position) caused her face to crumple up into abject misery. To add insult, he gave her a final, jovial pat on the knee and turned towards the door. Sam stepped back and edged towards the front door, flattening herself against the wall, hoping the coat stand would suffice to hide her from view. She could see him hovering at the threshold to the kitchen, watching everyone. Watching Jack. Then he turned and went upstairs. She heard his bedroom door close and only then did she finally allow herself to exhale, letting her body slump slightly against the wall for a moment. She went to rejoin the party but caught a glimpse of Andrea and paused. She made a pitiful sight and, although Sam wasn't in the habit of feeling sympathy for others, she felt it now.

Entering the sitting room, she plucked out a couple of tissues from the box on the coffee table and perched on the arm rest next to Andrea.

'Here, take these,' she said, holding out the tissues. This brought on a renewed bout of crying, making Sam regret her actions. She got up to leave but was restrained by a clammy hand on her arm.

'Please don't go,' said Andrea, looking up at Sam with the same pathetically hopeful expression she had given Nick. And for a moment, Sam saw what Nick saw; felt the same position of power he must have felt when looking down on this snivelling, weak cow and in that instant, she knew. She was capable of matching his cruelty; of inflicting the same misery. She could so easily be like Nick and it terrified her. She lowered herself down onto the arm rest and waited.

'Thanks,' Andrea said, wiping her nose with the back of her hand, the tissues left unused in her lap. 'You're so nice. You and Jack – I was watching the two of you, you make the perfect couple. I said so to Nick why can't you be nice to me, like Jack is to Sam? Why can't you come and dance with me and introduce me to everyone and bring me a drink? So I don't have to stand there on my own feeling awkward and stupid and d'you know what he said to me? He said he didn't give a shit about me or my feelings and I know he meant it. Oh

God, Sam, I love him so much, why does he have to be so nasty?'

All this came forth from Andrea in a jumbled, high-pitched torrent, making Sam feel even more uncomfortable. She hadn't signed up for the role of agony aunt. Not knowing what to say, she picked up the forgotten tissues from Andrea's lap and waved them in front of her face.

'Oh thanks, you're so kind,' she said, as if seeing the tissues for the first time.

'Why does he have to be so nasty?' she repeated, finally using the tissues to blow her nose. Sam was damned if she knew so smiled in what she hoped was a sympathetic manner. It must have been construed as such by Andrea who, much to Sam's alarm, suddenly leant her head on her arm. Sam knew the normal reaction would have been to put her arm around Andrea at this point – embrace her or pat her back. But looking down on the top of her greasy hair, she felt repelled. Thankfully, it seemed it was enough for Andrea that Sam was just there and, apart from a listening ear, no further requirements seemed needed. She listened as Andrea, in her strange, childish voice, spoke about how controlling Nick was over her, about how she couldn't seem to do anything right to please him.

'He ... likes to play games, just silly stuff but ... well ... sometimes he, he goes a bit too far, it freaks me out.'

'What does he do?' Sam prompted, fascinated.

'Oh, it's nothing. Forget I said anything,' she said, emitting a nervous laugh. 'I shouldn't have made him so angry, it was my fault. But he was ignoring me and I don't know anyone else here, so when Steve started dancing with me, I just let him. Not 'cos I fancied him or anything, but because I was lonely and I'd drunk a lot. I tried saying that to Nick but he wouldn't listen.'

She blew into the tissues and took a deep, shuddering breath.

Sam was getting annoyed at the strands of Andrea's hair tickling her arm and the weight of her head was really beginning to get on her nerves. But she closed her eyes and willed herself to remain still. She wanted to hear about Nick, *the real Nick*, no holds barred. She waited.

'It's not that he shouts or anything, it's ...' Andrea looked up suddenly, 'I can trust you, can't I?'

Of course you can't, you stupid retarded bitch. Sam nodded and was amazed to see Andrea returning her smile, somehow reassured that she was the chosen one to pour out her dirty little secrets to. She leant back a little as Andrea continued, 'He said I might as well go back to my old ways and start charging. He told me to go and tell Steve what I could offer. Said he could drum up some more custom and take a cut.' She blurted out.

Sam leant forward, unable to contain her surprise, 'What ... you mean Nick wanted you to prostitute yourself?' she asked incredulously, shifting her position so that Andrea could no longer use her arm as a headrest.

'It's ... It's what I used to do,' Andrea said, lowering her head, her voice just above a whisper. 'I'm not proud of it.'

'Oh,' said Sam, flatly, not knowing how else to respond.

'My mum kicked me out seven years ago when I got pregnant,' Andrea said, her head still down, twisting the tissue in her hands.

'What a bitch,' Sam said without thinking. She held her breath, hoping she hadn't offended Andrea, but was relieved when Andrea laughed.

'Yeah, I know, right? But I can't blame her really. I was a total nightmare for years and she just had enough of me.'

'What did you do?'

'Well, I went and kipped on a friend's sofa for awhile but then I had to leave and I was skint so ... I had to make enough money to live on.'

'No, I meant about the baby.'

'What? Oh, I ... I got an abortion.'

She said this with a shrug of her shoulders, but Sam heard the way her voice trembled and felt another uncharacteristic pang of sympathy for the sad, pudgy woman.

'I'm sorry,' she heard herself say and was surprised to find she actually meant it. 'Why did you tell Nick?' she asked, curious.

'Because I trusted him,' Andrea said simply. 'I still do. He was so sweet when I told him. He didn't judge me or anything, just held me and said it didn't matter. I've never had that before from a bloke –

you know, where you feel ... accepted. D'you know what I mean?'

'Yeah, I do,' Sam nodded, thinking of Jack. She knew exactly what Andrea meant.

'I'd love to have a baby now. I think it would be good for me and Nick.'

For the second time, Sam was nonplussed. The thought of having sex with Nick turned her stomach, but the thought of actually creating a baby with him was too much; another *him* in the world, with *his* blood coursing through its veins. That same smile, snub nose and cruel, watchful eyes.

She was aware that Andrea was now looking at her; a strange expression on her face which made her wonder what her own features were displaying. She tried to smile.

'You and Jack would make lovely little caramel babies.'

Sam blinked rapidly, digesting the comment before tipping her head back and laughing.

'I'm serious,' said Andrea, 'You two would make seriously cute babies.'

Sam shook her head. 'I don't want kids' she said. And it was true, she had made a promise to the ten-year-old girl staring sullenly back at her from the cracked bathroom cabinet mirror. She remembered the moment vividly. Her mother had promised to take her on a day out to the zoo, a birthday treat. She had worn her favourite jeans, the ones with the embroidered flowers at the bottom, and matched them with the bright purple hoodie from Pops. With her newly braided hair, she felt so cool as she carefully applied a layer of lip gloss (nicked off Theresa – but she deserved it, just leaving it out on the school desk like that, so careless). But then she had walked into the sitting room and seen her mother curled up in a trembling ball on the settee and marched straight back to the bathroom where she wiped off the lip gloss and vowed she would never dare have a family of her own, because how could she be sure that she wouldn't turn out like her pathetic, weak mother?

'I'd better get going,' Andrea said, edging herself off the chair and straightening her crumpled dress.

'Aren't you going to stay over?'

Andrea shook her head. 'No, Nick doesn't want me here. He told me to go.'

'You can stay on the sofa if you want?' Sam said, again feeling a stab of sympathy, but also thinking how pissed off Nick would be to see her there when he came downstairs later that morning.

'Thanks, but no,' Andrea said firmly. Sam followed her to the front door and waited whilst Andrea rummaged through the jackets on the coat stand.

'Found it,' she said, smiling. 'Thanks so much,' she said, hugging Sam tightly. 'I hope we can see each other again sometime. Say bye to Jack for me.'

'I will,' said Sam, walking Andrea to the gate. She stood, her smile changing to a sneer as she watched Andrea's retreating figure. How Andrea could be so pathetic and weak to put up with Nick's warped behaviour; - to endure the *nasty games* he played to '*freak*' her out – she would never understand. Andrea turned suddenly to wave goodbye, her hand froze in midair when she saw the look on Sam's face. Sam didn't bother to alter her expression this time. Slowly, she turned and walked back into the house.

Straightaway she noticed the group of bitches surrounding Jack as she stood at the threshold to the kitchen; flicking their hair; retarded, over-exaggerated expressions on their fucking stupid shiny faces. Anything to get his attention.

Nick was also there, standing beside him, laughing loudly at something Jack had said. *Nick.* She turned away, but not before he saw her – his cruel little eyes glittering – he lifted his cup and toasted her with a crazy smile. She turned away, almost tripping over a stray balloon in her haste. She wondered how he had managed to come back downstairs without her noticing but then realised he must have snuck down when she was with Andrea. She imagined him lurking near the sitting room; his ear pressed up to the door. Listening. Not that she gave a fuck. She hoped he had heard Andrea pouring out her dirty little secret. Surely it would give him something to worry about, her knowing. Dangling that little titbit of knowledge over his head, the fact that she knew he was going out with an ex-prossie. But then the deranged smile he just gave her suggested not.

Feeling suddenly drained, she trudged upstairs – a mixture of alcohol and tiredness making it an effort to lift one foot after the other. She had wanted to tell Jack she was going to bed, it felt wrong just leaving him. But then she would've had to say goodbye to the rest of them and she really couldn't give a fuck. They could go to hell for all she cared. Especially *Nick*.

She brushed her teeth and washed off her makeup, ignoring someone knocking at the door. They knocked again so she shouted, 'Fuck off!' and took her time to wipe the foundation from her face. By the time she came out whoever was there had followed her instruction and fucked off. *Good*, she thought.

Breathing a sigh of relief, she closed the bedroom door behind her and went over to the window to lower the blinds. It wasn't until she had taken off her dress and was about to slip into bed that she noticed it; an object peeking out of the duvet, the top of it resting on her pillow. She scrabbled for the lamp and switched it on, her heart racing. In the yellow glow, she could now make out what it was, a small, perfectly wrapped present, resting suggestively on her pillow. Her stomach started to churn uncomfortably. It had no right to be there, intruding on her space, making her feel jittery. She perched on the side of the bed and stared at it, contemplating whether to leave it till she'd had some sleep and felt better prepared for what was inside. Because she knew of course who it was from; he'd tried to get her to open it earlier and now she wished she had, when she'd been full of energetic optimism for the day ahead. Hesitantly, she picked it up, turning it round cautiously in her hands as if it might explode at any moment. She leant over and placed it carefully on the floor but then picked it back up – finding the thought of it just sitting there, waiting whilst she slept, unsettling.

There was a card sellotaped to the present and she decided to open that first. There was a picture of a dog on the front staring back at her with cartoon googly eyes and a superimposed grinning human mouth. Inside, it simply said 'Happy Birthday Sam. Have a good one. Nick' She stared at the words, trying to find some nasty, hidden meaning but could find none. It was just an innocent birthday card after all.

For a moment, she stared at the present before ripping at the paper with a vicious force, wanting to get it over and done with as quickly as she could. She gasped as her hand struck something hard and sharp. Whatever it was had pierced her finger, causing a tiny circle of blood to bubble up from the skin. Instinctively she put her finger in her mouth and sucked it, savouring the iron tang. Cautiously, she removed the rest of the paper to reveal the tiny stone figure inside. She stayed quite still for some time. Her eyes were wide open now – the tiredness she felt only a few moments ago entirely gone. It was the sharp, elf-like ear that had caught her finger.

Picking up the figure, she lifted it up towards the lamp so she could see it more clearly. The amount of detail carved into the stone was impressive for something that could have only been about three inches in size. Slowly, she traced a finger over the ridges of its cold, stone body, the sharp little teeth and claw like hands. Stretching over to the corner of the desk, she propped it up against the edge of her mirror, making sure it was facing her. She wanted it where she could see it.

Laying her head on the pillow, she stared at it until her eyes became heavy, each blink becoming slower and more effortful. The last thing she saw was its evil pixie face grinning back at her. The Lincoln Imp. Nick. Their faces merging into one as she finally slid into unconsciousness.

Chapter Thirty Seven

It's moving.

She's sure of it. The stone wall is moving. It swells then contracts, expands and shrivels. In ... Out ... In ... Out ... In ... Out. It is a living, breathing thing, glistening in the limited light from the air bricks, like it's sweating. She tilts her head to one side and concentrates. Yes, she can hear it breathing too. In ... Out ... In ... Out. A rhythm that starts to lull her to sleep but then the wall doesn't contract, instead expanding, swelling, bulging, sucking all the oxygen with it and she can't breathe. The stone mass starts to quiver and makes a rattling sound, like Sarah's last breaths and if she were able, she would have screamed. But she has screamed a lifetime of screams and has nothing left to give. She pulls her arms tightly around her and tries to stop the constant shivers that haven't stopped since witnessing Sarah's death. He took the blanket afterwards and ripped off the dress she was wearing, what was left of it anyway, leaving her naked. But she has found something to cover her, a top wedged into a crack in the floor behind the stairs. It is red with blue flowers. She doesn't know if it belonged to Sarah, or another wretched soul, and although it is stained with blood, she put it on and felt less exposed. She looks down at the top now, to distract herself from the moving stone mass that has resumed its rhythmic breathing and prefers to think it is Sarah's; that she hid it in an act of defiance: to not let the monster take everything from her.

'Why did you let it happen?'

She jumps, her head snapping upwards, eyes straining to see in the fading, weak light. She can't believe she didn't hear the scraping sound of the sacks being shifted above: the precursor to the devil's descent. She hasn't had time to take off the top and curses inwardly. Maybe he won't notice, she hopes, because she doesn't want to consider the consequences if he has.

'Come now, girl, stop cowering in the corner and speak to your old man.'

It can't be. She squints in the direction of the voice and sees that yes, it is him. The familiar outline of her dad; somehow impossibly perched on the two-legged stool, defying the logics of balance. She attempts to get up but her legs won't obey.

'Dad! Daddy? Is that really you?'

'Can you see me?' he says, taking a pull of his pipe. She nods.

'Can you hear me?' She nods again. 'Well then, it must be me. Why did you let it happen?' He says again, leaning towards her.

'Why did I let what happen?'

'The poor girl. She's dead, isn't she?'

She glances in the direction of the body. She hasn't looked at it since Sarah took her last, rattling breath and she clasps a hand over her mouth at the sight. The once emaciated form has started to bloat; there is a red, foamy substance leaking from the gaping mouth. The remaining eye is white and staring: unfocussed but at the same time, accusatory. She looks away from the hellish sight and back towards her dad. His head is tilted downward and slightly to one side in that way of his when he is waiting for an answer. But she can't put into words what she has witnessed: the sounds and smells of ripping, cracking and burning flesh and bone; the inhuman noises that Sarah made, giving way to choking, wheezing and gurgling as her vocal cords gave up. That was the price to pay for their act of defiance, for trying to outsmart the devil; she had to watch whilst he slowly destroyed what was left of Sarah and now she sits, too weak, too traumatised, to do anything other than wait for what is to come.

'You couldn't protect her, could you? Just like you've never been able to look after your own flesh and blood. You're weak.'

Denise nods and starts to cry; hearing her own father voice the truth she has always known deep down. She leans forward and holds out her arms.

'Daddy? Please help me. Oh God, please help me.' She can't see him anymore, her tears blurring her vision, but when she wipes them away with the backs of her hands, she still can't see him. He is no longer there.

So she sits back against the wall, feeling it swell and shrink, hears it breathe In ... Out ... In ... Out ... In ... Out ... and waits for what is to come.

Chapter Thirty Eight

Sam was woken by the sun's rays seeping through the slats of the blinds; by the strength of the light, she knew it must be late. A glance over to her alarm clock confirmed it was after midday. The sight of Jack made her start, she hadn't noticed him sitting at the desk. He was hunched over, looking at something.

'Morning. I mean afternoon,' she said, pushing herself up in the bed. He turned and smiled at her.

'Cool little fellow, isn't he?' he said, holding up the Imp. Sam started at the sight of the grotesque figure grinning at her. She had hoped it was just a dream, but seeing it now, in the bright summer sunshine, it looked very, very real.

'Nick must really like you, you know,' Jack said, swooping down and planting a kiss on her lips. 'He doesn't usually do presents.'

'How d'you know it's from Nick?'

'This?' Jack said, a quizzical expression on his face. Sam stared at the creased card he was holding and wished she'd ripped it up into tiny little pieces, or better still, burnt it. But instead, Jack had found it near the bin, where she'd aimed it and missed.

'You know how I feel about him,' she said.

'Yes, you've made that clear. But please consider giving him another chance; he's really not that bad.' Sam detected an edge to his voice as he placed the card carefully on the desk but then he suddenly leant forwards and covered her face and neck in the gentlest of kisses. She closed her eyes and was beginning to relax until Jack cupped her face roughly, his eyes focussed intently on hers.

'Will you give him another chance? For me?' He said in that low, unfamiliar voice that unsettled her.

She had no intention of doing so but nodded.

How could she possibly explain how receiving Nick's present had made her feel? What the Imp symbolised for her? She could hardly make sense of it herself. Jack didn't know about the morning chapel – her special place where she could be close to Pops; the hours she spent in the cathedral, taking strength from the cool, hard stone and the stained glass windows. And of course, the Lincoln Imp, her fascination never waning as she stared and stared at the small gargoyle carved into the stone. No one knew about it. So how could Nick possibly know? How could he know that she saw *him* when she stared at the Imp? Their evil little faces merged into one on the cathedral wall. But then she thought of the increasingly brazen way Nick looked at her, even in Jack's presence; his eyes boring into her as if seeking out her very core, until Jack caught his eye and something unspoken would pass between them. Of course Nick knew what the Imp meant to her, he could see into her soul. Squeezing the bridge of her nose, Sam attempted to stop these unnerving thoughts from roaming through her head, making it hurt. There was no way on this earth she could ever bring herself to like, or trust Nick, not even for Jack. But at least he would be moving out soon, so long as Jack wasn't about to renege on his promise.

Her mood lifted slightly, suddenly remembering the mug she had picked up in the Highbridge. It was just the thing to give him a little push in the right direction.

'I've got Nick a present too,' she said, a little too brightly. 'Why don't we give it to him together?'

'What is it?' Jack asked, and Sam couldn't blame him for the suspicious expression in his eyes.

'Oh, it's just a mug I saw in the Highbridge yesterday,' she said, keeping her tone light.

'Well that was nice of you,' Jack said, smiling. She smiled sweetly back.

Nick was already in the kitchen drinking coffee when they went downstairs.

'Morning. My my, we are looking a bit worse for wear!' he said, staring pointedly at Sam. 'You look like you could do with a good strong cup of coffee. I've just brewed some. Help yourself.'

'Thanks for my ... present,' Sam said, smiling through clenched teeth. Nick nodded. 'What made you think of it?'

'Glad you like it. Have you heard of the legend of the Lincoln Imp?' he said abruptly, ignoring her question. Sam was about to reply but Nick continued, 'It was sent from the Devil to cause havoc in the cathedral, but was turned to stone by an angel before it could get up to any real mischief. I fucking love that story, and the cathedral. I go there often, have you been?'

Sam felt sickened as she thought back to all the times she'd been in the cathedral and the probability that he might have been there at the same time; lurking behind the stone columns; watching her. Looking at him now, leaning against the counter and sipping his coffee, she was sure of it. He'd definitely seen her there. Or had he followed her? She shuddered.

'Yes, I've been,' she said stiffly.

'Great, isn't it? I picked him up in the shop. I don't know, something about it made me think of you,' he said, winking at her.

'What's that supposed to mean?' Sam snarled.

'Well we've got you something too,' Jack interjected, presenting Nick with the gift bag.

An uncomfortable atmosphere prevailed as Nick slowly took the bag, his gaze fixed firmly on Sam. But then he grinned. 'What's this then?' he said.

'Open it and see,' Sam said, forcing herself to smile.

She watched, transfixed, as he opened the gift bag and pulled the mug from its nest of colourful tissue paper. The blank expression on his face changed to one of bemusement as his eyes rested on the picture on the mug – a house, the words NEW HOME boldly printed in blue below.

'Is this supposed to be a hint then?' he said, holding the mug up to Jack. Jack blinked several times, his eyes fixed on the mug before turning to Sam.

'Oh ... sorry!' said Sam, clasping her hands to her mouth in mock bewilderment. 'I thought Jack had already spoken to you about leaving.' She deliberated over the words, feeding off the look of uncertainty on Nick's face as he turned to Jack.

'Look mate, I was going to tell you today. I didn't—'

Whatever Jack was going to say was interrupted by Nick, hurling the mug to the floor, making them both jump. He then stormed off towards the stairs and, to Sam's disgust, Jack went trailing after him.

She let out a low whistle, looking at the broken pieces of porcelain at her feet. What a waste of a nice mug, but at least it had served its purpose, she thought, bending down to brush up the pieces.

Pouring the last of the coffee into a mug, she leant against the counter and listened out for any signs of an argument coming from upstairs but it remained eerily silent; she moved hesitantly towards the bottom of the stairs, curious to see what was going on up there but quickly turned back into the kitchen when the door to Nick's room opened.

He thundered down the stairs and she saw a flash of him as he passed the kitchen, on the way to the front door, a large canvas bag in tow. Moving closer, she saw him reach for the handle, about to open it. But then he paused and lowered his hand. 'I might be leaving your little love nest, but I'll never be far away, you know that don't you?'

And with that final parting, he opened the door and left. For a moment, she stood stock still, not quite believing he'd gone and half expecting him to reappear – 'I'm back! Only joking!' – a demonic grin lighting up his evil face. She stood waiting, listening for any signs of his return, but there was nothing. She pressed her forehead against the cool, frosted pane of the door and slowly exhaled. She lifted a shaking hand to her face and wiped the tears that had started to flow from seemingly nowhere, only just realising how badly Nick's malevolent presence had got to her. Maybe she wasn't as strong as she thought. But it was finally over. Even if Jack insisted on still meeting up with him, she knew she would have to learn to cope with that – the fact remained that she'd won. She turned round and, closing her eyes, leant back against the door, listening to the sounds on the other side, a child laughing, a car engine revving, a coarse, female voice shouting – it was all music to her ears. When she eventually opened them, she saw Jack standing at the top of the stairs, his top half in shadow where the sun didn't reach. She couldn't make out the expression on his face.

Chapter Thirty Nine

Sam caught sight of their reflection in the shop window and smiled. Jenny was right, they made a striking couple; what was it she had said? Black and gold. She looked up at Jack and her breath caught momentarily. He looked so good; so much better than the image she held of him in her mind when she wasn't with him. The sheer physical presence of him never failed to take her by surprise. She squeezed his hand.

'Nervous?'

'No.' She shrugged, 'A bit.'

He squeezed her hand back. 'You'll be fine.'

She really hoped she would be fine – that was the problem. Actually wanting to make a good impression wasn't a predicament Sam often found herself in. Not until she met Jack anyway.

They walked through the central arch into the grounds of the cathedral and Sam pulled on Jack's arm to slow him down. She could never walk past the cathedral without stopping to take it in, from the magnificent wooden doors, working her way up, and taking in the intricate stone carvings and windows, right up to the uppermost points of the towers – the way the clouds moved through them made it look like the cathedral itself was moving, making her feel momentarily unbalanced. She felt herself begin to sway slightly and tightened her grip on Jack's arm.

'What is it with you and this place?' he said, smiling down at her, but he didn't attempt to move until she was ready and she was grateful for that. Things had been a bit strained between them since the mug incident.

Jack's pace slowed as they reached the parade of houses at the back of the cathedral.

'Right, we're here,' he said. Sam followed his gaze to the beautiful house nestled in the centre of the parade. It was the duck egg blue one with the ornate wrought iron balcony – her favourite. She couldn't believe it! Her hopes of giving a good first impression plummeted as she remembered the haughty woman, looking down at her with that glacial stare.

'Come on, let's do this,' said Jack, taking her hand and crossing the road and before she had time to think, he'd lifted the shiny brass knocker and given the door several sharp raps. Jack exchanged a look with Sam. 'It'll be fine,' he whispered.

The front door was opened by a man who looked uncertainly from Jack to Sam for a moment, as if deciding what course of action to take before ushering them both in. As she passed through the door, something made Sam look up – a flicker of movement between the balustrades. She saw a woman looking down at her from the balcony above; the same woman with the unforgiving bob, her frosty blue eyes regarding Sam as she followed the man into the house.

'Come on through,' said the man. 'It's good to see you son,' he said, clapping Jack's back.

So this is Jack's dad, Sam mused. She had to admit, it was a surprise. She had expected a suave, older version of Jack, yet she was walking behind a slightly rotund man who was short, well, shorter than Jack anyway, with thinning hair that had been carefully styled to try and conceal a large bald patch at the back of his head. She noticed how red the patch looked; vulnerable somehow, much how she was feeling lately, not sure where she stood with Jack since Nick had left. She took in her surroundings as they moved through the house; the grand chandeliers hanging from the high ceilings, art work hanging from picture rails that looked like they belonged in a gallery – so different to the Ikea prints she'd picked out with her mother. It was all so old and expensive-looking and she suddenly felt overwhelmingly out of place in her Primark sandals and New Look dress.

'Come on through to the garden,' Jack's dad was now saying, turning to beam at Sam. 'The dahlias have just come into bloom.'

Sam gasped involuntarily as she stepped into the garden; it looked like something out of one of those period dramas. An array of plants fighting for space all bloomed in the afternoon sunshine and there was a pond filled with water lilies, looked over by the statue of a naked woman. It was all so breathtakingly beautiful.

'What do you think of the dahlias?' Sam looked blankly at the enquiring look on the older man's face. She didn't have a clue which ones were the dahlias.

'Yes, you've been incredibly busy, haven't you darling?' Sam whipped round to see the woman – Jack's mother, standing at the door to the garden, a cigarette in one hand.

'I'll get you an ashtray dear,' Jack's dad said. Sam noticed his voice sounded strained.

'Lovely to see you, sweetheart,' the woman said, stepping down into the garden, ignoring her husband. She went to Jack and tilted her head to one side, offering her cheek for him to kiss. Her eyes remained fixed on Sam.

'Mother, this is my girlfriend, Sam. Sam, my mother, Jane.'

'Nice to meet you,' Sam said, deciding against offering her hand to shake. It seemed so formal. She wondered if the woman recognised her, remembered giving her that frosty stare before shutting her out of view with her expensive, heavy curtains.

Jane nodded slowly, her thin lips stretched tightly into a smile that went nowhere near her eyes.

'And this is my dad, David.'

'Pleased to meet you, dear,' he said, doing a strange little bow.

'Let's sit outside, shall we? Such lovely weather,' said Jane, linking her arm through Jack's. Sam followed.

'Err ... I got you these,' said Sam, proffering a bunch of roses towards Jane.

'I told her not to bother, you could open a garden centre with what you've got here,' Jack laughed.

'Indeed,' Jane said. Sam followed her gaze to the wall of rose bushes, each one displaying spectacular blooms in pink, white and yellow.

'Put these in water, dear,' Jane said, holding out the bunch to

David. 'And could you get us some drinks?' She didn't even look at him as she spoke, which Sam found odd.

'So how are you finding Lincoln? Jack tells me you lived in London previously,' Jane asked, settling back in her chair and taking a long drag on her cigarette. Sam watched her flick the ash on the ground, ignoring the ashtray David had placed on the table beside her.

'I'm really liking it, thanks, it's much more peaceful than London.'

Jane took another long drag of her cigarette before grinding the stub into the ashtray. David immediately picked it up and went into the house where the sound of chinking glasses could soon be heard.

'I don't know why he bothers doing that,' said Jane, her eyes rolling upwards. She produced another cigarette from the sleeve of her cardigan and held it, unlit, between her fingers.

'Where do you come from?' she asked abruptly, her blue eyes – so like Jack's, but yet so different – bored into Sam, causing her to shift uncomfortably in her chair and cross, and then uncross her legs. From experience, she knew where this was going.

'Tooting, south London.'

'No, I meant originally?'

Sam closed her eyes briefly and took a deep breath. There were many occasions where she was made to feel *other*: on a school trip to Eastbourne, the old woman at the ice cream kiosk reaching over to touch her hair, like she was some kind of specimen; the seedy man in a nightclub, licking his lips before saying *hey sexy, I like exotic girls, where do you come from?* `Even more so in Lincoln; *where are you from? No, where are you reeeaaaallly from?*

China, I'm from China, you stupid fucking bitch. Where are you from?

'I was born and bred in London, and so was my mum. Po— My granddad was from Jamaica. I never knew my dad.' *There we go, bitch – satisfied? Or shall I get out the family tree for you?*

Jane nodded, apparently satisfied.

David approached the table and carefully set down a tray with a jug and glasses. The ashtray was also there, sparkling clean.

'Here we go, who's for Pimms?' he said, beaming at Sam. Jane brought the cigarette she was holding to her mouth, prompting David to retrieve a lighter from his trouser pocket. Bending down, he lit the cigarette.

'Would you believe I don't even smoke?' he said, smiling at Sam and revealing a row of crooked, yellow teeth.

Sam had to quicken her pace to keep up with Jack's long strides; he hadn't said a word since they'd left his parents' home. She glanced up at him now, wondering if she'd made him angry somehow, shown him up in front of his parents. Maybe not though; he'd been distant towards her since Nick left – acting all sullen; even after she thought they'd managed to clear the air (over two bottles of wine – her pleading forgiveness for her little stunt with the mug; pouring out her feelings about how much Nick freaked her out; how he had to leave otherwise she couldn't see a future for them both). She thought Jack had got it at last; finally understood that although he wanted the best for his friend, his friend, sadly, didn't wish the same for him. But the next morning, she woke up to find Jack had already left the house. No note with a silly drawing on the desk, or text message saying he would meet her for lunch. He was up and out early most mornings and back late – a 5 o'clock shadow on his usually smooth chin. He looked troubled.

When he was in, he would stay downstairs, waiting until she'd gone upstairs, and sneak into the bedroom when he thought she was asleep. She heard him, of course, but regulated her breathing to make him think he'd succeeded.

It had occurred to her that maybe he'd had enough of her and wanted to finish it, but then why take her to meet his parents? She glanced up at him again, his jaw clenched, he looked so unhappy. So she was surprised when he stopped abruptly and put his arms around her, holding her so tightly she gasped.

'I'm sorry,' he said, the words muffled against her neck.

'What for?' she asked, reaching up to gently touch his cheek.

'For my parents. For being a prick,' he said, with the faintest of smiles.

'Are you still angry with me about Nick?' Sam blurted out. She hated having to say his name but if another uncomfortable conversation was needed to make things right between them again, she was willing to have it.

'Nick?' he said, a look of genuine surprise on his face. 'It's not about him and I'm not angry with you,' he said, cupping her face in his hands. 'I could never be angry with you, well ... not too much.' Sam closed her eyes as he bent down to kiss her.

In a small booth towards the back of the Magna Carta, Jack finally opened up about what was troubling him; how he was set to fail his final year at uni and how ashamed he felt.

'You see, Sam, I'm not the great, perfect guy you thought I was – I'm a stupid, fucking failure,' he said, jabbing his finger savagely into his forehead. 'And I've got no excuse. I've had everything on a plate since the day I was born. I did well at school, not the top of the class or anything like that, but I did OK, enough to please the parents anyway. But uni's eluded me. I just can't get my head around it.'

Sam caught his hand and pulled it towards her, kissing each finger. 'Why didn't you just say you were struggling?'

'Because I'm the popular boy; the one who does well in everything,' he said with a sad smile.

'What will you do?' Sam asked, squeezing his hand.

'Fuck knows,' he shrugged. 'Maybe follow my dad into the antiques world? He has connections. That's the benefit of having successful parents,' he said bitterly.

'You are not a failure, OK?' Sam said firmly, learning forward and grasping his other hand.

'Well if you say it like that, then I suppose I can't be! I've just got to pluck up the courage to tell my parents. Dad will be OK, but my mother ... she's another kettle of fish altogether.'

Sam smiled. She hadn't heard the term 'kettle of fish' before, but caught the gist. Jane Sutton was a formidable and wholly unpleasant woman; even by her own standards, and she found the way she interacted with Jack's father strangely unsettling.

'Shall we stay here and get some dinner?' she said, her stomach beginning to rumble, and although she felt for Jack, she couldn't really understand why he was so bothered about uni; at least he had wealthy parents to fall back on. But looking at his sweet face now, she knew she would never say anything – how could he ever understand what it was like to be in real deep shit when he'd been cushioned by so much money?

'Could do, but I'd rather go home and cook you something nice – make up for being a jerk.'

Sam nodded and they both got up and left the Magna Carta.

They went into the Co-op where Jack picked up steaks and wine and whilst he was pondering over a Cabernet and a Malbec, Sam went off in search of a dessert. Halfway down an aisle, she smiled at the sight of a familiar figure, rummaging through various jars on a shelf, much to the annoyance of the young girl stacking a shelf nearby.

'Edith!' she exclaimed, taking in the elderly woman's pristine blouse, the sharp edges of her pleated skirt ironed to perfection, and her hair scraped back with a severe looking clasp. Sam was relieved to see her back to her former self.

Edith whipped round, her hard stare softening slightly when she recognised Sam.

'Well well, fancy seeing you here. Aren't you supposed to be at work?' The old woman said.

'Not today, Edi— Miss Mowbray. How are you?'

Edith gave an indignant sniff, 'Very well, thank you,' and she added, in a raised voice, 'I'd feel even better if I could get hold of the gravy granules that are actually in date!' This, she directed at the girl stacking a shelf opposite.

The girl turned her head towards Edith and gave her a withering look. 'As I've already said, all the items are in date and the ones with the shorter use-by dates are put to the front to reduce waste.'

'Well, I don't call one month an acceptable amount of time to get through a jar of gravy granules. Maybe if I had the misfortune of having a great oaf of a husband and a string of greedy little ankle grazers, guzzling gravy with their roast dinners like there was no tomorrow then yes, it is feasible that a jar could be got through in that amount of time. But I'm on my own, see, so tell me, how am I expected to get through this?!' Edith held up a jar of the gravy granules and shook it at the girl who rolled her eyes and stormed off, abandoning her shelf stacking duties.

'Here, let me get another one for you,' said Sam, struggling on tip toe to reach the jars at the back of the shelf.

'It's no use, I've tried that,' said Edith impatiently. 'They do the shelves like this on purpose. Bloody fascists!'

Sam muffled a laugh, and continued with trying to reach the jars. She was glad Edith couldn't see her; she didn't think the old woman would take kindly to her finding the situation so amusing.

'Can I be of assistance?' said Jack, appearing in front of Sam. He gave Edith one of his dazzling smiles which was met with a hard stare.

'This is Jack, my boyfriend,' said Sam, feeling a mixture of pride and embarrassment at saying the word 'boyfriend' out loud.

Edith gave him a cursory glance up and down. 'Well, you look like a big strapping lad, can you reach me that jar at the back there?' she nodded towards the shelf. Jack obliged, easily reaching one of the coveted jars and handing it to Edith. She gave a curt nod, her eyebrows raised slightly as her eyes swept momentarily over the contents of Jack's basket.

'Well, I haven't got time to stand here all day,' she said, by way of farewell. Glancing at Sam, she said, 'I will probably see you at the health centre, that's if you deign to show your face.'

'Of course, Miss Mowbray,' Sam said, delighted by the woman's blatant rudeness.

'Lovely to meet you, Miss Mowbray,' said Jack, giving her another dazzling smile. Edith sniffed and turning on her heel, stalked towards the till. She turned back once, throwing a curious glance in their direction. Sam gave a small wave but Edith did not reciprocate.

'Jeez!' said Jack, shaking his head as they left the shop. 'I can't believe that's the same woman you talk about so fondly. She's a dragon!'

'Yes,' said Sam, smiling. 'Yes, she is.'

As Edith looked on at the retreating couple, it suddenly clicked into place, she knew she'd seen that face before. The boy with the hero good looks and the angelic smile. Her memory wasn't what it used to be but she remembered the way he would study the girls when he thought no one was looking. She also remembered his needy little friend, trailing after him in the playground like his second shadow. Turning back to the counter, she slowly placed the items into her shopping trolley.

****

When they got home, Sam noticed a parcel had been pushed through the letterbox. Unable to think of anyone who might send her a gift, Sam ripped it open. Inside was her mother's pendant. With it was a handwritten note and an official letter from Children's Services.

> The lady said it was you what saved me and Lee and Mummy. And this is yours, becos I saw from the stairs you try to get it when Daddy was standing on your hand. I asked if I could send it back to you, to say thank you.
> Layla xxxxx (your sort of sister)

The official letter explained that as a result of her report, the house in Tooting had been visited, where the scrawny, hollow-eyed mother was found actively bleeding from wounds inflicted by Eddie. The children were malnourished and showing signs of abuse, so all three of them were moved to a shelter, while a warrant was out for Eddie's arrest.

Sam was awash with emotions. After all she and Jack had been through, it was great to finally have the pendant back and she was looking forward to giving it to her mother. She also felt a huge sense of relief that the children were safe and that she'd been part of rescuing them. But Eddie was out there. And if he had a list of names of people who might have acted to see his children removed from his care, Sam knew her name would be right at the top.

Chapter Forty

Sam placed the extra special M&S lasagne in the oven and went upstairs to take off her make-up. She had the place to herself as Jack was on a lads' weekend in London. She wondered if Nick would be joining him, probably, but she hadn't asked Jack. It seemed so much easier just not to bring up the subject of Nick, and then she could pretend for a while that he didn't exist. But despite her best efforts, he was still there, in the darkest recess of her thoughts – smiling his evil little smile, just for her.

However, she wasn't going to ruminate about him tonight, she promised herself. It was a rare weekend on her own in the house and, although she loved being with Jack, it was nice to have some time completely to herself. She had the evening planned: first of all, lasagne, washed down with a large glass of Chardonnay (already chilling in the fridge) followed by a soak in the bath and a catch up with her *Sex and the City* box set – or maybe just an early night; it had been a long day with an early shift at the health centre followed by an afternoon of lectures. But first of all she was going to take off her make-up – something she didn't usually do until just before going to bed. She didn't want Jack to see all her imperfections under the glare of the lights.

After scrubbing her face clean, she went into the bedroom to get her dressing gown. With it still being light outside, it took her a moment to notice that her bedside light was on, which was odd, she was always careful about switching off lights before she left the house and Jack had gone early, wanting to set off before the rush-hour traffic started. She walked round to her side of the bed and reached down to switch the light off. It was then that she noticed him. The little stone Imp, perched against the base of the lamp, grinning. Sam froze.

After the party, she'd put the Imp at the back of one of the desk drawers - out of sight, but never quite out of mind. She'd wanted to throw the evil little grotesque away, but somehow she could never bring herself to do it and often found herself pulling it out from its dark resting place and staring at it for what seemed like hours, running a finger over the contours of its inhuman body. But she always put it back.

Yet here it was. Its stone eyes fixed on hers. She was sure she could hear it chuckling.

Nick. She knew it had to be Nick. But hadn't he given the house keys back to Jack? Maybe not. Was there any way it could be Eddie? Playing a nasty game, messing with her mind before he pounced. She felt a chill then, creeping up the base of her spine, wending its way up through her chest and shoulders, wrapping around her temples and making them ache. What if he was here right now? Hidden from view, watching. She pinched the bridge of her nose tightly, tight enough to bring some clarity to the situation. *Get a fucking grip*, she told herself before picking up the Imp and hurling it across the room.

'You don't scare me, you fucking evil bastard!' she screamed, launching herself at the wardrobe doors and wrenching them open. She ran from room to room, like a whirlwind, opening every door and every cupboard before rushing downstairs to do the same. She wasn't scared anymore. She was on fire. She was invincible. If she encountered Nick or Eddie now, she knew she could kill either of them. Plunge her acrylic tipped thumbs into their eyes, piercing them as easily as balloons.

Finding nothing, she ran back upstairs and started the process again. When she had finished, she pressed her forehead into the wall, hoping the cool sensation would lower the raging fire inside her. She willed her ragged breathing to slow and, after a few moments, was beginning to feel calmer but then the shrill beeping of the smoke alarm started, making her head jerk back uncomfortably and the flow of adrenaline return.

In the kitchen, she slid slowly down the wall until she was in a crouching position and again, focussed on regulating her breathing, grateful for the silence having dealt violently with the alarm and taken the burnt lasagne out of the oven. Looking up, she could see that the smoke alarm was beyond repair. She also noticed the surrounding ceiling hadn't fared too well either, with dents and scrapes visible from where she'd missed her target with the household broom. She cradled her head in her arms for a moment, feeling totally exhausted now the adrenaline had left her body. After counting to a hundred, she got up and went to inspect the lasagne. A quick sift through the blackened remnants revealed there was no point in trying to salvage any of it. At least there was the Chardonnay.

She took the wine into the living room and poured a large glass. Downing it in one go, she immediately poured another. It wasn't until she was halfway through the third glass that she finally began to feel the effects of the alcohol ebbing through her veins and making her feel fuzzy. Her eyelids fluttered a few times before becoming too heavy to open.

She sat up on the sofa feeling momentarily disorientated before her consciousness caught up. It was dark outside and a glance at the clock told her it was now 11pm. The cold chill she'd felt earlier returned and she pulled a cushion to her, hugging it tightly for comfort. She didn't feel invincible anymore. The thought of staying in the house alone all night suddenly terrified her – she knew she couldn't do it and the only place she could go now was to her mother's.

****

Sam considered ringing the doorbell but then instantly decided against it. Even though she wasn't living there anymore, her mother would never expect her to wait to be let in and besides, it was now after midnight. Entering the small living room, she was surprised to find it in darkness. Her mother usually left the light on. Fumbling for the switch, she felt a slight pang of anxiety run through her veins.

Something wasn't right. Had she run away from the spectre of

Eddie only to find him here?

An unfamiliar shape loomed in the darkness, causing her to gasp as she clawed desperately at the wall to find the switch. Where the hell was it? She cursed inwardly. The shape seemed to be closer now. Was it moving? Finally, she felt the cold plastic of the socket and jabbed at the switch, illuminating the room and breaking off one of her acrylic nails in the process.

Surveying the room, she cursed silently to herself for being so stupid. The threatening shape was instantly transformed by the light into a box, sitting on the kitchen table. Moving towards it, she peered into the already opened package: 'Electric home steaming hair kit', read the label. Sam smiled; her mother had been going on about having one for ages.

Relieved, she inhaled deeply, but abruptly stopped mid-breath. Finding the Imp out of its usual hiding place had freaked her out more than she thought.

Something about this place still wasn't right though. She couldn't quite put her finger on it. Everything was in its usual spot, she noted, walking into the kitchen and surveying the small area. She forced herself to take a couple of deep breaths in an attempt to calm her nerves. Feeling like a glass of milk (something she thought she'd long grown out of), she opened the fridge and there on the middle shelf was the familiar blue bowl – the one designated for making pancake batter.

'Strange,' Sam muttered to herself, bringing the bowl out and setting it on the counter. It wasn't like her mother to make pancakes for herself and she couldn't have known that Sam would be paying an unexpected visit. Instinctively, she peeled back the cling film stretched tight over the bowl and brought it up to her face. Almost immediately, the comforting, familiar smell enveloped her nostrils and she no longer cared why her mother had made up the batter, she was just glad that she had.

Tip toeing up the stairs, Sam found herself pausing outside her mother's room and again had the feeling that something was different somehow. Not right. She pressed her ear against the door and listened. Silence. She shook her head and went to her room;

her nerves were frayed from the events of the evening and now her imagination had gone into overdrive. *Got to get a grip* was her last thought as she finally drifted into sleep.

Sam woke the next morning with a jolt. She'd slept fitfully, with every lapse into deep sleep interrupted and resulting in periods of wakeful confusion as she tried to make sense of the short, crazy dreams she was having. In the last one, her mother had been talking to Pops, pleading with him to give her one more chance as she cradled a baby in one hand and a bottle of vodka in the other. Pops had sprung from his chair all sprightly – nothing like the skeletal form with the shrunken eyes he had become in the last few weeks of his life – and was shouting at her mother as he tried but failed to grab the baby.

She sat up in bed, thankful for the clear image of Pops, despite the unsettling dream. It was strange but she couldn't help feeling that she'd heard another male voice in her dreams. But it didn't seem like a dream – it felt real and much closer.

She was about to lay back down when she heard it. It was done very quietly and she could've easily been mistaken. Except for the familiar squeak the front door made as it swung shut; it didn't matter how slowly or carefully it was closed. It always made that sound.

Sam jumped out of bed and rushed to the window, dragging the curtains to one side. She looked to the left and saw the street was deserted as far as the eye could see. Her eyes darted to the other side and just caught sight of a flash of blue disappearing into Occupation Road.

Pulling on her dressing gown, Sam ran downstairs, nearly crashing into her mother at the bottom in the process.

'Whoa! What's got into you?' her mother said, smiling as she caught Sam in an embrace.

'Didn't you hear the door?' Sam replied, pulling away from her mother, noting how radiant she looked. Positively blooming.

'The door? Oh, it was just the local paper. Seems to come earlier every day!' she said, holding up the *Lincolnshire Herald* as evidence.

Sam looked at her mother suspiciously, wondering why the hell she was talking in that weird sing-song voice. Then an awful thought suddenly struck her, causing a chill that seeped deep into her bones. What if she had started using again? But no, her eyes were clear and she wasn't shaking and unsteady. She just seemed ... happy.

'You don't seem that surprised to see me.'

'Well, your jacket and bag kind of gave it away,' her mother laughed, pointing to the neat row of hooks at the bottom of the stairs.

'You look different,' Sam said, stepping closer to her mother.

'How so?'

'Just ... really good.'

'Oh,' her mother said, suddenly flustered as she brought her hands up to her face. 'It's probably the new face cream I'm using,' she said, patting her cheeks. 'I'll put the kettle on,' she said, turning towards the kitchen.

'How come you made pancake batter?' Sam wasn't about to let her mother off the hook that easily. She noticed her mother hesitate before picking up the kettle and placing it under the tap. An awkward silence prevailed, which Sam was determined not to fill, as she leant back against the counter to scrutinise her mother with folded arms. She was wearing a dressing gown Sam hadn't seen before – lacy and expensive looking, and her hair was up in a hastily put together bun, a few escaped tendrils curling round the nape of her slim neck. Briefly, Sam was tempted to place her hands around that slim neck, as she had before. To tighten her grip and render that throat incapable of pulling in oxygen. Just briefly.

'Do I need a reason to make myself pancakes?' her mother said, turning round to face Sam. She was smiling, but Sam thought she noted an edge to her mother's voice that hadn't been there before and wondered if somehow, her mum had read her thoughts. She hoped not. She unfolded her arms, suddenly conscious of her body language.

'No, but it's not something you would usually do, is it?'

'And how could you possibly know that, Sammy?' her mother said, slamming the kettle onto its base. No mistaking the edge to her voice this time. 'You're never here! But do you know what? It's ok. I've got used to being here on my own. And if I want to make myself pancakes, I bloody well will!'

There was another silence whilst mother and daughter stared each other out from opposite sides of the tiny kitchen. And then came the sound of laughter. Sam wasn't sure who started first, but she soon found herself bent double, clutching her sides as tears rolled down her cheeks and then her mother held out her arms and Sam rushed into them, not knowing until then how much she needed to be held; to be reassured that everything was going to be OK.

Later, sitting at the table, watching the steam rising from the pancakes piled high on the plate; Sam couldn't remember a time when she felt so close to her mother. She had left in such a rush; she'd forgotten to bring the pendant. But she knew that an explanation would be needed when she did give it back and that would involve having to talk about Eddie. So she was grateful for just being able to sit together, eating pancakes and enjoying the peace while it lasted.

Chapter Forty One

Sam entered the health centre earlier than usual; she'd ended up staying at her mother's for the remainder of the weekend, not wanting to return to Jack's empty home. She didn't think she could face it if the imp had somehow moved again and she wasn't even sure where it had fallen when she'd thrown it. She would have to go there straight after her shift finished though, to clear up the mess she'd made before Jack returned that evening. Not for the first time, she wondered whether to tell him about the imp being moved and that she was sure it must have something to do with Nick, but then that would invariably lead to Jack defending him, as he always did.

'Morning.'

Sam looked up, jolted from her thoughts. It was Edith, standing rod straight in front of her.

'Good morning, Miss Mowbray,' Sam smiled. She looked at the list on the screen.

'You're seeing Dr Cunningham; she's running on time so should call you in soon.'

'I should hope so too, seeing as I'm first on the list! I really don't care much for Dr Cunningham's sloppy timekeeping. Not a patch on Dr Simmons.'

'I'm sorry to hear that, Miss Mowbray. I do try my best,' said Frances, who'd managed to walk right up to Edith without her noticing. She looked over at Sam and winked.

Edith went to follow Frances to her consultation room but stopped abruptly and turned back to face Sam.

'Meant to say, I remember your young man.'

'What was that, Miss Mowbray?' said Sam, looking up from her computer screen.

'The man I saw you with in the Co-op. I assume you're courting?'

'Oh, you mean Jack? Yes, we're ... courting,' she said, smiling at the old-fashioned term.

'Yes, yes,' said Edith impatiently, 'I was a dinner lady at the school he went to. I remember him well now, one of the popular ones with his looks. He liked messing around with the girls. You'd best keep an eye on him, he's trouble.'

Before Sam could say anything, Edith turned on her heel after Frances.

Sam placed the moussaka in the oven and ran upstairs to have a quick shower. Jack was due back any time now and it had taken longer than expected to tidy up, with the company of the radio turned up loud to distract her from thinking too deeply about her state of mind at the time she'd created the mess. But it was all tidy now. Everything back in its place, apart from the imp whom she found lying face down under the window. She left him propped up against the mirror on the desk: a place she could keep an eye on him.

'Delicious,' Jack said later, taking another large mouthful from his plate. 'I should go away more often.' Sam looked up from her plate to see him winking.

'Watch it, cheeky,' she said with a laugh; 'and the moussaka's thanks to M&S, I'm afraid.'

'Well, here's to M&S,' Jack said. Sam laughed as they clinked their wine glasses. It was so nice to be just the two of them – finally. And she was glad she hadn't said anything about the imp, it would've only made for a bad atmosphere between them.

'What did you get up to then?' she asked, taking a sip of wine.

'We-ell, that would be telling,' Jack said, tapping the side of his nose.

'No, really, I want to know,' she said, trying to keep her tone light. Jack put his fork down and reached for her hand.

'C'mon, Sam, I already told you it was for Jimmy's birthday. He booked an escape room experience, it was a right laugh and in between that and going to watch the rugby, we sat in pubs and drank too much. And if you're wondering if Nick was there, then the answer's no. I haven't seen him since he left after the party.'

Sam nodded. She already knew Nick hadn't gone away. He'd been here. Playing his nasty games.

'Well, I might have to put a stop to you going away. I need you here where I can keep an eye on you.'

She'd meant it as a joke, but although Jack kept his hand in hers, she felt his grip loosen.

'What do you mean, keep an eye on me?'

'Oh it's nothing, I'm only joking,' said Sam quickly. She so desperately wanted to keep things good between them: a new start now that Nick had left. 'It's just something Edith said today, about recognising you. She was a dinner lady at your school.'

Jack raised an eyebrow. 'Really?' he said, sitting back in his chair. 'Can't say I remember her. What did she say?'

Sam shrugged. 'Only that you used to mess around with the girls and that I should keep an eye on you.' She laughed but Jack didn't join her, he just sat there, looking at her quizzically.

'I don't know why she'd say that,' he said eventually. 'Fucking bitter spinster.'

Sam was shocked by the sudden vehemence in Jack's voice.

'Mind you, all the dinner ladies were dragons,' he added, standing abruptly and collecting their plates. 'I think it's part of the job description.'

Sam watched as he placed the dishes in the sink and started to wash up. His white T-shirt showed off the beautiful contours of his shoulder blades and his tanned, lean arms. She loved his fluid movements, the way he stood with his head bent in concentration. She loved him.

Moving towards him, she circled her arms round his waist. She felt his body stiffen slightly but kept holding him till she felt him relax.

'Coffee?' he asked, turning round to face her. She shook her head.

'No, but there is something else I'd like,' she said, taking his hand.

Later, as they lay in bed, she was about to ask Jack why he'd got so angry about Edith's comment. It wasn't as if it affected her feelings for him in any way. But then her phone pinged. It was her mother – an invite for pancakes and coffee at 11 am the following Sunday. Sam stared at the message, wondering why her mother had suddenly taken to sending her formal invites when she was used to popping over whenever she felt like it.

'Oh well, pancakes and coffee it is,' said Jack when she showed him the message. 'Maybe she's just trying to establish a more formal arrangement for visiting – she probably just wants to make sure you don't catch her in a compromising position!'

'You mean with another man?' Sam sat up in bed. 'No way! She would've told me!'

But then she remembered how things didn't feel quite right on her last visit; the flash of blue disappearing into Occupation Road; the strange, awkward interaction with her mother and the pancake batter; and suddenly she wasn't so sure.

Chapter Forty Two

Lincolnshire Herald

Sarah Hollins: Police Re-Enactment to Go Ahead

Sarah Hollins has now been missing for six months and the police have admitted that they are struggling to find any leads in the case. She seems to have disappeared without trace. They are planning to re-enact the last known hours of her life, in the hopes that this will trigger a memory for any potential witnesses. Were you in Lincoln that day? Did you see a girl alone or with someone? Can you be there next Friday to see if it triggers a memory? Get in touch to tell us your story. She was wearing jeans and a bright red T-shirt with blue flowers as well as wedged shoes.

Sam looked at the young woman staring back at her from the paper; her eyes gleaming and full of life. She looked like a nice person, Sam thought, absently tracing the outline of the now familiar picture of Sarah Hollins with her index finger.

'All ready?'

Sam jumped at the sound of Jack's voice, not having heard him come down the stairs and enter the kitchen. Placing her coffee mug down on the newspaper article, obscuring the picture of Sarah Hollins, she smiled and said, 'Yes, I'm ready.'

Standing outside the two- up two-down, Sam looked up at Jack and shrugged her shoulders before giving the door a few short raps. It was strange knocking at her own door – her mother's door now – but it felt too intrusive to just let herself in. It would be something she'd just have to get used to.

She knew something was up as soon as she stepped inside. Her mother looked stunning, wearing a dress she hadn't seen before; her long hair flowing in loosely tonged curls and her nails painted in a hot red shade.

'What's all this in aid of then?' she said grudgingly. 'Is this a special occasion or something?'

As if on cue, there came the sound of the toilet flushing. Sam's head snapped up in the direction of the stairs. So that was the reason her mother was all dolled up; Jack was right after all, she'd found herself a new man. But what if he turned out to be like all the rest? She pushed the thought away and forced a smile. If he was a bastard, she'd know straightaway and she'd deal with it.

'It sounds like there's something you need to tell me,' she said in a teasing tone, expecting her mother to break into a huge smile. But she wasn't smiling and had started twisting her hands together in that way of hers. Sam's heart started to beat rapidly, memories of Eddie's many returns shattering her expectations.

'Mum?' she prompted, trying to keep her voice even. Still, her mother didn't respond, just carried on staring back at her with a stupid expression on her face. Sam felt it then, the overwhelming urge to grab her mother's shoulders and shake a response out of her. Her hands started to twitch so she stuffed them in her jeans' pockets, finding the pendant within. Now didn't feel the moment to return it.

'Denise? Are you OK?' said Jack. Her mother's eyes flickered in his direction and she opened her mouth to speak but then came the sound of footsteps on the stairs.

'Morning,' he said, flashing a grin at Sam as he moved towards Denise, placing an arm proprietarily around her waist. Sam felt herself begin to sway and reached out to the dining table to steady herself. She looked over to Jack for reassurance, that she was somehow dreaming or seeing things. But he didn't return her gaze; he too was staring. She followed the direction of Jack's eyes to him: the new man in her mother's life.

Nick.

She let herself be ushered onto a dining chair. She drank coffee and ate a pancake from the plate offered, mechanically chewing the pieces to a mush till they could be swallowed. She listened to the sound of her mother's voice, nervously explaining how she hadn't planned this. Neither of them had. They'd bumped into each other in the town centre and gone for a coffee. They'd got on so well, they'd arranged to meet the very next day for lunch and it had progressed from there. They'd discussed the age gap and both agreed it didn't matter; life was too short to pass up on happiness.

'I wanted to tell you, Sammy, I really did,' she heard her mother say as she reached forward to hold her hand. Sam snatched her arm away.

'But Nick thought it would be best if we told you both together,' her mother carried on in a faltering voice.

I bet he did, Sam thought, glancing briefly in Nick's direction, taking care not to look at his face. He had his hand casually draped round the back of her mother's chair. Suddenly Sam knew why the house hadn't felt right on her last visit. She thought she might be sick then, might actually choke on the piece of pancake in her mouth. She knew she'd never be able to eat them again and concentrated on swallowing the last mouthful before speaking.

'He was here last weekend, wasn't he? The night I stayed over,' she said, looking directly at her mother for the first time since Nick made his grand entrance.

'Yes.'

'Why didn't you tell me then?'

'I ... I should have. I'm sorry,' her mother said, glancing at Nick. 'It's just that Nick said you didn't hit it off so I thought it would be best to wait. And we were having such a nice weekend, Sammy, I can't remember the last time we spent so much time together. I just didn't want to spoil it.'

Sam sunk back into her chair, avoiding her mother's hand as she made another attempt to reach out to her.

'Please, Sammy, it's not such a big deal, is it?'

'What about Andrea?' Sam said, ignoring her mother as she looked Nick directly in the eyes. Those cruel, little eyes.

'We split up.'

'Really? I thought you'd moved in with her.'

'I did for a while but it didn't work out.'

Sam held his gaze, determined not to blink.

'It's true, Sam, he's renting a bedsit. I helped him move.'

They all looked at Jack who, until then, hadn't spoken a word; his gaze fixed steadily on Nick, his expression inscrutable. Sam's spirits plummeted further at the thought of Jack meeting up with Nick without her knowledge and the fact that he was helping him meant they must be on amicable terms. It had been too much to hope that she could break their bond after all.

'So, he's living here now?' Sam asked tersely, breaking the heavy silence that prevailed.

'No, Sammy,' said her mother at the same time as Nick said, 'Not yet.'

Sam stared at the two of them in disgust before grabbing Jack's hand.

'Come on, we're leaving.'

'I'll call you Sammy,' her mother said, as Sam wrenched open the front door. She hesitated and looked back to see her mother's pleading expression. She dug into her jeans pocket and produced the pendant.

'Here, a little present for you,' she said through clenched teeth, practically flinging the pendant into her mother's hand. As Denise gasped in delight, and started to ask questions, all Sam noticed was Nick standing there, a leering, lascivious grin on his face. She shuddered and stumbled out of the door.

She was managing to keep it together, putting one foot in front of the other, breathing in, 1, 2, 3, out, 1, 2, 3, until Jack stopped walking and pulled her into his arms, holding her whilst she screamed into his chest and tightening his grip around her till she finally stopped trembling. They remained silent and Sam counted the reliable beats of Jack's heart until she was able to regulate her breathing. She pulled away and, without a word, they carried on walking.

'So, you really didn't know?' Sam finally said, after gulping down the last of the wine in her glass. Jack shook his head slowly, refilling her glass from the bottle he'd bought. They were sitting in the Magna Carta and it wasn't until she began to feel the dulling effects of the alcohol that she felt she could ask the question.

'Jeez, Sam, do you really think I'd keep something like that from you?'

'Well, you didn't tell me about helping him move,' she spat back at him; she couldn't help it.

'I didn't tell you because every time I mention his name, you flip.'

'No I don't!'

'You do! Your mood changes and you shut down, so I've just got used to not mentioning him and that way we can pretend he doesn't exist. Isn't that what you wanted?'

No, I don't want you to pretend, I want it to be real! she wanted to hurl back at him. Instead, she squeezed her eyes shut for a few seconds, willing herself to stay calm.

'I don't want him near my mum, Jack, she's vulnerable,' she said, her eyes still closed.

'I know. But so is he. Look, I'll go and talk to him. I'll make him see sense, I promise.' She felt his hand grip hers. 'Sam? I promise. OK?'

Sam opened her eyes and nodded.

Chapter Forty Three

Sam walked out of the cathedral, blinking as her eyes adjusted to the bright sun. She'd lost track of the times she'd been inside the cool, dark morning chapel which she'd started regularly attending again since that dreadful Sunday morning two weeks ago, trying to blot out the sight of Nick; the cruel glint in his eyes as he draped his arm proprietorially around her mother. A nauseous lump formed in her throat each time she let herself think about it.

She hadn't spoken to her mother since; not answered her calls or returned her messages. The only way she could keep even vaguely sane was to cast her mother and that little creep from her mind. Jack had spoken to him but not had much luck as far as she was aware; they'd argued and now weren't on speaking terms – at least that was a positive.

She could only hope that her stupid, gullible mother would soon see sense and end it and put her own flesh and blood first, just this once.

She stopped off at the Co-op on the way back and picked up a packet of coffee and croissants; the usual weekend breakfast they shared whilst watching the morning cookery programmes. Her heart lifted at the thought of snuggling up to Jack on the settee before deciding how they'd spend the rest of the day – her almost perfect life. If it wasn't for *him*.

She had her key poised, ready to insert into the front door, but before she could, it was flung open and Nick came stumbling out.

'Hey!' she shouted as he barged past her, almost sending her flying into the hedge. He glanced in her direction and sneered.

'I actually pity you,' he shouted, before storming off.

'Fuck you!' she screamed after him, not caring if the whole street heard. Slamming the gate closed, she walked back towards the door, shaking her head in bewilderment at the audacity of the creep; he was even wearing Jack's blue jacket.

Shutting the door behind her, she was about to call out to Jack, but stopped when she saw him storming down the stairs, hands clenched into fists, his face so contorted with anger, Sam hardly recognised him. It took a moment before he noticed her and when he did, he stopped abruptly, a startled expression on his face and he lowered his gaze. He seemed uncomfortable, almost embarrassed.

'Hi,' he said, running a hand through his hair, recovering himself. After a moment's hesitation, he moved to stand in front of her. His hands were still clenched, so she took them in hers, gently unfurling them.

'What is it? Why was he here?'

She watched with a growing sense of dread as Jack shook his head, his eyes cast downwards.

'Jack, what's wrong?'

'We ... er, I need to sit down, get my head around this.'

Sam led him towards the kitchen table, where he sat, slumped with his head in his hands. She watched him, arms folded, and braced herself for whatever he was about to say, counting down in her head from twenty. But when she'd got to nine and he still hadn't said anything or made an attempt to lift his head, she busied herself with making coffee, putting an extra scoop in the cafetière; it needed to be strong. Whatever Jack was about to say, she needed to be prepared. Glancing over at him, she could see he was trembling slightly and wondered what on earth it could be. He was beginning to scare her.

He didn't notice her putting the croissants on the table, or the mug of coffee she placed in front of him. There was no reaction whatsoever. She started to imagine the worst case scenario; maybe Nick had proposed to her mother, or got her pregnant. The latter definitely being the very worst, the one thought that kept inveigling its way into her head ever since she'd found out about their dirty little affair. She felt the beginnings of a scream at the back of her throat and took a gulp of coffee which was too hot and scorched her mouth. At least it suppressed the scream. For now.

Maybe Jack would go on sitting there with his head in his hands. For one mad moment, she hoped he wouldn't say anything and then she wouldn't know and they could continue living in their little bubble; carrying on as if everything was just fine. Except of course that couldn't happen. She had to know. Jack looked up then, as if reading her thoughts. He looked so pale and his eyes had lost their usual sparkle. She reached her arm out towards him.

'He had a visit from the police,' he said flatly.

'What?' She slammed down her coffee mug, her other arm retreating from his as if it were contagious. Whatever he was about to say, she wasn't expecting *that*. 'What about?' she asked, wondering why he couldn't meet her gaze and, when he didn't reply, an awful thought flitted through her mind, making her cold.

'Is it to do with my mum?' she said with growing trepidation and when he still didn't reply, she knew.

'Oh my God, what has he done? I've got to see her!' she wailed, rushing to grab her trainers from the shoe rack. She cursed herself for not having done more to protect her mother from Nick, how could she have been so stupid?

She angrily wiped the tears that blurred her vision and stumbled towards the door, but stopped when she felt Jack's steadying hands firmly on her shoulders.

'Sam, slow down, it has nothing to do with your mother,' he said, turning her around to face him. 'It's about the missing woman, Sarah Hollins. The police think Nick might be involved.'

Chapter Forty Four

Stunned, Sam let herself be led back to the kitchen where she lowered herself shakily onto the chair. Needing something to do with her hands, she clasped the coffee mug in front of her, feeling the warmth seep into her skin. Not that it offered any comfort.

She blinked a few times, trying to process the unexpected information.

'What exactly did he say to you?'

'Just that he doesn't know anything. He wanted me to come to the station and provide an alibi for the time she went missing, but I wasn't with him that evening.'

'He wanted you to lie?' She gripped the mug harder, resisting the urge to hurl it at the wall. 'You don't fucking believe him, do you?' She could hear the hysterical tone in her voice and hated herself for it.

'Christ, I don't know, Sam. He wanted me to provide a false alibi, to lie to the police. I feel like I don't know him at all anymore. Not since he started seeing your mother behind my back.'

'Don't you mean behind *my* back?' Sam said, through gritted teeth, struggling to control her anger. Somewhere inside her, she knew this wasn't Jack's fault. She didn't want to be angry at him, but she couldn't help it. How could he be so blind to the fact that Nick was not only a warped little creep, but could actually be dangerous? She forced herself to take a deep breath.

'So where was he really?'

'What? Oh, when Sarah disappeared? He said he can't remember.'

'And doesn't that worry you?' She gripped the mug harder still, her knuckles paling.

'Of course it fucking does!' He was shouting now. Good. She wanted him to be as angry as she was. Angry with himself for being such an idiot to count Nick as a friend.

'So does my mum know anything about this?!' she shouted back. 'Did it occur to you that she could be in danger?'

She had finally failed in her efforts to stay calm, slamming her fists on the table. She stood up, knocking her chair over in the process. She knew where she had to be.

'Where are you going?'

'Where do you think?' she snapped, reaching for the front door handle. 'I have to tell my mum! I'll have to stay over and sort out getting the locks changed.'

'Hang on, don't you think that's a bit drastic?'

'No! No I don't!' Sam screamed, shrugging off Jack's attempts to hold her. 'He has a track record, or have you forgotten? *The girl from school?* Or maybe he only goes for women called Sarah then my mum doesn't have anything to worry about!'

'You're being irrational now. Sam, please!'

'*Sam please, Sam please what?*' She pushed Jack away as he attempted again to take hold of her.

'He's dangerous, Jack. I know it.'

'I'll come with you,' he said, as she got to the front door. She whirled round, about to scream no. That she would sort this out on her own. But the way he looked at her - the concern conveyed in his beautiful blue eyes, went some way to dampening the mounting fury inside her.

'I'm sorry,' she whispered finally, pulling him to her and burying her head in his chest. She stood completely still for a moment, listening to the rapid beating of his heart. 'I don't mean to take this out on you. I know you're scared, aren't you? You don't have to pretend you're not.'

'I don't know what to think at the moment, Sam. I just can't believe Nick could be involved.'

His voice broke slightly and Sam felt his chest shudder as he tried to contain his tears.

Less than half an hour later, they pulled up outside Denise's house. Sam was about to open the car door but stopped as Jack placed his hand gently over hers.

'Please break this to her gently,' he said. 'I know you hate the idea of her and Nick together, but she cares for him and she doesn't deserve this.'

Sam couldn't be sure how she would react when she saw her mother, but nodded. After several knocks at the door with no answer, she pulled her set of keys from her bag.

'Mum?' she called tentatively, before moving through the front room into the kitchen. 'Mum?' she called again from the bottom of the stairs. As there was no response, she climbed the stairs and stopped outside her mother's bedroom, listening for any signs of life from the other side of the door. There was only silence, so she opened it. Nothing out of the ordinary, she thought, her eyes sweeping the room. She moved towards the bed to straighten the crumpled duvet but stopped when she felt her phone vibrate in her pocket.

Hi Sammy, I'm sure you've heard about Nick by now. I don't want to believe it, it's crazy. I've gone away for a few days to sort my head out. Please don't worry about me. I'll be in touch soon. Thank you for getting the pendant back for me, I don't know how you did it but it's the only thing keeping me going.
Mum x

She stared at the phone for a few moments, deliberating whether to text back. She had so many questions to ask – where would her mother have gone? How would she fend for herself? Her fingers hovered over the screen, but then what was the point? She didn't know her mother anymore; she was a stranger to her ever since she'd started a sleazy affair with Nick. Closing the door to her mother's room, she walked heavily back down the stairs.

Chapter Forty Five

The following days dragged by with no further news about Nick's involvement with the missing woman and, despite the calls and texts to her mother, Sam still had no idea where she was. She'd briefly considered going to the police and had discussed it with Jack. He'd been supportive about it – told her to do what she thought best, but she could tell by the expression on his face that he thought she was getting prematurely worked up. And he was probably right; her mother was a grown woman after all and if she needed some space to sort her head out, then Sam would leave her to do just that. Besides, she didn't have much choice in the matter. But the niggling thought kept creeping back, uninvited. The feeling that she was missing something.

The alarm went off at 7 am, signifying yet another morning with no communication from her mother; over a week now and the longest she'd gone without being in contact. Sam reached over to switch off the alarm and then turned over to cuddle up to Jack for a few minutes before getting in the shower. But his side was empty, a note left on his pillow to say he'd gone out early to go to an antiques fair with his dad. She vaguely remembered him talking about it now, nodding her head distractedly over dinner; her thoughts all the while on her mother's whereabouts.

She lay back on her pillow and sighed, missing her usual morning cuddle with Jack, feeling his arms around her was the best part of the day. Slowly, she got up and made her way into the bathroom to get ready for work.

Anna was leaning on the counter when Sam entered the staff room, engrossed with something in the *Lincoln Gazette*.

'Morning,' said Sam when it was apparent Anna hadn't noticed her.

Anna looked up, a blank expression on her face before she smiled.

'Oh hi, Sam.'

'Something interesting?' Sam asked, moving towards Anna and peering down at the paper.

'It's about Sarah, the missing girl,' Anna said, pointing to the article. 'The police finally have a suspect.'

She carried on speaking but Sam didn't hear her as she craned her neck over the paper, only just managing to restrain herself from grabbing it out of Anna's hands. The article stated that a Caucasian man in his late twenties had been arrested yesterday evening in connection with the disappearance of Sarah Hollins.

'Hopefully they can find out what happened to Sarah and give some closure to the family. It's such a shame her mother isn't here to see this.'

Sam nodded numbly, her eyes fixed on the article. So there it was, in black and white: the affirmation that she was right about Nick. She wondered if Jack knew.

She walked back to her desk and looked at the list of appointments. Edith had been a no-show which was strange; she never missed an appointment.

Time seemed to go ever so slowly as Sam checked in patients, made further appointments and answered enquiries, all on automatic whilst her mind whirred with the news. She'd sent Jack several messages, but he hadn't replied. Finally, he would now have to face up to the fact that his so-called friend was an evil bastard. She was relieved that at least he'd sorted out changing the locks, a sure sign that he was taking the recent revelation seriously.

Finally, her phone pinged with a message, it was Jack.

Hi baby, so sorry I've only been able to message u now but signal really bad here. I've stayed on a bit longer with dad, so don't wait for me to have dinner. Btw, I can't believe it about Nick, it's fucking crazy! Talk when I'm back.

She replied before tucking her phone in her bag and retrieving a packet of paracetamol. Her temples felt tight with tension – the usual precursor to a migraine and she wanted to nip it in the bud.

When her shift was over, Sam couldn't face the thought of going back to an empty house so she headed to her special place; the one place where she could feel close to Pops.

The musky scent of timeworn stone enveloped her with a welcome familiarity and she paused for a moment, taking in the magnitude of her surroundings. Instead of turning into the morning chapel, she found herself drawn to the back of the cathedral, where she stopped and looked up at the little creature grinning down at her. She returned his smile.

'Cheeky little fellow, isn't he?'

Sam jumped at the sight of the vicar who had sidled up to her from nowhere.

'I wouldn't know,' she said curtly, annoyed by the intrusion, and started to make her retreat, afraid that he might start preaching to her.

'Have you seen his friend?'

Sam stopped and turned back.

'Up there, just to the right, see?' She followed the direction of the vicar's pointing finger.

It took only a moment to locate the other grotesque, its hooded eyes looking down at her from a lopsided face. Two horns ran centrally from its forehead and curled sideways to meet long, pointed ears. Unlike the imp, it wasn't grinning.

'Not many people notice that one,' the vicar said, obviously pleased to have caught her attention. 'I like to point him out,' and with a brief nod, he walked past Sam to greet a parishioner.

She stood planted to the spot for some time, wondering how she could have missed the sinister creature staring down at her. That niggling feeling she hadn't been able to shake since her mother had gone AWOL had now changed to an insidious sensation that invaded her body and made her shiver.

Eventually, she walked back to the morning chapel and, after lighting a candle for Pops, she took a seat in one of the wooden pews. Closing her eyes, she tried to focus her mind and hold onto the vague recollection that had been floating around her subconscious.

The first thing she noticed on opening her eyes was the other candle in the sand pit, placed next to hers. The second thing was that the main door to the cathedral had been left ajar, causing a gust of wind to disturb the flames, threatening to extinguish them completely. Sam jumped up and ran towards the entrance, pushing her way through a group of annoying tourists that hindered her progression. Standing outside, she surveyed the area in mounting desperation: an old couple, walking with faltering steps across the cobbles; a man perched on the wall, watching his dog; a figure in a blue jacket in the distance, weaving through the crowds. And then it clicked – the image that hovered tantalizingly on the periphery of her mind.

She ran as fast as she could up Steep Hill, only stopping when she got to her mother's front door. Feeling sick from the exertion, she fumbled in her bag, praying the set of keys were still there and that she hadn't left them in the other bag she often used. Thankfully they were and, with a trembling hand, she let herself in.

Her legs wobbled as she took the stairs two at a time. Entering her mother's room, she looked behind the door and saw it was indeed what she had glimpsed when she was last there – the same blue jacket. Stepping closer, she ran her hands down the insides and pulled out the tickets to the student comedy night they'd gone to. Leaning in, she rested her head on the jacket and inhaled the familiar scent.

Jack's scent.

How had she not noticed it before? Taking the jacket off the hook, she held it to her and slid slowly down to the floor, determined not to move until she'd worked things out in her head. Pulling out her phone, she called Jack; there would be some explanation as to why his jacket was in her mother's room, she just needed to hear his voice to reassure her. No answer. She tried again. And again. The wall felt good behind her, something hard and unmovable that made her feel secure but after a while, she started to feel an ache at the back of her head and became aware that she was banging it against the wall over and over again. She stopped, but soon realised it felt better to carry on – the rhythmical thud felt soothing.

It was in between the rhythmical thuds that she heard it – the unmistakable squeaking of the front door. She froze and listened for any further movement, wondering if she could be so stupid as to have left the front door open. Slowly, she eased herself up from the floor and peered round the door.

Hovering at the top of the stairs, she was only met with silence; making her wonder if she'd been mistaken. Carefully avoiding the step with the loose floorboard, she slowly made her way down the stairs but nearing the bottom, she heard another sound – the sound of something moving fast and towards her. In blind panic, she turned and started back up the stairs, but her leg was being held, hands gripping it like a vice, pulling her so that she fell forwards. She attempted to scream but found a hand had made its way to her mouth from behind.

Chapter Forty Six

'Shut the fuck up!' a familiar voice hissed in her ear. Sam tried turning to face him but couldn't move her head. She closed her eyes and started to count – like she used to when she was little. His hand was still over her mouth and with her nose pressed against the stairs, she could hear her own breath coming out in rapid bursts. Managing to adjust her head slightly allowed more air into her lungs.

'I'm not going to hurt you, I swear. I just need you to listen. I didn't take that woman. I don't know her. I swear!'

She felt the rush of his words, hot against her ear.

'Sam, please,' he said, his voice breaking slightly as if he were about to cry. There weren't many other options so she gave a slight nod – as much as her head would allow in the awkward position.

Breathing heavily, she turned and sat back on the stairs, looking at him, half expecting to see those cruel eyes taunting her, like the Imp. But the usual glint of nastiness was gone, replaced instead by something desperate and vulnerable.

She ignored his outstretched hand and grasped the banister to haul herself up. They stood still for a moment, appraising each other, and Sam briefly considered using her higher vantage point to boot him in the chest. Her leg itched at the prospect but then he looked down and said, 'I'm really sorry for scaring you like that but there's something you need to know.'

****

She stood and watched Nick make the coffee, placing heaped teaspoons into mugs along with several sugars. 'Good for the shock,' he said, turning briefly towards her. It disgusted her – the way he was so familiar with locating everything, like he'd been living here for years. Her mother and *him* in their little love nest.

'You're bleeding. Here,' he said, passing her some kitchen roll. 'I'm really sorry,' he said again, as she dabbed at the trickle of blood from her nose.

'How long have you had that jacket?' she asked, dully.

'What?' he looked down as if noticing it for the first time.

'I thought you'd borrowed it from Jack.'

'Nope, believe it or not, this belongs to me.'

Sam moved aside as he walked past her to the table, setting down the mugs of coffee. Reluctantly, Sam joined him, pulling out the chair furthest away from him.

'That's clearly a problem for you, isn't it?' he said, shaking his head. 'Even now, with all this shit happening, you're just bothered about me wearing Jack's fucking stuff?'

Sam flinched as he slammed his mug down, wondering if she could make it to the door, but she'd have to be quick and there was no guarantee she could make it before he got to her. And what then? If he was capable of kidnapping a woman, he could be capable of anything. She didn't want to think of what he'd done – was still probably doing – to Sarah Hollins. And then, of course, there was the other Sarah he'd held captive at school.

He followed her gaze and pushed his chair back against the far wall. 'Go on then, be my guest,' he said, gesturing towards the door. 'I'm not stopping you.'

She made to stand, but then, looking at him; the pleading, desperate look in his eyes and the way his hand shook as he lifted his mug; it was apparent he was in more of a state than her. Sinking back down into the chair, she knew she needed some answers and started with the most important one.

'Did you know about Jack and my mother?'

'Oh yes,' he said bitterly, 'A couple of weeks ago, when I came round to see why she was suddenly giving me the cold shoulder. He tried to make out he'd just popped in to try and mend bridges between you and her. But I saw the way she looked at him, the way most women look at him. I never stood a chance. Jack can't resist, you see? He can't handle it when I'm happy.'

'I ... I don't understand how he could do that to me,' she said, wiping a tear that was threatening to escape. She wouldn't let him see her cry.

'It's not about you, haven't you realised that yet?' He stood up and started to pace the floor. 'I told you before – me and Jack go way back. I know him better than anyone, well, at least I thought I knew him.'

He slumped back into his chair, deflated.

'Do you know where my mum is?'

'No, I just got a text saying she was going away for a few days and not to bother getting in contact.'

They both jumped at the sound of a police siren, only relaxing when the sound continued past the house, becoming fainter as it retreated into the distance.

'I didn't take that woman,' he said with sudden urgency, his eyes boring into Sam. 'But I know who did and you have to believe me.'

Chapter Forty Seven

Sam focussed on a spot on the wall as she listened to Nick describe a man she didn't recognise. A man who manipulated and controlled every aspect of Nick's life; who made him whip himself when he had 'misbehaved'; who, on one occasion, wouldn't let him go to the toilet so he had to sit through assembly in trousers stinking of piss. A man who, when they were school boys, got him to play nasty tricks on the girls, taking it a bit further each time, despite his own protests. Until the day came when he was made to take the blame for locking a schoolgirl in a room and torturing her; a decision that changed the course of his future.

She continued to stare at the spot on the wall till her vision blurred, prompting her to finally blink. Her head felt heavy and dull and she wished she could just go over to the sofa and curl up into a ball and stay there until everything made sense again. There was no way Jack could be capable of doing the things Nick was telling her, so why on earth was she just sitting there digesting his cruel lies?

But then she thought of the rare glimpses of Jack when his mood flipped, gripping her tightly as he spoke in that low, unfamiliar and unsettling tone: the knowing looks exchanged between Jack and Nick, a secret world she wasn't part of: How, according to Edith, Jack liked *messing around with the girls* and that he was *trouble*. All these things were worrying, yes, but didn't amount to Jack being some kind of monster.

'W...why are you doing this?' She finally asked, her voice wavering. Nick raised his head to meet her gaze.

'This is not a game, Sam. He said quietly, but fervently. 'This is not about me getting one over on you, or trying to come between you and Jack. I am telling you the truth'. Sam considered getting up then and leaving. She needed to confront Jack with what Nick had told her and then he would hold her in his arms and reassure her that everything was going to be OK. They would go to the police and report her mother missing then deal with whatever came next together. She stood up, resolute in what she was going to do but then Nick whispered,

'I loved him. I still love him.'

He leant forward and rested his head on his arms. She could see he was trembling.

'He was the popular boy – the one that everyone looked up to and when I was with him, my sad, shitty life was more bearable'.

There was a moment's silence as Sam slumped back into her chair.

'You mean you love him ... like sexually?'

'It's not like that. I don't know how to explain it, I ... yes; I have feelings for him that I've never had for other men. Or women.'

'So you were just playing games with my mum to get at me?'

Nick lifted his head. 'Maybe at first, but then we got close. I really like her, Sam. We were good for each other and if Jack hadn't interfered, it could've been serious.'

'But I'm not here to talk about my relationship with your mother. I've been set up for kidnapping that woman, Sam. I didn't even know she was missing till I was arrested. Then they let me go and I thought that would be the end of it – a case of mistaken identity, you know? But some of the questions they asked, it was weird, like they knew too much about me and then the police turned up again this morning with a warrant to search my place.'

'How come they let you leave?'

'Because I said I needed a piss and jumped out the bathroom window.'

Sam shook her head in disbelief. 'But if you're innocent, why would you do that?'

'Because they'll find something!' Nick shouted, slamming his fists into the table, making her jump. 'Jack will have made sure of it! But I'm not going down for him again; this isn't a stupid school game anymore!'

'But ... but how would Jack do that? *Why* would he do that?' She was shouting too now, unable to contain the conflicting emotions rampaging through her; trying to reconcile the Jack she knew – the man she loved, with the total stranger Nick was describing.

'To teach me a lesson of course! To punish me for being with your mother and not following his rules!' He got up and started to pace the room again.

'But I'm stronger now, you see?' Sam flinched as he got up and stood over her, lowering his head to hers. 'He knows it and he doesn't like it. I'm not playing by his rules anymore; I'm a loose fucking cannon!' The tone of his voice rose, making him sound manic and there was spittle gathering round the sides of his mouth.

'That still doesn't explain *how* though, does it?' Sam said, through gritted teeth.

'Let me briefly tell you about Ellie Stanmore.'

Sam met his gaze uncomprehendingly.

'I didn't know her surname back then. She was just Ellie – a girl Jack mentioned he was seeing, then suddenly wasn't. And then there's news of a girl gone missing: Ellie Stanmore. I make a joke in the pub about how I hope it's not the same girl Jack's seeing. Paul and Joe laughed, Jack laughed too, but he gave me this look and I just knew. We never talked about it; I suppose I didn't want to know.'

Not wanting to hear anymore, Sam stood up, pushing past Nick to the back door. If she didn't get out into the open, she felt like she might start to scream and not be able to stop.

The geraniums were still flowering, but the marigolds and impatiens were either dead or dying, she noticed, standing in the small back yard. But then what had she expected, leaving them in her mother's care. She turned slightly as Nick came to stand beside her.

'I know this is a complete mind fuck, Sam. I've had longer to take it all in, but you have to get your head round it now because I haven't got much time. I'm in trouble, more trouble than I've ever been in and you're the only one who might be able to help.'

Sam laughed then, a raw, barking sound she didn't recognise.

'I know, ironic, isn't it? We're not exactly best buddies but I'm sure you'll agree we can put aside our differences for now?'

'How can I be sure you're not just making this all up?' she said, kicking one of the pots so it toppled, spilling soil onto the concrete.

'Because I saw what he did to Sarah.' He said it so quietly, Sam almost thought she'd misheard him.

'Go on?' she said, not really wanting him to; not really sure how much more she could take.

'I hung around because I didn't know what to do. I couldn't just leave her locked in the room and I couldn't open it, so I went and found the caretaker. He had to carry her out and he would've had to be made of stone to do that without weeping.'

'What ... what did he do?' said Sam tremulously.

'Let's just say she was scarred for life.'

He was still speaking but all she could hear was the whooshing sound of blood in her ears.

'How fucking could you?!' she screamed, pushing her fists into Nick's chest. 'How could you stand by and not say anything?'

Nick grabbed her wrists and pulled her towards him. 'I don't know, it all happened so quickly and Jack twisted it in my mind, making me feel like it was all my fault and that he's the one who had to come to my rescue. He's good at that. And I *still* fucking carried on loving him!' His voice cracked and Sam could see the tears pooling in his eyes. Those cruel eyes that had once observed and taunted her were now desperate and she lowered her head; she had to look away. They stood for a moment in their strange embrace before he spoke.

'I thought ...' His voice broke again and he made a sound like he was clearing his throat. 'I thought it might be just a phase he'd grow out of. But then Ellie went missing – if it even was the same girl he was seeing. And now I find myself being framed for this woman's disappearance, only a week after Jack came round – acting all nice, like he wants to be friends again.'

He held her tightly till she raised her head and looked at him, their faces barely an inch apart.

'Do you think he's got my mother?'

Chapter Forty Eight
Two days earlier

Edith Mowbray shut the door on the outside world and cast a cursory glance around her cottage. Having lived there her whole life, she was familiar with every nook and cranny; every creak of the floorboards and the hum of the boiler warming the pipes for the central heating (a much later, and happy introduction to the cold, dank rooms). Edith switched it on now, a frivolous decision considering it was summer, but it felt colder than usual and as she got older and her skin got thinner, she found herself predisposed to switching it on any time she felt the need. It was a treat, she told herself – much like the chocolate éclair she eased out of the paper bag and placed onto one of her mother's fine china plates.

She hadn't had many treats in her long life, having been brought up by parents with strict, Victorian values with never enough money to buy new things. She'd always lived by the 'make do and mend' motto. Being the eldest, she had it tougher than her two brothers; leaving school at thirteen to help her mother with the piles of ironing and needlework she took in to make ends meet. Whilst her brothers took off, leading their lives as they pleased.

She hadn't always led a humdrum existence though. There was a brief moment of excitement in her life when she was in her early twenties and had not yet lost the shiny glow of optimism that can only be felt by the young. She had encountered the most handsome man she'd ever set eyes on.

Inspired by Britain's call to help out with the shortage of workers following the war, he'd travelled thousands of miles to the

'Motherland' from Guyana (a place she'd never heard of) to work for the postal service. He was living in London at the time and it had been pure chance that she'd met him on a rare night out - a dance in the local church hall whilst he was visiting his cousin.

They had danced the night away; he swept her off her feet – literally. They met up secretly several more times before he went back to London. He would pick her up round the corner from her house in his cousin's battered Morris Minor and they would drive out to Saxilby, Holton-Cum-Beckering, Burton Waters – wherever they fancied in the time they had together (she could usually get away for a couple of hours without rousing her mother's suspicion).

They wrote to each other when he went back to London – his experiences of taking turns to use the sink and hot plate in a room he shared with three other men; 'no mean feat, Edi,' he'd write.

She sat back in her armchair and smiled.

'Edi.'

Anyone else abbreviating her name would've been met with a curt response, but the way Raymond said it, in his gentle, musical tone, made it sound different.

They met a few more times over the course of a year; whenever he could take the time off to travel to Lincoln. It was maybe the third occasion that they slept together. His cousin giving up his room for the night; such a kind gesture. She had said she was going to babysit so her friend could go on a night out with her husband and her mother had no reason not to believe her. And that was that.

If she'd known then that that was going to be the most wonderful, climactic time of her life, she would have grabbed those moments, turned them into something more.

He had asked her to marry him. Only once, the morning after, entwined in one of the two single beds in his cousin's small room. He had told her he'd saved up enough to rent a room of his own. Asked her to move down to London with him. Straightaway she'd said no; she had too many responsibilities, being the main earner since her mother's arthritis slowed her ability to sew and iron. Not to mention the fact that she would be disowned if she introduced a black man to the family.

But now, all these years later, so many lonely days and lonely nights spent in the same, overstuffed armchair, reminiscing. She often wondered how different life could have been.

She reached for her cup of tea, cursing under her breath when she realised she hadn't even made one. Her memory wasn't the same these days, even before that dreadful infection that had sent her doolally for a while. At least that had got sorted.

Waiting for the kettle to boil, she glanced over to the calendar on the wall. *Dr's appointment 10.30 am* was written in bold red for the next day – a small shiver of contentment rippled through her body. The only engagement for that month, it was sometimes the only human contact she had, apart from ticking off the useless staff at the Co-op.

She so looked forward to going to the health centre – not that she wanted any of them to know it. Her interactions with the black girl, Sam (*was that short for Samantha?*), were especially enjoyable, and she sensed the feeling was reciprocated. Maybe, in another lifetime, she would have been friends with that girl – or could have even been her mother. She shook her head for being so sentimental and poured boiling water into the waiting cup.

Still feeling cold, she checked the dial on the heating, not trusting herself to have actually put it on. But no, it was set to twenty-one degrees. There was definitely a draft coming from somewhere though, but that was to be expected in such an old cottage. With a shrug of her shoulders, she buttoned up her cardigan and walked back into the sitting room.

She noticed the chocolate éclair straightaway. It was still on the side table where she'd left it, but there was now a bite out of it. She knew her memory wasn't so good nowadays but she definitely hadn't taken that bite. She stepped further into the room, her eyes fixated on the éclair.

'Hello, Miss Mowbray.'

Edith dropped her cup at the sight of him. Had he been there the whole time?

'So sorry to give you such a shock. I know it's not good for the heart, especially for someone your age. Delicious cream cake, by the way.'

It took a few seconds to register who it was, but then it clicked. The boy with the face of an angel. She suddenly felt lightheaded and gripped the side of the armchair to steady herself. *Have to keep your wits about you, Edith.*

'What the heck are you doing in my house?' She was disappointed to hear her voice waver; how feeble she must look in front of him.

'You really must remember to shut your windows properly, Miss Mowbray, otherwise it makes it so easy to slip a hand through and reach the key in your back door – so conveniently placed.' He stepped from the shadow of the door and smiled; the light revealing his glacial eyes. She couldn't help it, but she started to tremble.

'Get out. Get out of my—' She was abruptly cut short as he moved in a flash towards her, placing a hand around her throat.

'Now now, Miss Mowbray,' he said, shaking his head. 'You remember the rules: no shouting. Do you remember? That's what you always used to say to us in the corridors, like you owned the school. Even though you were just a dinner lady.'

Her chest rattled as she fought to get air into her restricted lungs. She attempted to ease her fingers under his hand, but he laughed and tightened his grip. When a darkness started to cloud her vision, he suddenly let go, letting her slump to the floor.

'What do you want?' she rasped, clinging to the armrest. 'There's money in the kitchen. In the drawer by the sink.'

He laughed again. 'I don't want, or need, your money, Miss Mowbray. I'm not a petty thief.' He lowered himself down to her level. 'What I want is for you to learn a lesson. Your last and most valuable lesson.'

She gasped as he grabbed her hair and jerked her head upwards. His eyes seemed several shades darker close up. She remembered those eyes, the way they watched the girls at school, so different from the other boys, with their shy, furtive glances. He didn't notice her watching him; the unsettling, brooding way he observed those girls, like prey. It had troubled her so much that she went to the head master, only to be told in a patronising manner that none of the teaching staff had raised any concerns; that he was a popular, well-adjusted boy and that perhaps she would do well to keep to her responsibilities as a lunch time assistant.

She wished she'd managed to warn Sam – not the vague comment she'd made the last time she was in the health centre, but properly. Suddenly, she realised that that is what she would do. Must do.

She felt his grip loosen slightly and impulsively kicked out; glad she hadn't got round to taking off her shoes, as her foot made contact with his ankle, tipping him off balance. How she got up so quickly she didn't know. She stumbled out towards the kitchen, no point going to the front door as she always locked it from the inside and couldn't be certain where she'd put the key. She knew she wouldn't make it to the back door but if she got to the kitchen, she could get hold of the carving knife. Just maybe.

She made it into the kitchen but suddenly felt both his hands grab the back of her head, snapping it back with such a force, she felt her hair tearing from the roots. She was as powerless as a rag doll as he slammed her head into the counter. A flash of indescribable pain bolted through her body before she slumped to the floor, feeling the cold quarry tiles pressing against her cheek. *You're in real trouble now, Edith,* she hazily thought.

'Oh dear, Miss Mowbray, what a nasty fall. I think your head is bleeding,' his voice floated down from somewhere above her.

Her gaze fell on the clods of dust that had gathered under the stove, intermittently blocked by a pair of training shoes pacing back and forth across her vision.

The fear that had gripped her was gone now, replaced by a cold numbing sensation spreading through her body. Her vision began to blur but she was struck by something under the stove - something shining out against the dirt. Her heart lifted; it was the brooch from Raymond. She was so upset when she'd lost it, so angry at mislaying such a precious gift. The emerald twinkled and the memory of their first dance came back to her so vividly and so happily, a tear fell, disappearing into the blood gathering on the tiles.

Earth Angel. She hadn't heard it in over forty years, but it was like Marvin Berry was right here, singing it for her and Raymond.

Her handsome Raymond. How she wished she'd said yes. She tried to reach for the brooch, but her arm wouldn't obey.

He was speaking again, his voice sounded so far away.

'I really don't like people bad mouthing me, Miss Mowbray, especially to my girlfriend. I have a reputation to keep up. You wouldn't ...' His voice floated away and all she could hear was the whirring sound of helicopter blades. She wondered where it was coming from.

Cold. She felt so cold now. What was she trying to do? That was it – she had to warn Sam (*was that short for Samantha?*), warn her of the devil that she was courting. She felt herself stir, her body parts finally starting to obey her brain.

But something was stopping her. Something heavy.

'Oh dear, Miss Mowbray, does that hurt? Never mind, let's put you out of your misery.'

Jack smiled, lifted his foot and slowly pressed it down on her neck.

Chapter Forty Nine

He indicated right at the small junction that would take him onto Wragby Road and was surprised to see two cars in front of him, their indicator lights blinking in the misty dawn light. There were never usually cars on the road at this time of day. No matter, he thought, humming along to the song on the radio. He hadn't heard it before – it had a good beat and he tapped his fingers on the steering wheel in time to it. The song finished and the DJ announced it was going to be a beautiful day. He glanced through the window and nodded in agreement. The mist was already beginning to clear to reveal an azure sky.

A few minutes later, he turned onto Barnaby Lane, leaving the two cars ahead of him to continue their journey, as he knew they would. It was extremely rare to see another vehicle around here, except for the odd tractor that he occasionally had the misfortune of getting stuck behind. But not today, thank God. He turned the radio off – fed up with the DJ who clearly enjoyed the sound of his own voice to the detriment of his listeners. Besides, the signal usually went a bit funny in this part of the countryside. He pressed down gently on the brakes as he passed the derelict building.

It used to be a school, Uncle Monty had told him. The only school for miles around, serving all the children from the surrounding villages. That was until a fire devastated the building, killing a teacher and several children in its wake. All that had happened over forty years ago now, but yet there it still stood with its blackened windows and hollowed-out rooms. He'd gone inside once, with Uncle Monty, whilst out on one of their long walks. He smiled, remembering how enjoyable those walks were; Uncle Monty made them such an adventure. 'Now where would my favourite nephew like to go today?' he'd say, which was a running joke because he was Uncle Monty's only nephew. Nevertheless, he liked to think that even if he'd had other siblings or cousins; Uncle Monty would've still considered him the favourite.

Uncle Monty always shook his head when he asked if they could go to the school. 'Please, Uncle Monty, we don't have to go inside. We can just walk around it,' he would plead, in his unbroken, child voice.

'No, my dear boy,' Uncle Monty would say firmly. 'It's an unsafe structure that should have been knocked down years ago.'

'But you've been inside.'

'Only for a quick inspection and, besides, I'm an adult. I can weigh up the risks to myself and make that decision. But I can't be taking you there, your mother would have me hung, drawn and quartered!'

He laughed as Uncle Monty pulled his funny death face. 'But Mummy doesn't have to know and anyway, I'm seven now and I'm big enough to weigh up my own risks.'

He'd pulled himself up and folded his arms to look as serious and grown up as possible, but Uncle Monty only laughed. That made him angry. Really angry.

'Well I'll go there without you and if I have an accident, Mummy will blame you!' he shouted, stamping his feet. He was aware he was behaving like a spoilt brat which he really didn't want to do. Not in front of Uncle Monty, who was always so calm and affable. He pressed his fists into his eyes to stop from crying. When he opened them, Uncle Monty was regarding him, one bushy eyebrow raised.

'Well, we can't have that, can we?' Uncle Monty finally said.

'Right, let's do it,' Uncle Monty said, with a sudden slap of his knee. 'But not a word to your mother. Are we clear?'

He nodded enthusiastically. There was no way he was going to disturb Mummy. Especially not when she had one of her headaches. They always seemed to come when Daddy was away for work; making her all snappy and short tempered. But he didn't mind. No, not at all. Because it meant he got to spend precious time with Uncle Monty.

They would drive up to his secluded little cottage where Uncle Monty would make them thick wedges of cheese on toast after which Uncle Monty would say, 'You're looking tired, little sis, why don't you have a nap by the fire and I'll take the little man out for a while?'

'Well, if you're sure that's all right,' Mummy would reply, smiling gratefully as Uncle Monty tucked the soft blue blanket around her and, before he'd even finished stoking the fire, her eyes would be closed, her usually clenched jaw loosened.

It took exactly one hour and thirteen minutes to get to the school – he knew this because he checked his watch as they left Uncle Monty's house, checking it again as they entered the grounds of the school. He'd felt hugely relieved at finally mastering how to tell the time, being one of the last children in his class to do so; it had started to get embarrassing.

Mummy had taken him for tests to see what was wrong with him. Of course, she tried to pretend they were normal; that every child had them. But he wasn't that stupid. He'd been able to tell the time for a few weeks now, yet he was still being taken to Dr Hogarth's clinic, where he would sit in his office and play strange games whilst being asked strange questions. And although he always tried his very best, he always left the sessions with a sense that he had somehow failed and the worried glances exchanged between Mummy and Dr Hogarth didn't go unnoticed, however hard they tried to reassure him that everything was fine – that he'd done really well.

But thankfully the visits to Dr Hogarth stopped when he eventually got Mummy to bend to his way of thinking; that there in fact was nothing at all wrong with him. He'd had to teach her a few lessons along the way, of course – a few lessons to make her realise the roles were reversed and he was in charge now.

A quick glance in the rear-view mirror confirmed there were no other cars on the road behind him, although it wouldn't have mattered if there were, he would have simply carried straight on and come back when it was clear. Navigating carefully around the potholes, he drove down a narrow lane past the derelict school towards the outbuildings behind.

The school and surrounding buildings had been built in the

early 1700s, Uncle Monty had told him, and used to be a county school for poor orphans - a pioneering venture for the time, led by an optimistic philanthropist, Thomas Jacobs. Sadly, the venture failed to survive his death and the buildings were used as a correctional facility and later, a workhouse. It wasn't until the mid 1800s that the site was mostly demolished and a new, smaller school built. However, Uncle Monty told him, with a twinkle in his eye, some of the original structures remained and the wall that enclosed the playground was in fact the original prison wall, albeit reduced in height and parts removed to make space for new entrance gates.

He'd got so excited by the school's history, he could hardly contain himself as they made their way along an old bridle path towards the school. He'd had to break into a run at times to catch up with Uncle Monty, who strode ahead, pointing out various trees and birds with his walking stick. He would nod, and glance hurriedly at the rook's nest or pheasant Uncle Monty was pointing out to him but inwardly, he couldn't care less. He just wanted to get to the school.

Now, he steered the car into a narrow gap between two of the outbuildings and came to a stop, letting the engine run for a few more moments before turning it off, enjoying the contrast of complete silence. Closing his eyes, he smiled and savoured the moment; the precious moment of not knowing.

Would she be dead or alive?

Chapter Fifty

He jumped out of the car and squinting his eyes against the sunlight, surveyed his surroundings. Travellers had taken the copper pipes and the lead from the rooftops a long time ago, so he wasn't bothered about coming across any trespassers and even if he did, it wouldn't be a problem as this was *his* land now and he had the right to chase any opportunists away.

Uncle Monty didn't tell him he'd acquired the school and surrounding land till much later, when he turned eighteen; a 'development opportunity' that never reached fruition as Uncle Monty died a year later.

He made his way to the last outbuilding, not much bigger than a shed, and pulled open the door. He had considered making it more secure initially, but eventually conceded that it would only draw attention to it and besides, no one would find what the shed was housing – not without foreknowledge.

Uncle Monty had led him round the inside of the school, the parts that were still accessible anyway. He'd found it thrilling, better than anything he had ever experienced, as he took in the sight of blackened wooden desks and the remnants of books and a clock on the wall, its hands forever stuck at 10.20 am. He had even come across a lone tennis shoe and wondered if it had belonged to one of the children who'd died in the fire.

But if he found all this thrilling, what Uncle Monty was about to show him exceeded his wildest dreams although, as he reluctantly left the school to follow Uncle Monty, he didn't know it at the time.

He walked the short distance to the back of the shed, where thirteen large sacks of coal were stacked on the floor. He knew how many sacks there were – having moved them numerous times over the years. He took off his jacket and hung it on the nearby hook he'd put up for the purpose; moving the bulky sacks was a strenuous task that left him sweating from the exertion. He didn't mind, it was good exercise and kept his arms strong and defined – his appearance and ability to attract others to him were vitally important and he couldn't have, *wouldn't have* meddling old witches like Edith Mowbray stating otherwise.

The last few weeks had begun to take their toll on his usually flawless complexion though and Sam had noticed, but thankfully she seemed to buy his cock and bull 'woe is me' story about his failing studies, although he hated having to portray a vulnerable, weak side of himself. He viciously kicked one of the bags, not liking the way he was feeling; the anger that descended so suddenly and took every last ounce of his reserve to quash and not overspill and reveal itself. He straightened up and took a few deep breaths, visualising what he was about to behold. This was his most special of moments and he wasn't about to let his emotions crowd his thoughts and spoil it. Eventually, his head cleared and, with a smile, he resumed moving the sacks, humming a tune under his breath.

Before Uncle Monty had opened the door to the shed, he had turned and bent down to peer at him from eyes almost obscured by his bushy white eyebrows and made him swear that he mustn't tell his mother, or anyone else about what he was about to see. Searching for the hint of a twinkle in Uncle Monty's eyes, he was confronted with the sternest of looks that made him feel suddenly very grown up and, he hated to admit it, even then – slightly scared. He'd nodded gravely and promised on his mother and father's life that he wouldn't tell a soul, and felt honoured that Uncle Monty had chosen him to share whatever it was he was about to reveal. They had solemnly shook hands before Uncle Monty opened the door to the shed.

It had been used to store surplus desks and garden tools, Uncle Monty said, leading him to the back. He watched as Uncle Monty then stamped his feet and declared that this was it – the important thing he was going to reveal. It took a moment for him to notice the trap door under Uncle Monty's black boots, mostly obscured by dirt and dust and he watched on in amazement as Uncle Monty proceeded to open it to reveal a rusty metal staircase that disappeared into darkness.

He'd watched Uncle Monty descend the steps, his torch lighting the way down.

'Come on, boy, you're not a scaredy cat, are you?' he'd said, peering up at him. He shook his head vehemently and followed Uncle Monty down into the gloom. It was a narrow staircase and all he could see was the back of Uncle Monty filling the space in front of him, his broad shoulders brushing the damp stone walls on either side. He glanced back at the receding square of light and briefly considered chickening out, but Uncle Monty's voice floated up from the darkness, telling him to get a move on as they didn't have much time before Mummy woke up and would start worrying about where they were. So he continued down the stairs, the light from Uncle Monty's torch illuminating his way.

When he'd got to the bottom, Uncle Monty had waved his torch around the space until he'd let out a triumphant 'Aha!' and swiftly moved away, momentarily leaving Jack in darkness. Then, just as he'd thought he could stand it no longer, shivering in this cold, dank space, there was light – only weak, from a camping lantern fixed to a wall, but enough to finally see his surroundings.

He had listened, transfixed, as Uncle Monty told him the school was in part erected on top of an old basement that used to be part of the prison and at that very moment, they were actually standing in one of the rows of prison cells that had remained intact.

He'd run his hand along the wall and was easing off some of the peeling paint when Uncle Monty said, 'Bad things have happened here, can you feel it?'

He'd turned to see Uncle Monty looking at him strangely – a look of excitement making his eyes dance. And then he'd known, he didn't know how, but the feeling was so strong he'd really believed it to be true: Uncle Monty wanted to do bad things, or maybe he had already done bad things – things he didn't have the words or imagination to describe in his young mind. He'd known he should feel scared, but he found it excited him too. He looked at Uncle

Monty and nodded, returning his smile.

Now, opening the trap door, he felt that same thrill ripple deliciously through every cell of his body, making him feel so very grateful to be alive on this earth and in this privileged position. It was evident by the stench that she was already dead as he descended into the darkness but, flipping the light switch, he bent down and checked her pulse, just to make sure.

Sarah Hollins was indeed dead, bless her soul. He stroked her stiff, cold hand with affection, thinking of all the things she'd done to stay alive. It hadn't been easy getting her to that stage. Not being his usual type, she'd been so much more of a challenge, taking a lot longer than expected for what he liked to call his 'bespoke behavioural conditioning' to kick in.

But he knew he couldn't live with himself if he didn't take up the chance to finish off what he'd started all those years ago.

He looked down at the dirty rag tied around her leg and gently prized it open. The smell made him gag, but he couldn't take his eyes off the gangrenous, rotting flesh, resulting from an infected wound (self-inflicted, for his pleasure). She'd had such spirit, not like Ellie who gave up on life almost the moment he'd brought her here, whimpering in a corner, barely making any attempt to follow his orders.

He stroked her cheek, the undamaged side of her face that he hadn't worked on and emitted a low whistle. From a corner where the light didn't quite reach came a scraping sound that advanced hesitantly towards him.

'Come closer, my sweet,' he said, smiling encouragingly, but there was no further movement.

'Now,' he said sharply, slapping the floor beside him and was pleased to see his command being obeyed.

'Good girl,' he said, patting her matted hair before throwing one of the dresses he'd selected from her wardrobe onto the floor beside her. 'Now put this on, it's time to take you home for a good wash, don't you think?'

Chapter Fifty One

'Come on, hurry up!' he was beginning to wish he hadn't bothered now and just left her there, but he needed help with getting rid of Sarah's stinking carcass. He'd done it all on his own with Ellie's, hurting his back in the process as he dragged her body out of the basement and into the car.

He backed out into the shed and lowered the body to the floor. Looking at the gibbering wreck hunched in front of him, he considered booting her back down into the basement. His leg twitched at the thought of her bones crunching on her fall down, but he resisted the urge.

It hadn't taken much for Denise to fall for his charms – a meaningful look here, a lingering hug there; suggesting to Sam that she invite her along with them for coffee or lunch. And later, calling round on his own for cosy little chats which soon led to a kiss on the sofa, before he led her upstairs. It was all going so well, she was so easy to bend to his will; the perfect candidate for his powers of persuasion and so very, very needy.

But then he'd gone round one morning with Sam, and Nick was there, his arm draped around Denise, grinning like a Cheshire cat. That had been a huge surprise and he really didn't like surprises. Sitting at the table, across from the happy couple, and maintaining a calm exterior whilst wanting to bludgeon them both to a pulp had taken every last reserve of control, but he'd managed it somehow.

Of course it was all to get at him, their little act. An attempt to get more of his attention. He'd expected it from Denise, the stupid, underhand bitch, but *et tu, Nick?*

Nick: The perennial loser. The last boy to be picked for a team in the PE line up. Yet he'd seen the potential in that introverted skinny boy with scraped knees and a snotty nose and taken him under his instruction to become his greatest achievement by far.

He couldn't pinpoint the exact moment Nick had begun to change; the stubborn glint in his eyes as he wilfully disobeyed his orders, even declining the reward of letting Nick into his bed, where he would sometimes turn a blind eye to Nick's tremulous fingers as they explored the contours of his body. But his newly defiant behaviour definitely escalated when Sam came onto the scene. She seemed to be a catalyst that brought his nasty, shit-stirring traits to the fore. It was apparent that Nick fancied her from the start whilst also hating her for being his girlfriend, and for a while, it was fun observing the way the two of them interacted with each other; their little cat and mouse games were so amusing. Then Nick had gone into his room and left that freaky little imp for Sam and it stopped being amusing. But when Nick started seeing Denise behind his back, he had had to face the fact that it was time to finally cut him loose. Nick had gone too far.

It was risky, he knew, to frame Nick for Sarah's disappearance, as it would invariably draw unwanted attention to him, being Nick's closest friend and the link to what happened at school. And he'd been so very careful over the years; studying the next successful candidate for weeks, even months before making a move, dazzling them with his perfect smile – *Hi, I'm Jack* – they didn't stand a chance. Of course, not all of them met the same fate; it would soon leave an obvious trail to him if they did. He'd completed four of his projects so far – five if he included Denise.

But he'd taken a huge risk with Sarah, spotting her at the Christmas market one day, her arm linked through her mother's. How happy she'd looked, only the faintest of scars showing through her rosy cheeks as she bought some tacky Christmas decorations. He'd wanted to take her there and then, the stupid bitch, but instead, he'd bided his time, tracking her routine until the right time came, stealing up behind her as she walked back from her late shift.

His interest in imprisonment and torture had been spiked by his introduction to the basement and Uncle Monty's tales of what the prisoners would have endured. However, as he got older, he wasn't so sure if Uncle Monty had actually been regaling his own experiences and, by the time he felt confident enough to ask him outright, it was too late, Uncle Monty was dead.

So he kept his thoughts to himself, satisfying his growing urges with the little tricks he used to play on the girls at school, but without a doubt, none of them compared to his encounter with Sarah; extracting the exquisite smell of her fear, even with his amateur methods. But he'd honed those methods, learnt from his past experiences and had improved.

The plan was to stop for a while until Nick got sent down and the dust had settled. He hadn't meant to take Denise, not yet anyway, but she'd gone and spoilt his plans, smiling smugly at him as she served pancakes round her naff little kitchen table, Nick's fingers playing with the tendrils of hair on her neck. She would have to pay dearly.

'Stand up,' he barked to the crouching figure. She raised her head slightly but didn't move, so he grabbed her hair and pulled her up.

'What the fuck have I told you?' He didn't want to lose it, not now. He breathed in and exhaled slowly.

'T ... to do what you say,' she whimpered. 'I have to do what you say.'

'That's my girl,' he said, feeling his temperament restored. 'Now get in there,' he jerked his head towards the car boot. Her eyes widened in surprise and horror but one nod from him and she climbed into the boot, next to Sarah's wrapped up carcass.

'It isn't a long ride,' he said with a smile, before slamming the boot shut. He was about to drive off but felt his phone vibrate in his jeans pocket. The signal was patchy in these parts, but he could get reception in some areas. 'Wow,' he chuckled, seeing the numerous missed calls from Sam.

Sam: the anomaly in his life, his warrior queen. The one girl he didn't feel the compulsion to hurt; the one girl he'd invited to move in with him and introduced to his parents; the girl who'd had a nightmare childhood and survived. She was an absolute bitch, whilst at the same time so loving and protective. The way she'd looked at those simpering whores at the party, hanging off his every word like their lives depended on it, if looks could kill. Phew! He supposed what he felt was something akin to love, not that he had anything to compare it to.

He was met with the sound of static as he tried to retrieve Sam's message. Never mind, he thought, there was still work to do and she would just have to wait.

Twenty minutes later, he reached Uncle Monty's cottage, which was conveniently set back from the lane, sheltering behind a long row of conifers. He came to a stop at the end of the driveway by the pond and opened the boot. She had her eyes shut and was shaking.

'Out we get,' he said, hauling her up and setting her down. He was pleased to see she immediately lowered herself into a crouching position beside him and he bent down to stroke her hair.

'I had so many plans for you,' he said, kneeling down to her level and lifting her chin so she had to look at him. 'So many plans.' He shook his head.

When he'd met her for the first time, in a snivelling state about her lost pendant, he couldn't quite believe this pathetic excuse for a human being was Sam's mother; she had victim written all over her, as if her only purpose in life was to be dominated and hurt by others. She was literally handed to him on a plate and he couldn't help himself, as she responded so shamelessly to his subtle advances – even from that first meeting, in her house where she smiled coyly at him through her crocodile tears.

She didn't deserve to be Sam's mother.

Chapter Fifty Two

Together, they lifted the body from the boot, not that Denise was much help; she was shaking so much by now, she kept losing her grip, nearly causing them both to fall into the mud but somehow, he managed to keep a leash on his temper. Once the body was positioned where he wanted it, he instructed Denise to collect some rocks, pointing to a pile of them stacked up by the shed. She started to crawl towards them but stopped when he whistled.

'Get up. You'll need to be upright to lift them.' He rocked back on his heels, watching her scramble to her feet, and started to hum.

When she'd eventually collected enough rocks, he loosened the polythene wrapping and placed several of them between Sarah's legs before binding the polythene with rope. Now came the tricky part of getting the body down the steep, muddy bank and into the pond. When he'd disposed of Ellie's body, he had almost fallen into the water too and he didn't want a repeat performance. Fastening a length of rope to the car's tow bar, he signalled to Denise to help him push the body down the steep slope. He half hoped the momentum of the weighted body might send it straight into the pond but instead, it slithered to a stop, half submerged in the murky water.

He cursed, realising he'd have to go down there. 'Stay there,' he said, pinning Denise with a menacing stare.

Cautiously, he lowered himself down the slippery bank and with a prod of his foot, pushed the bagged body further into the water, watching until it disappeared beneath the surface.

Despite the earlier predictions of it being a fine day, it had started to rain, and he was glad to finally enter the cottage. Apart from a lick of paint here and there, he'd done nothing to change the interior, as it reminded him of happy days spent with Uncle Monty. Instructing Denise to stay on the mat, he walked through to the living room and filled the fireplace with a few logs and coal from the scuttle. Although it was the height of summer, the evenings were always chilly here and the fire would also prove useful for what he had in store for Denise. He retrieved the poker from the fire stand and smiled. But first things first; he wanted her to be clean and fed before he went to work on her but there was so little time, just one day instead of the usual weeks or months. He would have to savour every moment.

Placing her in the hot scented bath water, perhaps a little too hot judging by the whimpering and squirming, he scrubbed her clean, enjoying submerging her head to wash her hair; enjoying the desperate look on her face as he got carried away and held her under a little too long. As her eyes were beginning to bulge, he let her back up, considering whether to finish her off there and then as she flailed and spluttered like a ... well, like a woman who'd nearly drowned. But no, he would show some decorum, take things slowly. Uncle Monty would approve, he was sure.

He led her to the bedroom and selected a dress from the wardrobe – the tight purple one that made her look like a hooker. He held it up to her and smiled, thinking back to how excited she was when she first wore it – a sexy new dress bought just to please him. Quite pathetic really.

He looked at her now, standing naked and shivering; rivulets of water making their way down her body. That body, as yet unmarked, apart from the few bites and bruises he'd inflicted, was standing before him: a taut blank canvas waiting for his artwork. Her wet hair was now curly and just above her shoulders, he moved towards her and ran his fingers through it, gently untangling any knots, thinking how much younger she looked without it straightened. Holding her in his arms for a brief moment, he closed his eyes, wishing he could have longer with her.

But the clock was ticking; along with Ellie's ring and Sarah's silk scarf, he had planted Denise's pendant in Nick's seedy little bedsit and if the police were doing their job properly, they should have found them by now. He would have to act fast.

Once she was dressed, he crushed a small amount of the sleeping pills into a glass of wine and watched her drink it. He'd estimated the amount, hoping his guesswork was right – he wanted her conscious later. Placing her on the bed, he tied her arms and legs together and pulled the blanket up round her shoulders.

'There, you can't say I don't treat you right,' he smiled, before kissing her on the cheek. 'I have an antiques fair to get to now, but don't worry; I'll be back as soon as I can.'

Seeing her eyes begin to drift, he didn't expect a response and, although he didn't think it was needed, he proceeded to gag her – just in case.

****

Jack arrived back at the cottage later than expected, but it had been worth taking the time to shake hands and exchange pleasantries with the numerous old boys his father introduced him to – delighted with his only son's sudden interest in the world of antiques. He feigned curiosity as one bore after the other blethered on about the importance of checking for the purity marks on old jewellery, or looking out for the slight imperfections in carved objects, indicating that the item was indeed carved by a human – this was slightly more up his street, albeit carving flesh instead of inanimate objects – all the while thinking about the woman in the tight hooker dress tied to his bed.

He opened the door to the bedroom and was pleased to see Denise stir and open her eyes.

'Not long now, my sweet,' he beamed.

He seared two steaks and opened the bag of salad. It was a couple of days past its best but never mind, it would have to do.

'Time for dinner,' he said, looking down at Denise's recumbent figure. Her eyes flickered in his direction but quickly looked away. 'Come on, up we get,' he said, yanking her upright and loosening her ties. 'No time to play coy,' he pulled her roughly into a standing position and gave her backside a hard slap.

'Well, isn't this nice?' he said, lighting a candle. Without warning, he grabbed her arm and held it over the flame. 'Isn't it?' he said, menacingly, only letting go when she shrieked out, 'Yes, yes!' He poured wine into their glasses – more for her, she was going to need it. 'Cheers,' he said genially, clinking his glass against hers.

'Now eat,' he said, with no trace of his convivial tone. Except, despite his previous lessons, she didn't obey and kept whimpering, making the all too familiar fury bubble up inside him.

'I said eat!' he roared, as he seized her hand and clamping it down, scored the skin between her thumb and forefinger with his steak knife. She screamed a high pitched, agonised wail that sated his rising fury.

'There there,' he said softly and reaching for her napkin, wrapped it round her hand. He didn't want blood seeping out all over the table; the messy work would have to take place outside. Cutting a piece of the steak, he slid it into her mouth. 'Isn't that nice, see?' She gagged at first, but then started to chew. 'Good girl,' he said, cutting up another piece. He was about to place it in her mouth when he heard his phone ringing from the living room, one of the few places to get reception in the cottage. 'Excuse me,' he said, patting Denise's arm.

It was his mother and for a brief moment, he considered not answering, but it wasn't like her to call for no reason.

Chapter Fifty Three

Sam repeatedly smashed the knocker down with all her might, not caring about the curious glances from passersby; they could go to hell. It was maybe by the ninth smash of the knocker that the door was finally opened and she was confronted with Jane in a dressing gown, her icy blue eyes clouded with sleep and her usually sleek bob frizzed unflatteringly around her gaunt face. A glint of recognition flickered across her face, but a warm welcome wasn't forthcoming.

'Why the hell are you making such a racket? Were you trying to knock the door down?!'

'I'm sorry to disturb you like this.'

'So am I. I've got one of my migraines and was just getting off to sleep. What is it?'

'I need to speak to you. Can I come in?' Sam stepped towards the door, afraid that Jane was about to slam it in her face. 'Please Jane, it's urgent.'

Jane scowled, but opened the door a fraction to let Sam through. She focussed on a matted spot of hair at the back of Jane's head as she was led down the hallway into a room lined from floor to ceiling with books.

'Well?' said Jane, turning abruptly and making it clear Sam wasn't invited to sit down. 'What is it?'

Your son is a fucking psycho who gets a kick out of kidnapping women and might have hurt my mother. Bitch!!!

'I ... I have something to tell you about Jack.'

She watched Jane's expression rapidly change from disdain to concern, to shock – her eyes widening as Sam recounted what she'd just found out.

Jane lowered herself carefully into a chair, her face cast down. She remained silent and for a moment the only sound to be heard was the rasping of her bony hands as they clasped and unclasped in her lap. Sam worried that it was all too much to process and that she wouldn't be able to get anything useful from the older woman. But then Jane looked up, her gaze focussed with alarming clarity on Sam, like two lasers boring into her.

'And you actually believe my son could be capable of this?' she said, her voice low and measured. 'Of abducting and torturing women; of sleeping with your mother? Just on the say so of his so-called friend?!' She moved to the window and adjusted the blind, reducing the fading sunlight and plunging the room into gloomy semi-darkness.

'Nick's very unstable, did you know that?' she said, whipping round so abruptly, Sam took a step back. 'Had to be sent away to some place for juvenile delinquents. Jack was the only one who stood by him, has always stood by him, and been a pillar of support. And this is how he repays him?'

Her voice shook with such conviction, making Sam realise how ridiculous it all seemed. Of *course* Nick was lying! Collapsing into the nearest chair, she wondered how she could have been so gullible. She knew, at first hand, what a warped, twisted creep he was, almost from the first moment she'd encountered him. The way he'd entered Jack's bedroom and leered at her. And now he wanted her to believe – did make her believe – that Jack was the one who was dangerous.

But then Jack's jacket crept back into her mind - so out of place in her mother's room. She raked at her head, hoping to remove the unsettling image but it refused to budge.

'Sam ... Sam?'

She was brought to with the gentle tap of Jane's hand on her knee. 'I'm sorry to see you so distressed, but it really isn't necessary. I don't know why Nick is doing this to Jack, the one loyal friend in his life – he's obviously a very disturbed young man.'

Sam looked up, surprised at the level of warmth in Jane's voice.

'I need to go to the police and tell them I've seen Nick, and I'm going to report my mum missing. It's just not like her to go off somewhere on her own, I think something's happened to her.' Jane didn't say anything at first, regarding her with an inscrutable expression on her gaunt face.

'Well let me get dressed and I'll take you there, but first I'm going to make you a hot sweet tea – you're in no fit state to go anywhere just yet.'

Sam was about to protest, but felt her legs give way as she tried to stand up. Her encounter with Nick must have shaken her up more than she'd thought, and then there was Jack's blue jacket, hanging up in a room it had no place to be. She so desperately needed to speak to Jack.

'Here we are,' said Jane, entering the room with a tray. She offered Sam one of the dainty teacups and perched on the edge of the desk. An uncomfortable silence prevailed, only disturbed by the clinking of fine china as Sam drank her tea as quickly as she could without scorching her throat. She had to get to the police station.

'I need to speak to Jack,' she said, fumbling in her bag for her phone. 'I can't get hold of him.' Dialling the number, she let it ring until it went to the sound of Jack's voice apologising for being unable to take the call and asking her to leave a message – she didn't. When he did eventually look at his phone, he would already find three messages and at least twenty missed calls.

'God, why won't he answer?!' she slammed her phone on the desk in frustration. 'Can you call David?' she said, suddenly realising that of course, Jack was with his father. 'He went to an antiques fair with Jack, didn't he tell you?' she continued, feeling exasperated with the vague expression on Jane's face.

'Of course, I'll try now,' she said, rising from her chair. 'Give me a moment, my phone's upstairs.'

Sam nodded, her eyes following Jane as she left the room. She drained the last of her tea and placed the cup back on the tray, her eyes settling on a gold framed photo of Jack and his mother as she did so. Jane was seated, hands placed primly in her lap, her hair longer and lighter. Jack stood behind her, his hands gripping her shoulders in a way that looked wrong somehow; too grown up for his young age. They were both smiling; two sets of blue eyes looking out to the camera.

The pounding ache in her head was still there, but didn't seem so insistent, a fatigue taking its place, making her feel drained and lethargic. She walked over to the chaise lounge by the window and ran her hand over the dusky pink velvet. It felt so soft and inviting, she curled up on it, revelling in the softness of the material against her cheek. Her eyelids felt so heavy, it was a sheer effort to keep them open. Even when Jane re-entered the room, she couldn't seem to pull herself together.

'Sorry for keeping you waiting, I thought I might as well get dressed whilst I was upstairs. No luck, I'm afraid.'

'With what?' said Sam, struggling into an upright position.

'Getting hold of David. Nothing to worry about, there's never a good signal in some parts of Lincolnshire. Oh dear, are you all right?'

'I ... I'm fine,' said Sam, trying, and failing to get up from the chaise lounge.

'You poor thing, it has obviously been a terrible day for you. Here, let me help.'

Sam placed her arm around Jane's bony shoulder, feeling guilty at putting her weight on such a fragile frame but not able to do anything about it. She reached out for her phone as they passed the desk, but she missed, instead knocking it onto the floor. She contemplated bending to reach it, but Jane carried on moving towards the door. Never mind, she thought; she could pick it up later, with Jack.

It was getting dark as they stepped outside, making Sam wonder how long she'd been at the house, she tried to remember when she'd got there. The cathedral bells were chiming and she tried to keep count but couldn't, her thought processes were having the same problem as her limbs – slow and heavy, making her stumble as Jane helped her towards a racing green Jaguar.

A man was walking towards them and came to a stop as they got to the car. Sam recognised him but couldn't think from where. She couldn't think full stop. He raised his hand halfway in greeting and she attempted to reciprocate but her arm wouldn't obey. It wasn't until Jane was guiding her into the back seat that the man's name came to her. Colin. It was Colin, wearing the familiar duffel coat that he seemed to wear whatever the season, and a puzzled expression on his face as the car pulled away. She made another attempt at waving but failed, hoping at least she was managing to smile as they rounded a corner and Colin disappeared out of sight.

Chapter Fifty Four

'Mummy? What is it?'

Jack listened to his mother relay what Sam had told her; how she had fallen for Nick's lies and actually believed that *he* was behind the abduction of Sarah Hollins.

'I mean, how could she think you could be capable of doing such a thing?! She really doesn't know how lucky she is to have you in her life, she's ...' There was a shrillness to her voice that Jack didn't like and he held the phone away from his ear for a moment before taking a deep breath.

'Mummy.' She was still ranting. 'Mother!' he said, raising his voice, relieved to finally have silence. He pinched the bridge of his nose, fighting to stay in control of his mounting fury. 'Where is Sam now?'

He heard his mother draw breath. 'Why she's still here. I couldn't let her leave in such a state, so I gave her one of my pills to calm her down.'

She spoke with such self-assurance, he laughed; only his mother could do something so unhinged and think it was perfectly normal.

'Wow! But why did you do that? Why not just let her go to the police?'

'Because ... because I didn't want her saying those things about you!'

'But you convinced her that Nick was lying, didn't you?' There was a brief silence; he could almost hear her brain working to formulate a response.

'I ... I couldn't be certain,' she said, the former self-assuredness missing from her voice.

'Mummy?' he said, in a warning tone, 'That isn't a good reason to drug my girlfriend.'

'All right, all right! I just thought I could give you more time to ... to get matters in order before she goes to the police. Her mother's missing, did you know about that?'

A longer silence prevailed as Jack considered his response. There was no doubt in his mind that his mother knew him – *the real him* – but what lengths was she prepared to go to, to protect him?

Mummy had come across the personalised necklace bearing Sarah's name – a little memento from his time spent with her in the old costume room at school and, he must admit, he'd thought it was all over then as she stood over him in his room with the incriminating object dangling from her fingers. But instead, she'd turned on her heel and marched downstairs and, from his window, he'd seen her throw it in the bin. Well strictly speaking, it was something wrapped up in a plastic bag, but he was pretty certain it must have been the necklace.

And though nothing was ever said out loud, that was how it was to be between him and Mummy; an unspoken agreement that she would turn a blind eye to his misdemeanours. Mummy dearest, who saw the real him from a young age, and accepted it – well, to the extent that she was unlikely to betray him. However, he didn't think she could stomach the stark truth of what he did and a small part of him didn't want her to know. He came to the realisation that he would have to alter the course of his actions.

'No,' he said eventually. 'Denise isn't missing.'

****

Sam could just about make out a row of trees in the fading light. She didn't have a clue where she was, but they were definitely somewhere very rural. She could see the back of Jane's head, bobbing up and down as she navigated the car along a narrow, uneven path and Sam groaned as her own body was jostled from side to side. The migraine had subsided slightly, morphing into a dull ache that thrummed at her temples.

She couldn't make out what was happening, though she vaguely remembered Jane helping her into the car.

'Where are we?' she croaked, her throat dry.

'My brother's house, well actually, Jack's now,' Jane said, slowing to a stop.

'Why did you bring me here? I have to get to the police station!' Sam said, struggling to sit up. Jane turned and smiled coldly.

'There's someone you might like to see first.'

Then she saw him, walking towards her, a concerned look etched on his beautiful face, and she knew that everything would be OK. Jack would make all that had happened OK.

She fumbled for the handle and propelled the door open with a force that took her by surprise. But as her legs met the ground, she soon found they hadn't caught up with the rest of her body as she started to fall.

'Easy, baby' Jack said, rushing to her side and effortlessly scooping her up into his arms.

'Nick ... Nick, he told me it was you and I believed him. I'm so sorry.'

'Hey, you have nothing to be sorry for, Sam. Sam, look at me?' Sam looked up and saw the love, so evident in his clear, blue eyes and felt ashamed for ever having doubted him. 'You have nothing to be sorry for,' he repeated.

'Now let's get you inside, it looks like it's going to rain.'

They entered the cottage and Jack led her through a large hallway and into a living room with an open fire. She took a seat on the faded leather sofa.

'Can I get you something to eat?' Jack said, kneeling in front of her.

Sam shook her head. 'Just some water.'

'Mother?'

'The same, please.'

Sam watched Jack leave the room before turning to Jane, who was in an armchair with her legs crossed, staring vacantly into the fire.

'What just happened?' Sam said, leaning forward. 'I know it was early afternoon when I came to you and now it's nearly dark.'

Slowly, Jane's eyes moved from the fire and focussed on her. She looked suddenly very old and nothing like the self-assured, indomitable woman Sam had first met, as she appeared to struggle with assembling her thoughts. She opened her mouth and might have been about to say something when Jack re-entered the room.

'Here we are,' he said, setting a tray with two glasses on the coffee table. Sam immediately picked up a glass and took several large gulps.

'I'm so sorry about what happened,' Jack said, sitting beside Sam and putting an arm around her shoulders. 'I didn't realise how dangerous Nick is – I should've been there for you.'

Sam looked up to see Jack's face, contorted with anger. 'I think he's got my mum, Jack, we need to tell the police.' She reached for her bag but remembered her phone was still in Jane's study.

'I think it's better if we go to the station in person. I'll drive us there and we can make a statement together.'

Sam nodded and stood up, expecting Jack to follow suit, but when he didn't, she lowered herself back down onto the sofa, noting a strange expression flit across Jack's face. She looked over to Jane, who continued to stare vacantly into the fire, rubbing her bony hands together.

'Why are you here?' she said, feeling something unpleasant creeping up her spine. 'What is it you're not telling me?' She thought about Jack's coat, hung up behind her mother's bedroom door and how he hadn't answered her calls or messages and her head started to pound with a greater determination.

'Come with me,' Jack said, holding his hand out to her. 'And I'll show you.'

Sam took Jack's hand, relieved by its reassuring warmth, and let herself be led out of the living room and back into the hallway. He moved towards a closed door, but stopped before opening it.

'Sam, I need you to trust me' he said, placing his hands on her shoulders. She wasn't sure what to think, but nodded. Jack opened the door and held a finger to his lips, indicating to Sam to be quiet as she entered the room.

Her eyes were immediately drawn to a figure, lying in the bed, an unfamiliar mass of tight curly hair obscuring her face. But she instantly knew who it was.

'Mum? Mum!' she exclaimed, pulling away from Jack's restraining hand.

'Mum?' she said louder, pushing the hair back from her mother's face.

'She's out for the count, I'm afraid,' Jack said, placing a hand on Sam's shoulder.

'Come, let's leave her to sleep,' he said gently, leading her out of the room to a rustic kitchen with a large, wooden table where she found herself being ushered into a chair whilst Jack busied himself with making coffee. He placed a mug in front of her and she wrapped her hands around it, relishing the searing heat as she listened to what he had to say.

Jack had come across her mother in town a few weeks ago, coming out of the seedy pub near the train station. According to him, she'd been really wasted and he had to take her home in a taxi where she confided to him about Nick and how the way he was treating her was making her scared. Sam nodded, thinking back to the night of the party and what Andrea had told her about the games Nick liked to play that 'freaked her out'.

'She told me she'd started drinking again and nearly accepted an offer of cocaine from a man in the pub. I was going to tell you, Sam, but she begged me not to,' he said, running a hand through this hair. 'She said you'd been through enough and didn't want you to worry, so I agreed not to say anything but only if I could check in on her to make sure she was all right.

'I tried talking to Nick, to persuade him that she's a vulnerable woman and to end it with her, but he wouldn't listen.' He reached out and gripped her hand.

'I was going to tell you, I swear, Sam, but then Nick suddenly became a prime suspect in that missing woman case and when Denise found out, she told me she had to get away from him; she didn't feel safe in her house anymore. 'So I said she could stay here.'

He rubbed a hand over his face. 'Christ, Sam, it's been a

nightmare keeping all this from you. I realise now, I should have told you straightaway, but it's been hard coming to terms with the fact that my closest and oldest friend is a criminal.'

'Yes, you should've told me,' Sam said stiffly.

She glanced over towards the sink and noticed the two wine glasses side by side on the counter.

'I think the best thing to do is let your mother stay here for a while, at least until Nick's been convicted.'

'No,' said Sam firmly. 'We all need to get back and tell the police everything that's happened. My mum needs to tell them how much he scares her, its important evidence!'

'I think Sam might be right, Jack.'

They both turned round to see Jane, standing in the doorway.

'Keep out of it,' Jack said, his voice uncharacteristically harsh. There was a moment's tense silence before Jane collected her bag and, giving Jack a reproachful look, left the cottage. Jack followed her out into the rain, leaving Sam alone with her thoughts. Hesitantly, she stood up and went back to the bedroom.

'Mum? ... Mum, can you hear me?' she said, prodding her mother. There was a groaning sound, but her mother's eyes remained closed. She pulled back the duvet and gasped at the sight of blood, oozing from a bandage on her mother's hand.

'Mum? Wake up!' she said, shaking her mother and seeing her eyes at last begin to open.

'What happened to you?' she said, pushing the hair from her face. Her mother opened her mouth and made some unintelligible croaking sounds.

'W ... wa ... ater,' she finally managed, moving her arm out of the bed. 'Down there.'

'It's OK, I'll get it for you,' Sam said, bending down to pick up the glass her mother was evidently trying to reach. As she retrieved the glass, she noticed a purple garment poking out from under the bed and pulled it out. It was a slinky figure-hugging dress – the type of dress that screamed *Fuck me*. She held it closer and breathed in the familiar scent of her mother.

Denise's eyes met hers briefly before looking away, but Sam

wasn't about to let her off that easily, whatever state she was in.

'What the fuck is this?!' she said, shaking her mother, this time violently.

'Sammy!' her mother whimpered; 'Sammy, I'm sorry! Sammy, Sam—'

She had to stop the sound of her mother's weak, pathetic pleas so she gave her a sharp slap across her face, followed by another, and another, before she felt Jack's arms around her, pulling her away.

She let herself be led, once again, into the living room, sliding her arm away from Jack's outstretched hand. She clasped her hands together to stop them from trembling.

'What the fuck's been going on between you and my mother?' she hissed, fixing Jack with a hard stare, determined to get to the bottom of whatever was going on.

'Oh God, Sam, I didn't want you to find out. Not with all the shit that's happened.'

'Go on,' she said, shrugging off his arm from her shoulder. 'Tell me.'

'I ... I came here after the antiques fair and she was all dressed up and trying to... well ... she was very drunk, but ...'

'Why did you leave her with alcohol?' Sam interjected.

'I didn't! She found an old stash of my Uncle Monty's vintage wine in the pantry. I forgot it was there.'

She looked into his blue eyes, trying to fathom what he wasn't saying; because there was definitely something he was holding back.

'What about the jacket I found in my mum's bedroom today? *Your* jacket!'

'What?' he said eventually, a nonplussed look on his face.

'The blue one.'

'Oh my God,' Jack said, slapping his head in realisation. 'The fucking bastard!'

He punched the sofa and stood up. Sam didn't think she'd ever seen him so angry.

'Nick, it was Nick. He must have put it there, or, wait a minute, are you sure it was mine? He has the same one, you know.'

'It was definitely yours.'

'God, Sam, I should have listened to you when you said you didn't like him. He's fucking poison!'

He went to sit in the chair opposite her and covered his face with both hands. 'Please say you believe me, Sam. Please.'

Before Sam could reply, the door flew open, the sudden rush of air causing the dying fire to spark and crackle. Her mother was standing in the doorway, pulling at the unfamiliar dressing gown wrapped around her.

'Sammy!' she whimpered. 'Don't listen to him, he's l ... lying!'

'What the hell?!' Jack said, jumping up from his chair. 'Why would you say that? After all I've tried to do for you!

'Sam, your mother is the one that's a fucking liar, you have to believe me!'

Sam looked from Jack to her mother and for a moment there was only the sound of the rain battering against the windows with increasing strength, the crackling fire and her mother's weeping. And she would have believed him. If she hadn't caught it, in that split second she happened to look his way as her mother spoke – the brutal expression that flickered across his face, causing him, in that briefest of moments, to look like a complete stranger.

Chapter Fifty Five

Slowly, Sam stood up and walked towards her mother, placing an arm around her waist just in time, as she started to slump to the floor.

'I don't know what you've done,' she said, turning to face Jack, 'but I'm leaving now, with my mum.'

'Jesus Christ, Sam! Really?! Are you *really* going to take her side? After all she's put you through; a miserable childhood, the constant looking out for her. She just *takes, takes, takes.* Don't you see that? Look at her – she's pathetic! She doesn't deserve you!'

Sam looked down at the top of her mother's head, resting against her arm. Jack was right, she was a pathetic excuse for a mother, she'd never been there for her and now, here she was, trying to get Jack to sleep with her.

But there were *two* glasses on the kitchen counter. The uninvited image hovered in her mind, the image of them sat cosily together drinking wine. She felt her mother pulling away from her.

'He's evil, Sammy. He ... he kept us in a cellar and ... he killed her! He killed Sarah!'

Her mother collapsed to the floor and she did nothing to stop her this time. The apprehension she was feeling quickly morphed into a cold, stabbing fear that made her limbs feel heavy and she was terrified that her muscles had stopped working altogether, leaving her no option but to sink to the floor beside her mother.

So Nick was telling the truth: Jack was the monster.

She regarded him, standing there, and tried to decipher any semblance of the man she thought she knew – the man she loved.

Then his features disappeared altogether as the room was plunged into darkness. Her mother screamed. She was aware that

Jack was moving towards them. She lunged forwards, instinctively balling her hands into fists. It was timed well, as her hands made contact with Jack's chest, pushing him away with a force that sent him stumbling back and crashing onto the coffee table.

'Come on!' Sam screamed, pulling her mother up and grabbing her arm. She held her free arm out in front of her as they made their way into the dark hallway. She could just make out the front door in the gloom and headed towards it, yelping out in pain as her hip struck something hard and solid.

'Mum, please!' she sobbed; struggling to haul the extra weight as she limped blindly forwards. Somehow she made it to the front door and, for one awful moment, predicted it would be locked, but she yanked the handle downwards and it dutifully opened.

Sam struggled to remember the direction she had come into the cottage and found she had no recollection as she stared wildly into the dark, open space. The rain was so heavy now she was already soaked through. She carried on moving as fast as her mother allowed, hoping that if they made it out onto the road, she could flag down a car, or find another house. Anything.

Except she wasn't moving forward anymore, but slipping and sliding, her screams combining with her mother's as they tumbled downwards. And then she felt water and screamed again as she scrabbled to find purchase in the viscous mud.

Suddenly, patches of the surrounding area were made visible by flashes of light; the dark, soupy water and the trees above the steep muddy bank all illuminated momentarily before receding into the inky blackness. The light then swept across her immediate area before settling on her. She put an arm up to shield herself from the piercing beam now trained on her face.

'Thank God! I thought you'd gone into the water! Are you OK, baby?' She was far, far from OK but nodded numbly. 'Sorry I took so long, I was looking for the torch. The blackouts round here never fail to take me by surprise.' He tutted. 'Oh dear, it doesn't look like your mother's in a good way.'

Sam followed the beam of Jack's torch as it moved from her face to the figure of her mother, lying a few yards away. She could just make out the trickle of blood that ran down the side of her face.

'Mum! Mum?!' she wailed and started to crawl towards her mother's lifeless figure. Her body was submerged from the waist down in the water.

'Mum, please wake up,' she sobbed, trying but failing to pull her mother up out of the water. She could see a large gash on her mother's temple and saw the culprit – a sharp, bloodied rock protruding from the mud.

'Sam, Sam? Just stop for a moment and listen to me. Please?'

She looked up towards the dark outline of Jack's figure.

'The pond is very deep, so please, just keep still whilst I get the rope.'

Sam hesitated a moment before nodding, it wasn't like she had much choice after all. She was, yet again, plunged into darkness as Jack turned back towards his car. Without taking her eyes away from the dancing light of the torch, she traced a hand around her mother's head, her fingers exploring the glue-like mud until they struck the rigid contours of the rock. Easing it out, she clenched her jaw tight and plunged it into her calf, hoping against hope that she hadn't nicked any vital arteries. The pain was indescribable, but it had to be done. It had to be convincing. With trembling hands, she placed the rock behind her before the light from Jack's torch returned.

'My uncle told me the pond is eight feet deep, you know,' he said, in a conversational tone. 'He tried keeping fish in there, but they all died from the lack of oxygen.'

'Right, I'm throwing the rope to you now.'

Sam made a show of attempting to move towards the rope before stopping to clutch her leg.

'What's the matter, baby?'

He sounded genuinely concerned, Sam thought, as she looked up in the direction of the light. 'I don't think I can move my leg.'

She pulled up her trousers to reveal the oozing wound underneath and hoped that it looked as bad as it felt.

'Oh baby, that doesn't look good. OK, don't move, I'll come to you.'

Yes, you come to me, she thought, watching as he once again disappeared into the darkness.

'Right, I've tied the rope to the car,' he said and, with his back to her, proceeded to climb down the bank. Without a moment's hesitation, Sam retrieved the rock and hobbled as fast as she could towards the outline of Jack's descending figure and as soon as he was in reach, she flung herself upon him, howling, as she smashed the rock down indiscriminately again, and again, until he finally stopped squirming. She rolled off him, her breath coming out in ragged gasps, her heart feeling like it was going to explode from her chest as she fought to retain control of her bodily movements. She saw the light from the torch and started to drag herself towards it, but her movements were abruptly curtailed. Somehow he was on top of her, pinning her down into the mud.

Struggling to get air into her lungs, Sam knew she didn't have much time before she suffocated in the thick mud. She arched her back with all her might and then jerked her head upwards, relieved to feel the back of her skull connecting with the angular bone of Jack's chin.

She turned in time to see him fall back into the water, the sound of the splash almost drowned out by the rain.

Coughing to expel the mud from her mouth, she slithered towards the torch and shone it at the space she'd seen Jack disappear, but apart from the raindrops dimpling the water, there was no other movement.

Slowly, painfully, she took hold of the rope and cautiously made her way back to her mother's side. Only her head and shoulders were now visible as she'd slipped further into the water.

'Mum?' she said shakily, gently stroking her mother's cheek, 'Mum, please wake up. I don't think I've got the strength left to get us both out of here. Please get up.'

But her mother remained unresponsive to her pleas. Wiping the rain from her eyes, Sam reached her arms under her mother's shoulders and started to pull but she wouldn't budge. She seemed to be caught on something.

Holding onto the rope to stop herself from sliding into the pond, she reached her other arm further into the black water, in the hope she could set her mother free from whatever was ensnaring her.

She found her mother's hand and gasped as it gripped hers.

'Mum! Thank God! It's OK, I'm going to get you out of here.'

But something wasn't right, as she felt her mother's hand tighten its grip and pull her down.

'Mum! Stop! You're hurting me!'

It was then she realised that the hand didn't belong to her mother, as the pale fingers broke the surface, attached to hers. She screamed and managed to break her hand free from Jack's grip; the rope her only saviour from slipping into the water. Her mother started moving then, sliding further down into the dark mass.

'Mum!' she wailed, grabbing at her mother's head, and then her hair, but it was no use, she couldn't stop her from being pulled under. She held onto that last fistful of her mother's hair until her own head was nearly submerged – the water entering her nostrils, causing her to splutter, until her hand started to lose purchase on the rope – the only thing stopping her from joining her mother in the cold, cold water. She looked up at the sky; at some point it had stopped raining and she could see the stars.

And at that moment, she made the decision to let go.

Epilogue

Seven months later

Sam places a lid over the pan of linguini and lowers the heat to a simmer.

'Ready in ten minutes!' she yells above the sound of music blaring from Tanya's room. Emily pokes her head out from behind her door and grins.

'Smells delicious! I'll be out in a minute.' She disappears behind her door and Sam hears the whirring sound of Emily's hairdryer. She rolls her eyes and sets three plates on the little kitchen table.

'Fuck!' she exclaims, remembering just in time to take the salmon off the heat. It's a new recipe she's trying; another one to add to her ever expanding repertoire.

'Smells gorgeous, babe!' says Tanya. 'Shall I do the honours?' she pulls a bottle of Prosecco from the fridge and proceeds to open it. 'Emily! Hurry up!!' She shakes her head. 'That girl spends half her life on her bloody hair!'

Sam laughs. 'If I had hair like that, I'd be the same!' They both turn as Emily enters the kitchen, her hair an explosion of curls that fall all the way to her lower back. 'Soz,' Emily says, plonking herself down at the table.

Sam waits till the Prosecco has been poured then raises her glass, 'Big congratulations to you both, you deserve it.' They clink glasses. 'Don't go expecting any special treatment though.' She does her best 'resting bitch face', making Emily and Tanya break into laughter.

Sam observes them affectionately as they shovel the food into their mouths, making appreciative noises as they do so, and thinks back to how much they annoyed her at first; always rehearsing their lines and bursting into song in preparation for the next big audition. But now she couldn't imagine living without the noise. She also realises that she mustn't have been a barrel of laughs in the beginning; a sullen presence within their carefree domain. But they had welcomed her into the flat, introducing her to the bright, airy bedroom that had recently become vacant, and slowly chipped away at her defences with invites to join them clubbing, for brunch, or just to sit and watch crummy romcoms with a bottle of Chardonnay – until she not only got used to being in the company of other people again, but was actually finding she enjoyed it.

They were going out tonight, to celebrate Tanya and Emily getting parts in The Lion King; their first big West End show – a reward for all the rehearsing and auditions (and subsequent rejections) in-between their long waitressing shifts. She was busy too; with her admin job at a Physiotherapy practice and a part time course in business management (having realised that she wasn't cut out for Counselling – it was hard enough keeping her own fucked-up mind in check, let alone the minds of others).

That was one of the things Sam was indebted to Frances for - putting her in touch with Tanya, her niece. Although she'd expressed a wish to return to London, Sam had been reticent about sharing with anyone else, rather visualising herself renting a bedsit; believing she needed to be on her own. But Frances had gone ahead and arranged a visit to the top floor flat off the Caledonian Road – driving Sam down to London herself to make sure the meeting went ahead. And Frances had been right of course, in her infinite wisdom. She could see what Sam couldn't: that being on her own would be the worst thing after what had happened – she needed to be in the company of others.

But the most important thing that Frances had done was to restore her back to life – nurturing and bolstering her mental health where the counselling sessions had failed.

Sam had turned up for work a week after her mother's funeral in the mistaken assumption that she was OK; that she could cope. But on first sight, Frances and Alan had exchanged concerned glances (she supposed it was her skeletal frame and the mismatching shoes that did it) and had frogmarched her into the nearest examination room where it was decided that Frances would take her back to her own home, where Sam stayed for two restorative months, having long, often very difficult discussions around the farmhouse table in the beautiful cottage Frances shared with Dora, her partner.

It was Colin who had first alerted the police. Dear Colin, who found it so difficult and stressful to steer off his familiar run of sentences, explaining in stilted words to a frustrated police officer how his mother told him that if something doesn't look right, he should always tell the police. And where he failed in words, he excelled in his memory; reeling off the number plate of Jane's car and the time and direction they took off.

Then it was Nick who gave himself in, providing the next layer of information; relaying all that he had told Sam, which mustn't have been easy, she had to admit.

But the last, and most vital layer of information, had come from Jane, no longer able to shy away from what her son was, as she drove back through the dark, country lanes. Something she had known since he was a child but kept buried under her cashmere cardigans and austere manner until she could contain it no longer, causing her to swerve at the last minute off the Wragby Road and towards the police station.

The police found Sam that night, crouched at the top of the bank, still clutching the rope like her life depended on it. How she had made it back up, she still doesn't know; the events of that night present themselves in distant hazy patches, memories that feel like they don't belong to her: the moment where Jack's mask fell, revealing the monster within; the trickle of blood down her mother's head; looking up at the stars, and her decision to let go. She likes to think that Pops was one of those stars, looking down on her and giving his blessing for her to stop in her futile quest to save her mother; to put herself first for once.

Her mother.

The pathology report evidenced she had died from a head trauma before entering the water; there was some comfort to take from that, she supposed.

She lit one last candle for Pops the day before she left Lincoln, taking a seat in the pews and closing her eyes – thankful for the clear picture of him in her mind. She had come out of the cathedral to find Nick sitting cross-legged on the wall, his head tilted to one side.

'I didn't want to spoil your special moment,' he said, with no trace of the familiar sarcastic glint in his eyes.

'Here,' he said, holding out a small package to her. She'd taken it hesitantly, not sure what to do if it turned out to be some cruel trick. It wasn't, she discovered as she unwrapped the layers of paper to reveal the silver pendant; one of the items Jack had planted at Nick's bedsit. He'd found it before the police arrived. 'I wanted to give it to you in person,' he said, smiling.

It turned out Sam wasn't the only person leaving Lincoln the next day. Nick was going to move into his sister's flat and apply to become a custodian for his niece. 'I owe it to her to try,' he said with a shrug of his shoulders, noting the sceptical look on Sam's face. The parting was strange; she had felt an inexplicable urge to suddenly hug him, maybe a feeling of closeness at the bond they shared as survivors of Jack's evil. But the feeling was short-lived, as she stood facing him in the grounds of the cathedral, and she made no attempt to move closer. They had exchanged numbers, but both knew they would not stay in touch.

Sam looks at herself in the mirror and brushes a hand tenderly over her neck, where the pendant spends the majority of its time. She has inserted a picture of Pops, opposite the one of her grandmother. There's a framed picture of her and her mother that she keeps in a drawer – the last one of them together, taken in the Highbridge cafe on her birthday, similar faces smiling into the camera lens of her mother's phone. She isn't ready to put it up. Not yet.

The pendant takes her back to Eddie, too. He had tried so hard to find her and that had been his undoing. The police had found enough drugs stashed in his house to prosecute him for dealing and together with the evidence from Layla and Lee's mother, that was enough for a warrant. Eddie, enraged in his quest to locate Sam and Denise, was pulled over by the police for driving too fast. He'd been arrested and his trial had been straightforward. He was guilty on all charges and was facing a lengthy prison stretch.

Shaking Eddie's image from her head, she puts her jacket on and fixes the brooch to the lapel, the green stone twinkles in and out from the dark material, reminding her of the beautiful colours of the cathedral's stained-glass windows. She re-checks the delicate clasp; like the pendant, this is a much-treasured thing that has come into her possession. A gift from one of Jack's other survivors.

When she went to visit her in the nursing home, Sam couldn't help but burst into tears at the sight of Edith Mowbray propped up in her bed. Sam had thought she was sleeping and, on leaving a farewell note on the bedside table, was making a quiet exit when Edith had stirred – her eyes looking vaguely in Sam's direction until they focused with a sudden clarity.

She lifted her head, her mouth open, as if to speak, but then slumped back into the pillows.

'I'm so, so sorry, Miss Mowbray,' Sam said, rushing to the old woman's bedside. Perching on the armrest of the chair, she laid her head gently on Edith's arm and wept.

'There, there,' Edith whispered over and over again. 'There, there.' And when her tears finally began to subside, Sam sat up, pulling a tissue from her pocket, feeling guilty for offloading her grief onto such a frail, old woman.

'It's ... not your f...'

'Please don't tire yourself out, Edith,' Sam said, alarmed at Edith's breathlessness.

'It's n....not your fault.' Edith repeated, closing her eyes briefly.

Sam smiled and took Edith's hand in hers and they sat on in silence regarding each other for a moment before Edith spoke. 'In there,' she said, pointing shakily past Sam towards a set of drawers. 'I have ... some ... thing for ... you.' She rested her head back on the pillows and closed her eyes again, obviously exhausted.

Sam turned towards the drawers and pointed to the top one. 'In here?' Edith opened her eyes and nodded.

She gave a little gasp at the sight of the emerald brooch, nestled in a small black box.

'It's ... it's so beautiful. I can't take it though, there must be someone else you'd rather give it to?'

Edith gave an imperceptible shake of her head.

'For ... you,' she said, her voice barely raised above a whisper.

Heeding the steely firmness in Edith's eyes, Sam decided against declining the brooch and closing the box, placed it inside her bag.

'Thank you, Edith,' she said, moving back to the bed. Edith raised an eyebrow.

'It's Miss ... Mow ... bray to you.'

Sam leans into the mirror for a closer inspection and brushes a light dusting of powder over her face; not the multiple layers of foundation she used to cake on in a bid to hide blemishes that were never there. She is learning to accept what she sees.

'Are you nearly ready yet?' Tanya shouts. 'The cab will be here any minute.'

'Coming!' Sam replies, in unison with Emily. She picks up the little figure and runs a finger over the rigid contours of its stone body. She places it back on her dressing table, returning its grin.

They tumble out of the cab, holding onto each other for balance as they negotiate the sleet covered pavement in their sky-high heels. The bouncer ushers them in ahead of the disgruntled queue – one of the advantages of looking the way they do. Sam feels her heart beating in time to the music, the vibe is positive and she pulls her girls in for a hug – it's going to be a good night.

THE END

Acknowledgements

I would like to thank Susan Yearwood for believing in my writing and taking my first draft to the next level.

Thank you to Joffe Books for short listing Unpleasant Creatures for the Joffe Books Prize for Crime Writers of Colour 2021. This was a huge boost to my confidence and made me see myself as a credible writer for the first time.

Thank you to my mad, wonderful family: My parents for instilling a lifelong love of books with weekly visits to the local library and the bed time stories; Kirsty, for her creative input and unwavering belief in me; my husband for egging me on ('when are you going to get that bloody book finished!') and Tom, for the crash course in using Instagram and for....well....being Tom!

And thank you to anyone who has read my book, it's amazing to think of it out there and I hope you enjoy it!

About the Author

I have always loved reading but my drive to write was inspired by my English teacher, who told me she had loved one of my short stories so much, she took it home to read to her family.

It has taken me a long time to realise that writing is really all I want to do, and being a finalist in the Joffe books competition 2021 made me realise that I'm actually quite good at it!

I used to work as an Occupational Therapist in the NHS and my many years experience of working in the Mental Health sector informs a lot of what I write. I am fascinated by what makes people tick and I enjoy creating characters that don't necessarily fit under specific labels.

Being mixed race and having grown up in Tottenham, I depict characters from different racial, cultural and economic backgrounds in order to illustrate real life.

Although I touch on some of the situations that my characters face - due to their colour, - I do not want these situations to define them or for their experiences to become politicised or tick a diversity box. I want readers from all backgrounds to engage and connect with my characters.

Extract from my new novel
Twenty nine years ago

It has started to drizzle as I exit Marylebone station and I pause for a moment to search for my umbrella, desperate to put a barrier between the droplets of rain and my newly blow dried hair. A woman shoves past me and glances back in my direction, her lips curled into an ugly snarl. 'Jeez!' I mutter under my breath as I'm jostled by several other commuters before locating my blasted umbrella, releasing the catch and stepping out into the morning rush.

The sleepy little village I left at precisely 6.15 this morning is in such stark contrast to the onslaught of noise, traffic and people, I am a little discombobulated and I afford more jostling and 'tuts' as I turn this way and that, struggling to get my bearings. And briefly, I consider turning around, stepping onto the next train back to Kidderminster and on sinking into the worn out seat of my faithfully waiting Ford Fiesta, bawl my eyes out at yet another missed opportunity. But only briefly; it's not an option. I can't afford to let these pessimistic thoughts take root in my mind. I start to walk in the direction of a main road, matching the determined gaits of the smartly dressed city workers. If I play my cards right, I too could be joining them. I pass a swanky looking wine bar, closed of course, due to the early hour, and imagine meeting colleagues for drinks after work; chinking glasses and exchanging anecdotes; making new friends and finally getting on with my life. A huge umbrella clashes with mine, nearly sending me off balance in my unfamiliar high heels. 'Watch it!' I shout, but the arsehole holding the umbrella does not acknowledge me, simply strides on down the middle of the pavement like he bloody owns it. Two little girls trail after him, dressed in private school uniforms, their straw boaters wilting in the rain. They are maybe five and eight to my untrained eye and look thoroughly miserable. No wonder with that fucker for a dad. I catch the older girl's eye and smile, she looks down and pulls her sister along. I nod, recognising the protective gesture all too well. I must try to remember that London is not the same as our little village; it isn't the done thing to smile at strangers, especially children. People might get the wrong idea.

I come to a set of lights; a gull's cry rings out shrilly in-between the abrupt beeps of the pedestrian crossing and the blasting of several car horns as a man on a moped weaves in and out of the line of traffic at an alarming pace. I am jostled once again by the fast moving Londoners; an obvious loser in the race. It isn't until I get to the other side of the road and away from the din that I hear my phone, ringing against my hip in my coat pocket. A quick glance at the screen confirms my worst fears: It's mother. With a huge amount of self restraint, I resist the habit of a life time and stuff the bloody thing back in my pocket. I haven't told her about the interview – a role as a social policy advisor for Westminster council; a role that, if I get it, will take me away from the sleepy backwater I have had the bad fortune to grow up in; away from the responsibility that weighs so heavily on me, threatening to suffocate me at times. This interview is a chance at a new start. A new life.

I enter the glass fronted building fifteen minutes early and make my way towards the sign that says reception, conscious of the clacking sound my heels make on the shiny floor. A man is speaking to the woman behind the reception desk, she swishes her glossy long hair and blinks rapidly as she looks up at him in a ridiculously overt way which makes me cringe inwardly. But it isn't until he turns in my direction, alerted by her gaze, that I see why she is acting this way. He looks at me with green eyes and smiles, causing me to emit a girlish titter that I manage to disguise with a cough. He nods his head before moving away. The sound of the woman clearing her throat brings me back to why I'm here.

'Hello, I'm here for an interview' I say to the receptionist, peeling my lips back in response to her overly bright, superficial smile. She's about to speak but stops when the insanely gorgeous looking man reappears, proffering his hand.

'Ah, you must be Ms Brookes, pleased to meet you. I'm Paul Gilder, one of the panel who will be interviewing you. We spoke on the phone?'

'Oh!, y...yes!' I manage to sputter, taking his hand which feels smooth and firm. He has a solid grasp, reminding me of his. An unwelcome frisson fires up in my groin and ripples through me and I pray that I'm not blushing. Now is not the time to be behaving like a stupid girl with a childhood crush.

'Are you ready for me?' I say, forcing myself to hold his gaze and drop my tone down a notch.

'Not just yet' he says smoothly. 'Please take a seat and Lucy can get you a coffee, or a tea?' He raises his perfectly shaped eyebrows and I am about to say coffee when my phone rings.

'Sorry' I mutter, pulling out my phone from my coat and cutting the call. Paul Gilder smiles, revealing a perfect set of teeth, just the right shade of white without being ostentatious.

'Not a problem, you have plenty of time to get back to your caller, I need to prepare a few things in any case so will leave you in Lucy's capable hands.'

I turn down Lucy's offer of a coffee and head to the toilets. It is only when I am safely enclosed in one of the cubicles that I pull out my phone and retrieve the three voicemail messages left on it. All from my mother.

I hold the phone reluctantly to my ear and listen.

****

'So, now you know our backgrounds and roles within the team, please tell us a bit about yourself and what attracted you to this post?'

I shift uncomfortably in my chair, trying but failing to appear thoughtful and engaged whilst struggling to drown out my mother's messages. She had sounded apologetic in the first one, said she was sorry to call me so early, to just call back when I could. By the third one, she hadn't bothered to go upstairs or out to the garden, so I could clearly hear the noise: the rhythmical keening sound. The sound that indicates another trip to the doctors, or the hospital. The sound that makes me want to curl up into a tight ball. The sound that makes me wish you were never born.

I mumble my way through the interview, frequently asking for questions to be repeated or rephrased so I can formulate answers that are too short or vague and clearly not wowing the panel in front of me. When the painful process is over, I retrace my steps back to the station, not bothering to put up my umbrella, there's no point now, I have no one to impress. I stare blankly at the moving scenery from the train window, noticing nothing but the persistent growl of my stomach. I was going to treat myself to a breakfast somewhere nice after the interview but wanted to get out of London quickly, a desperate need to get away from the city of hopes and dreams, it holds no place for someone like me.

I can't help envisaging another scenario, where I leave the interview knowing I've clinched it: I tell everyone over dinner and dad looks me in the eye and says 'Well done love, I'm proud of you'. Instead of treating me like an afterthought, I'm finally the centre of attention as I clink my wine glass with him. But thanks to you, that's not going to happen now. Thanks to you, I am now sitting in the worn out seat of my Ford Fiesta, bawling my eyes out at yet another missed opportunity.

How I wish you had never been born.

Printed in Great Britain
by Amazon

56584854R00179